PRAISE FOR NAJA MARIE AIDT

“The emotions unleashed . . . are painfully universal. Yet you know exactly where in the universe you are. This is the hallmark of great short stories, from Chekhov’s portraits of discontented Russians to Joyce’s struggling Dubliners.”
—Radhika Jones, *Time*

“Without question one of the best—and possibly the best—story collection(s) of the year, Aidt’s [*Baboon*] appears for the first time in English after winning a major Nordic prize. Prepare to brave the darkness.”
— Jonathon Sturgeon, *Flavorwire*

“Undoubtedly one of the most intelligent writers of the contemporary literary world, Aidt is also clearly one of the most compassionate—and therefore one of the most important—voices in fiction. How she bears the weight of such empathic descriptions of her characters, who we feel for as though we had stumbled directly into their lives, is a credit to her brilliant insight into the human condition.”
— Jordan Anderson, *Music & Literature*

“This collection is for those who delight in the eccentric and the atmospheric; Aidt inspires readers to read between the lines.”
—*Publishers Weekly*

“A major literary event.”
—*Los Angeles Review of Books*

“Unusual, laconic languag … You are faced with a universe tha … idt.”
—

ALSO BY
NAJA MARIE AIDT

Baboon

ROCK, PAPER, SCISSORS

NAJA MARIE AIDT

TRANSLATED FROM THE DANISH BY K. E. SEMMEL

OPEN LETTER
LITERARY TRANSLATIONS FROM THE UNIVERSITY OF ROCHESTER

Originally in Denmark as *Sten saks papir*

First edition, 2015

Library of Congress Cataloging-in-Publication Data: Available.
ISBN-13: 978-1-940953-16-8 / ISBN-10: 1-940953-16-2

Literary quotes within the novel are sourced from:
Epigraph: "The Tenth Elegy" by Rainer Maria Rilke, trans. by Stephen Mitchell. / *Blade Runner* (Film), screenplay by Hampton Fancher and David Webb Peoples. / *The Collected Poems of Frank O'Hara*, edited by Donald Allen. California UP, 1995. Poem used: "Jane Awake." / *The Essential Haiku Versions of Basho, Buson, and Issa*, edited and with verse translation by Robert Hass. Ecco Press, 1994. / "Ode to Celery" from *Landesprache* (1960) by Hans Magnus Enzensberger, trans. K. E. Semmel. / "I laugh as if my pots were clean" from *My Life* by Lyn Hejinian. Green Integer, 2002. / "All Souls" and "Death Fugue" from *Poems of Paul Celan*, trans. by Michael Hamburger, Persea Books, 1988. / "Ninth Elegy" by Rainer Maria Rilke, trans. Stephen Mitchell. / "We Two, How Long We were Fool'd" from *Leaves of Grass* by Walt Whitman. Norton Critical Edition, 1973.

This project is supported in part by a grant from the Danish Arts Foundation.

DANISH ARTS FOUNDATION

This project is supported in part by an award from the National Endowment for the Arts.

ART WORKS.
arts.gov

Printed on acid-free paper in the United States of America.

Text set in Bembo, a twentieth-century revival of a typeface originally cut by Francesco Griffo, circa 1495.

Design by N. J. Furl

Open Letter is the University of Rochester's nonprofit, literary translation press:
Lattimore Hall 411, Box 270082, Rochester, NY 14627

www.openletterbooks.org

And we, who have always thought
of happiness rising, *would feel*
the emotion that overwhelms us
whenever a happy thing falls.

Rainer Maria Rilke, "The Tenth Elegy"
(trans. by Stephen Mitchell)

ROCK, PAPER, SCISSORS

A man cuts across the street in the city center. It's drizzling. The traffic is earsplitting and intense, from shouting to dogs barking, from roadwork to the wailing of ambulances and the cooing of doves, from children screaming in their strollers to the metro rumbling beneath the streets, from hyperactive teenagers to the muttering homeless, from buses to street hawkers. Thomas crosses the street, a thin leather portfolio tucked under one arm, an umbrella under the other, and on his heels a plump, blonde woman hustles to match his pace. When she's almost at his side she clutches his jacket, her cotton coat flapping behind her like a tail or a kite, and glances about wildly. A car races toward them at high speed. She gasps and lunges ahead, and at last they're safe on the sidewalk, and Jenny lets go of Thomas. She says, "Can't you use the crosswalk like a normal person? You almost got me killed." Her eyes are wide and bright.

"Have you been crying?"

"I wasn't crying."

"It looked like you were crying back there."

"Maybe I was crying on the inside. I was dying of hunger." She raises her chin defiantly and begins to walk. Thomas follows. They head down a side street, away from the noise, a long, narrow street, poorly lit. It's 6:30 p.m. and darkness expands around them. The air is cool. A raindrop pelts Thomas's cheek, and before long they're seated opposite one other at a table in a small restaurant. Thomas's eyes roam across the objects between them: a green ceramic bowl filled with olive oil, a breadbasket, salt and pepper shakers, a carafe of water, and two mismatched glasses. Jenny's chubby white hand fidgets with a napkin. Then she leans back and looks at him. "What did you think about the lawyer? Should we hire him?"

"Do we have a choice?"

"I guess not. Why were you so late?"

"I don't know. Maybe I was hesitant."

"Hesitant? Why hesitant?"

He smiles at her and lights a cigarette. "Does it even matter now?"

"Do you have to smoke?"

"Yes."

"Are you even allowed to smoke here?"

"Yes. What are you going to eat? You want a glass of wine?"

"I want a Bloody Mary. And pasta with pancetta. And a salad. Remember the olives we had the last time we were here? You think we can get them again?"

The waiter, a stooped older man with wavy black hair, takes their orders and disappears into the kitchen. When the door swings open, Thomas sees two young men, one hunched over some steaming pots, the other grappling with a frying pan. In the warmth of the kitchen, their faces gleam with sweat. But it's cool in the high-ceilinged room they're in. Thomas shivers. A middle-aged woman behind the bar polishes drinking glasses. The restaurant isn't even half full. "Remember when Dad brought us here the night of the accident, after you'd been to the emergency room? We sat over there." Jenny points at a table next to the window. "I think it must've been this same waiter, back when he was young. You were pale as a sheet. How old were we?"

"I was eleven, you were nine."

"And we got to order whatever we wanted. All I ate was chocolate cake. Three slices." She laughs suddenly and loudly. "Ha! You were pale as a sheet, though nothing had happened. Nothing serious. Bumps and bruises. Just a few bumps and bruises."

The waiter sets steaming plates before them. The bartender places a red drink, a pallid stalk of celery poking out of it, in the middle of the table as if it were meant to be shared.

"Just a few bumps and bruises," Thomas repeats slowly, pushing the drink toward Jenny. "That's one way to look at it."

"Oh, don't be so dramatic. Eat your food. Cheers."

She raises her Bloody Mary so that the lamplight shines through the red liquid. "Ha! Just a few bumps and bruises!"

"That actually looks like blood," he says, pointing at the glass with his fork. Then he bores into his oxtail and shovels the sauce with his knife. The waiter limps back carrying a half-empty bottle of red wine along with a plate of olives. But Jenny isn't happy. "They aren't anything like the ones we had last time. Plain, tasteless. I bet they got them at the local supermarket. Try them yourself. Everything gets worse over time, everything, everything. Doesn't it?" Thomas refuses to try the tasteless olives. He takes a swig of wine, and says: "Dear Jenny, you're always complaining. Everything doesn't get worse over time, everything gets better. We're rid of Dad, for one thing. Think about that. And he'll never come back. Except in our most terrifying nightmares."

"How can you be so mean? You've always been mean. It's a constant, neither worse nor better with time. But everything else gets worse. Love and marriage. Our bodies fall apart. Hideous! Things get uglier. Doors, buildings, chairs, cars. And silverware." She pokes her fork at him. "Yup, even silverware gets uglier and uglier, and people get uglier and uglier. Just think of Helena and Kristin's twins, how they dress so tastelessly you wonder if it's a joke. They sent a photograph at Christmas, Kristin must have taken it—she's such a terrible photographer—and . . ." She stops abruptly, sets down her fork, and smoothes her shirtsleeves. Then she looks directly into his eyes. "You're also getting uglier. You really are. You were handsome once. You looked like Mom and her brothers."

"Can we talk about something a little more uplifting?" Thomas smiles at Jenny, but she shakes her head, and says: "I don't know. I'm not doing so well. You think we can save a few odds and ends from Dad's apartment before it's cleaned out?"

"There's nothing there, Jenny. Just a few ugly, ugly things." He smiles again, and now she too smiles, despite herself. Her teeth are yellow, her mouth wide and red. A sudden gleam in her green eyes.

"I want the toaster. It's special to me."

"Then take it. No one will know. What do you want with an old toaster?"

"Come to think of it, did he have anything personal in his cell?"

Thomas lights another cigarette and shakes his head. The bartender's playing some strange music, a kind of languid disco.

"A notebook and a stack of porn mags. His watch."

"What was in the notebook?"

"Nothing. Doodles and some phone numbers."

"He didn't even have a photo of us?"

"Don't be childish, Jenny. Of course he didn't have a photo of us."

"I want dessert. And coffee."

Jenny orders ice cream and coffee for them both. She devours hers greedily, starting with the maraschino and then working her way through the layers of ice cream, chocolate syrup, and whipped cream. One moment she resembles a little girl, the next a broken, overweight prostitute. A charming prostitute, Thomas thinks, surprised. He imagines how she'll look in twenty years. The skin of her cheeks will be slacker. Her hair will be thinner. Maybe her hands will shake. Casually he glances at his phone. No messages.

"How's Alice?" he asks.

"She's got a new boyfriend. Again. I don't like him." She licks the last of her ice cream off her spoon. "You should see how he gropes her in public. He's reckless." She looks out the window. It's pouring now. Runnels of water stream down the enormous panes. "It's not easy having kids, Thomas," she says dreamily, still holding her spoon. Then she collects herself. "Well, anyway, I'll go pick up the toaster tomorrow." She tries to smile, but he can tell she's on the verge of tears. He takes her hand and squeezes it, feigning solemnity:

"Take the bus right to his door, Jenny."

She can't help but laugh. A moment later, she squints at him, giving him a hard glare. "Okay," she says. "Listen. This is how it was: We sat right over there, at the table by the window, and Dad said: 'Order whatever you want.' He didn't care, he said. At first I didn't believe him, but he was serious. You remember that? He snorted and groaned. Sweat dripped from his temples down his cheeks. Remember how sweat used to run down his temples? Who'd called him anyway?"

"You know. Someone from the emergency room. I waited for hours. Do we need to discuss this?"

"Yes, we do. Dad visited you in the emergency room, then what?"

"Jenny . . . let it go." Thomas stares resignedly at her.

"Come on. Then what?"

"Something *had* happened. I sprained my left arm, banged my head, and injured some vertebrae."

Jenny leans back smiling patronizingly, almost gleefully.

"It's true," Thomas goes on, annoyed. "And the first thing he said to me when he walked into the room was, 'What the hell have you done now?' He didn't care that I'd been hit by a car. He thought it was my fault."

"Did you walk in front of the car, or what?"

"No, and you know it." Thomas feels anger surging in him, his voice growing shrill. "It was speeding, it turned the corner, it hit me, I landed on the hood. You know all that. Maybe the sun blinded him. It *was* spring."

"Who was blinded by the sun?"

"The driver! But it wasn't my fault." Thomas sighs loudly. "I was going to buy bread . . ."

"Yes." Jenny flares her nostrils and turns away, eyebrows lifted. "I waited for you in the hallway. Waited and waited. But you never came."

"Like it was my fault!"

"I'm not talking about fault. I'm just saying you never came. I was so hungry my stomach hurt. I just sat there, squatting, leaning against the wall. Remember how dark it was in that foyer? How deep it was? The bulb on the ceiling, the brown walls? Ugh, they were really brown. When you were alone in there, it was like they were alive. There were shadows and . . . black holes."

"Black holes?"

"Yes. Black holes. I was so scared." Jenny's eyes are moist now.

Thomas shrugs. He signals the waiter, orders another coffee.

"I was scared, Thomas," Jenny repeats, earnestly. "Look at me."

"He was wasted," Thomas said.

"No, he wasn't. You're blowing things out of proportion again."

"Yes, he was. He was wobbly on his feet. You think I couldn't tell when he was drunk? And you could too. He stank. Listen, Jenny. I had a concussion, a black eye, a scraped head, and a sprained arm, and all he did was stand there wobbling and blustering like an idiot. He stared at me, he stared out the window, he sat down, and he stood up again. He hobbled around the room in that uneasy way that made us nervous, and that—"

Smiling, Jenny shakes her head.

Thomas points at her. "It *made* you nervous, no matter what you say."

"But I wasn't even there!" she interrupts him.

"No, but *I* was, and he just walked over to me and grabbed my arm. 'Let's go,' he said, despite the fact they wanted me to spend the night at the hospital. It was embarrassing, but he didn't care. He yanked me out of the bed and shoved me into the elevator. I remember that shove clearly, because I had so many bruises on my back. Then we went home and picked you up—"

"In a taxi," Jenny interrupts.

"He didn't say a word the whole ride."

She straightens up when the waiter pours her coffee. She says, "I remember that. The taxi. How we drove here and could order whatever we wanted."

"And why do you suppose that was? Was it a punishment or a celebration?"

"I don't know. What do you mean by 'punishment'? I ate as much chocolate cake as I could, but *you*," Jenny points at him. "You just sat there moping—and what did you order again? Soup?" She snickers. "Soup! It made him angry. But c'mon, it's so weird to order a ridiculous bowl of soup, the cheapest thing on the menu, when for once you could have whatever you wanted."

"I was sick!" Thomas sets his cup heavily on the saucer. Then he lowers his voice. "Can we just drop this? Why do you *want* to talk about this?"

"Drop what? You had soup, you didn't touch it, he got angry, and then you fell off the chair."

"I fainted, Jenny. I was nauseated, I was freezing, I was in pain, my head was spinning, I couldn't eat that fucking soup." His voice is a savage hiss, but Jenny laughs again, lightheartedly.

"You fainted because you were hysterical! Don't you think? That's what I think."

Thomas shakes his head, stares at Jenny, lights a cigarette, and blows air through his nose.

"Okay," Jenny says. "We won't talk about it anymore. But the chocolate cake was really good. And you were so pale when you came to. Ha! He almost had to carry you to the car, though he didn't want to. Then, as if that wasn't enough, you threw up on the living room carpet when we got home. All because of a few bumps and bruises."

"It was a concussion!" Thomas practically shouts. "A *concussion* for God's sake."

They stare at each other a moment, then each loses focus. Thomas zones out, his eyes resting on two men bent over their pasta. One of the men dabs his mouth with his napkin; the other says something, and the two laugh at the private joke. Thomas smokes greedily and drains the last of his cold, bitter coffee. Jenny gnaws at her pinky nail. She goes to the bathroom. Thomas thinks of his father's kitchen, the toaster. The smell of the kitchen, the sound the cupboard next to the stove made when you closed it, how it stuck when you tried to open it. And the toast that would pop up, almost always too burnt at the edges, was like coal against his teeth, like tinfoil. He asks for the check. Jenny returns and begins to rummage in her purse. She fishes out a tube and slathers her hands with cream. A faint odor of menthol spreads around them. Then she begins to talk about her night shifts at the nursing home. About her modest salary and Alice and her friends who eat all her food. "What am I going to do?" she says, raising her hands only to let them drop heavily to her side. Thomas is exhausted, doesn't say much. He pays, and they say goodbye outside the restaurant. Jenny is under a red umbrella, and Thomas is under a black one. Rain lashes the sidewalk with such force that it bounces off as if it were coming from both above and below. She offers him a key. The word *Dad* is etched onto a small piece of blond wood attached to the key ring. "I'm going out there tomorrow," she says.

"Say hi to Alice!" he calls out as she walks away. She raises her arm dismissively but doesn't turn back. Maybe she's begun to cry.

For a moment he feels a prickling jab of tenderness for the plump, swaying body disappearing around the corner. Then disgust. Then tenderness again.

At home Patricia's sitting in front of the computer, her coat on. Her striped scarf has fallen to the floor. She leans forward, craning her neck, her face to the screen. The hallway light spills into the half-lit living room. She's put a bowl of oranges on the coffee table. The cat sleeps in the armchair. Thomas stands in the doorway observing her. "Hey," he says finally. She glances up. "Oh, hi baby. I'm almost done. Sorry, it's just these pictures for the catalog. The graphic designer *keeps* putting them in wrong . . ." She stares silently at the screen, he stares at her back. The living room: still life of woman with averted face. Thomas goes into the kitchen, where a tower of dishes is stacked up. He washes his hands and drinks a glass of water as he gazes out the window. He can see the river and the lights on the other side of it. A lightning bolt flashes across the sky, a thunderclap booms far away. It begins to rain. "How'd it go?" Patricia calls out. "Okay," he mumbles, putting down his glass. He walks into the bedroom and sits on the bed. He picks up his pillow and buries his head in it. This is how I smell, he thinks, it's me, this aroma, the smell is me, it's what I give off and what I leave behind, traces of my aroma: me. I am here. I am in the pillow. It's frightening. Then Patricia appears in the doorway. "What are you doing?" He tosses the pillow aside. "Is something wrong?" She's taken off her coat, and her hair is gathered in a ponytail. There are wet splotches on the knees of her stone-washed jeans, and her mascara has left black marks around her eyes. Must be from the rain. "You look tired," he says. "Have you even had dinner?" "I had a sandwich on the way home. We don't have any bread." She sits beside him. "You have sauce on your collar." He nods. With her nail she scratches a little at the dried sauce. She strokes his cheek. She puts her arm around him. "Where'd you eat?" she asks softly. "At *Luciano's.* Jenny insisted." He puts his arm around her, and they sit like that for a while. He can't stop thinking about how stiff and clumsy it feels. They undress in silence, she brushes her teeth, naked—he's already in bed—and she brushes her hair. "How's Jenny? Was she impossible? And what did the lawyer say?" Patricia sits on the edge of the bed and touches his arm. She has goose bumps on her thighs. Her dark hair scatters across her face when she yanks the hairband from her ponytail. "Are you free of your father's debt?" He closes his eyes. His body is heavy as lead. His heart beats languidly, as though drugged.

"Yes. If there is any," he says, his voice raspy. "We've renounced everything. There shouldn't be any problem. The county will pay for his funeral. But Jenny's insisting that we have a ceremony."

"Oh, no."

"Why 'oh, no'?" He speaks with difficulty. It feels as though half his mouth is anesthetized. Patricia lies beside him on her back. The duvet rustles when she gathers it around her.

"It's just . . . the people who'll attend. You know. That guy Frank," she says in disgust, "do you think he'll come? I'm sure he will. And the fat one, what's his name again?"

He's almost asleep now, his leg jerking, halfway into a dream about a circus. In it he's moving slowly through high grass, getting closer and closer. He hears music. The grass is crawling with grasshoppers.

"Thomas?" She tugs at his arm. "Thomas. We should have sex now. It's been weeks."

"I can't," he mumbles, "I'm sleeping . . ."

He hears her distant sigh, then rolls onto his side. And he's back with the circus. A girl on a carousel screeches with joy; she resembles Jenny. He senses the grasshoppers' presence, a tickle, a sound, at once claustrophobic and alluring, and in the dream he regards his dirty, sunburned hand and realizes that he's a boy, not a man as he first thought.

The next morning he wakes at dawn. The sun's shining through the slats in the blinds. Patricia's fast asleep, her mouth open. Apparently she's been pulling at her hair again, which she sometimes does in her sleep, because it's completely rumpled on the left side. A strange habit. Carefully, he touches her shoulder. Her breasts look like two pink cupcakes. For a moment he feels a strong desire for her. Then it fades. He crawls out of bed, makes coffee, showers, shaves, and gets dressed. Patricia stumbles sleepy-eyed into the kitchen and sits at the little table in the corner. He pours her a glass of juice. "When will you get home tonight?" she asks. "Can you stop at the store on the way back? We don't have anything. Buy some good bread."

She has a late meeting, so they arrange to make dinner at eight. He slurps the last of his coffee, then kisses her neck and cheek; she pulls his mouth to hers and pushes her tongue into it. He's brushed his teeth, she hasn't. "Get a bottle of wine, too," she says, smiling. He removes his coat from the hook and stuffs the folder under his arm. He leaves the umbrella. Outside the air is mild and fresh after last night's rain, the plane trees' dense cluster of branches providing comfortable shade all the way to the train station. He loves their mottled trunks. He smokes a cigarette, and feels wide awake. He cuts across the street. Thomas O'Mally Lindström cuts across the street whistling with the sparrows circling overhead, after which he turns the corner and disappears into the darkness, down a long, dingy stairwell on his way to the train.

Dressed in a light-blue shirt, Maloney kicks the coffee automat. His curly hair is still damp following his shower, or maybe it's his sweat.

Thomas suspects that he's screwing Annie, their employee, and maybe they've just had a tryst in the back room. Maybe Maloney's got high blood pressure. He's grown heavier over the past few years, and he sure likes his fats and salts. These are the kinds of thoughts rumbling through Thomas's head when Maloney shouts: "I hate this machine! Peter! Peter! Go get some coffee. Milk and sugar. You need money?"

Thomas shakes his head, smiling.

"It's always on Fridays, have you noticed that? Always on fucking Friday when you fucking need your coffee the most. I'm calling the company to let them know they can pick up their machine and shove it up their asses. I won't pay another penny on the installments for this piece of shit." Maloney's already on his way out of the office. "Are the deliveries arriving today? Did you talk to them?" he shouts. Thomas follows him. Maloney flicks the switch for the chandelier, Eva rolls up the vacuum's hose; they exchange a greeting. She says, "Have a good weekend" in her oddly whispered, self-effacing way, bowing her head shyly—but what could she be shy about?—and dragging the vacuum cleaner into the hallway. She can't be the one he's fucking, Thomas thinks, inserting the key in the register. Now Maloney's on the phone with the company that delivers their stock, and it sounds as if they aren't coming today. He slams down the receiver and sighs. "Why does everything have to be so fucking difficult?" It's a big store, a desirable location, and it's been a paper and office supply shop for nearly one hundred years; they've maintained as much of the old, dark wood as possible. The chandelier hangs from the huge rosette on the ceiling, which is cleaned thoroughly with a toothbrush, and they've carefully renovated the built-in cabinetry with room for especially fine decorative paper and gold leaf. The broad wooden planks have been polished and lacquered. When they opened the store, Thomas spent weeks lying on the floor sealing the cracks with tar. That was a warm summer, he recalls, and I hadn't met Patricia yet. Maloney was young and trim in those days, and he was dating a nougat-skinned beauty whom he consistently referred to as "the sex kitten." In the evenings they drank beer at a café around the corner and discussed how rich they'd be if they did everything right. Right. What the hell is right? Thomas wonders. For a moment he feels the urge to kick the coffee automat—since it'll have to be returned anyway. Instead he sits behind the counter and turns on the cash register screen. Pale sunlight cascades through the tall windows. Morning traffic rumbles in the distance. "Soon people won't have any need for paper," Maloney says. "Who writes a letter nowadays? Who can even write by hand? Tell me. And books? They're on the way out, too. People sit around fiddling with their stupid digital devices on the train. Have you noticed that? *Wuthering Heights* and Thomas Mann. It's a joke. He and the Brontë sisters would turn in their fucking graves."

"Maybe they do."

"What?"

"Turn in their graves." Thomas looks out the window. Sees Peter balancing coffee cups and a bakery bag, a cigarette dangling from his mouth.

"Did you know that Peter smoked?"

"No. Nor do I fucking care," Maloney says. "What a goddamn morning. I think I'll go home."

"That must be why he's always chewing gum. To hide it. The smell."

Maloney calms a little once he's had two cups of coffee and gobbled a chocolate croissant. There's an enormous zit on Peter's cheek. Annie's wearing a red dress that accentuates her wide hips; her arms are thick, and her mouth is small and narrow, with thin, tight lips. "Okay, we're doing inventory today. You do rows one through four,

Peter. Annie, you do the rest." Thomas nods at her. "Don't count the pasteboard. We've ordered more."

"But they haven't arrived yet," Annie says.

"No, they *haven't*," Maloney says, sourly. "Turn in your lists to me before 1:00 P.M. We need to send our orders by 3:00."

"It's usually before 4:00, isn't it?" Annie raises her chin and looks at Thomas.

"But today it's before 3:00," Maloney says, and Thomas asks: "Are we doing the books?"

Maloney nods, then dries his cheek with the back of his hand. "I'll start."

A moment of silence. Everyone's thoughts seem to turn inward, sleepily holding their breath as if it was very warm. But it isn't very warm.

"What time is it?" Peter asks.

Maloney points at the wall clock behind them.

"Oh, yeah," Peter says. "Sorry."

Annie stands and moves her big butt into the store.

They open at 9:00 A.M. Annie and Peter begin, shelf by shelf, holding their lists under their arms. They look like two well-behaved students. Or assistants at a library. But Annie already looks older than when they hired her only a year ago—as if working in the store has worn her down. Thomas cleans the pen and pencil jars. Standing behind the counter, he gazes around the high-ceilinged room, letting his eyes roam across the products. He thinks: Half of everything here is mine. I *have* done it right. Then the door opens, and a mother with two small boys enters. They're looking for tissue paper, felt-tip pens, and a printer cartridge. Between customers Thomas reads the newspaper, and at 10:30 he goes out to the sidewalk to smoke. It's windy. Rotten leaves billow in the air and swirl around the street; the sky is suddenly dark and overcast. Earlier he'd found a notice in the local paper: "Convict Found Dead in Prison." He tore it out and shoved it in his pocket. As long as Maloney doesn't start in about selling party supplies, he thinks, extinguishing his cigarette on the sole of his shoe. That has never been the purpose of Maloney & Lindström. I should also quit smoking.

Annie hands in her list before Peter does. Thomas is hungry. He drifts about aimlessly, adjusting things on shelves. Not surprisingly, the two small children left their greasy fingerprints on the silk paper. He flips over the two most visible packages. A group of twelve- or fourteen-year-old girls tumble through the door giggling and at once filling the store with their exclamations and shrill voices, their all-encompassing noise. With their eyes made up and clinking armbands. He doesn't have the strength to deal with them. He makes eye contact with Annie and signals for her to watch them. It's not unusual for girls that age to steal. Small flocks of girls, and always during lunch break. He suspects they go into all the stores on the street, one by one. Last time a girl stole a handful of panda bear erasers and one of the big electric pencil sharpeners. She had hidden them in her hat. He would have called her parents, but she cried in such a shameful, desperate way that he let her go. He finds Maloney staring out the office window. "What's up?"

Maloney starts. "Halfway there." Thomas closes the door and sits on the edge of desk. "Are you sleeping with Annie?" Maloney stares dumbly at him, then bursts into laughter. "Thomas!" he says, "What are you talking about? Annie! What thoughts you have in your little head." Grinning, he leans back, stops laughing. He eyes Thomas. "What's going on with your dad? Did you talk to the lawyer? Yesterday, right? Let's go get some lunch." Maloney's in the habit of asking questions and not waiting for a response. They retrieve their coats from the hallway closet and tell Peter they're going on break.

Maloney orders a sandwich with extra bacon, Thomas the soup of the day and a salad. They sit in the far corner, as usual. "They're coming to pick up the coffee automat on Tuesday," Maloney says, shoving a rather too large bite (bacon smothered in mayonnaise) into his mouth with his finger. "I let them have it, this little underling who sounds like someone jammed a carrot up his ass, telling me all about the rules—when the fucking piece of shit doesn't even work."

"Maloney . . ."

"Someone has to make sure things work."

"My sister's taking the death pretty hard." Thomas hears how formal he sounds—the death—but he can't say "my father's death." He can't say "my father."

"Oh, Jenny with the blonde hair," Maloney mumbles, chewing energetically. "I did bang *her*, though it was a long time ago now. But Annie? How could you think that? Ha! She's gained weight, hasn't she? Your sister? So has Annie for that matter."

"She has to go to the apartment, she said."

"Jenny's so . . . *emotional*. Isn't she? Tears and laughter mixed into one. It's like she can't quite control which emotions connect to which expressions. What is that called again?"

"Histrionic."

"No, sensitive. It's a charming character trait." Maloney looks at him while cleaning his teeth with his tongue.

"It's almost over, Tommy. When are you dumping him in the ground?"

"Tuesday."

"I'll come if you want me to. You haven't touched your soup." Maloney wipes his mouth with his napkin and drains his soda. With two fingers he lifts a leaf of lettuce from Thomas's plate, then lets it drop. "I remember Jacques. His glistening gray suit. Was it grease? Was it greasy? Is that why it glistened?" He glances up from Thomas's salad. "I'm coming to that shitty funeral, whether you want me to or not, okay?"

"Okay."

They stop a moment to admire the show window, which they're both happy with, before they enter the store. It's 2:00 p.m. Customers are beginning to arrive. It's already busy: Annie works efficiently behind the register, while Peter advises people, retrieves items from the storeroom, and crawls up the ladder if anyone wants something from the top shelves. Thomas feels a momentary pang in his stomach, a rapping in his soul, a delight for the store, for its bustle, for the fact that they actually own this place. That he's *made it this far.* That he's risen out of the shithole he grew up in. That the store's actually *successful*, the employees, *their* employees, his shelving system (his own certain sense of style). That they *don't* have carpet on the floor. Satisfaction for his satisfaction, oh, satisfaction for satisfaction. Because recently a kind of lethargy has crept into him, a certain undefined disquiet or boredom (is it boredom?). But at this moment a twinge, a pang, when he strolls through the store nodding at customers and warmly greeting the sweet visual artist with the studio around the corner; she's looking for colored acrylics and can't find the magenta or the ultramarine. He calls for Peter, and Peter immediately goes to the basement, and the visual artist smiles gratefully. Walk down the short hall, open the office door, get the rest of the accounting done before closing time. He's just sat down to it when Jenny calls.

"Oh, Thomas . . ." He can't tell whether she's sniffling or there's some other sound in the background. "Oh God, it looks awful here . . ."

"What looks awful?"

"This place looks AWFUL, Thomas."

"Are you in the apartment?"

A strange sound emerges from her.

"Of course it looks awful there. What did you expect?"

She snorts hysterically.

"Call a taxi, Jenny, go home. I'm hanging up, and you're calling a taxi. Okay?" He hears her sitting down on something soft and creaky. Must be the armchair.

"C'mon, Jenny."

"I can't."

"You can't what?"

"I can't stand up."

"But you just sat down."

"How do you know that?"

"I can hear you."

"What can you hear? You can't hear anything! You have eyes in the back of your head, you spy!"

"You're sitting in Dad's moth-eaten armchair staring at the television."

"There's no television here anymore." Her voice quivers. "Someone took the television, Thomas. The apartment's been ransacked. Everything's gone, everything. It's so dusty here, so disgusting . . ."

"Of course it's dusty. I'm hanging up now. Call a taxi."

"Don't you give me orders! You always give me orders. I've never been allowed to decide ANYTHING for myself. Always you. Or Dad. Or some other fucking stupid bastard!" Jenny breathes excitedly into the phone, seething. He has never heard her say *fucking* before. Now her mouth is close to the receiver, her voice dark and husky, thrusting the words: "They have ta-ken the tele-vis-ion, Tho-mas."

Maloney enters the office. He glances curiously at Thomas. Thomas writes "Jenny, hysterical" on a slip of paper.

"I'm hanging up now. Bye, Jenny. Bye." He hangs up.

"I need to pick her up," Thomas grumbles. "I don't know if I'll be back today."

He gets to his feet, snatches up his briefcase, and removes his coat from the hallway closet. Then he rushes through the store without saying goodbye to anyone, despite the inquisitive look Annie gives him. The glass door glides closed behind him. He lights a cigarette, hails a cab. Before the cab arrives, he gets Jenny on the phone again. Howling now and incoherent.

The last time he saw the apartment was many years ago. It's in a narrow, indistinct redbrick structure squeezed between two taller buildings, the tallest of which is now apparently equipped with balconies. Small trees have been newly planted on each side of the street. A woman carrying a child strapped to her chest leaves the playground across the way. The playground is also new. A fire station used to be there. He remembers the constant howling of the sirens when he was very little. Then it'd been razed, leaving an empty space where local kids hung out in great, squealing flocks, and where he and his friends built a fort made of boards (and one summer, in this fort, they'd smoked their first cigarettes, which they took turns stealing from their fathers). But the building looks the same. The windows haven't been replaced. There's no intercom. Even the door with its chipped blue paint is the same. Thomas shoves it open with his foot and steps into the stairwell. A steep stairwell adorned with something that was once a wine-red runner—now so filthy it's nearly black. The wood creaks under him, the timer light clicks off. He locates the light switch and continues up to the fourth floor accompanied by the ticking of the timer light. As children, he and Jenny couldn't reach the switch, so they had to feel their way forward in the darkness. He puts his hand on the railing. The hand recognizes each turn, each crack, each unevenness. The pungent odor of rot and mothballs is so familiar that he doesn't even notice it at first. But suddenly it nauseates him. His father's apartment door is open.

Jenny's sitting in the dark on the edge of their father's unmade bed, staring at the wall. The curtains are closed. The floor is strewn with papers, clothes, overturned lamps, and shards of glass. The air is thick with dust. A dresser has been knocked over, and the arm of a shirt sticks out from one of its drawers. Thomas enters the living room. There's more light here. The television is missing, and so is their father's record collection. The coffee table is also gone, as well as the silverware—the hutch is open. A dish with a flower motif, which belonged to their grandmother, has fallen to the floor and cracked down the middle. An apple core lies beside it. He goes back to the hallway and closes the front door. The nasty odor of decay wafts from the little kitchen. The apartment has been empty for probably a month and a half. Jenny stopped by only once after their father was arrested, to water the plants. But someone else has clearly been here. Thomas goes to Jenny in the bedroom. She's still sitting on the bed, now with their father's pillow in her lap. He squats before her. "Come. Stand up. I'm taking you home." "Someone broke the lock," she whispers, running the back of her hand across her mouth.

"It doesn't matter, Jenny. Stand up." He takes hold of her hand and tugs on it. But Jenny won't stand.

"What have they taken?" she asks.

"I have no idea. There's nothing here."

"The coffee table and the television," Jenny whispers.

He clutches her arms and hoists her forcefully to her feet. "We're going now. C'mon." She sniffles. Leans heavily against him. He wraps his arms around her, embraces her. She smells of warm, spicy perfume and nervous sweat.

"Don't be afraid. There's nothing to be afraid of. It's over. He's dead, it's all over. We don't need to worry about anything."

"Oh," she moans, "oh, oh, oh. I'm so tired. I'm so tired." Thomas guides Jenny through the living room, where several wilted cacti with long, gnarled limbs are collecting dust on the windowsill. Now he notices an armchair lying on its side. It's been slashed, and he can see the gray lining inside. In the stacks of paper on the floor is a photograph of their mother. "The toaster," Jenny says, tottering out to the hallway. He picks up the photograph and puts it in his pocket. Jenny's already in the kitchen. He follows her. A swarm of tiny flies buzz lethargically in the sink. The smell is unbearable. Something indefinable and gelatinous has formed a green stain on the kitchen table. Jenny braces the toaster under her arm and gets to her feet. She stares at the floor as though turned to stone. Thomas shakes his head. "No. Don't do that. C'mon," he says, brusquely. "You're coming with me." And she actually follows him, but when they reach the hallway, she pauses again and slides her hand along the dark brown wall. "See," she says. "Here it is." She takes his hand and guides it across the cracked paint, and he can feel the inscription that Jenny etched into the wall the evening he'd gone to the emergency room. *Thomas is stupid.* She laughs suddenly and loudly. Then she slides to the floor with a thump and begins to sob. He doesn't have the energy to console her. He leaves her there and returns to the bedroom, where the smell is less offensive. He rights the overturned dresser and opens the drawer, the one with the shirtsleeve poking out. Inside he finds their father's threadbare sweaters, his socks bundled in pairs, and a few pairs of underwear. The air is thick with dust and stale, stuffy heat, combined with the stink from the kitchen, sour and abominable. He checks the other bedroom, still furnished with bunk beds plastered in stickers, the ones they'd slept in as kids and also when they were older, when he was much too tall to sleep in it and had to curl into a fetal position. Standing stock-still, he regards the fading green wallpaper and its minute white vines. All the sleepless nights he laid waiting for their father to come home. Jenny's uneasy sleep, her getting up and pawing around on the floor looking for her pacifier whenever she'd dropped it. Her whimpering. And then the relief he felt when he finally heard the key in the door, and Jacques's heavy footfalls crossing the wooden floorboards, on the way to the kitchen for a beer. This was followed by the smell of cigarette smoke billowing through the apartment. He can almost smell it now, can almost hear their father rummaging in the living room. Then he's overcome with dizziness. He staggers across the room and parks himself on the lower bunk, dropping his head between his knees. "What are you doing?" Jenny stands in the doorway, her raised eyes moist with tears. After a moment she sits beside him. The thin, stained mattress slumps under her weight. She begins to hum. Then she says, "Look, my little goldheart!" She sounds like a five year old. She runs her index finger over the sticker. "And the angel and the purple smiley face Aunt Kristin gave me . . ." Something seems to move at the outer edge of his vision, but when he turns his head there's nothing. He stands. "Let's go," he says, panic-stricken, grabbing Jenny and towing her along, but she won't come with him, she wants to return to the bunk bed. She says, "Stop it, Thomas," and goes limp, holding onto first the bedpost and then the doorjamb. But he tugs, pulling her all the way into the hallway. Just as she's about to stumble over the doorstep, he punches the door and kicks it. "Fucking hell," he shouts, "Fucking piece of fucking shit!" He kicks at the door again. "Piece of shit!" Kicking harder, the wood snapping. He yells, "I hate this shitassfucking place!" He's hot now, he wants to set fire to the entire building, he wants to choke the life out of Jenny; he kicks the door again, buckling the frame, anger thundering through him.

"Thomas," Jenny whispers.

"FUCK!" Thomas roars. The neighbor's door opens and an old woman sticks her head out. "I'm calling the police!" she cries in a shrill, thin voice. Jenny steps toward her. "But it's just us, Mrs. Krantz. Thomas and Jenny, Jacques's children, you remember us, don't you?" Thomas balls his fists and breathes heavily, clenching his teeth. Mrs. Krantz hesitates.

"You scared me."

"Jacques is dead," Jenny says.

"Jacques is dead? Jacques O'Mally?"

Thomas starts down the stairs. He hears Jenny speaking in a low voice, suddenly clear and normal, almost ingratiating. "Mrs. Krantz, have you heard any strange sounds coming from the apartment recently? It looks like it's been burgled. Have you heard anything suspicious?"

"Burglars?" Mrs. Krantz stutters nervously. Jenny continues, "Yes, it's awful. Have you heard anything? Can you remember seeing or hearing anything?" Thomas can't stand Jenny constantly repeating herself. Mrs. Krantz, he notices, has come all the way out into the hallway. She's wearing a hairnet over her wispy, curly hair.

"Have you heard anything coming from my father's apartment?"

"I don't hear so well," Mrs. Krantz says, tugging on her long earlobes. "Everything gets worse over time, everything, everything. It's hopeless . . ." She squints and points down the stairs at Thomas. "Is that your brother? I remember him."

"But you haven't heard anything?"

Mrs. Krantz shakes her head. Thomas's legs itch. If Jenny says "have you heard anything" one more time he'll scream. Then he'll murder her.

"We need to go right now, we have things to do," he says curtly. "C'mon, Jenny."

"It was so nice to see you again," Jenny says, offering her hand to the old woman.

At last Jenny totters down the stairs, the toaster under her arm. Mrs. Krantz waves her bony gray hand, and Jenny waves back. Thomas is already outside in the sunlight, his cigarette lit. His pulse gallops. A thin layer of cold sweat covers his back and belly. Instantly he's drained. The sun hammers down through a blue sky, blinding them; they sit side by side on the stoop, overwhelmed by discouragement and exhaustion. Jenny steals the cigarette from Thomas and takes a deep drag. "You don't smoke," he says, grabbing it back. "Can you believe Mrs. Krantz is still alive?" Jenny says. "She was such a loathsome bitch, a mean, nasty, wicked bitch. Remember that time she claimed we'd tortured her ugly mutt?" Thomas nods, but Jenny continues, agitated. "Just because we were friendly enough to walk the dog when she was sick!"

"I remember, Jenny."

"Remember how he beat us that night? And now here she is, being all nice to us. The loathsome bitch! I should have punched that pig right in her face." Thomas looks at Jenny. She looks angry. Then comes a faint smile and a moment's life in her green eyes. He smiles tiredly. She squeezes his arm. A bus drives past, spraying them with dirty gutter water, but they remain seated. The afternoon sun is getting lower. For some time, they are quiet. School's out and kids are scurrying cheerfully down the street. The boys tease the girls, the girls tease the boys. Bodies hopping and dancing and running and jabbing and slapping and pinching and gesticulating. A red-haired girl leaps onto the back of a skinny boy. Thomas suddenly feels rinsed and cleansed by the loud and happy cries of laughter from the herd. Then he remembers they're not allowed to be here. They don't have access to the estate. When he stands, his left foot's asleep and his knees are stiff. Only now does he notice how cold the air is. "Don't tell anyone we were here," he says, squeezing Jenny's arm.

He walks with Jenny to the station and takes the bus back to the store. It's almost completely dark now. Maloney's done with the accounting. The shipment arrived today after all, and now it's in place. The chandelier's yellow light makes the store seem smaller and cozier. Annie's on her knees sorting something in a cabinet, Peter's leaning against the ladder blowing an enormous bubble with his chewing gum, then it pops in his face. He seems more stooped than usual. Thomas drops into a chair in the office, sighing. "Have a pastry," Maloney says. He's sitting with his legs propped up on the table and riffling through a catalog. He pushes a plate filled with cream cakes toward Thomas. Thomas pokes at a strawberry with his teaspoon, then sets the spoon down. "Someone was in the apartment. Everything was ransacked."

Maloney peers up from his catalog. "Junkies?"

"Maybe."

"Maybe it was a while ago."

"But it looked recent."

"How could you tell?" Maloney sets his feet on the floor and inches closer. His gut bumps against the edge of the table.

"There was an apple core on the floor. It wasn't dried up, it was fresh. Only a tiny bit of brown."

Maloney leans all the way back in the boss's chair: one long, fluid motion. "You sound like an amateur detective. Some kid could've tossed an apple core there, especially in that neighborhood. Don't you think you should close the book on your father's story?" A strip of Maloney's stomach is visible between the elastic of his pants and his shirt, which has slid up.

"He never did a goddamn thing for you while he was alive, and I'm sure it'll be the same now that he's dead. You look like someone who needs a drink. We can ask Annie to lock up."

They sit at the bar. The bar wraps around them in a very safe and inviting way. Thomas is on his second martini, while Maloney slurps the last of a piña colada. The girl behind the bar smiles at them under sharply trimmed, bleached bangs, and the music is just their style—as if she knew precisely what they liked. And now they're acting kind of goofy, unrestrained. Thomas has nearly forgotten about the break-in and Jenny's naked, frightened face. His glance lingers on the girl's eyes, which are dolled up in black. Are they blue or gray? Maloney says, "Maybe Peter's gay." And Thomas says he thinks Peter's a virgin. "But the kid's twenty-two years old, for God's sake." And Thomas says, "You can't talk about anything but sex." "What about you?"

Maloney answers, and then Thomas's cell phone rings for the third time—he's ignored it until now; it's Patricia. "I need to take this," he says, pushing the door open and stepping onto the sidewalk as he grapples with his cell. Cool wind whips at his face.

Patricia's already home, she says, it's past 8:00, and they'd agreed to have dinner. Did he buy wine? Bread? Chicken? Vegetables? Thomas stabilizes himself against the wall with his left arm. "I'm coming," he says. "I'm taking a taxi right now. I'll bring Chinese. And beer. I'm sorry, hon, I lost track of time."

"I don't want Chinese," Patricia says angrily, "and you sound trashed."

Maloney isn't at all happy that Thomas needs to go, but he doesn't even stand up when Thomas gathers his things and pays the bill. They say their goodbyes. Maloney calls out, "See you later!" Thomas trudges up and down the street, but there's no available cab. Through the steamy glass door he can see Maloney seated among a group of younger men and women, whom he's already begun to entertain with wild gesticulations. Out here it's cold as hell. Thomas heads toward the wider boulevards, buys beer and cigarettes at a deli. He's freezing and shivering, and finally a taxi pulls along the curb. It's a pleasant ride through the city. I love the lights and the darkness, he thinks, lights and darkness, and just like that they're at the door of his building. It's all too quiet here, he thinks. And I haven't bought any dinner, I can't go home without any dinner. Thoughts like flies and stinging insects: Where are my keys? An apple core, the stench in the kitchen. If she doesn't want Chinese, I need to go all the way down to the tapas place, it'll take at least fifteen minutes.

When he balances through the door with a tall stack of takeout containers resting on the palm of his right hand, he drops his key and is almost dumb enough to bend down and pick it up and thereby drop the containers with all the food, but he manages not to. His head's buzzing. He licks his lips, a raspy dryness in his mouth. The long hallway is high-ceilinged, painted white. He hears Patricia approaching from the living room in her bare feet. She pauses a few feet away. "Sorry," he says, forcing himself to smile. "It's been a strange day." She tilts her head. The light lands on the left side of her face, the high cheekbone, the ear. "I was wearing a dress, but I took it off." She tosses her hair back, lifting her chin. "I thought we were going to have a nice evening."

With his back he pushes the door shut, then sets the containers on the low table under the mirror.

"And we will, won't we?"

He catches a glimpse of himself, ruddy-faced, bags under his eyes. Then he advances toward her, and reluctantly she falls into his embrace. "You smell like alcohol," she says into his neck, "and I'm hungry."

She's wearing something that looks like pajamas, but he's not certain they are pajamas. Silk that hangs loosely from her, no doubt very expensive. Patricia spends a lot of money on clothes. Patricia wants a baby. Patricia's ambitious, but she wants a baby. She crawls onto the sofa and bites into an artichoke heart. She raises her beer to her mouth and drinks. Then, shifting herself, she points at the tapenade. She'd like some of that, too. In the blue armchair Thomas sits arching forward, longing for a cigarette. But then he'd have to go all the way down to the street, and that wouldn't be the best thing to do right now; it'd be downright rude. He shovels some lettuce into his mouth and bites into a hunk of bread, realizing that he hasn't eaten anything since lunch. When Patricia's full, he eats what's left in the containers, and when he's emptied the containers, he leans back, lethargic and sleepy. Patricia, apparently no longer angry, asks how his visit to his father's apartment went. He can't muster the strength to tell her how it looked, so he tells her about Mrs. Krantz instead, trying to make it sound light and funny. "Her voice sounds like . . .

like some screechy kid pissing in a potty." Where that came from he doesn't know, but Patricia smiles, her eyes growing friendlier. "Did she sound like the screechy kid or the piss hitting the potty?" she asks. Thomas returns the smile. Staring into each other's eyes, they are in harmony, everything they have together is in that moment, a fraction of a second. Then Thomas glances away. "I have no interest whatsoever in going to the funeral. I'm considering not going. Why should I go? For whose sake?"

"For Jenny's, I guess."

He doesn't answer that.

"Do you think your aunt and Helena will go?"

"No. But Jenny's probably invited them. I can't deal with Jenny either, for that matter. All of this means nothing to me, I don't want to be involved."

"But Thomas. Isn't it best that we go, get it over with? At least then you'll never regret not going."

"But I can regret that I *went*," he says, standing. The city glimmers in the darkness, under a yellow half-moon. Patricia sighs and collects the containers.

"We'll go out afterward and have some champagne, just you and me. We'll celebrate when it's over," she calls out on her way to the kitchen. Slap, slap, the soles of her bare feet against the wooden floor. Water running in the sink. She's rinsing the plates, no doubt. Thomas opens the window and lights a cigarette. He leans across the cornice and blows smoke into the cold, damp night air.

Patricia returns to the living room. She stops, preparing to say something, but hesitates. Instead she says, "Want me to put my dress back on?"

He turns toward her, making sure the hand holding the cigarette remains outside. "You don't need to. I'd be fine if you just took your clothes off." She regards him solemnly. Then she smiles and begins to undress. He doesn't have any desire for this at all, but now there's no way back. So ridiculously compliant of him, just because he felt guilty for coming home late, for smoking indoors when he's agreed not to, for not making dinner for her, for not talking with her. For coming home drunk like a loser. Now she's naked and standing in the center of the room, her fair skin almost golden in the half-light of the reading lamp. He looks at her hips, her pubic hair, her smooth thighs. He looks at her belly, a little distended. Her breasts and her long arms, her slender throat. Her skin is slightly wrinkled right above her knees. Her eyes are so black. He takes a deep drag of his cigarette, then tosses it away. He thinks of Annie's big ass and quickly begins to remove his pants—he needs to be fast now, when, miraculously, he's erect—and soon he's spinning Patricia around and draping her over the sofa. He gets on his knees behind her and eases into her, his eyes closed; she gives herself to him, she's soft, he pulls her close, and just when he's about to come everything grinds to a halt. He notices a fly on the wall and wonders what it's doing alive this time of year, then images of his father's apartment rush through his mind, the bunk beds, the smell, it nauseates him, he draws himself out of her, lies on his back on the floor, turns his head away when he hears Patricia sit beside him, sure that she's either eyeing him worriedly or accusingly. Soon he hears her stand and go to the toilet. He feels his spine against the floor, the pain. He's tall and thin and bony. His shirt curls up along the hem. He's still wearing his socks. But a little while later, after they've gone to bed, she does everything she can to be good to him, patiently and expertly, so expertly that even though he doesn't feel up to it or want to, she succeeds; she knows his body, knows precisely which stimulations arouse him, and he gives in at last. He's relieved that it feels good to enter her. She makes faint, delicate noises, and he sees her quivering eyelids. When he finally comes, with enormous relief and oddly jarring grunts, her eyes are radiant now, her gaze fixed and sated. She removes a stray lock of hair from her mouth, tucks the duvet around him, and turns out the light. Then they fall asleep.

On Saturday morning Thomas wakes early, his heart thumping, stressed, uneasy. It's 6:00 A.M., still dark outside. Patricia sleeps with a hand on her belly, and the bed smells like old man. He rolls over, tries to get his pulse under control. Can't. He goes to the bathroom, drinks water. Then back to bed. Falling asleep seems impossible, yet he must've slept, because it's suddenly light outside, and he's dreamt, and now it's 9:30. Patricia's up, and his telephone beeps with a text message. Drunk with sleep, he reads, "you need to help me, the toaster doesn't work, j." For God's sake, she's got to stop this now. Instantly, he's pissed. Feeling the tension in his neck, he kicks off the duvet. "stop it," he writes. "aren't you sweet, thanks a lot," Jenny replies. He curses under his breath and steps into the shower. He pulls on pants and a sweater, clean socks, running shoes. In the kitchen Patricia sits swaddled in her duvet, reading the newspaper. She drinks coffee. She's bought bread and butter at the bakery. There's also juice. "Good morning, honey," she says, sliding over so that he can sit on the bench. She's done the dishes. A half-empty bottle of beer rests on the kitchen table, and she's put the food containers in a garbage bag and swept the floor. But she didn't use the dustpan: dust and crumbs are heaped in a little pile in the corner, near the sink. Thomas pours coffee and butters his bread. Jenny texts, "knew I could count on you." He falls for it every time. She feigns helplessness and insinuates that he doesn't care about her, and so he comes leaping to her aid after all, motivated by a guilt he has no reason to feel. But not this time, hell no. "fine," he responds, skidding his cellphone across the table. "What's going on?" Patricia asks, looking at him. "Nothing. It's just Jenny. She's obsessed with the stupid toaster."

"Toaster?"

"I can't explain it. And it's boring! Ridiculous. She's trying to manipulate me, as usual. I guarantee she's bored. Alice is off with her new boyfriend all the time, she says, and Jenny just sits staring at the wall." He hears how hotheaded he sounds, how loudly he's talking. Already he regrets it, but he can't help himself now.

"She's working, though, isn't she?"

"Yes, but when she's not working. She works the late shift. All she does is eat, all day. And stare. That fatty." Thomas slams his cup on the table. "I'm going for a walk." Patricia looks at him, surprised, then returns to her newspaper with a shake of her head. He's almost never angry. Now he's boiling with rage. He takes the stairs down from the sixth floor, tramping hard on the steps, pounding his fist on the elevator at every level. Luckily he left his cellphone back in the kitchen, otherwise he would've called and given her an earful. The temperature outside is colder than yesterday, the wind's blowing from the west. A plastic bag dances in the gusts. He should've worn a jacket. He fishes his cigarettes from his pocket and finally gets one lit after several attempts. Fucking wind. Maybe the door of his father's apartment was busted a long time ago. Maybe it was just some junkies, like Maloney suggested, who'd stolen the silverware and a few pieces of furniture, or some drunken second-hand shop dealer, or some boys, or maybe all of the above in several rounds. Maybe it really was some kid throwing an apple core through the door on his way down the stairs. But it was in the living room. Thomas turns a corner and the wind lashes his face. The park on the other side of the street seems gloomy in this gray weather. An old woman with two small dogs is practically flying through the air. A band of youths hang around the benches at the park entrance. Farther down the street there's an ambulance, and the EMTs are maneuvering a stretcher into the vehicle. His rage dissipates once he's trudged around the block. Yet he still has no desire to go upstairs to Patricia. He decides to go grocery shopping. The supermarket is filled with families chugging around with large carts and piling them with items. There's a line at every register. The families with children appear to be buying groceries for the entire week: milk, bread, frozen foods, cereal, huge packages of toilet paper. Thomas removes products from the shelves, but the entire time his ears ring with a high-pitched note of irritation. And when he puts his items onto the belt—goat cheese, red onions, crackers, sparkling water, and a whole bunch more—he suddenly stops. Every single one of these people will die. Every single person, no matter how old they are. The ones babbling cheerfully, clowning around, having a good time, arguing and talking, or lonely or hunted or sad or happy or relieved—even plain joyful—they will all die. Maybe soon. They'll lie like wax figures in some morgue. Their insides and their flesh will swell and rot, bacteria will explode inside their bodies and make them stink like dead cows in 95-degree heat. He looks at a dark-skinned, middle-aged woman behind him, at the young blond man at the register, at a grandfather holding his small grandson's hand. They'll all be disgusting corpses. Maybe very soon. The grandfather actually looks like someone who might kick the bucket any day. The kid could run in front of a car. The woman could have a terminal illness without knowing it. Him too. Even him. Maybe he's got cancer. He slides his card through the machine and grabs his bags. He has a headache, a hangover, and stiff legs. The glass door glides open and nudges him back onto the street with a puff of warm air. Son of a bitch. Their father lay with his eyes closed, his dark hair combed back; one of the guards had found him, dead as a doornail on the floor. Heart attack. A white sheet covered his body. When they removed it, he was wearing prison garb. "Yes, that's him," Jenny had said, though no one had asked them to identify the body. She took a step back and squeezed Thomas's arm. He felt nothing but loathing. There he lay, a corpse, already pallid and stiff. He recognized with a cool indifference some of his own features: Yup, that's how I look, too. It was as if their father resembled a boy or a young man, and yet didn't. His features were smooth, wrinkle-free. The dome of his forehead, his jutted chin, his broad mouth, his thick lips. His face expressed nothing. It was clear that he was no longer a human being. Yet it was unmistakably him. The body, a form for the life that had been inside him, like a mold one lifts a cake out of. The cake had been eaten. Their father's big hands were crossed over his abdomen; they'd probably struggled to set them just so, or maybe they'd hurried, as soon as he'd been declared dead by the prison doctor. With a sudden tenderness, Thomas imagined several female officers with keys and pistols in their belts standing over the deceased, washing his ears, cleaning his nails. Arranging him, getting him *ready*. But it was the nurses who'd fixed him up. Those hands unnerved him; they were the same ones that had filled so much of his childhood. The hands he and Jenny had kept a close watch on, the entire time, those fast, unpredictable hands. Their father wore the ring with the black square on his little finger. He'd inherited it from his big brother, who'd been in the foreign legion and died when he was twenty-six, and he'd always promised Thomas that it would be his some day. "When the time comes, you'll get the ring, Thomas. Before my brother got it, it was my father's. When I die, it'll be yours. And your son will have it after you."

"But you can't die," he'd said, anxious. He was seven years old.

Their father had laughed out loud. "Ha! I'm not planning on it!"

Thomas wanted nothing to do with the ring. They must've forgotten to remove it when they prepared his body. Jenny squeezed his arm. "He looks so different," she whispered. She'd visited him at the prison, so she must've known. He hadn't seen his father's face in many years. Outside it was cold, but the western sky was soft pink, golden. The bushes shivered when they walked toward the road. Thomas had taken the package containing his father's possessions from the cell; they'd just handed it to him, without asking whether he wanted it or not. He could have chucked the whole thing in the garbage can on the way home, but the package now lay at the bottom of the bedroom closet, on top of his shoes. He'd first realized he had it when he got home. Later he'd opened it and found the pathetic dirty magazines, the notebook with telephone numbers sloppily scratched in, and the watch with the worn leather strap—which the old man had owned for as long as Thomas could remember. Every time he raised his arm to smack him or Jenny, or just raised his arm threateningly, pretending he was going to hit them—which was almost worse than the punch itself—he'd seen the reflection of light on the face of the watch and tried to tell what time it was. As a way of shielding himself. Like whistling when you were being beaten. Or reciting a verse in your head when you were being yelled at by the teacher, in front of everyone. Later he sang pop songs to himself, but around his sixteenth birthday nothing worked anymore, and so he began to fight back. Though he was taller and bigger than his father by the last year he lived with him, his father was almost always superior, except the one incredible time when Thomas had managed to haul him down to the floor and sit on his chest staring directly into his eyes, hissing: *You will never hit me again, you bastard.* He was agitated by so many emotions that he nearly lost his breath. As well as a strong desire to cling to his father's body, to feel his arms around him: tears, love. Their father had only smiled and shook his head, clucking his tongue. And Thomas stood and walked to his room. The next day he ran away from home.

Wind rips at the enormous white tarpaulins covering the façade of the adjacent building. He still has no desire to return to Patricia, but he can't stay out here. A woman opens a window on the second floor. He meets her glance for a moment, then her face disappears behind a checkered cloth that she shakes out vigorously. Crumbs and fluff billow in the air like snow. He takes the elevator up and carries the grocery bags into the apartment. The bathroom door opens, and Patricia exits with a towel around her head. "I'm sorry," he says.

"Every time you walk through that door you say 'I'm sorry'."

"I know," he says.

"Did you go to the store?"

"Just picked up a few things." He turns and grabs the bags and walks down the hall. He gives her a quick peck on the cheek as he passes by; she smells like fresh laundry, but there's also this hint of earthiness, of wet soil, which he always finds off-putting. He sets the bags on the kitchen table and checks his cellphone. Jenny has called several times. She's sent three text messages: "please can't you help me?" and "I'll take it to the shop then" and a half-hour ago: "aunt k called." He hears Patricia setting up the ironing board in the living room. With the phone in his hand he opens the bedroom door. It's cool and dark in here. He sits on the bed. His clock ticks faintly. He doesn't *want* to call. After a short time, Jenny answers, out of breath: "What do you want?"

"What's up with the toaster?"

"It doesn't work."

"Why are you obsessed with it? Why do you want that old piece of shit? Why are you harassing me?"

"Am I harassing YOU? I think you're harassing me. Why won't you help me?"

"Don't waste your money taking it to the shop, that's crazy. Don't waste your money on him."

"He's dead. It's my toaster now."

"Don't you hear how ridiculous that sounds, Jenny?"

"Should I hang up now? Stop it, Alice, I'm on the phone!"

"What's she doing?"

"Badgering me for money. Won't you just look at it?"

"Only if you tell me why you're so obsessed with it. Why didn't you take a painting instead? Or Grandma's dishes?"

Patricia stands in the doorway, a stack of creased shirts over her arm, and looks at him sharply. Then she leaves.

"Because," Jenny sighs, her voice softening. "That is, because, you know, it meant a lot to me when I was a child. When we made toast. We lived on bread, Thomas. It was magical to me, it could make plain things interesting. Toasted bread was fragrant and tasty, especially if we had butter or jam. I know it's nostalgic. But it's a good memory. For me, at least."

Now it's Thomas who sighs. "A good memory. Do you really mean that?"

"Yes." Long silence. "I'd like to hold onto that good memory."

"It sounds like you've taken a course on positive thinking."

"I haven't. I'm just thinking that I might as well make the best out of it."

"Out of what?"

"Well—I don't know. Everything." They fall silent. He hears Alice clattering in the background, and a television. Jenny clears her throat.

"Okay," he says. "I'll look at it. Will you be home in an hour and a half?"

"I'm always home, Thomas."

They hang up, and he sits staring at his shoes. Then he stands and walks back to the kitchen. While he puts his groceries in the fridge, Patricia comes in. She says, "You seem very strange."

"What makes you say that?"

"Because that's what I think."

"Are you trying to start a fight?"

"No."

"Have I done something wrong?"

"No. But you seem strange."

"Oh, Patricia. Stop. I'm just not quite myself."

"How so?"

"Restless. Odd."

"What do you mean 'odd'?"

"Claustrophobic."

"Claustrophobic? Do you want to talk about it?"

He looks out the window. "I'm going over to Jenny's soon. I promised I'd help her with something."

"I'm going with you."

"You don't have to do that. I won't be long. We can see a film later."

"Don't you want me to come with you?"

"That's not what I meant."

"Well, then I'm coming with you." Patricia gives him a look, challenging him to tell her she can't come. Her eyes bore into his. "It's been a long time since I saw Jenny and Alice." Thomas glances at the floor. And so Patricia gives up her ironing and goes with him. The sky's blue, and the green river water reflects the treetops and the silhouettes of houses. The train screeches slowly southward, out toward the suburbs that form a broad and frayed ring around the city: public housing high-rises and wide swaths of rundown row houses, body shops, storage sheds. Huge factories surrounded by barbed-wire fence, smaller industrial plants. A junkyard here, a warehouse with a big wind-swept parking lot there, a lumberyard, then more of the tall cement towers where people are crammed together beneath ceilings thick with asbestos, the best of which have access to a boxlike balcony. Though she's now on a sugar-free diet, Patricia has bought an apple pie. She squeezes his hand. They walk through the streets where young men hang out in front of delis and fast food joints. A whiff of beer and smoke wafts from the bars; they pass the shopping plaza with the movie theater, where people stand in line at the ticket window. A gaggle of women scowl at Patricia when she stops to pick up her silk scarf. The elevator rocks threateningly. It snails its way up to the eighth floor. It smells of piss here. They look at each other the entire way up, but say nothing. Alice opens the door. She seems surprised. "Look who's here!" But she gives Patricia a hug and lets them enter. For a moment Thomas thinks: She looks like Mom. But that's probably just his imagination. Alice is small and slender and has a prominent nose and a pretty, curvy Cupid's bow like her father. Her golden-brown skin is smooth and fine, her dark eyes almond-shaped and a little crooked. She's shaved her head. A snake tattoo threads its way up over her neck to the back of her head. She's only just turned eighteen. Dropped out of school, unemployed. For a moment, Thomas recalls her sitting on his lap when she was little. The way she'd held onto his neck when he carried her. Now she steps to the side so he can enter the apartment. And here comes Jenny, smiling, from the kitchen; she looks hot and sweaty, her lipstick seeping into the small wrinkles near her mouth. She sees Patricia and says: "*You're* here?" Patricia smiles and hands her the pie. The kitchen is a mess, and a large pot simmers on the stove. "How nice. I was just making some soup." Jenny washes her hands. "I thought Thomas might want some lunch, but maybe you've already eaten?" Thomas leans against the fridge. One can see a long way from the kitchen window: the forest in the distance, high-rises, other parts of the city. When he leans forward and glances down at the area between the buildings, his stomach lurches: networks of trails, a playground, parked cars. A few children run across one of the fields wielding a kite on a string. It swirls in the air and flutters back and forth in the wind, and it looks as though they can barely hold onto it. He turns. The soup is sludgy and gray, and smells nauseatingly of cabbage and pork fat. Patricia converses politely, Thomas watches a flock of geese. Or are they ducks? He goes to the living room, where the curtains are drawn. Darkness, low furniture, a whole lot of embroidered pillows on the sofa. On the wall a number of faded drawings from when Alice was a kid, signed with large, clumsy letters. *For the world's best mom. Congratulations Mom.* A reproduction of a picture of a deer standing beside a lake. A framed photograph of himself and Jenny. In it, they are young and standing under a tall tree. Jenny's skinny. She's wearing a white dress and her thick reddish-blonde hair spills to her waist. He just looks like an overgrown boy. They hug each other, smiling. Their feet are bare. Maloney was the one who'd taken the photograph. Light flickers between the green leaves. A walk in the woods. A very long time ago. It smells stuffy in the apartment, and he wants to open a window, but marches down the hallway toward the bedrooms instead. The shelving units have seen better days. A bunch of bric-a-brac, some books, washed-out bed linens and towels in untidy stacks. A door is ajar. Alice is lying on her bed with a man. Thomas hurries back to the kitchen. Jenny has ladled up the soup, there's no way out of it now. "Alice and Ernesto! Lunch!" Jenny shouts. "Is that her boyfriend?" Patricia whispers. Jenny nods, and rolls her eyes and shakes her head resignedly. They sit around the little camping table. Jenny passes out pink napkins adorned with teddy bears. Thomas grinds peppercorns over his bowl. Unidentifiable chunks of fatty gray meat bob around in the murky liquid. He lifts a piece of overcooked cabbage with his spoon and lets it fall back into the soup. What is she thinking, serving such dog food. She knows that he—that he can't. That he has better taste than this. That this is . . . The kids drift in. This Ernesto is only a head taller than Alice, but he's broad and muscular. His hair is short, black, and shiny. He greets them politely, introduces himself. He must be older than Alice, Thomas thinks, feeling discomfort, both at the soup—which actually tastes like food served at an institution—and Ernesto's hairy hands, one firmly planted on Alice's thigh as he shovels soup into his mouth with the other. Alice stirs her spoon around her bowl and picks at a piece of bread. "How are you doing?" Patricia tries. "It's been so long since I've seen you." "Really good," Alice says. "Are you still looking for work?" Alice nods disinterestedly. "No, you're not," Jenny says. Ernesto glances up. Alert. Solid jawline. "And how about you?" Patricia regards him with interest. "Are you a student? Are you in college?" All of a sudden she sounds rather strident. He smiles curtly. "Hardly," he says in a calm, friendly voice. "I'm a musician." "Really, how exciting—are you a singer?" He shakes his head. "Drummer." So that's why he's so muscular, Thomas thinks, clearing his throat. "Ernesto plays in a really cool band," Alice explains, pushing her bowl aside. "They're super awesome. You can listen to them online, if you want. They're called El Pozo." She stands. "They just sit around, doing nothing at all," grumbles Jenny. "You don't do a thing. I don't know how you can stand it."

"Thanks for lunch," Alice says.

"There's an apple pie," Patricia says. "If you'd like to eat some later?"

Alice vanishes into the hallway. She's in an awful rush. Ernesto turns in the doorway and, smiling, reveals a relatively nice set of teeth. There's a noticeable gap between the front two. "Thanks for lunch, Mother Jenny." Then he's gone. Jenny and Thomas exchange glances. "*Mother Jenny?*" he says softly. "What the hell does he mean by that?"

"I have no idea," Jenny says, ladling more soup into her bowl.

"Doesn't he have a mother?"

"I don't know."

"He seems sweet," Patricia says, raising a yellow-brown drinking glass to her mouth.

"He's not. He's a snake."

Patricia swallows, then puts down her glass. "Why a snake?"

"I can just tell. He's lazy and slimy. They just lie in bed all day fooling around. Alice is being dragged down to his level. Into the mud. Before him it was another guy. He was actually worse. An arrogant bastard, to put it mildly. She's got a new boyfriend all the time."

"I can find out if we have a job for her at the museum."

"If she's even able to handle a job," Jenny says bitterly, putting her spoon down. "I honestly don't know what I should do with her. She hates me."

"Oh, stop, Jenny. She doesn't hate you," Thomas says. He's irritated, dark waves in his belly. "She's only eighteen."

"But where does he live, this Ernesto? Here?" Patricia asks.

Jenny gets to her feet and rinses the bowls. "It seems that way, doesn't it?" Patricia wraps a lock of her hair between her fingers; no one says a word. Patricia glances curiously at Thomas, but what does it *mean*? He needs to smoke, he can't breathe, he has to leave. "The toaster," Jenny says coolly, "it's over there." She nods in the direction of the big closet at the end of the kitchen table. "Can you please look at it now?"

Thomas fiddles with a little fucking screwdriver. The women are seated in the living room drinking tea and eating apple pie. As far as he can see, Jenny's drawn the curtains—which is better than nothing. The door's ajar, but he can't hear what they're saying. Are they laughing? Yes, Jenny is, and now Patricia too. The toilet flushes. Heavy steps in the hall, it must be Ernesto. The toaster is unbelievably greasy and revolting and littered with old crumbs. That he's really sitting here prying it apart in this kitchen fills him with disgust—that he's agreed to do it. Insanity. That old feeling of deep-seated anger at Jenny and all the guilt that comes with it hits him like a slap. It's so incompatible. The sobbing. There's no development in our relationship at all, he thinks. It's as if her entire personality exists to play the role of victim, huge and hollow, for my benefit only. So I can fill the holes with my shame, my strange, indebted need to protect. The screwdriver slides from his hand, he's warping the screws. He props the toaster between his knees, braces it tight, and tries again. It's big and clumsy, probably at least as old as he is. He has no idea how you pry such a thing apart, he just keeps unscrewing the screws and removing all the parts that come loose, when the screws no longer hold them together. Suddenly it breaks in two. The shell of thick plastic falls apart. Thomas gawks at the guts of the toaster. And all at once he jerks his head back.

Fastened between the now detached outer shell and the heating coils, on either side, is a thick packet wrapped in tinfoil and taped carefully together with clear, yellowed tape. At first he simply stares. Then he manages to pry them out. He hears Patricia's voice approaching. Feverishly he stuffs the two packets under his shirt, then under the waistband of his pants. When she steps into the kitchen, he's back to sitting over his work, replacing the screws in the tiny holes. And what part belonged where? He hadn't organized the pieces in any manageable way. He's beginning to sweat.

"Is it tricky?" she asks, filling the pot with water.

"Nah," he says. "Not really."

Patricia sets the pot on the stove and turns on the gas jet. "Tell me when it's boiling, okay?" Then she leaves again.

He's warm and cold, his heart races, his hands tremble. What the hell did he find? A mass of disjointed thoughts swirl through his brain, but there's no up and down to anything. What the fuck is it? Who put the packets there? What the hell's in them? He screws and screws with the terrible doll's screwdriver that keeps rotating crookedly on the thread, and now Jenny comes out and stands beside him, her hands at her side.

"Can you figure it out?"

"Well, I've taken it apart and put it back together, at least," he mumbles. "We'll see if it works."

"Could you tell what was wrong?"

"Nope," he says, tightening the last of the screws. "It probably just doesn't work. Broken."

He puts the toaster on the table, and Jenny immediately grabs it and plugs it into the outlet above the table.

"Oh, look!" She claps excitedly. "It works! I said it would! Oh, thank you, Thomas. Look, it works!"

And it does. The small coils glow orange. "Patricia, come out here. Your man is a genius with a screwdriver. Come see!"

They all stand admiring the rather smoky toaster. A burnt odor hangs in the kitchen.

"Can you smell it? Oh, I love that scent. Right before the toast pops up."

She's crazy, Thomas thinks. The pot whistles. Patricia pours water in the teapot. Excited now, the women return to the sofa.

"Come on, Thomas, have some apple pie!" Jenny's eyes are lit up like a child's.

When he clambers to his feet, he can feel the packets against his belly. What the hell's in them? He yanks the cord of the stinking toaster from the plug and walks stiffly out to the others.

Jenny suddenly looks more like a diva than a washed up, underpaid, slovenly, scarred at-an-early-age, frustrated nurse's aid. She throws herself upon the leather couch, props a leg on the easy chair, and her dress slides up to reveal a fleshy, milk-white thigh. Her cheeks are flushed and she seems both lazy and shamelessly sensuous. Thomas can tell it makes Patricia uncomfortable. Even Jenny's voice is sultry. When Alice enters with a mug and plops down beside Patricia, pouring herself some tea, Jenny's motherly love knows no bounds.

"Did you tell Thomas and Patricia who sent us a letter yesterday, sweetie?"

"Just a letter from my dad." Alice slurps her tea cautiously.

"Isn't that incredible? Alice and I couldn't believe our own eyes, isn't that right, sweetie?"

"From Ahmed?" Thomas interrupts, nearly choking on a bite of pie. "Why?"

"Yeah, Alice. Why?" Jenny smiles, her eyes half-closed.

Alice puts her mug down. "He wanted to tell me I have a little brother."

"What?" Thomas straightens up. "Where?"

"The letter was sent from his mother's address," Jenny says. "If she's still alive, or if he's moved into her house, he didn't say."

"He sent a photo. It's a cute kid," Alice says, her face breaking into a little smile, a brief flash that vanishes almost instantly.

"He looks like you did when you were a baby, sweetie. A beautiful child. And you look like Ahmed."

"She also looks like you," Patricia says, "and your mother."

"Did he send money?" Thomas asks.

"Nah."

"You haven't heard from him in ten years."

"No, but now we *have* heard from him." Jenny smiles. As if it was something to smile about, Thomas thinks. Ahmed let his daughter down. The tinfoil crackles against his belly whenever he moves. Carefully he leans back in the wobbly chair.

Jenny takes a deep breath and slowly exhales. "In our family the men don't take very good care of their children. It's a tradition. But you don't have any children, Thomas, so you don't count."

Patricia mumbles: "Not yet, in any case," and Alice sits up, says: "Not all the women take good care of their children, either, as far as I can see."

"What do you mean, Alice?" Jenny struggles to sit up straight. "Why do you say that?"

"As far as I know, your mother left you two."

Jenny sinks back again. "Right, well, but we had Aunt Kristin."

"Oh, did we now?" Thomas looks at Jenny

"She was a consolation of sorts. In any event, we lived with her that summer."

"That was a week at most."

"I hate it when you're so superficial, Mom," Alice says in a high, clear voice. "It's unbecoming."

"Hey, now," Jenny mutters.

"Aunt Kristin let you live with your father. She couldn't handle you two. You told me yourself. And your father was a bastard."

"Exactly," Thomas says, smiling at Alice. "He was a bastard."

"Exactly," Alice says, returning the smile. Suddenly there's a connection between them.

"Hang on," Jenny says. "Aunt Kristin wasn't much older than you are now. Of course she couldn't keep us . . ." Now it seems as though Jenny's about to fall asleep. Her eyes fall shut.

"Do you have a smoke, Thomas?" Alice asks. He fishes a crushed pack from his breast pocket, and offers one to Alice. They light their cigarettes. Patricia glares at him disapprovingly, but it's oh so good to feel the smoke in his lungs. Alice ashes on an empty pie plate.

"Are you sad that you never hear from your father?" Patricia asks.

She shrugs. "I used to be. But not anymore. Since I don't really know him, I couldn't care less."

"Be happy you don't," Jenny snuffles. "But he's got himself a cute kid, just like you were once." Did she drink port before they arrived?, Thomas wonders. Or popped pills? Does she pop pills?

"She still is!" Patricia squeezes Alice's shoulder. "Please visit us soon. You can bring your boyfriend, if you'd like." Alice seems younger and happier for a moment. She leans against Patricia and wraps an arm around her. Then, suddenly, Ernesto is standing in the doorway in his undershirt. "There's pie?" he asks, showing everyone his toothy smile.

Thomas and Patricia push open the door to the street and are almost blinded by the light. Thomas glances up at Jenny's windows, and sure enough, he sees a flapping arm; he returns the wave. They take a left toward the station. Patricia draws inward, says nothing. Thomas discreetly shoves his hand under his jacket and shirt and touches the packets. The tinfoil seems to have loosened here and there, no doubt there's plastic underneath. Their father lay on a plastic sheet. Jenny insisted that the nurses dress him in his own clothes. So they did. Meanwhile they waited outside, and it took a long time. Maneuvering such a rigid cargo of flesh and bones must be strenuous work. The sounds in the hallway were hard and raw. The entire time he felt one little shock after another: a door slammed shut, then voices, then footsteps coming or going. As though all sounds were magnified. Jenny clutched the sleeve of his jacket and wouldn't let it go. They stared at each other, but said nothing. She hung on his sleeve. Then the nurses returned, each of them flushed and warm. One disappeared, while the other began removing a thin rubber glove from her left hand. Her disposable smock rustled softly. "So he's all set," she said. Jenny thanked her, clasping her hands in her own. An ambulance was called. They could see him here or at the hospital chapel. But Jenny wanted to see him in his "usual surroundings." Their father now wore a torn, dark-blue shirt and gray flannel pants. But the nurse had left the yellow windbreaker hanging on a chair. It was made of nylon. Maybe she'd considered how, when he was shoved into the oven, the flames would shoot through the windbreaker with its raging fire. Thomas tried to imagine it. Raging fire. Within seconds, the material would curl up and melt and the stench would be terrible.

"Would you like to sit with him for a bit?" the nurse asked kindly. "I can bring another chair."

"No thanks, we'll stand," Thomas replied.

"The car will be here shortly." She smiled, then was gone. The door closed.

"I hope we can find our way out again," Thomas said. Jenny eyed him reproachfully. Then she tugged at the white sheet covering their father's shins, and the toe tag appeared, neatly cinched around his right big toe with a little bow. His naked feet looked awful. The nurses hadn't clipped his nails. Thick, horny yellow nails on crooked toes.

"Gross."

"Thomas!" Jenny put the sheet back. There was an overly sweet, nauseating odor in the cell, mixed with Jenny's spicy perfume. They stood there. An odd silence. The very silence, Thomas thought. The innermost essence of silence: the silence of death. Everything ends. Everything has ended. A long time passed and a short time passed. The late afternoon light fell softly through the armor-plated window. A glimpse of greenish sky. The cell was impersonal, lacking any trace of their father, who had lived here for four weeks. Maybe the staff had cleaned it up before they'd arrived. The nurse popped her head in the room. The car was ready. Jenny sniffled and shot a final glance at the body on the cot. When they exited the cell, they saw two porters rolling the folded-up stretcher from one end of the hallway to the other; they also saw the thick plastic body bag their father would be stuffed into, but they didn't stop to see him being wheeled off. The nurse followed them out and shook their hands. Then they signed a piece of paper, and the package with their father's possessions was placed into Thomas's hand. The heavy doors fell shut behind them. Jenny looked about for the ambulance when they were outside in the fresh air, but neither one of them could see it. "Maybe it's parked on the other side of the prison," Jenny said. A bird tweeted cheerfully in a tree above them. "Don't you think? Don't you think there's a parking lot on the other side?" She sounded so anxious. "Yes, probably," he said. She tucked her arm under his. "I'm quite certain there's a parking lot over there, aren't you?" Then they walked along the huge, wet lawns observing the green and rose-pink sky, and as though automatically they headed in the direction of the train station cafeteria, where they sat next to the window and ordered the weak coffee they served with a whole lot of sugar. They froze like icicles.

"We're parentless now," Jenny said, her lips quivering. Then she went silent. It was as if they were children again, slouching wordlessly at a small gray table under a slightly too-bright source of light. Just like they used to in the evenings in the kitchen at home. There's something childish about us, Thomas thought. That's what we have in common.

Patricia clutches his arm and picks up the pace. The sun's so clear and strong that it stings their eyes. In the light, her dark hair has a reddish sheen. She squeezes his arm. "Can you and Maloney hire Alice for the store? She needs to get out of that apartment. You think she could clean, or something?"

"I don't know, we've already got Eva, you know. I can't just fire her. And every position is filled. Peter's apprenticing. We won't be rid of him for another two years."

"I just think we ought to help her, Thomas. She's smart enough, don't you think? And after all, she's your only niece. And mine. She's the only child in the family."

"She's not a child."

"Yes, she is. An overgrown child."

"Didn't you mention a job at the museum?"

"I'll look into it tomorrow. I just thought it would be good for her to spend time with you, that you could maybe train her."

He scrutinizes her.

"What?" she asks.

"Do you really think it'd be good for her to spend time with me? Don't you think it'd be better for her to get away from all this shit as fast as she can, especially her mother and her family? She's young. She could get the fuck out of here."

"Get away? How? With what? They're living off nothing. Now they have this Ernesto eating their food, too, it looks like."

"And some food it is."

"Yeah, that soup was something else."

"It was inedible."

"But back to Alice—she'll have to save up some money before she can start her own life. Wouldn't you agree?"

They've reached the platform and can see the approach road as well as scattered fields planted with evergreens. In other places the evergreens are interspersed with wild, young deciduous trees and thickets. A yard with tall stacks of brown cardboard surrounds a shed and the squat gray building of a recycling center. To the right of that, a discount supermarket. They can just make out the river that snakes around Jenny's part of the city. As if the river's avoiding this tainted area, where the schools are terrible and the child mortality rate, poor nutrition, learning difficulties, criminality, and drug abuse are well above the median. Jenny has lived out here since Alice was born. Back then there was hope; there were new constructions—parks, playgrounds, schools with façades painted in bright colors. There was a community center, a library, a sports arena. Here, it was believed, the children would play in the fresh air and the adults would help each other build a real community. Everyone would thrive. In less than twenty years the whole project has hit the skids. Now there's neither money nor the will to do anything about it. All the idealistic students who'd begun their lives out here have long since departed, handing the area to those forced to remain.

"Isn't that right, Thomas? She needs to save money."

He nods distractedly.

"Could you at least talk to Maloney? He knows Jenny too. Would you do that?"

"Okay, okay. I'll try."

"Should we to go to the movies?"

The train rolls in. Before he does anything else, Thomas wants to go home with his packets. But of course he can't say that.

That's how he ends up seeing a two and a half hour-long film, as the packets dig deeper and deeper into the skin of his belly. He doesn't dare shift them. He tries to fall asleep. Patricia squeezes his now clammy hand and eats popcorn with the other. The film has prolonged stretches without dialogue. It's set in an attractive but crumbling city. Patricia whispers: "Look at that. See how beautifully it's filmed." Every sex scene turns Thomas on, and that doesn't help ease his discomfort. He slurps soda, which gradually grows lukewarm and flat, and then he dozes off, but Patricia yanks on his arm. "You're snoring!" He wants to straighten himself up in his seat, but he can't because of the packets. When the film's over, she insists that they eat a proper dinner after eating that awful soup, and she pulls him through the streets and down alleys and even deeper into the oldest quarter in the city down more alleys, until they stand outside the narrow, black-lacquered door of a little restaurant. There she orders kebab and several salads and a bottle of red wine that has a thick and revolting taste of raisins and barrels of oak. Still, they swig it down rather quickly, and when it's empty, Patricia takes his face in her hands and pulls him across the table, planting a wet kiss on his mouth. "I love you," she says hoarsely, smiling in the glow of the candlelight. "Last night was amazing. You're so wonderful, honey."

He leans back in his chair. "I thought you said I was strange?"

"You are strange. *And* wonderful."

"So are you. Are you ovulating?" He can't help himself.

"If I'm ovulating then that's my business." Patricia glares at him, cool, disappointed. "And if you want to know when I'm ovulating, then you'll have to pay attention to my cycle yourself. And if you don't want to get me pregnant when I'm ovulating, then you'll have to take care of that yourself. I love you even when I'm ovulating, Thomas. But seriously, why must you ruin my happiness at being here with you? Why do you feel this need to do that?" As she talks, she shakes her head slightly.

"You know very well it has nothing to do with you, hon. I just don't want kids. We've discussed this a thousand times. I don't want kids, Patricia. I really don't."

"And I just don't get that." She stands. "You're mean, Thomas." She turns and disappears behind a red curtain. Probably the bathroom. For a moment, he's afraid she'll leave. Mean, yes. That's exactly how he feels. In the full sense of the word's two meanings. He hopes she'll return soon so he can go to the bathroom, because he needs to shift the packets. It feels as though they've gnawed an open wound into his skin.

When Patricia returns, a hurt expression on her face, Thomas stands and goes behind the curtain. The bathroom's impossibly small, and he can barely squeeze in. Once he's able to close the door he can hardly turn around. The stench of urine hangs in the air, the light is low and intimate, the walls adorned with dark purple, velvet wallpaper. There's a cracked mirror over the microscopic sink. He fumbles with his zipper and nearly drops one of the packets onto the floor. In the muted light it's impossible to see whether or not they've damaged his skin, but it feels that way. He has this irrepressible urge to open the packets, but it would take too long to get them sealed up again, so he settles on examining one with his hand (it *has* to be bundles of money) and shoves them into the waistband of his pants, next to his groin. His heart races, a sweet chill ripples up his back and his neck. Shivering, he washes his hands under a thin jet of cold water and goes back to the table, but Patricia's gone. The waiter bustles worriedly about: "Your wife left. Here's the check, sir. I hope you enjoyed your meal." Thomas pays the tab and just manages to see Patricia turn the corner. He reaches her only when they've come to more heavily trafficked streets (the packets prevent him from running), and it's obvious that she's been crying. She curses at him, cries again, she's unhappy, she doesn't understand him. She plants a seed of guilt, he feels guilty, he feels angry, he feels restless. They take the bus home. Patricia sniffles a lot, and a nearly-orange moon rises in the dark sky like a faint half circle. He consoles her and apologizes, but Patricia turns away and jerks her hand back. "I think I'll die if I have a kid," he says. "That's the dumbest thing I've ever heard," she mumbles thickly. "I really think you need help, Thomas." At home she goes to bed immediately, and he knows he ought to sit at the edge of the bed, talking to her gently and calmly, reassure her that he loves her. But he can't do it. Instead he locks himself in the bathroom and, when he's finally removed both the tinfoil and the plastic film, quickly forgets about Patricia. He sits with ten bundles of bills in his hands. New crisp bills. Big bills. Five bundles in each packet. He counts them. His hands tremble. The money must have come from their father's final, measly coup. Though he doesn't know the details, he guesses that someone double-crossed him and got him busted. Soon it becomes clear that the coup hadn't been so measly after all. He counts the money again. It's an enormous sum. His head spins. Jacques must've been involved in something huge. Something truly dirty. Carefully he sets the bills on the bathmat, parks himself heavily on the edge of the tub, and lights a cigarette. Goddamn. What do I do? I'll take the money to the police, nice and easy, on the way to the store tomorrow. He stares at the laundry basket. No, I'll hide the money. No, I *won't* hide the money. I'll give the money to Jenny. No, that's too dangerous, and she wouldn't be able to handle it. I'll hide the money anyway. Now his eyes wander across the black mosaic floor tiles. No, I won't, I'll take the money to the police. I'll give it to charity. No. For God's sake, how dumb can a person be. I'll ask Maloney to hide the money. Someone will come looking for it, don't be naïve. But not at Maloney's—no one would look for it there. He closes his eyes. In no way can he involve Maloney in this—Maloney can't keep his mouth shut. I definitely won't say anything to Jenny.

Or Patricia, either. I'll put the money in a safe deposit box at the bank. Like I'm in some fucking *movie*. Idiot. I have to think about it. I'll decide in the morning, I'll sleep on it. The old fool, hiding money in the toaster. He probably felt like a gangster, smart and resourceful. The idiot. It was almost as though Jenny had intuited the money was in there, but she couldn't have known that. Thomas flushes his cigarette butt down the toilet and slides the window open a tad. He pulls a bill from one of the bundles and holds it up to the lamp. It's legit all right. Watermark and all that jazz. He packs the money back up and tiptoes down the dark hallway. He pours himself a tall glass of whiskey in the living room and gulps it down, grimacing. It occurs to him that there's an old microwave in their storage unit in the basement. He smiles. He thinks: *I'm smiling like crazy because I am crazy.* We might as well stick to kitchen appliances, he thinks, if that's the way the old man wanted it. I'll put them down in the microwave then. He draws his keys out of his pants pocket, carefully closes the door behind him, and takes the elevator down. The basement is dark as a cave. He fumbles for the light switch and suddenly he can't remember where their storage unit is. Every unit is numbered, one after the other in a system of hallways running lengthwise and crosswise. But which number is theirs? Is there some sort of system? There are iron doors with bars for each of the small compartments. Through these bars he can see moving boxes and worn-out furniture. It's not here. Or here. He begins to sweat. The heat from the boiler room is unbearable. The smell of dust clings to his nostrils. The light clicks off. He turns the corner onto a new, long hallway. And another. This one's like a passageway, narrower than the others. His footfalls ring metallically on the hard floor. At last he catches sight of an orange plastic chair that he'd used in his kitchen before he moved in with Patricia. And there are the boxes filled with summer clothes. And the microwave, way in the back. He can feel his heart hammering. In with the bundles, close the oven, slam the door shut. A thought rumbles through him: Is this secure *enough*? He's about to open the door again—because of course the money should be taken to the police, what is he thinking? what kind of person is he? But now he wants to get out of the basement. Now he's panicking. What if he can't find his way out again? The bundles will have to stay there until morning, in any case, and nothing will happen to them between now and then. Desperate and downright afraid, he bumbles around the basement searching for the exit. He keeps finding new hallways, new light switches that click off, new fucking signs on doors with new combinations of numbers. He wants to be calm and composed, but he's not calm and he's not composed. At last he finds a door and enters an unfamiliar stairwell. Out on the street he lights a smoke. His torso is wet with sweat, and his throat is constricted; it's as if there's an iron hand wrapped around his chest, squeezing him, as if someone shielded behind iron is screaming in his face. In the silence of the street at night, he can see that he's wandered off, down in the basement, in the completely opposite direction of his own door. He's four doors from his own. It almost makes him smile—it's so laughable, this. His watch shows quarter after 1:00 A.M. The wind has settled. How long did he stumble around in the darkness like a scaredy-cat? Slowly his breathing returns to normal, his pulse calm. A scooter motors noisily past with two youths on it, the girl tightly clutching the young man; each wears a black helmet. He catches a glimpse of the girl's long legs in skinny jeans. Her blonde hair spilling down her back. The moon vanishes behind a dark cloud. His shadow towers long and ghostlike on the street. When a humpbacked old man with a squeaky, nasal voice calls to his dog on the other side of the street, Thomas jumps, frightened. "Come, Bingo, you old scoundrel. Come to Papa." Later in the night, rain begins to fall, heavy and monotonous. A powerful sense of unreality trails him into his dreams when he finally falls asleep close to morning, just as the first sliver of daylight wedges through the blinds. He dreams of the basement, and once again: the little girl on the carousel, her facial expression now distorted; grasshoppers everywhere; the sensation of suffocation; stagnant warm air.

The following morning the wind has picked up again. Patricia goes to yoga at 10:00 A.M. She doesn't seem angry with him, but she's quiet. Thomas wanders anxiously through the apartment the entire morning. He can't think about anything else but the money in the microwave. At 11:30 he's so jumpy that he decides to go for a jog, to rid himself of his unease. Against a strong wind, he pants around the park four times. More than once he has to stop for a drink from the water fountain. The sun breaks through the layer of clouds. When he returns, Patricia's listening to music. It sounds like Schubert. She's scrubbing the kitchen sink.

"Tina and Jules are coming to dinner at 7:00. They're bringing Stella."

"What's the occasion?"

"No particular occasion."

"You didn't tell me anything about this."

"Tina called just now and I invited them over. Is that okay?"

He pulls a bottle of sparkling water from the fridge.

"Are you angry about it? Why are you angry? They'll put Stella to bed and probably go home early. It's been so long since we've seen them."

He pours water into a glass and chugs it.

"Thomas?" She dries her hands and puts them on his shoulders from behind. "What's wrong?"

"I'm tired and confused and don't have any particular interest in sitting around talking about literature and recipes while a two-year old races around makes a mess of everything," he says somberly. "My father just died."

She sighs. She sits on the edge of a chair. A short time passes before she says anything more. He thinks: She's making an effort.

"I'm really sorry. I didn't think his death affected you all that much. I thought you were mostly relieved. But—"

"I *am* relieved!" Thomas has an uncontrollable urge to be left in peace. Schubert's piano sonata worms into his brain in an unbearable way. She sets the scouring pad aside and removes her rubber gloves.

They sit opposite one another at the small, black-stained table; the water faucet drips, and large gray cloud formations flit swiftly across the sky. The sun disappears behind the clouds and the light in the kitchen changes, like a curtain closing on a stage.

"Do you want me to cancel?"

He shakes his head.

"We can invite Maloney to join us, if you want. And Jenny?"

"Hell no!"

Her eyes darken, and she looks down.

"I'm just not myself, Patricia. I can't explain it. Weird things are happening."

She props her elbows on the table and looks directly into his eyes. "What do you mean?"

"I don't know." He fiddles with a box of matches, scratches at the sulfur. "But I'll survive this dinner." He attempts a smile. Takes a deep breath. The nape of his neck tingles unpleasantly. He thinks again of the money.

"Okay. I'll do the shopping and make dinner. I thought we could broil a turbot in the oven. With melon and raspberries for dessert."

He nods.

"Do you want to take a shower first?" He shakes his head. She squeezes his hand and leans across the table to put her free hand on his cheek. "You're warm. You don't have a fever, do you?"

He doesn't have a fever. Still seated, he stares out the window listening to her clattering in the bathroom, blow-drying her hair, opening closets and cupboards in the bedroom. He sighs, thinking: "You should be drinking champagne and dancing on tables, you're free, a free man. You've just inherited a considerable amount of money." But he has no desire to dance. He stands up and turns off the music in the living room, crawls onto the couch, and pulls a blanket all the way up to his chin, still miffed about having dinner guests and Schubert, and he's amazed at how his body instantly grows heavy as lead, how his breathing almost at once becomes slow and calm, how his lower lip relaxes, slips down, how a little drool trickles from his mouth and splotches the pillow, how the wet stain grows cold against his cheek. He wonders how his body can go from being agitated to being calm so quickly. Off in the distance he hears a train. A truck slowly and loudly—a kind of snort—rumbles down the street, and the whole time the wind, the wind: howling and whistling like a huge, unthinking creature racing through the world without knowing what it's supposed to do.

It feels as though only a few minutes have passed before he hears the key in the door. Startled, he sits up. Patricia walks past the living room, bottles clink, water runs, something is plunked heavily on the table. He lies down again, closing his eyes. Wafting from the coffee table is the scent of oranges. Soon she enters the room carrying a bouquet of purple tulips in a vase, casual, relaxed, wearing a tight-fitting dress, her eyes are dark with makeup. She looks stately, mature, formidable. She sets the vase down on the low shelf, rearranges the flowers a bit, and then admires them. She stands stock-still, as if lost in thought. When he shifts slightly on the couch she turns, surprised. "Oh, you're on the couch? I didn't realize you were there." Thomas takes a shower and gets dressed. Pulls a sweater over a white T-shirt. He slumps on the kitchen chair while Patricia prepares the fish and washes the lettuce. The radio plays pop music and commercials. They share a ham and mustard sandwich. Staring at him from the cornice is a dove. He runs his hand through his hair. Patricia sets the table in the living room and uncorks the wine. He promises to mix the drinks when the guests arrive. But he doesn't want drinks. He gets to his feet, restless. "Is there anything I can do?" he asks. Patricia shakes her head. "Just sit down and relax." Not long after that he removes his sweater, puts on a blue shirt, and thrusts his socked feet into a pair of black shoes. There's still that crawling sensation under his skin, as if the rustle of the money has moved directly into his body; it's unpleasant, a sweet tingling that makes him short of breath and hyper alert. His short nap has put the wheels in motion again, the swirl of his thoughts, the trembling, that feeling of the clear divide between himself and the room he's in, hysterical joy, suddenly, but also a thick clump in his throat that he wishes he could spit out. The guests will be arriving any minute.

Back in the kitchen he pulls out the vodka and the cranberry-grapefruit juice. He removes some limes from the fruit drawer in the fridge. He prepares Sea Breezes. "But it's not summer," Patricia says. "Exactly," he replies. The fish is in the oven, everything's ready. Patricia pours him a glass of red wine, and it occurs to him that it's been a long time since he had a smoke. Maybe he can get in a quick trip to the street before Tina and Jules arrive with their pampered tot. Patricia seems happier now. He kisses her neck (and hates himself for thinking: I'm kissing Patricia's neck, it's a *gesture*); she squeezes his arm with one hand while removing her apron with the other. "I'm going to put some music on," she says. "But not Schubert," he says. "No, not Schubert," she says, smiling and disappearing into the living room. On the street the wind continues to blow, but not as strongly. The darkness is charcoal-gray, dense. It's drizzling. The humidity's rising again. He leans against the wall, sucking smoke deep into his lungs. The sharp, bitter taste of tobacco fills his throat.

A couple leaves the building on the opposite side of the street; they seem to be in love, clinging to each other, laughing. Jules's car rolls up to him. "You standing there poisoning yourself?" Tina waves from the backseat. And then they begin to unpack, the kid and all the things that are, apparently, needed to take a toddler out for a few hours: some kind of device that can be put on a chair so that the kid can reach the table, a diaper bag, another with baby bottles, a little blanket, another bag, an apron made of oil cloth. Thomas tosses his cigarette butt into the gutter.

Up in the apartment, they toast and converse and chase down Stella, who's drawn to the bathroom, though her mother won't allow her in there because the "floor is slippery, you could fall and hurt yourself." They sit at the table and the guests praise the fish. "It's just right, not at all dry. I love the herbs you used. Is it marjoram? Chili? Ginger?" and the wine is nice, and the big white plates, the silverware—"Is it new?"—and Patricia's good taste when it comes to furnishing the apartment. "It's impossible to keep the place in order when you have a child in the house," Tina says, almost apologetically. "We pick up all the time and still it doesn't help." And Jules adds: "Hell, we might as well let it stay messy." But Tina doesn't agree. "Then you're just giving up." Patricia nods and smiles and takes a sip of wine, while Thomas drains his sea breeze.

"We can never find anything. She's got this compulsion to move things around. Recently it was the car keys. She can reach the top of the cabinet in the foyer now . . ."

"Right," Jules breaks in, "that's where I usually put the keys."

"Now he keeps them in his pocket," Tina goes on. "But when I have to use the car and he's not home, it's a problem."

"Why don't you have a spare set?" Patricia asks.

"That's a good question. We did, but we think Stella tossed them in the trash," Tina chuckles.

"In the *trash*?" Patricia says, shocked, giggling. "What a little scoundrel!" Thomas is truly bored. Jules grumbles off and on. Then Stella howls, alarmingly loud, and they all get to their feet and run in separate directions. "Where are you?" Tina shouts nervously, and of course Stella's in the bathroom. She's lying in the bathtub, her legs splayed along the sides of the tub, red-faced, screaming piercingly. Evidently she'd crawled up onto the edge and slipped in headfirst. They console her and babble. Stella bawls heartrendingly on her mother's lap and they all look only at her. Chubby red cheeks, bright shiny eyes, a sweep of curls and ears fine as tiny, rose-pink shells. They wipe away her tears—even the tears seem cleaner than an adult's tears. A large bump has begun to form on her forehead. She rubs her eyes and suddenly stops howling. She's caught sight of some candles on a low shelf, and decides she absolutely has to go investigate; her little body squirms and fidgets to get down. Tina lets go of her only to stand up immediately and follow her. "No, no, no. You'll burn yourself. Hot. Stella will burn her fingers." Then Patricia rushes in with ladles and plastic bowls and energetically shows her how she can drum on the bowls. "Music!" Instantly and eagerly Stella's absorbed in a new activity, but only for a moment. Thomas glances at Jules, who fills his wine glass to the rim and chugs it down greedily. "Great wine," he mumbles. His eyebrows have grown bushier. He has gray hairs. But his eyes are the same, ice-blue and insistent. He's a few years older than Thomas.

They eat fruit and drink coffee. Tina takes Stella into the bedroom to put her to bed. It takes a long time. Meanwhile Jules talks, not surprisingly about literature, his voice gravelly and sloshed. "The biggest problem at the moment must be this tendency to write autobiographies purporting to be novels. It bores me more than words can say." Jules is an incarnate fan of the Big Story. How a younger man can be so conservative is beyond comprehension. He's not really old-fashioned in any other way. For many years he was an editor at a large publishing house, but he lost his job when Stella was a baby, and now he earns his living teaching at a couple of universities. Is he bitter? Old fashioned? No, Thomas thinks, and observes Jules, now withdrawn, rubbing his nose. He stayed home with Stella when she was a baby, for seven months. It's only when it comes to literature that he's conservative. But is he? Or does he just not buy into all the fads? In the exact same way that he himself insists on selling paper in a virtually paperless era, even displaying his wares in the old dark cases? Does it make him conservative? Is he conservative? Jules has stopped rubbing his nose. Tina returns, blinking at the light, an almost victorious expression on her face. "She's asleep!" It's now 9:30. With a sigh, she sits.

"You truly belong to the old world, Jules," Patricia laughs.

"You can say that again," Tina says, draining the last drop of her coffee. "What are you all talking about?" She's an economist with a full-time job; she earns a lot of money, much more than Jules. Jules was fired because he was too selective. Too passionate, but his "passion" wasn't the kind that brought the publisher a lot of revenue—he rejected nearly all of the manuscripts that fell into his hands. It was said that he worked against his own self-interest. But, as he slumps across the table now, he appears gentle and nearly transparent. Patricia says something about poetry and images. Then she talks about a novel she read that made a lasting impression on her. It was both autobiographical and very moving. Jules shakes his head. "Not my thing."

"But have you read it?"

"Certainly not. Nor will I ever . . ."

He turns toward Thomas, his eyes swimming: "Tell us a funny story, Thomas. How's it going at the store? Do you and Maloney get drinks after you close? Do you make good money?" Thomas begins loudly rattling off all sorts of stuff. He grins hysterically at things that aren't especially funny. He gets to his feet to illustrate how Peter and Annie walk. He's filled with an energy he can't control, and now he mimics Annie's voice. Patricia looks at him, aghast. Thomas is standing in the center of the room. Then, just as quickly as the mania had come over him, his bubble bursts; exhausted, he sinks into his chair. I'm myself again, he thinks, relieved. And then: *Myself*? *Who*? Patricia continues to stare at him. Thomas figures that they've gotten past the literature portion of the evening amazingly fast, which means they'll soon be talking about recipes. But in this he's wrong. Because Patricia says: "Thomas's father just died." And Jules and Tina turn and gaze at him quizzically. "Oh, no," Tina says, covering her mouth with her hand.

Later, Jules nevertheless returns to the subject of autobiographical literature. "People have got to stop their naval-gazing bullshit and write real stories. What the hell is wrong with fiction? The idea that it's truer and more real to write about yourself is nothing but the unreflective extension of individualism and the childish self-centeredness of our stunted generation. We've *let* ourselves be stunted. There's no will, rebellion, or idealism in us. No solidarity. And now, apparently, we feel the need to spew our self-absorbed, narcissistic, self-pity over literature as well. It's enough to make you vomit!"

"What do you mean by 'self-absorbed, narcissistic, self-pity'?" Tina asks, glancing at Thomas, who shrugs. But before they get an explanation from Jules, Patricia begins to speak. "Maybe fiction is old-fashioned, maybe the novel as a form isn't especially interesting anymore. We see the same thing happening in the visual arts. The personal vision, the private story, the individual finds a greater truth, and so does the recipient—"

"The *recipient*? Oh, SPARE ME! I've just answered your question!

It's not at all true, and those goddamn private stories belong in a fucking diary or on some tasteless reality TV show!"

"But Jules, at least listen to what she's saying . . ." Tina looks tired.

"Besides," Jules continues, undaunted, "everything you're saying was disproven long ago. I'm talking about the novel as a form of art. As a concept. The great novel. The autobiographical tendency shows that today's 'literati' don't dare trust fiction, don't dare trust art as a creative power, they don't understand it and so don't bother with it. They just say it's unusable because it's not 'true'! It's too damn dull, narrow, and populistic! And completely spineless!"

"Autobiographical works can also be great literature. You're the one who's old school. Why this focus on *the great story*? What kind of crap is that?" Patricia raises her voice. "How can you rule out the possibility that the novels you love include autobiographical elements? Of course they do! And those writers who say they're writing autobiographical stories can be lying. No one knows that. But does it even matter? Anything that's presented in an interesting way is valid. What matters is the form. The way the material is shaped. *How* it's used. That's what makes art! For example, the book I read," Patricia says, pointing angrily at Jules, who immediately interrupts her: "Obviously novelists can draw on their life experiences, but to insist on it as if it were a fucking hallmark! No, you're confusing things, believing it's so fucking modern." Swaying in his seat, Jules reaches for his glass. "You're a lemming, Patricia!"

"C'mon, Jules. You can't say that," Tina says feebly. She lowers her head in shame and picks at her napkin. Patricia shakes her head obstinately and drains her glass. Thomas admonishes himself: *You've got to say something. Your silence is painful.*

"How can you teach literature to young people when you have that attitude?" he asks. "Do they put up with it? Don't they just sit there staring at their electronic doodads and each other while you lecture?"

"Shit, I'm teaching them what's worth knowing. The great classics of world literature, and by that I mean proper books, and it's completely irrelevant when they were written. And luckily not all contemporary writers are shit. On the contrary, Patricia! This is just some kind of pathetic tendency that we'll all have forgotten about in fifty years. The problem isn't the autobiographical part. The problem is calling it literature, to put it ahead of fucking literature! That's how stories are being reduced for God's sake!" Shouting now, Jules gets to his feet.

"No, they don't!" Patricia tries to talk over him. "Polyphonies arise. Multiple voices! It's an investigation into what a narrator can do. A narrator isn't necessarily one voice. This is about new ways of understanding identity. It's also happening with visual art!"

"STORIES ARE BEING REDUCED!" Jules throws his arms in the air.

Tina shushes him. Then she addresses him sternly, as if to a dog: "Sit." And Jules sits.

Patricia sighs. "But it *is* literature, Jules. You can't deny that."

Jules shakes his head, cursing. Thomas can still hear Jules's and Patricia's voices, their rising and falling; they sound more subdued now, but he can no longer make out what they're saying. It's just sound. He's gliding through the darkened basement. He can feel the money against his belly. His heart hammers hard and irregularly, and on his way through the darkness he bumps into something. A body. A large, warm body blocking his way. And then, as if bellowing from some deep cave, a voice booms right in his ear: "Who's there?" There's a choking embrace. Flesh, damp skin, matted hair. He's trapped by bones and flesh. He's held in this embrace, this strong and living thing that won't let him go. But is it alive? Or is it a zombie? He starts, frightened, and is yanked brutally from his seat of his own volition and tumbles to the floor. The others stare at him curiously. "What happened?" Patricia asks.

He shakes his head. "I just need to go to the bathroom."

He splashes water on his face and washes his hands. He breathes deeply, tries to suck the air all the way to his diaphragm. But the presence of the overwhelming body hangs inescapably on him. There was nothing human about it, and yet: *Who's there?* And what is it? What was it? He's tipsy, but not drunk. Or is he? Did he fall asleep? Was he dreaming? He returns to the others, who've apparently not changed topics. Jules shouts: "Pass me a smoke, Thomas!" and impatiently extends his hand. "If they don't want to learn anything, then they can just piss off!" He looks up, a wild expression in his eyes. Tina glances apologetically at Patricia, and Thomas lets Jules have a cigarette, though smoking is forbidden in the apartment. Tina glowers in dismay as the two men smoke, no doubt thinking about her daughter, the pure, unblemished body in the bedroom.

"There's a lot written about the body," Patricia says. "We also see it in the visual arts. Gender, the body, a new understanding of the biological condition. It's quite different from the theory observing gender and body as something learned, something one bears on you. Now you bear it *in* you. It's really interesting. And . . ." "I completely disagree," Jules coughs. "It doesn't have jack shit to do with gender and body. Let's have more gender and body, but not if one has to hear some fucking narcissist or other befouling one's brain with his ridiculous life story."

"You're hopeless," Patricia grins, setting down her coffee mug. "Yes, he is," Tina smiles, relieved. No, he's not hopeless, Thomas thinks. And now you can go home. I can't take any more. But they make no motion to leave. Jules looks as though he needs to cool off. He smokes and stares out the window.

Tina hurriedly asks how Patricia's doing, and she explains a little about her work with the next big exhibition at the museum. She's the director of the museum store. They're about to order related art books. She's having trouble getting the exhibition's poster ready, and the catalog's still unfinished, the graphic designer is impossible. Chitchat. Something about a yoga teacher. Vacation plans. A few spiteful remarks about a mutual girlfriend's divorce. Jules has zoned out, disheartened, tired. He's dropped ashes onto the floor. Finally Tina stands. "We should go home now. Stella gets up at 6:00 A.M." Reluctantly, Jules rises. They gather Stella's things, which are scattered around the apartment. It takes an eternity. At last Tina scoops up the sleeping girl. Patricia tucks the blanket tightly around her. Jules is already out in the hallway. "I'm sorry," Tina whispers. "I don't know what got into him."

"There's nothing to apologize for," Patricia says, caressing Stella's cheek. "We're friends." Thomas follows them down and helps them pack the trunk. Stella whimpers sleepily in her car seat. Jules gives Thomas a long, firm hug. "Good to see you," he breathes, "and stay away from that book Patricia read. Not only does it sully the reader, it sullies itself. It's unbearable, Thomas." He seems genuinely unhappy. Then they drive slowly, as though in search of something, down the street. He shouldn't be driving, Thomas thinks, the man's drunk. But it's too late now. He lights a cigarette and walks around the block. The streetlights are orange. The light forms soft, particulate clusters under the lamps. Everything seems surreal. As though the law of gravity has been abolished, and at any moment he could float up into the night sky. It's not windy anymore. The feeling of the animal or the body, or whatever it was, has finally left him. He feels completely empty. Like being surrounded by some other species, he thinks, that's what it's like. Upper class snobs. I'm still only just barely a part of that world. I'm playing myself. But I'm not anything more than what I'm playing. Never ever. It's disgraceful. He grinds his cigarette with his foot. Then it starts to rain. A fine, insistent rain.

Back in the apartment Patricia has cleared the table; there's a cross breeze because she's airing out, and the apartment is ice cold. She's already begun washing the dishes. When he enters the kitchen she turns, her hands dripping. She looks directly at him. "I want a baby, Thomas," she says.

He awakes in a daze, a nasty taste in his mouth, the telephone ringing in the living room. Patricia's side of the bed is empty, her duvet having slid halfway onto the floor. His body seems petrified: warm, immovable. Naked, he gets to his feet. The telephone rings a second time. It's Maloney.

"Where are you? It's 10:00 a.m. We're getting a big delivery in half an hour. Are you sick, or what the hell's going on?"

He mumbles a promise to hurry. His cock hangs loose and pale between his legs. His pubic hair's crawling toward his bellybutton, as though on its way to his head. Scratching his back, shivering, he stumbles to the bathroom, turns on the shower. Patricia left no note on the kitchen table, as she usually does whenever she leaves without first waking him. After Jules and Tina had gone, he'd been too worn-out to discuss having a baby versus not having a baby, and she'd become irate and disappointed, telling him that he had no dreams for the future, that he had zero ambition. He'd gone to bed. Had collapsed and practically fainted into sleep.

A half-empty cup of coffee and a small bottle of red nail polish are the only traces of her. He downs a glass of water and eats a banana as he buttons his shirt. Outside the rain has ceased, but the air is bone-chillingly cold and full of moisture. He trots to the station and is barely able to squeeze into the packed train car, where people stand like sardines in a barrel, with their bodily odors and their bad breath and their pretty faces and their ugly warts; with their youth and their age and their illnesses and their morning eyes, full of disgust or indifference or radiant with resolve and expectation. He presses himself between a fat businessman reeking of aftershave and a schoolgirl wearing an enormous backpack; she's listening to music and holding the safety bar to keep her balance. The backpack thumps into Thomas each time the train halts. He's never late. Now he'll have to listen to Maloney ribbing him the rest of the day. But Maloney's in ridiculously good spirits this Monday, bursting with energy and barking orders; he and Peter have already begun unpacking the delivery, which sits in a small mountain of cardboard boxes on the floor right inside the door. Annie slashes them open with a box cutter, removing items, while Maloney makes sure they've gotten what they've ordered and paid for. The atmosphere is good, focused; only Peter, as usual, is slow and shy. Thomas joins in, and the work agrees with him. It's simple, it's manageable: most of the boxes need to be taken to the basement and the products arranged properly, shelf by shelf, by number and name. The slick boxes have to be shoved into place and stacked and organized. Thomas knows the basement like he knows his own pocket; it's their treasure chamber, and it has nothing in common with the dark, dusty labyrinth he'd rushed around in Saturday night. Now it feels as though that never happened, that it was all a dream, a fantasy, a figment of his imagination. He grows warm, he puts eight boxes of plastic folders on the shelf, he presses the felt-tip pen against the cardboard and writes the folders' colors clearly and legibly on the front of each box. They'd started doing this after they hired Peter. He was never able to find the right colors; maybe he's colorblind. Maloney's whistling a tune down the aisle near the glossy paper. Hunched over, Peter lugs the heaviest boxes of paper downstairs. "We're also missing H4 and B2 upstairs," Annie says, clearing her throat. "And recycled Double Demy gray." "What about white?" Maloney calls out. "Didn't that bookkeeper buy the last of it yesterday?" Annie goes upstairs to check. But there must be customers in the store, because she doesn't return. Thomas follows Peter up the narrow stairwell to bring the rest of the stuff down. They've often discussed replacing this stairwell with a new and wider one, so they could haul a dolly up and down and spare their backs. But Peter's young and fairly strong. And isn't that why you have an apprentice?, was how Maloney put it when Thomas brought up the idea. He needs a cigarette. He tugs the last boxes through the store and out to the hallway. Peter sticks his pale, acne-scarred face through the hatch, ready to grab them. They work in silence. Thomas hands Peter the boxes, Peter balances them down the steps. "I'll take it from down here!" Maloney shouts from within the depths of the basement, though they could've heard him easily if he'd used his normal voice. But Maloney needs to make noise, to shout. There's no life without noise—that would be his motto if he could formulate it. But that's the thing with Maloney, Thomas thinks. He doesn't even know it. He doesn't know much about himself, it doesn't interest him. Maloney acts and suffers and parties and rages and loves and hates, and it's all noise. Is this an expression of a simple, beautiful life? Now he thrusts his red face past Peter, who's struggling with a large box. "Time we have some friggin' coffee!" "Now?" Thomas says, "Shouldn't we finish first?" But Maloney can't wait. Peter has to brace himself against the uneven basement wall as Maloney's corpulent body presses him out on the edge of the stairwell. Here he stands, teetering and about to fall. It's a long way down. "Be careful, Peter." Thomas points at the pale-faced apprentice, who at that moment lets go of the box and grabs hold of something. The box lands with a heavy thud on the basement floor. "What the hell was in that?" Maloney asks, squeezing himself up the stairwell. He stands beside Thomas, huffing now. They stare down through the hole in the floor. "Sorry," Peter says. "But I was about to plummet." "Plummet? It's not a damn mountain. What's in the box?" Peter looks almost frightened. "Come here, kid." Maloney offers his hand and hoists Peter up. "I think it was glass," Peter whispers. "Candlesticks." Maloney sighs heavily and walks into the office. "Go down and check whether or not it's all smashed," Thomas says.

Thomas stands in the doorway of the office and gets Maloney's attention. "Who ordered candlesticks?"

"I did."

"I thought we agreed no party supplies in the store."

"Candlesticks are not party supplies. Candlesticks are decorations."

"Decorations are party supplies. Besides, we don't sell 'decorations,' either."

"C'mon, Thomas. They're damaged now anyway. I'll cover the costs."

"I don't like the thought of you ordering tasteless things behind my back."

"For God's sake, Thomas."

"You know how much I hate party supplies."

"And I love them. The kitschier the better! Novelty toys and clown noses! Balloons and fake beards! Bibs for grown men with pictures of naked ladies!"

Thomas shakes his head, grumbling.

"But candlesticks aren't kitschy," Maloney continues. "I've carefully selected them so that I wouldn't offend your aesthetic sensibility. They'll sell like hotcakes."

Maloney looks at Thomas. Then Thomas turns to leave and bumps into Peter, who's returning to give his report.

"Fourteen red candlesticks smashed, eight transparent, seven green, and only two blue. All in all, one hundred twenty-nine candlesticks aren't broken. I've thrown out the damaged ones and noted them on the purchase order. Thirty-one pieces were lost."

"Good work, Peter. Go out and have yourself a smoke now." For a moment Peter looks flustered, but then he goes. A wide smile crosses Maloney's face.

"They're even *tinted*?" Thomas says.

"They look awesome," Maloney smiles, propping his legs up on the desk. "You can take a few home to Patricia on my tab."

Time passes. Lunch and more coffee. Maloney takes a nap on the office floor, his legs tucked under the desk. Toward evening, Thomas assists Maloney in filling the empty slots on the shelves by putting out the recently received products. Envelopes, letter paper, notebooks. They discuss arranging a spring cleaning of every shelf and cabinet, but when? And can Eva do it by herself? Can they afford to hire additional staff to do it? If they decide to go ahead with it, Thomas thinks they should be on-hand to make sure everything stays in order and nothing gets damaged. He imagines Eva emptying a bucket of dirty, soapy water on the gilt-edged paper that he now holds in his hands. "We did it last year with Peter and Annie," Maloney says, dropping to one knee to fill the pencil cases in a metal box on the lowest shelf. "We didn't even pay them extra, did we? That was drudge work." They decide to speak to Eva. "Because *I* won't do it again, I tell you," Maloney announces once he's on his feet again. After that, he entertains Thomas by telling him about his trip to the bar over the weekend. He'd played pool and drunk piña coladas, then he'd gone to a different place and had beer and played more pool, until a few guys he knew showed up with some women. They'd wound up at some place with live music, where they danced, and Maloney found himself dancing, mostly with a girl named Lauraine, who was very blonde and a little older. "But she had these fantastic hips." He succeeded in coercing her home with him, and they'd executed a *coitus uninterruptus*, despite the fact that he'd been piss drunk. "You can keep the *coitus uninterruptus* part to yourself next time," Thomas says. No longer does he see images of water spilling onto letter paper, but Maloney in his bed having sex in the gray morning light; he imagines the gently intertwined flesh, hears the half-choked sounds. "I think it was quite a feat," Maloney remarks cheerfully. "But I slept all Saturday, and Sunday I washed clothes, did that sort of thing. Then Jenny visited me in the evening."

Thomas stiffens. "Jenny visited you? Why?"

Maloney shrugs. "I think she just needed to talk."

"But you haven't even seen each other for years."

Maloney smiles. "You don't know anything about that. Love doesn't fade that easily."

"Jesus. I don't understand anything."

"There's nothing to understand. She just swung by. Wanna get out of here?"

According to the clock, it's already past 7:00. They're finished now and carry the empty boxes to the door. Thomas slowly dims the chandelier. The fading sunlight is gorgeous, and dusk gradually begins to appear in the corners. Maloney gets their jackets and locks the door behind them. They haul the boxes to the recycling container and break them apart.

"I'm in the doghouse with Patricia," Thomas says, turning up his collar. "She keeps bugging me about having a kid."

"Would it really be that awful?"

"Yes. You don't want one, either. Right?"

"I'm not like you. You've got Patricia and your good taste. All I've got are dubious encounters with bleach-blondes and a one-bedroom apartment with a 'nice' view. Ha!"

"But I really don't want one, Maloney. You know that. I mean it."

"Go home now and talk to her. Are you having a mid-life crisis or what? I'll see you in the morning. Remember to set your alarm clock."

Maloney clasps Thomas's arm as he talks. Then he pats him gently on the shoulder and pulls his hat over his forehead. Then he's gone. Thomas braces himself against the wind and heads toward the train station. What's Jenny up to? Why does she need to talk to Maloney? He feels violated, misled. But how? Confused and exhausted, he piles into the train, squeezes in between people and their smells. My life is one continuous repetition of activities and tasks. Maybe I really *don't* have any drive, and now I'm going home to an unhappy Patricia, and that's all my own doing.

But Patricia isn't unhappy. She's set the table and is frying chicken and vegetables in the big wok. She looks vigorous and sexy; her mouth is the same color as her newly-painted red nails, and her skin's damp from the moisture in the kitchen. Thomas took the stairs up and he's out of breath, but greatly relieved, almost joyful. The apartment seems warm and cozy, and his anxious concerns about the money in the microwave and Jenny's visit with Maloney give way to thoughts of enjoyment, pleasure, food. He pours white port wine and fills glasses with seltzer, he slices a lemon and drops a couple wedges in each glass. Lots of ice. She puts the glass to her red lips and swallows the bubbly, refreshing liquid. "The catalog's finally finished," she says, pleased. "It's off to press tomorrow." They eat in the living room and watch a film after they've washed the dishes. Neither of them mentions yesterday's argument. They lie close to one another, their bodies intertwined on the couch watching TV. She fingers his earlobe, he plays with her hair. Suddenly she strips off her panties and goes wild. She stands, she drops to her knees, she straddles his face, she's wet and tart; she whimpers and moans and comes but is eager for more. His head tingles with arousal. This body is alive, he thinks, we're alive. Patricia's desire is overwhelming and unencumbered. She doesn't hold anything back. When she opens her mouth and growls or screams it's both frightening and ecstatic, a powerful force rising within her. She thrums and sweats and rolls her eyes. At last they fall together onto the carpet, exhausted; he pulls the condom off and ties it into a knot. Patricia's face is quite soft now and it fills his vision. But when they're lying in bed, it's the money he thinks about. What the hell do I do? Nothing, he thinks. Let the money stay where it is. His sore cock is shriveled up, shrunken, still moist. Patricia sleeps like a child under the white duvet. Oh, peace. Remember this now, he tells himself, you can relax, there's nothing to fear. We just have to get past that stupid funeral.

Tuesday morning is like gold flowing through the streets: a new warmth in the air, dust floating in the sunbeams, it's as if the sky has expanded overnight. The sounds of the city seem more cheerful, their resonance deeper. People seem happier, lighter. Look, a woman smiles broadly, a young man waits for an old woman with a walker, a child's brown eyes shine like chestnuts in the backlight. Spring's on its way, Thomas thinks, walking from home all the way to the store, because who wants to take the train on a day like this? How fitting that spring arrives today, the day the old man burns in hell. That works for me, there's hope, a new path to forge, free of old grudges. *Free of old grudges* is a strophe in one of the old man's favorite songs, a schlager from his youth, and Thomas can't help but smile, a kind of schadenfreude. Because *he*, Thomas, is the free one and not the deceased; that'll teach him (but what can a dead man learn?). These are the energies that buzz through Thomas O'Mally Lindström, who for the occasion is wearing a blue suit. He won't bury his father wearing black. He buys coffee in a grungy deli and smokes a few cigarettes. He crosses the street and takes a pleasant detour through a lush park, where mimes and young musicians are already performing, where people soak up sun on benches, where dogs yap and cavort on the triangular lawn. Jenny sends him a text: "remember, 1:00 p.m." And he responds: "why did you visit maloney sunday?" She answers: "mind your own business." Very much against his wishes, Jenny had an obituary printed. He discovers this when he's sitting in his office absentmindedly perusing the newspaper: *"Jacques O'Mally departed us suddenly. May his soul find peace. Children and grandchildren."* Grandchildren? But there's only Alice.

"She must've thought it sounded better in plural," Maloney says, his entire head stuffed inside the filing cabinet. "And it does, too. Children and grandchild—you can't write that."

"May his soul find peace. What the *fuck* is that?" Thomas snaps, shoving the newspaper aside. "She *is* nuts."

Maloney pops red-faced out of the cabinet and straightens himself up. "She's a drama queen, Thomas. Jenny loves drama. A funeral is an incredible drama. Think about it." Thomas groans. "I'm guessing it'll be a pretty entertaining afternoon," Maloney says, dropping into the boss's chair. Annie enters the office and says they're out of thumbtacks. But they were in the delivery yesterday. She can't find them. Send Peter to the basement. He's not at work. He's not at work? He had to go to the doctor, something about a rash. A rash? Annie doesn't know anything more than that.

Thomas wanders about the store for a few hours and assists some customers. He talks to the accountant, mails some documents, checks the ledger from last week. Patricia calls and asks for the chapel's address. Peter comes back from the doctor's; he has ringworm. This little nugget of news gets Maloney going. He slaps his thighs, howling with laughter.

"Ringworm is contagious," Annie whispers. "Did the doctor say anything about that?"

"We're not exactly in the habit of fondling Peter's torso, are we? Or maybe we are?" Peter looks down. Maloney bursts into laughter again. "Does it itch?" Annie says worriedly. Peter nods. "Go get some lunch, Peter, and order something for the worm. Put it on my tab! It can have whatever it wants. Oh, that's classic. Ringworm!"

Thomas sighs. "I apologize on Maloney's behalf, Peter."

"You don't need to do that," Maloney chuckles, ruffling his own hair. "I'd like a large turkey sandwich with extra bacon and pickles. Cranberries, but no tomatoes, please. They just make the bread soggy."

Peter leaves, and Annie washes her hands at the little sink in the hallway. Thomas gets her attention in the mirror. "We need to leave for a few hours this afternoon. We have to go to an interment." She nods, drying her hands thoroughly on a paper towel.

"I thought he was going to be cremated," Maloney says.

"He is."

"Then it's not an interment, Thomas. Loosen up, man!" Maloney shouts. "Jesus Christ, I'm hungry!"

They eat, and in no time the office smells like a classroom, boiled egg, sweating salami. The store is quiet. "Must be the good weather," Peter remarks, cautiously.

"We need to do a spring cleaning," Maloney says, food smacking in his mouth, "is that something you'd all be interested in?"

No reaction.

"We'll pay you, of course."

"You didn't last year," Annie says firmly.

"But we will this year."

"No thanks, I'd rather not," Peter says quietly.

"Me neither." Annie looks at Maloney, defiant, but Maloney's focused on holding his sandwich, which threatens to fall apart. "Why the hell didn't you ask them to put a toothpick in it, Peter? Look at this shit." He leans forward to snatch up a piece of greasy bread from the floor.

Peter slurps his cola. His Adam's apple bobs up and down with each gulp. "Well, I'm going back to work," Annie says, tossing her crumpled sandwich paper in the trash on the way out. Maloney belches and says: "We're off in ten minutes. Don't do anything I wouldn't do."

Thomas opens the window and sucks a pleasant breath of fresh, mild air into his lungs. "Did you order a new coffee automat?" he asks Maloney.

"Haven't ordered shit. Who would I call? I don't give a flying fuck about ordering so much as a glow-in-the-dark turd from that company, let me tell you."

"A glow-in-the-dark turd?"

Maloney begins to whistle. "What do you think we'll sing today? Jenny's got some tearjerkers in store for us, no doubt. Will there be a wake?"

"I hope not," Thomas replies, suddenly nervous. He expressly told her that he wouldn't spend a dime on this service. The city's covering it. They've refused to pay for the funeral director and the burial plot—Jenny because she can't, and he because it makes him happy. The old man's ashes will be heaped in the cheapest wooden urn they could find, and then dumped in an unmarked grave. But a wake? He hadn't considered that. He figured it was completely out of the question, that in the very least they would agree on *that*. And since Jenny doesn't have any money, he convinces himself that the probability of her arranging anything behind his back is minimal.

They take a cab, and Maloney's remarkably silent the whole way, as if he's told himself that the situation calls for it. Thomas glances at him, but he's pretending to be deep in concentration, his attention firmly and piously focused out the window. The city floats, still bathed in light, a kind of sunshine-rain, and they pass all the old haunts: Here he once sat with Patricia on his lap (the green bench under the linden trees); here he and Jenny picked up their father at a bar one morning; here the department store and his faint recollections of standing with their mother on the escalator, on the way up to buy a new dress for Jenny; here their grandfather's nursing home, which their old man referred to as the End Station ("Are you going out to the End Station to visit the old psychopath?"); and here the soccer fields, the big library, the music venues, the garages where one of their father's friends sold "used cars," the speakeasy in the back room, outside of which Thomas and Jenny hopped in puddles one interminable autumn day. Then the hospital emerges with its attractive, old central building and the newer additions of gray concrete. The network of trails and moss-covered lawns. Now they're close. The car slows on the smaller streets, with their row houses and simple one-story villas, and there's the cemetery with its headstones and crosses, with its evergreens and weeping willows and copper beech, half-rotten bouquets of flowers, the recently dug graves and their fresh wreaths. The car swings through a gate and follows the gravel road to the chapel. The crematorium is in the far back of the cemetery, as though hidden from the road. Thomas catches a glimpse of it behind some small, whitewashed office buildings, and he can't help but look for smoke furling over the bricks. But there's no smoke. Not yet, he thinks. The driver stops the car. One of the chapel's wing doors has been flung open, leading into the darkness. Jenny stands on the stairs wearing a dark-blue jacket. And a hat. "She's wearing a hat!" Maloney says, stifling a laugh. "Wow . . ."

"What did you expect?" Thomas mumbles, climbing out of the car. Jenny's cheeks are already wet with tears, she's wearing heels that are much-too tall, and black gloves. Her mouth glistens on her powdered face, orange-red and vulgar. Alice and Ernesto lean against the wall in the sunlight, smoking. Sharp, sharp sunlight now, very defined shadows. Alice raises her hand in a limp wave then lets it drop just as limply. A group of men stand a short distance away. At once Thomas recognizes one of them, Frank, their father's buddy of many years. He's grown thin and sallow. The obese man in sunglasses must be the one they always called Fatso. He's lost most of his hair, and has combed a few black wisps over his bald dome. Another, much younger man is wearing a baseball cap pulled down over his forehead, which nearly hides his face. He's smoking intensely, continuously lifting the hand holding the cigarette up to his mouth and then down again. He's tall and slender, muscular. Frank gives Fatso a playful shove, and they grin. A car rolls up in front of the chapel, and out steps Aunt Kristin and Helena followed by the twins, who must be twelve or thirteen years old by now. Two shy girls in matching windbreakers. It occurs to him how much Kristin resembles their mother. There's something elegant and practiced in her movements, her smooth full-bodied hair, now silver-gray, like a helmet atop her heart-shaped face. Jenny has already hugged Maloney and squeezed Thomas's wrist. He pulls himself free and goes to Kristin. She wraps her arms around him and holds him tight. "Thomas," she says into his jacket. "How are *you*?"

"Fine," he says. "And you? The twins have gotten so big."

She looks at him. "You never visit us. But we'll have to change that. I just told Helena that now we'll *have to* invite you to the house. We've reconfigured the barn, and there's room for all of you to spend the night. Or rather: *I've* reconfigured. Helena's not much for manual labor, as you know. Of course she's also been busy recently, you know, she got an order for a huge tapestry. We've put the big loom out in the barn . . ." She lets go of him: "My God! Is that Alice over there? She's all grown up!" Then he says hello to Helena, who's packed in something resembling a poncho, out of which she pokes her narrow, friendly face, a warm smile; she kisses his cheek. The twins shake his hand politely and regard him with their identical gray-green eyes. The expression in their eyes is different, but he can't tell which is which.

"Congratulations on your tapestry. Kristin just told me how busy you've been." Helena lights up. "Thank you so much. Yes, it's an overwhelmingly massive project, but I believe I've finally figured out what to do. It's an alter tapestry."

"Christ on the cross?"

Helena smiles. "No, the Holy Virgin at the well. And I'm actually happy about that."

Suddenly Patricia's at his side. "Are you okay?" she whispers, clutching his jacket. She says hello to Helena. The twins have sat down on the lowest step. Thomas wants to say something to Patricia, but a tall man with sharp features and a jacket a little too outsized for him approaches them with long strides. He introduces himself and offers his hand. "My condolences," he says. "You must be the son? I don't want to intrude, but my colleagues thought it'd be a good idea if I came. It was a bit of a shock to find him like that. I'd spoken with him only three hours earlier. I've known Jacques for many years—he visited us many times in his later years, after all. He looked a little tired that day, but he was in good spirits."

Thomas thanks him for coming.

"I thought you'd want to know his last words?"

Thomas nods.

"His last words were literally . . ." The prison guard sucks air through his nose. "He said: 'I think I'm too damn tired to exercise today.' And then he smiled at me. That's what happened. I think I'm too damn tired to exercise today. Didn't seem strange at all. Otherwise I'd have called the doctor, you know. I hope you understand." The man suddenly looks tense. A moment later, he relaxes. Thomas thanks him, says that he appreciates him coming. "Thanks for taking the time." "No problem," says the guard. "He actually got off pretty easy. It didn't look good for him this time. He was facing quite a sentence. The trial was set to begin in a few weeks."

"What was he charged with?" Thomas asks.

"Unfortunately I can't discuss that."

"How long do you think he'd have been in prison?"

"A long time." The officer nods. "Many years." The two men stand there. The officer rocks up and down on his toes. "Well, I think I'll go in and find a seat," he says, heading toward the chapel.

Patricia's standing beside Maloney and Kristin, who now has her arm around Jenny. Alice is talking to Helena. Thomas pulls a smoke out of his jacket pocket and paws around for his matches. But before he can locate them, Frank is right beside him, with his wrinkled, sun-ravaged face, putting a lighter to his cigarette. An odor of dust and cologne clings to him. "You've certainly grown since I last saw you," he says, smiling brashly. "We'll be sure to send your father off good and proper. I hear he died in his cell?" Thomas nods. "If you're gonna die, I guess it's not the worst way to go: Bang, you're gone. Am I right?" Thomas nods again. "But I'll miss him. We've been friends for thirty-three years. You know that, right?"

Thomas nods a third time. "Who's the one with the baseball hat?" he asks, indicating the group. "You mean The Kid?" Frank points, and the man looks up. Thomas catches a glimpse of his eyes and his broad nose. He must be in his early twenties. A lock of curly, reddish-brown hair sticks out from under the hat. "It's Luc, Fatso's nephew. Your father called him Luke. He worked with us before Jacques got busted. Did errands and that sort of thing. He's known your father since he was a little boy. And me of course. Good kid. He's a good kid. But I won't bother you anymore on a day like this. We can chat later. I'm offering everyone a round of drinks at my pub afterward. Jenny thought that would be the best thing. And it's the least I can do for my old friend." Thomas looks at him in disbelief. Frank takes a deep drag on his cigarette. "I've got a little place now, for my old age, you see. Your father just managed to approve of it before his arrest. The boss said, 'Okay, it's a good joint.' That was important for me, you know. Your father did enjoy having a drink now and then."

"You're right about that," Thomas mumbles. Frank laughs huskily and pats him on the shoulder. "You've always had a sense of humor, just like your old man. That's the way it should be!" His laughter morphs into a cough. He steps back. Thomas tosses his cigarette onto the ground. Jenny and the others have gone inside. Patricia motions to him: It's time. When he begins to walk, he hears Frank and the others following him. And now he hears an organ playing. Who the hell ordered organ music?

The chapel isn't exceptionally large, but the enormous windows fill the space with light. There's the casket. There's Ernesto playing the electric organ. Some kind of jazz, presumably. He's swaying rhythmically back and forth while tossing his head back, fully absorbed. Apparently, Jenny has arranged everything on her own. The funeral director, a tall, long-limbed woman in a tight skirt and cream-colored shirt, steps forward and offers a dry, warm hand. Then she returns to her position at the door. White walls, hard benches. No one says anything. Thomas slides in beside Patricia. Jenny's sitting in the first row, next to Alice. He hears Frank and his entourage clattering into their pew somewhere behind him. With people in scattered seats, the chapel seems empty and all-too enormous and hollow. Ernesto finally concludes his musical score, after a long and truly embarrassing improvisation that he apparently can't get enough of. That's followed by silence, during which every little sound in the room is amplified: shoes scrape the floor, benches creak, a cough is suppressed, a jacket is rustled. Jenny gets uncertainly to her feet, a piece of paper in her hand. Thomas grows ice cold. If he doesn't clench his teeth, they chatter. Jenny steps up onto the platform the casket rests on and turns toward the attendees. She lays her hand on the casket and quickly removes it, as if she's been scalded. Thomas notices the casket is adorned with scant decorations: a handful of roses, daisies, and some wreaths. He's freezing, shivering. Patricia looks at him out the corner of her eye and squeezes his hand. Jenny clears her throat and appears unhinged.

"First of all, I'd like to thank Alice's friend Ernesto for the beautiful music. Jacques loved jazz." Like hell he did, Thomas thinks. "And I'd like to thank you all for coming out today to say farewell to him." Thomas looks down at his knees. They're quivering. And so are Jenny's. She wobbles in her high heels. She braces herself against the casket for support. As if at any moment her fleshy body could collapse across it. "It's not easy saying goodbye, but we need to. Dad was . . . Dad was one of a kind. He wasn't always easy to have as a father, but . . . he was what we had. He . . ." Jenny is overcome by a fit of powerful, wet sobbing, and tries desperately to control it. She clears her throat. "He was also—a good and loving—father . . . No, I'm sorry . . ." She wipes the tears from her eyes and stares at her paper. She looks up, out over the audience, squints. Time seems to stand completely still. Will she throw herself to the floor? Will she scream? But then a small smile spreads across her face; she locks eyes with Thomas. And then in a suddenly firm voice, she says: "There was no one else besides him, for us. Now he's found peace, and I believe we should sing a song before we leave him. Or before he leaves us. But I guess he's already done that, so . . ." Jenny fumbles for her scarf, tugs on it. "Oh, yeah, I'd also like to let you know that Frank, Jacques's friend of many years, is offering everyone a round of drinks afterward at his place, Café Rose. You can get the address from me after the ceremony." She nearly stumbles as she walks back to her seat.

The twins sit leaning against Helena. One of the girls yawns. Patricia hands Thomas a sheet of light-blue paper. A cheap photocopy, just the sort of thing he despises. On it are the lyrics to the song they're supposed to sing. At the very least she could have asked me to do that, Thomas thinks, and has already guessed what kind of song it'll be even before he inspects the paper. Of course it's the song about old grudges. Jenny has drawn some unhelpful hearts and stars around the words. And a sun, for crying out loud, in the upper left corner. At the organ, Ernesto's having trouble finding the melody; he's playing haltingly and too quickly, and it becomes a rather disjointed performance: Frank and Fatso's voices boom, while everyone else adds their voices more tentatively, and in the center of it all, Thomas can clearly make out his and Jenny's own subdued voices; they know the song by heart. Jenny's voice hasn't cracked, as he would've expected; she sings in tune and in a clear and vibrant voice. When the song's finished, Jenny places a bouquet of orange flowers on the casket. Lilies, maybe. Tiger lilies. She waves him over. His steps are loud on the tiled floors, and he's seized with panic: everything seems distorted and loud. He thinks about the huge body that squeezed him that night Jules and Tina visited, the hair in his mouth, the warm, sticky skin that pressed against his own. His chest hurts. He struggles to breathe. He feels a strong urge to flee. All the while there's this sensation that, when he turns around, he'll come face to face with something so frightful and awful that it'll scare him to death. He doesn't dare turn around. To support himself, he leans against the pews. He stops walking. But Jenny motions for him again, impatiently. When he finally reaches her, he forces himself to turn around, and all that he sees are people quietly gathering their things and shuffling toward the casket. And there the two of them stand, one on either side of the deceased—the silent white casket made of veneer—he with a powerful sense of unease, Jenny like a kind of hostess, seemingly cheerful now. She steps aside to let the prison guard lay a single red rose on the casket. Frank and Fatso fumble with a limp bouquet of carnations that look like something they bought at a gas station. Handshakes and nods. Frank pats Jenny on the cheek. "Yeah," he says, "on this road we'll all travel." He sighs. He squeezes Jenny's arm. Alice is already on the way out, followed by Ernesto. They *are* tiger lilies. And now Thomas notices that the modest decoration, with daisies, is from the city. Apparently it's part of the package. A white banner made of a thin synthetic material: *Rest in peace.* All at once Luc is standing beside him. Carefully he lays a large bundle of blue hyacinths on the casket, near where the dead man's face must be—as if the strong odor should go with him to the grave, right up through his nostrils. The funeral director addresses them discreetly, her cheeks flushed.

"Usually we leave the flowers on the floor, but would you prefer them on the casket?"

"There aren't many anyway," Jenny says.

"That's perfectly fine. We'll just take the cards out." The hyacinths' scent is intense, at once nauseating and agreeable. The dress tightens over the funeral director's hips and derriere when she bends forward to remove the tiny envelopes from the three bouquets. Thomas spins around; it feels as though Luc's still standing right behind him, but he's gone. Thomas glances about, but he's nowhere to be seen. My reflexes are delayed, he thinks, and again this fear spreading from his gut. Then, suddenly, Kristin's smiling face is right in front of him. Now *she's* up here, and she grabs each of their hands. "You did great, Jenny," "Thanks." Jenny whispers like a schoolgirl. Kristin places a small bouquet of twigs with red berries on the casket. "They're poisonous," she whispers to Thomas when Jenny turns her back. A wide smile spreads across Thomas's face, and he feels a sense of relief running through him like a welcome breeze in the midst of something all-too warm and cramped. His belly flutters, his lips quiver, and his fear dissolves, vanishes. He wants to embrace Kristin and laugh. I want to laugh, that's what I want. I want to howl for a long time. Or blubber in her hair. There's a thick lump in his throat. Maybe it's not tears but a scream, he thinks. A powerful roar. Maybe he'll kick over the casket. I'll kick over the casket. I'll break him in two. He feels Kristin's hands clutching his waist. "Thomas," she says." Now he sees that she's also holding onto Jenny, now he hears Jenny whimpering loudly. "Come," Kristin says. "Let's get out of here. You two shouldn't linger. That's enough. Blow out the candles." "The candles?" He hadn't even noticed the wax candles, almost as tall as a man, on either side of the casket. Kristin counts: "One, two, three. Blow!" He looks at Jenny, she looks at him, she sobs, and in unison they blow out the small flames. Two thin columns of black smoke spiral upward. Kristin goes off to gather jackets. Then she leaves the chapel. Jenny's cheeks are blackened with mascara. The chapel's empty now, the air cloudy with tiny specks of dust, visible in the light from the open door. Sweeping light, floating dust. Again this silence in the room, mystical and endless, like outer space, or like a shed on a summer day when you're a kid, when you sit dozing and sweating under a cardboard box, when you sit under a cardboard box with a parched throat and dry, warm hands, sucking small puffs of breath and letting your eyes roll all the way up under your eyelids without closing your eyes. To be so silent and absent that you're almost dead. Thomas staggers. Jenny thanks the chapel officer standing at the door in his black suit. Thomas shakes hands with the funeral director. His own feels clammy and sweaty. She hands him an envelope with roses imprinted on it. "The cards that came with the flowers," she says, smiling. "My condolences." They go outside, but then Jenny turns and slips back inside. She tugs at the chapel officer's sleeve as he's closing the door. "Will he be cremated now? Soon? Are you cremating him now?" she asks breathlessly. "I can't answer precisely, unfortunately. But yes, it'll be either today or tomorrow, I would imagine. He doesn't have to go very far, after all. You can ask the funeral director, if you wish." He nods in the direction of the funeral director. "The woman over there." But Jenny responds with uncontainable tears, loud and mournful. The door closes behind them. Thomas takes hold of her; she leans against him and dampens his shirt, a river flowing from her eyes. She hangs on his neck, sobbing.

"Why are you crying?" he mutters. It only makes her cry harder. He can't say anything more. His throat constricts. He can only stand here with her; she's too heavy to maneuver down the stairs. There's too much weight on her now, a hefty girth, and here on the stairs, as if they're on a platform above the others, everyone will surely stare at them. And now he can't help but shed a tear himself, for Jenny and her miserable existence, for all that's touching about her, for all the shit that has preceded this bizarre moment, for the child under the cardboard box, for the heat, for the prickling light, for the body leaning against his, so completely surrendered, this aura of defeat emanating from her. In the corner of his eye, he sees Frank glance alertly at them. Then Maloney enters his field of vision. Gently he nudges Thomas aside and takes Jenny into his arms so that Thomas can walk down the stairs. Sucking snot into his nose, Thomas feels love for Maloney. That too is making him bawl; what's wrong with him? Patricia advances and gives him a forceful embrace. He puts one of his hands in her jacket pocket. His hands are cold as ice.

Little by little, the ragtag group pulls itself together and gets moving. Alice hops impatiently up and down, her teeth chattering. She's wearing all-too few clothes, her short jacket and her just-as-short T-shirt underneath it revealing her stomach. Ernesto puts his arms around her. "I'm hungry," one twin says to the other. "Me too," says the other. "C'mon, Mom, can we go now?" "I have bananas in the car," Helena says, finding her car keys. Frank helps Jenny give people directions to Café Rose. Kristin offers Thomas and Patricia a lift, because, as she puts it, "We're not going home yet, we have to see this through to the end." Maloney hails a taxi for Jenny, Alice, and Ernesto. The prison guard, who's been talking with Luc, gives his thanks. "It's back to the grind for me," he says, adding that he was happy to "be here." With his long legs he climbs onto his rusty bicycle and pedals doggedly down the alley.

The car smells of overripe bananas and dog. Patricia and Thomas have to sit with the girls on their laps in the back seat. "We'll skip seatbelts, for once," Kristin says, stroking Helena's head. "Drive carefully, love." Thomas feels chilled to the bone, he feels hunger and craves a cigarette, he feels nauseated and headachy. Too much saliva in his mouth, nerves that cause his eye to twitch. Kristin and Patricia chat during the drive, and every now and then Helena laughs pleasantly. The sounds penetrate Thomas, or rather they don't; he hears only gibberish, nothing makes sense. The sun's lower now, and he sees that the chestnuts have begun to bud; soon they'll bloom. Soon it'll be spring. Soon it'll be summer. "It'll be summer soon," he hears himself say.

"We can't wait until summer. You should visit us sooner than that—in the foreseeable future." Kristin hands the bananas to the twins. "Right, Thomas? You have to promise me. We need to talk." He nods. The twins shovel the bananas into their mouths and throw the peels onto the floor. "You're so dumb," one says.

"So are you," says the other. "Nina threw her banana peel on the floor!"

"Pick it up, Nina."

"So did she. *Idiot*," says the other one, what is her name again? "I hate you."

"Kids, knock it off, please. We've just been to a funeral."

"So what? She still threw it on the floor."

"And I'm not a *kid*."

"Maya!"

"How's school? Are you really in seventh grade?" Patricia's voice, mild and calm. Something to hold onto, Thomas thinks, trying to focus on that voice. He closes his eyes, but his eyeballs skate back and forth under his lids; he's too uneasy. They drive past the big parking garages, toward center city, then head west. Thomas feels Maya's windbreaker against his knuckles and fingers. Her hair touches his face each time the car makes a turn. It tickles unbearably. He wants to get out of this car. And just like that they've arrived. Everything becomes clear: Thomas recognizes the place at once; and strangely, it calms him. It's not far from his father's apartment, but it's in a neighborhood that hasn't been renovated yet. No young trees here. Old, whitewashed gray houses, bicycles lying on the sidewalk. A tobacconist, a seedy little grocery. A few dogs lie in the sun, their snouts resting on their front paws, waiting on their masters. And there's the bar on the ground floor of a tilting four-story building. Frank stands waving in the door. They tumble out of the car. With some difficulty Thomas gets to his feet. "Check out the curtains," Patricia whispers. "Do you think they even have a jukebox?" Bright orange curtains with a thin green strip. On the window is painted: *Beer wine music spirits.* What is the word "music" doing there? And below that: *One beer, One shot 10:00 A.M.-2:00 P.M.* Alice is making out with Ernesto, tonguing him without restraint. Jenny rubs the mascara from her eyes and reapplies her lipstick, the color of which matches the curtains perfectly, Thomas thinks. I'm cold as ice, he thinks. I'm not here. But Patricia takes his hand and leads him up a few steps and into the smoky room. Luc, whom Frank called The Kid, is working the bar. "Welcome everybody! You can order whatever you'd like, it's on me," Frank shouts, "I hope we'll have a lovely afternoon together." Maloney's already got his mitts on a pint. Small tables with red-checked cloths. A nauseating stench of toilet cleaner and alcohol. Three tables have been shoved together in the center of the room. "We've got some grub too," Frank continues. "A little buffet. Please help yourselves." The buffet consists of some bowls of chips and peanuts. Gummy bears and marshmallows. Pigs in a blanket. Ketchup and mustard in plastic bottles. A stack of paper plates and some red napkins, as well as a bowl piled with hardboiled eggs and red caviar. The egg yolks have a greenish tint, black edges. Thomas reels backward. The twins immediately begin gathering candy and chips. The others cluster at the bar. Luc's busy making gin and tonics; he pours beer and white wine, and cola for the girls. Luc's face: glowing. He has freckles across the bridge of his nose, creamy skin. Maloney asks for a shot of whiskey. Jenny watches Luc transfer boxed wine into a tall glass. She's still wearing her gloves when he hands her the drink. It's unbearable, Thomas thinks, ticked, all these people in this bar, my own family. This jovial friendliness. Trying to get on Frank's good side even as they look down on him—at best—and at worst, scorn him. It makes him sick. Thomas skirts the buffet table and goes outside. As soon as the door closes behind him, he taps a cigarette out of his pack, and with his face bathed in sunlight and his back against the wall, he tries to control his hot flash of anger. But before it's tamped down, Alice joins him. At first they smoke in silence. Then she says: "Are you actually sad?" He shakes his head vigorously.

"You think Mom's acting?"

"What do you mean?"

"You think she's pretending to be 'mourning'?"

"In a way, maybe. I don't think she's crying over our father, but over a lot of other things. That happens sometimes. I don't know."

Alice loses herself staring at the sky, she inhales a deep puff of her cigarette. She rubs her closely shaved scalp. Then she looks at him with eyes that burn, boring into him. "I need a job."

Thomas wrinkles his brow. "But you haven't finished school. Shouldn't you go back?"

She shrugs, flicks her cigarette away, and goes inside. Voices and laughter drift through the open door, then it slams with a thud. Thomas squats on the stoop and closes his eyes to the sun. His anger's gone, replaced with this strange feeling that everything's unreal; the law of gravity has been rescinded, and he's floating in an empty, colorless room. Some dogs bark, someone calls out of a window, a motorcycle roars way down the street, the sounds gathering into something very familiar, and for one moment he's back on his old street, ten years old, on the way to school with his books thrashing in his backpack and a taste of blood in his mouth, because once again he's bitten his lip too hard. Walking along thinking of pleasant aromas. Cinnamon, beef soup, applesauce. To stand under newly washed sheets flapping in the breeze, letting them envelop him. The coffee shop beside the school: the completely overwhelming pleasure he felt when the door was opened and the scent of coffee wafted into his nostrils like an explosion of aroma. The pure feeling of frost. The sun shined that day like it does today, spring, but the air was still cold, a shiver, and the previous evening he'd learned that their mother had died. Kristin had been the one who'd called; their father had answered. Thomas sat hunched over his homework in the kitchen, but the conversation thrust its way straight through division and geometry, there was no mistaking the subject. When their father hung up, Thomas heard him sit down in the armchair, the creaking and the crackling. Then silence. Jenny was already asleep. Thomas felt his own breathing growing thicker and thicker, the relentless deep freeze in his stomach intensifying. Their father turned on the television. Blood rushed to Thomas's cheeks. Through a film of tears he stared at parallelograms and triangles. He stood and crept to the door, where he saw their father's back and the TV screen. Some cowboys rode through a desert with raised rifles. "Was that Aunt Kristin?" he asked carefully. Their father grumbled.

"Was that about Mom?"

"You have good ears."

"But *was* it about Mom?" Thomas planted the sharp point of his pencil into his side. A thin, sharp pain. Their father turned halfway round to look at him. "Your mother's dead. She's been sick, and now she's dead. But it doesn't change anything. To us she's been dead a long time. Go do your homework now. It's late. I'm off soon."

Their father turned his attention back to the screen. Thomas struggled for air.

"She's not dead to me," he whispered.

"Maybe so, but now she is in fact truly dead. And you might as well get used to it." Then he raised his voice menacingly: "Don't stand there pouting, Thomas."

His father rose heavily and stood in all his bulk, tall and big-boned. He stared at Thomas. "You're not gonna stand there whimpering, are you?" His father sighed. "That doesn't make any fucking sense. Have you forgotten that she left you? We haven't heard a word from her since. Cut it out, goddamnit." He got his jacket from the couch, put it on, zipped it up, and lit a cigarette. He shoved his lighter into his pants pocket and exhaled smoke. He gave Thomas a hard, dark glare that sent him back to the well-lit kitchen. *Don't sniffle, don't say a word.* His clear snot dripped on the floor. Then he heard the door bang shut and again he stuck himself with his pencil, poking it deeply in the skin just under his ribs.

The next day was incredibly sunny. He didn't say anything to Jenny. Not before summer. He didn't want to make her sad. He kept their mother's death to himself, like a big, shaggy, twisted lump of darkness. It wasn't until August, when they visited Kristin in her apartment, that he learned what had happened. Their mother had been diagnosed with breast cancer and was dead six months later. She'd been out of the country and was buried in the city in which she'd died, Kristin said, according to her own wishes. She didn't want to be buried in the family plot. She didn't want to go home. Kristin had been with her during her final days, and she'd made sure that she'd been buried. "Did she say anything about us?" Thomas asked following a pause, in which Jenny scratched at a mosquito bite while humming and rocking in her chair and swinging her legs back and forth. But Kristin had just shaken her head. "No. She had so much pain that she couldn't really talk. She was taking a lot of medicine, which caused her to sleep a lot. But I'm certain that she *thought* about each of you." Thomas knew this was a lie. Something Kristin only said to make them happy. How would a lie make him happy? That same day, toward evening, Kristin had pulled him aside and given him a small photograph of their mother: She's sitting in a garden with him on her lap. Jenny's looking out from the baby carriage beside them. Their mother smiles to the camera. A teapot and some cups are resting on a table. Behind them is a tree with a thick, enormous crown. Their mother's one bare arm holds Thomas, the other rests on the back of the bench behind his head. She looks calm and laid back, almost tranquil. Her eyes are hidden behind large sunglasses. It was the same photograph he picked up from the floor in their father's apartment, when Jenny got her toaster. Thomas opens his eyes. Now he thinks about the money. The microwave in the basement. Christ. He gets to his feet. Patricia stands in the doorway: "Where did you go? Aren't you coming in? You can't leave me alone in there, it's not exactly fun." He mumbles an apology and follows her inside. She holds the door for him. The first thing he sees is Maloney shooting craps with Fatso at a table to the right of the bar.

After three glasses of cognac and one beer, Thomas wants to turn to Frank and say: *You need to tell me about the job that put Jacques away.* But Frank beats him to it. He bares his rotting, blackened teeth in a smile, waves Thomas closer, pulls him down beside him on the bench under the window, and pushes yet another glass of cognac across to him. He says, "I thought of something . . . have you and Jenny been out to Jacques's apartment recently?"

Thomas stiffens. "What do you mean?"

"I mean, you must've inherited some things, right? Maybe you went out there to look at the furniture and all that. Or didn't you?"

"No. We've inherited nothing. We've disclaimed everything, inheritance and debts."

"Huh. Jacques had debts? I didn't know that."

"Why are you asking?"

Frank raises his glass and sips, then leans back. He fishes a cigarette out of a shiny case. "Just curious, my friend. And because I forgot a bag of mine last time I was there. But it's just some dry cleaning, nothing terribly important. I seem to recall Jenny saying the two of you'd been out there, so I wanted to ask."

Thomas stares at him. He doesn't know what to say. His tongue is bloated and dry, pressed to the floor of his mouth. It doesn't want to budge. Frank lights the cigarette and sucks on it, running his hand through his hair; smoke climbs upward and dissipates into faint spirals under the lamp. He smiles. "How are you doing otherwise? Jenny says you own a business?"

Jenny apparently says whatever she wants to whomever she wants. Thomas takes a slug of the amber-yellow cognac, which burns wonderfully in his throat. His tongue wants to move now.

"Yes, thank you. It's going well."

At that moment the two men turn toward the sound of a boisterous whooping, Maloney stomping on the floor, apparently having won a round.

"That's my partner," Thomas says.

"It's good to have a partner," Frank nods. "Your father was a great partner. He had *class*. You know what I mean? You could trust that guy. Now all I've got is Fatso, but that's okay too."

He straightens up and drops his hands to his thighs. The veins coil like fat worms under his skin. "Did you know this place was named after Fatso's sister? She lives out in the country now, with some guy I think. You remember her from our street?" He runs his tongue around in his mouth, making smacking sounds, then rests his hands on the table. "She was a fine-looking woman. You remember Rose?"

Thomas nods.

"She was one pretty gal." Frank scrapes his cigarette through the ashtray and leans back again. "So you haven't found my bag?"

"No. We haven't. Sorry."

Frank stares at him. "That's too bad."

"Yeah."

Though his mouth smiles, Frank's eyes are hard and direct. "Then we'll just have to hope it turns up someplace else."

"Yeah." Thomas empties his glass. Frank turns toward the back of the bar, and zones out. There's a minute of silence. The sun blazes through the orange curtains. Fatso shakes the dice cup and the dice clatter onto the table. Luc says something to Alice, which causes her to hop from the barstool to illustrate something with her body. Standing on her tiptoes raising her hands toward the ceiling. They laugh. Thomas senses the pulse in one of his feet and wants to leave, but when Frank begins to rise, Thomas remains seated after all. He takes a deep breath. When he begins speaking, his voice sounds like a loud whisper. "Why was Jacques nailed? What kind of job was it? Was he doing it on his own or were you all involved? And what about him, over there?" He nods in Luc's direction.

Slowly Frank rotates his head. For one moment they look at each other, intensely. Frank's eyes gleam almost yellow. But a film of gray has dimmed the color in them. "The Kid?" he says.

"Yeah."

Again Frank's lips move into a dead smile. "The Kid was very close to Jacques."

Then all at once Frank's arms are around Thomas's neck. His armpits give off a hint of deodorant and dunghill. He squeezes Thomas, practically shaking him, upbeat but a little too tight. "Go fill your glass. There's more where that comes from." And with that Frank is quickly on his feet and slipping behind a curtain near the bathrooms. Fatso looks up from the dice cup and watches him go. Glances quickly and piercingly at Thomas. The Kid's pouring red wine for Alice and Ernesto. Patricia's in the far corner with Jenny, Kristin, and Helena. Kristin tosses her head back in laughter; Patricia has apparently said something funny. There's a tap on the window behind him, and when he snaps his head around, he stares right into the eyes of one of the twins. For a few seconds she locks eyes with him, solemn. Then her face dissolves into a smile, the light filling her eyes.

When he stands, he feels the alcohol's effect on his legs. His feet tingle. Up at the bar Alice puts her arm around him. "This is my

Uncle Thomas. And this is Luke." He nods to Luc, who nods back. "I thought your name was Luc. The beloved child has many names, I've heard." Luc nods earnestly. Thomas asks for another cognac. "Did you know that Luke knew Grandpa?" Thomas shakes his head. "He's actually known him since he was little, isn't that right, Luke?"

Luc beams. "He taught me how to fish."

"Did he now? I didn't know that he could fish."

"He was good at it. We almost always caught something." Luc's voice is surprisingly sonorous and pleasant, rising from deep within his belly.

"And where did you fish?"

"Sometimes we got out of the city, north to streams or lakes. But usually we fished in the sea."

Luc sets Thomas's cognac down with a little thump. His eyes are light brown, with some sort of greenish tint floating in them. Lush, coal-black eyelashes. Relatively nice teeth, only a single crooked tooth.

"Sea fishing?" Thomas says slowly.

An eager smile spreads across the young man's face. "Yes! From the quay down by the old industrial harbor, or we'd row out. But only during the summer. We'd put out nets to catch flatfish, and eel, but jig-fishing was always the best."

"That so? My father apparently had hidden talents." Another smile. Luc leans over the bar and braces his elbows on the countertop.

"What about the river? Did you fish in the river?" Luc nods. "Of course." Alice drops her cigarette butt into an empty beer bottle. "Isn't it strange, Thomas, that Luke knew *my* grandpa and I didn't?"

Luc: "He was smart. And patient. If you're not patient, you don't catch a thing. Rule number one."

"What else do you do? When you're not fishing?"

"Look at him," Alice says. "He's a bartender."

"Yes, I can see that."

Luc straightens up again. "I help out here and there wherever I'm needed. You know, many small brooks make a big stream."

"To stay with the metaphor," Thomas says.

"With the what?" Luc asks.

"Ignore him," Alice says, putting her hand on Luc's arm. "He's always got to be so clever. You're a walking dictionary, aren't you Uncle Thomas? I really looked up to him when I was little. My rich uncle who was so smart." Alice sniffles and sips her red wine. "You still are. Rich and smart." She draws a cigarette from Thomas's pack. "But you sure as hell didn't teach me how to fish. God, you know what else? Luke and I were born in the same month!"

Thomas: "Congratulations."

Luc: "With ten days and four years between us."

Alice: "Luke's four years older than me."

Thomas: "I see."

"We also live in the same neighborhood. How uncanny is that?" Alice leans back on the barstool, the lit cigarette between her fingers, and laughs. "It *is* uncanny."

Luc smiles.

"But I'm moving soon," she says, inhaling a deep drag.

"Where are you moving?" Luc asks.

"I've no idea. But I have to move soon, I'm getting sick of my mother."

Ernesto comes over. Groaning, he squeezes himself onto the stool beside Alice. "I keep losing! They're destroying me." It turns out that Fatso and Maloney have been playing for money the whole time. And they're not placing small bets. Maloney appears to be in his element. "Your friend's winning the entire pot," Ernesto sighs, drinking his wine. Thomas hears Frank's voice cutting through the women's conversation at the back of the café. He's standing with one arm around Jenny and the other around Kristin. But Kristin quickly removes it.

Patricia gives Thomas a long, telling glance. She wants to go home. So does Thomas.

"Thanks for the drinks," he says, offering Luc his hand. A firm shake, a warm palm.

"No problem. Come back another time."

"No!" Alice blurts out. "You're not leaving already, are you? We're going to dance soon." Alice wiggles her torso, apparently rather drunk. She embraces him, warm and playful, rippling with energy. Thomas says goodbye to everyone, except Frank. Fatso says: "You don't want to shoot craps? We didn't even get the chance to talk. Come back another time and get yourself a beer." Maloney gets to his feet and bearhugs him. "Quite a family you've got!" he whispers giddily. "It's like being on a sitcom, a TV show . . ." "A horror," Thomas mumbles and for one moment is on the verge of tears, feeling completely transparent and accessible to whatever and whoever. But only for a moment. The faces around him are unclear and wavering in clouds of smoke. "Have a safe trip home, okay?" Maloney clucks his tongue, hikes up his pants, and returns to his seat. "If this keeps up, I'll buy a round for everyone in the joint!" He broods over the dice, and Fatso shakes the cup. Maloney wins again. The twins have come inside and are hanging out beside the jukebox, one ganglier than the other. Boredom, pre-pubescence. Finally Patricia and Thomas are outside in the cool evening air. "It feels as though we've been in there for days," Thomas grumbles. "But it's over and done with now," Patricia says, squeezing his bicep. He's still a bit dizzy, but at the very least, the alcohol has relaxed his muscles. Thomas's mouth feels pasty, and he's not at all certain that anything is over with.

And yet he returns to Café Rose when Patricia falls asleep, her mouth hanging open, her dark hair fanning across the white pillow. He can't sleep. Something pulls him back. Like a sleepwalker, he sneaks through the apartment buttoning his pants and rooting around for his bicycle keys. The hallway smells of floor polish, and he thinks of the imminent spring cleaning; soon the store's floors will be polished. The streets are empty, and there's no traffic. He cycles through a red light, and rides on the sidewalks down one-way streets. His back-wheel squeaks, and the bell's about to fall off. To pull the cold air into his lungs. To ride fast. The alcohol like something simmering right beneath the surface of his skin. He locks the bike to a streetlight. It's 11:00 p.m., maybe everyone's gone home. But not everyone has gone home. In the center of the room Alice, piss drunk, is dancing with Frank to the sound of scratchy soul music, hanging on his neck like a young girl, affectionate and silly. Fatso has taken Luc's place behind the bar, and Maloney's still seated on the same chair shooting craps, now with Luc. Or Luke. Or The Kid. Ernesto has fallen asleep, his head resting on his arms. Surrounding him is a cluster of rowdies, who've commandeered the tables near the windows. "Thomas!" Frank shouts, breaking free of Alice, who tumbles backward and bumps against the bar. "Couldn't live without us, eh?" Thomas helps Alice to her feet, wakes Ernesto, and sends them home in a cab. From the backseat Alice screeches the jukebox's songs, while Thomas presses money into Ernesto's hand and guides him into the front seat. "Now make sure that she gets home and goes to bed, you got it? No detours." He gives the driver Jenny's address. The car glides down the street and turns the corner. He hopes she doesn't throw up on the leather seats. Thomas pushes the café door open. Maloney's now reeling on his feet, screaming at Luc. But Luc's not saying anything. He's leaning back in his chair, visibly pleased, shoving a wad of bills in his pants pocket. "You cheated! Admit it! You've been messing with the dice for the past hour!" Addressing Thomas: "Fucking hell, he's taken everything." Then, to Fatso: "You saw it yourself! He cheated!" To Luc: "Replay!" But Maloney has lost. Luc stands, zips his jacket, and says: "Thanks for the game, it was a pleasure." He raises his arm in greeting, smiles at Thomas, and turns. But Maloney leaps at him, heavy and breathless, wobbly on his feet, like a huge, injured animal. He knocks over chairs and grabs at Luc's back. Hissing something unintelligible and trying to haul Luc to the floor. But Luc is strong. He gets his arm free and reaches behind him, taking hold of the nape of Maloney's neck and pressing his skull forward against the back of his own head. He holds tight. The muscles of his sinewy arms flex under his skin. He presses. Maloney gasps. Fatso lumbers over good-naturedly and splits them apart. "Let go, now. Let go of the old man, Luke." He has a hand on Luc's shoulder. "You can let go now, boy." And Luc lets go. Maloney loses his balance and falls over, landing on his stomach. Thomas pulls him to his feet. "Maybe you should go home?"

Groaning bitterly, Maloney pats dust off his pants. "What about you? I do what I feel like doing." Luc is gone. Fatso's once again behind the bar. The little group that witnessed the fight now return to their glasses and cigarettes. To incoherent conversations and drunken lewdness. Maloney staggers to his beer glass, lifts it to his mouth. But it's as though he forgets to drink. "Fucking asshole, god-damn mother fucking upstart. Do you realize how much he stole from me? He *stole*, Thomas. I should've kicked his ass!" He sits on a barstool, his glass still half-raised to his face. Sighing deeply, slumping, and shaking his head.

Thomas grasps Maloney's arm and helps him to his feet.

He stands on the stoop, watching Maloney stumble down the street and curse under his breath. "See you tomorrow!" Thomas calls after him. Maloney doesn't respond, and suddenly there's something moving about the way he lurches away, alone, a strength in him, and Thomas thinks: *But what if he walks in front of a car,* and the thought scares him. So he trots after Maloney, catches up to his broad back, and hugs him, pressing his face into Maloney's jacket. "What the hell," Maloney mumbles. "You again?"

Fatso lights up when Thomas sits down at the bar. Pouring beer on the house, he wants to know what Thomas has been up to during the intervening years. "I almost didn't recognize you at the service today, but your eyes are the same. You got them from your father. You don't forget eyes like that." Fatso is sober and chatty, his shirt pulled taut over his round belly, his strong hands working swiftly and expertly with glasses, bottles, and beer taps. "The Kid has a good feel for craps, and I've seen many grown men go off on him because they think he's cheating. But he's just lucky. That's my opinion. When it comes to games he's unbelievably lucky. You know that old saying? If you're unlucky at games you must be lucky in love. That's not the Kid."

"Is he unlucky in love then?" Thomas asks, lighting a cigarette.

"Yeah, I guess you could say that. In any case, I've never seen him with a girlfriend. My sister's afraid he's gay. But I think she's . . . how can I say it? Overanalyzing. Rose is . . . No, he's just a loner. He's handsome as all hell, so it's not his looks."

"How old is he?"

"Twenty-two. You have kids, Thomas?"

And in this way they prattle on. Thomas discovers that Rose is addicted to pills, and that for long stretches of time The Kid lived with Fatso. Fatso explains mawkishly how close The Kid was to Jacques (and here Fatso wipes a tear from the corner of his eye), that Fatso's happy working in the café, that finally he's found a "measure of peace," that everything's more or less the same here on the street. "But we're getting older." For his part, Thomas talks a bit about his store and Patricia. "You've done well for yourself." Fatso nods in admiration. "You've always had a good head on your shoulders." All these clichés about how he's always been, as if Fatso had something to do with Thomas's "success," as if Fatso knows Thomas, as if he were Fatso's own son. "You've always done your own thing," et cetera. Thomas washes it down with more beer, but when he asks about his father's final criminal act, Fatso claps his mouth shut.

"What happened? Did he kill someone?"

"I can't talk about it, Thomas."

The bar's busy, their conversation continually interrupted, but Thomas doesn't move. A woman in a green polyester shirt with huge sweat stains under her arms leans her head on his shoulder and probingly gropes his thigh. He shoves her spidery hand away. "No! I won't keep my fingers to myself! You're so handsome . . ." One of the woman's eyes is badly crossed, and she clutches her Campari close to her chest.

"Did you visit him in prison?" Thomas asks when he's got Fatso's attention again. But Frank's standing right behind him now. Perhaps he's been there for a while. "You two having a good time?" he asks in a chilled tone, forcing his way between the woman in green and Thomas. "Move it, toots, you're blocking the entire bar." The woman slaps at Frank. Frank yanks her off the stool and sends her packing with a hard shove. Thomas waves Fatso closer.

"Listen, help me out. My father's dead and gone. You don't owe him anything. What kind of job was it? It must've been something big or more brutal than earlier? Why did he go to prison? He almost always got off. Or got a shorter sentence. Did someone rat on him? Did someone die? Did he kill someone? The guard said he was facing a long sentence." Thomas pauses. "C'mon, Frank. Help me out." Frank says: "You harping on that again?" The two faces are so close to him that he can smell them, and he inches closer, so close that he can feel the heat from Fatso's skin. He softens his voice. "I understand if you think it's weird, and maybe even pushy, but I really need to know about his final months. You two are the only ones I know who were close to him. I can't . . . find peace until I know." Fatso turns away. Then all at once Frank's face is right up in his, whispering in a raspy voice: "Let me tell you one thing. I want to be left alone to take care of my business. Do you understand that?"

Fatso wanders to the other end of the bar, where some young men are shouting out for beer. Thomas, shaking his head, says: "But who would I tell? The police? He's *dead.* The case is closed. I'm just asking for a small favor, between you and me, Frank."

"Do I owe you a favor? Listen, because this is the last time I'll say it: *I want to be left alone to take care of this establishment.* Whatever the cost. You got that?"

There's a pause. Frank breathes heavily and Thomas leans back in his seat, squinting.

"Are you threatening me, Frank? Is that what you're doing? This is my father we're talking about. Don't tell me you're threatening me. Who do you think you are?"

Staring hard, Frank edges closer. "I'm not threatening anyone. I wouldn't dream of it. I'm just telling it like it is."

"But you're not saying anything at all . . ."

"Maybe I think it's a little impolite of you to come roaring in here, abusing me. I wiped your ass when you were a baby, Thomas. I fixed your lunches."

"Like hell you did!"

"And I held this wake for your father today. You didn't have any interest in doing that, did you?" A bitter smile. "You haven't exactly been beating down his door, and if he was still alive you wouldn't give a shit about him. Or about us, for that matter."

Thomas wants to protest, but Frank raises his voice to a sharp hiss: "Now I think you should quietly get yourself another beer, on the house, and enjoy the rest of the evening. You don't got shit to worry about, Thomas, and you shouldn't go snooping around here. We want to be left alone. Do you understand that? Don't try to butter up Fatso, either. We'll make an exception today because you're Jacques's son, and because we've known you since you were a boy. But that doesn't give you the right to a damn thing. You got that? My patience has worn thin, Thomas. I don't want to hear any more from you. Stay away. You got that?" Frank stares at him with his old man's eyes. Thomas returns the stare. It's like looking into the face of a mangy dog. Something vicious and desperate. Something immeasurably wretched. Something that's nearing its end. Fatso glances at them from where he's standing, underneath an orange lamp. He appears to be chiseled from stone. Without a word, Thomas gets up and leaves.

It's like being a zombie. When they were children, he and Jenny had watched zombie films on TV, petrified, Jenny often crying and hysterical, but not even *that* could get them to turn off the set, not even the crying or the screaming, they couldn't get enough, they had to see the films through to the end, their eyes glued to the screen, and since then he's had a recurring nightmare about being chased by phalanxes of gray-skinned zombies, running from them, knowing they are *there* and going to catch him, no matter how many doors he locks in the dream to barricade himself: they always find him, these nearly faceless living dead with their slow-motion and insatiable bloodthirst, this ugly fantasy about immortality, but now he's the zombie, one of the living dead, that's how it feels when he can't wake, when he can't talk, eat, read. April passes. Thomas is wrapped up in a thick duvet. He's sluggish and indolent, his body practically rigid with exhaustion, his need for sleep seems unhealthy. Or that's what Patricia thinks, anyway. He slept most of the day following the funeral and that's how it's been ever since, now he's the one who takes a nap under the desk in the store's office, while Maloney orders Annie and Peter around. He's the one nodding off on the train home, his head heavy, dangling; he's the one who, freezing cold, crawls onto the couch and falls asleep in the middle of the news broadcast, only to stumble into bed later and pass out, sleep black and dreamless, as soon as his head hits the pillow. "Are you sick?" Patricia asks, worried. "Are you depressed?—Does it have something to do with me?" But Thomas can only shake his head tiredly. It's like hibernation. *I'm a bear. I'm a beetle.* Days and nights dissolve in a colorless slush: he walks around the store, mechanically moving objects from place to place; he hears Maloney's voice; he hears conversations about Peter's ringworm (which is apparently drying out after treatment with a fungicidal cream); he greets customers and deliverymen, bicycle and parcel couriers, the mailman and Eva, who, stooping, pushes the vacuum across the shiny wooden floors (she's consented to do the spring cleaning if they'll also hire her niece)—and organizing all of that sapped his energy. He orders products and sits silently during meetings with the accountant, while Maloney leads the conversation. He agrees to nearly everything, and forgets most of it later, his mind can't *retain* anything. He can't even bring himself to put up any resistance when Maloney, humming, decorates the show window with the small candlesticks of tinted glass. He goes to the doctor, Patricia forces him. "I feel a little like a zombie," he says, staring at the floor. The doctor laughs and takes his blood pressure, draws blood, weighs him, peers deep in his throat, jams an instrument into his ear, listens to his heart. His blood pressure is slightly higher than normal, but other than everything looks fine. Post-traumatic stress syndrome triggered by his father's death, the doctor concludes, despite Thomas's protests. He's advised to continue his regular lifestyle, including exercise and easily digestible, frequent meals. "Come back in a few weeks. If you're not feeling better, we'll discuss alternative treatment." Patricia looks at him in wonder. "Has your father's death really affected you this much? I thought you were relieved." He shrugs. His thoughts fly away from him before he even thinks them. They are mere hints of a rapidly evaporating substance, something you can just glimpse before it scatters to dust or air, exploding into millions of microscopic molecules and disappearing into space. He lies in bed and thinks about the money in the basement. I should buy something, he thinks weakly, turn it into something. Get rid of the money. But he can't bring himself to complete his thought, and he certainly can't muster the strength to go down to the basement. It seems so absurd that the money's in his old microwave, he almost can't believe it's there. And then, one radiant, clear morning at the end of May—when the cherry trees have long since bloomed, a veil of white and pink still hanging on the treetops, it's practically more beautiful than when the trees are fully in bloom, Thomas thinks, astonished at his first lucid thought in some time and, astonished at the joy expressed in that thought, just as he's putting change in the cash register—Alice shows up unexpectedly at the store. Her hair has grown out a little. She's got a green stud in her nose that flashes every time the sunlight hits it. Thomas offers to buy her a cup of coffee at the café across the street, but Alice would rather have tea, an omelet, sausages, and French fries. They sit opposite each other. She smiles brightly, looking alert and exquisite. Black nail polish, slender hands, light-brown neck.

"To what do I owe the honor?" Thomas asks, chugging his triple espresso so that he'll be a little more clearheaded.

"I moved," she smiles. "Luke found me a room with one of his friends. And now I really need a job."

"What does your mom say about that?"

"What can she say? I'm eighteen. I'm an adult."

"Are you?"

"Yes!" Alice looks directly at him. "She flipped, of course, she threw a jar of pickles at me, shouting and carrying on. But then she packed all my clothes and set them out in the stairwell. She changed the lock, too, but the next day she called and begged me to come home. Now it seems like she's accepted it. You know her. But she won't give me any money, and I'm seriously broke. I need to pay rent in fourteen days. They've let me owe them."

The omelet arrives. Alice squirts ketchup onto her plate and dives into her food. She stuffs a chunk of sausage into the folded-up omelet that's already in her mouth, then licks the grease from her fingers after she's swallowed, mumbling, "Sorry, but I haven't eaten since yesterday afternoon."

"Are you still seeing Ernesto?"

She nods.

"And where does he live?"

"With a friend."

"How's it going with his band?"

"Good. They've got a concert tonight. Do you want to come?"

"Maybe."

"Can you loan me some money? I promise to pay you back when I have a job."

"But are you even looking for a job?"

"Of course!"

Thomas promises to call her later and consider going to the concert. "Maybe Luke will come, too," Alice says. "We've become really good friends. He's super cool. Ernesto and I hang out sometimes at Café Rose and he's teaching Ernesto how to shoot craps and win."

"How do you teach that? The dice fall randomly. Does he have some sort of unique shaking technique, or what?"

Alice smiles. "I don't know. But it's kinda fun. He tells me stories about Grandpa and buys me drinks."

It annoys Thomas that she refers to his father as "Grandpa." He sucks air through his nose and leans back, tipping in his chair.

"What stories does he tell?"

"All sorts."

The chair lands hard on all four legs. "Listen. Your grandpa was a criminal and not a nice person. You shouldn't listen too much to Luc's glorifying nonsense. Half of it is probably a lie—all that stuff about fishing I guarantee is a lie."

Alice gives him a defiant look. "Wasn't it, like, a hundred years since you last saw him?"

"Wasn't he in jail because he was a fucking crook?"

"Thieves aren't by definition bad people. Maybe he changed. Besides, can't thieves go fishing too?"

"He was a mean bastard."

"But he read poems."

"What did you say?"

"He read poems. Poetry. That's what Luke says."

Thomas shakes his head vehemently. "Give me a break."

Alice lifts a French fry with her index finger and thumb and dips it extraordinarily slowly into her mouth. "I think it's a nice thing to think about. He loved Shakespeare's sonnets. Knew many of them by heart. He read Whitman. Have you ever read Whitman?"

"Of course I've read Whitman! Have you?"

Alice laughs. "No."

"He also read Borges. Mayakovsky and Celan. That's what Luke says. I think those sound like pretty names. Celan . . ."

"Celan? He needs to cut it out. My father never read Celan."

"Rilke, Mallarmé . . . Oh, he was supposedly obsessed with Rilke, according to Luke."

"Alice, this is crazy. You . . ."

"What time is it?"

"I don't know, but he hasn't read Mallarmé either—"

"Aren't you wearing a watch?"

Despite himself, Thomas pushes up his sleeve and glances at his watch. It's 10:00 A.M.

"Fuck, I've gotta go. I've got a job interview."

"Where?"

She winks. "Wouldn't you like to know!"

He stares at her face, unnerved. Lets his eyes glide down her forehead, cheeks, lips. Is she going to be a go-go dancer? A stripper? A hole to fuck? And why does he actually think that? She looks totally serene. Then her face cracks open and a childish, disarming, perfectly happy smile spreads across it. "Thanks for breakfast, Uncle Thomas." She sets her hand on his, which is slack and cold on the table—as if it didn't belong to his body. "You shouldn't worry so much about me. I'll manage. I'm feeling good now, much better than before. You know? I'm telling you, living at home was so depressing, I was fucking depressed. She drove me fucking crazy."

"Stop saying fuck all the time, Alice."

"Now it's kind of a relief. Now—now I am—full of hope, actually. Yeah, full of hope, that's how I feel." She stands and kisses him on the cheek. "Call me later, okay? Come with us tonight, we'll have a lot of fun." She moves easily and effortlessly through the restaurant, and the glass door slides shut behind her with a *swoop*. He stares at it for a long time. Now it's as though she's not been here at all, as if she were a ghost. But Celan? Rilke? He leans across the table, resting his head on his forearms. Oh, lethargic body. Oh, sleep. Then someone claps a hand on his shoulder and pulls him up. "No sleeping in a public place, young man." Maloney stands before him in all his girth, a Coke in his hand, looking at him warmly. "C'mon." Thomas gets to his feet and chugs across the street after Maloney. "Were you watching me and Alice the whole time?"

"Christ no, I just wanted a soda." Maloney spits out a piece of chewing gum. "I can't deal with anymore customers, you need to take over. All they do is complain. That visual artist returned an entire box of acrylics, one of the big ones. She claims they're 'dry.'" Maloney spins abruptly, and Thomas bumps into his belly. "What the hell does she mean by that? Who does she think she is? That's shit for us, they're goddamn expensive. It's a straight loss." He walks on, turns his head, raises his voice: "A *straight* loss!"

"Did you check the expiration date?" Thomas sniffles.

"Of course I checked the expiration date! They're good for another three years. Go see for yourself. I don't think they're dry at all."

"But they'll just need to be returned to Gross & Selvaggi, right? That can't be our problem."

Maloney groans. "Just have a look at them, okay? And what are we going to do about the coffee automat? It's enough to make me sick." He shoves the door open. Annie, who's standing at the register, glances up from her book; he strides past her, hunched over. "Fucking bullshit. I'm going to the basement. Peter! Inventory! C'mon!" Sighing, Annie returns to her book. Down at the end of the store, two teenage boys fumble with some of the expensive ballpoint pens. They probably write poetry too, Thomas thinks, just like fucking Mallarmé. An almost welcome stab of anger throws him off balance, his body tense as a bow; he clenches his enfeebled hands into fists and kicks a cardboard box. Annie lurches once again when he shoves open the door to the street with his hip and shoulder then closes it hard with both hands, suddenly irritated by the loose springing mechanism, the soundless sliding noise, tame, toothless, in every way an expression of an anesthetized bourgeois and political correctness. A door should *slam* shut, goddamnit, hard and resoundingly, like when an ax strikes a rock. He smokes a cigarette, feeling his body as something toughened, agitated, as if Maloney has broken through his sleepwalking and infected him with his continually seething stew of emotions. But Thomas isn't seething. He's boiling. He wants to kick something over and punch someone's face until it bleeds, gushing red. He wants to see blood. Because what the fuck's up with poems, and Luke finding Alice a room? Angrily he checks the box of returned acrylics, comparing them with the individual tubes they sell. Sure enough, the colors in the box are a little dryer than the newer tubes. He calls Gross & Selvaggi, fills out the return slip for the entire shipment of "artist boxes," and orders a new crate. After taking a deep breath he writes the visual artist, apologizes, says it's their fault. He'll let her know as soon as a new batch has arrived. She can kiss my ass, he mumbles to himself. But in the meantime he would like to offer her a small compensation, and he invites her to come see the pastels, charcoal, and watercolor paper. He doesn't send her an e-mail, he sends her a watermarked card in eggshell color (Conqueror, 40lb) with *Lindström & Maloney* printed in blackish-purple ink in the lower right corner, and he tells Annie to take it to the visual artist right away. From the basement emerges the sound of tearing paper and cardboard being split apart and folded up. Peter and Maloney are apparently cleaning up. Thomas slams the hallway door shut, startling the two teenagers who are still trying out ballpoint pens. Thomas takes a deep breath, leaning his head against the door-frame for a moment. Then he crosses the floor to them.

"Are you looking for something in particular?"

"Oh, no. We'd like to buy a gift for our friend for his confirmation. His name is Juan."

"Yeah, Juan Alvarez Garza."

"Uh huh. And, um, can we get his name inscribed on one of these?" the other says as a blush expands across his pimply cheeks. Thomas's anger is transformed at the sight of these cheeks. They move him, and now he's moved. His anger morphs into a kind of happiness. I'm going crazy, he thinks, maybe I'm manic-depressive.

"Can we have his name inscribed?" the boy repeats.

"Of course you can. Does your friend write poems?"

"What?"

"No, oh, poems, I don't think so . . ." says the blushing boy.

"Hmm. But maybe he'll want to write poetry after you two give him such a nice pen," Thomas smiles. The two boys stare uncomprehendingly at him. The blushing boy's teeth are locked in shiny silver braces. The other boy pulls his hat down over his forehead. "Well, then I think we should buy this one here," says the one with braces, hesitantly, pointing at a royal blue ballpoint pen behind the glass display case. "Don't you think?" The other boy nods. "Certainly," Thomas says. "Then we'll just have to make sure we spell his name correctly. I'll send the pen to the engraver. Unfortunately, we don't do that here." The two boys gape at him. "You can pick it up in about ten days. Does that give you enough time?" The boy with the hat nods cautiously. He fills out the slip with large clumsy letters, while the other boy pays the deposit with some crumpled bills from his pants pocket. They give a polite farewell and trip over each other's feet, flustered, on their way out of the store. The slow-moving glass doors disgorge them onto the sidewalk like a lump of meat. They stand there a moment, then the blushing boy begins shuffling off northward; the other one follows after him, his arms dangling at his side. Thomas looks at Annie, and starts laughing.

"Did you see them?" She nods, but doesn't understand why it's so funny. "Did you see his braces? How the other one pulled his hat down to look more like an adult? Man, they were awkward! But sweet." For several minutes Thomas shakes with laughter, he sweats from laughter, chuckles, coughs, spits, and gurgles. Thank God there are no customers in the store, he can't stop laughing, the thought of their gaping faces, puberty's bell jar, the stupidity it entails. "Did you see how thick they were?" and he continues to laugh, more and more, and now not only because of the boys, but from a deep and dark place, a hollow, dangerous place, now he can feel it, how it pulls on his body, a primordial soup, a desert, a volcanic eruption, horrifying, and Annie mumbles nervously: "What's so funny about it?" But that only sends Thomas off on a new fit of laughter, stomach cramps, tears, the laughter cleanses him, he can't do it anymore, and here come Maloney and Peter through the door with terror in their eyes, alerted by the sounds, the howls, and that too is funny, painfully funny, they cling to the door as if they don't dare enter the store. "What the hell's wrong with you?" Maloney says. "Nothing," Thomas pants, bending forward. "It's just those two boys, oh God, you should've seen them . . ." Several minutes pass, Thomas contorted by the wrenching of his body's howling, giggling, sputtering, and gradually his laughing fit subsides to a hollow moan. Then there's silence. Then it's over, and it's as though he steps outside of himself and sees a tall, sweat-soaked man in disheveled clothes, face flushed. Filled with shame. Maloney makes an effort to smile. "Good to see some life in you," he says softly, returning to the basement with Peter. Annie sits with her head bowed, nervously picking at a fingernail. The door opens, and an older gentleman wearing a gray suit walks in. Thomas escapes to the bathroom.

As if the insanity of his laughing fit hasn't quite released him, he chain smokes, oddly disquieted the rest of the afternoon. He calls Patricia and tells her that he'll be home late (which surprises her, this morning he was aloof and impossible to get a word out of, and now he wants to go out?). He calls Alice and promises to loan her a small sum, gets the address of the music venue, tells Maloney that he'll close up, and enjoys the solitude of the empty store after the others have gone home; he wanders around in the half-darkness between the shelves, running his hands over the rough watercolor paper, the smooth sketchbooks, the pencils' perfect hexagons and their sharp lead tips, and now the contours of the deckled-edge paper, dull and yellowy, the matching envelopes. His hands find calm by touching the clean, new things. He squeezes a cylindrical eraser and sniffs it, the fresh scent of a new pencil case, and the memory the scent evokes is powerful: shredding an eraser into tiny pieces, trying to eat it because it smelled so tempting, edible, and then the dry little disappointment once it entered his mouth. He activates the alarm and locks the door, and at 7:00 p.m. he downs a greasy meal of enchiladas accompanied by a mountain of deep-fried chicken wings, all of which he washes down with beer. The restaurant is a hole-in-the-wall, but it's filled with people eating or waiting to eat; there's a line at the register, where customers pick up pre-ordered take-out. Salsa music is playing, and the sound from the scratchy loudspeakers mix with the diners' loud conversations and the waiters' shouts to the kitchen staff, who now and then can be seen through a slot in the wall. Thomas stands out among the assembled collection of not very tall people. He sits at the bar and thinks about his meeting this afternoon with the visual artist. Upon receiving the card, she'd come immediately to the store, apparently satisfied with the invitation to choose a fitting compensation for the "dried-out" colors, but then her mood shifted abruptly, and once again she complained about the watercolors, saying that "it couldn't be right," and that normally she was very happy with their assortment and quality, that she'd never had any problems with even a "single piece of charcoal," but now she had to admit that she'd lost a great deal of respect for "the entire business." Thomas, still clammy and high-strung following his laughing fit, assured her that he was terribly sorry about the whole wretched ordeal, that the colors already had been returned to the manufacturer, and that it most certainly wouldn't happen again. "How can you guarantee that when you just told me that it's the manufacturer's fault and therefore the manufacturer's responsibility?" she asked, rolling her eyes in exasperation, the whites shot through with fine red threads. "That's simply not possible." His anger returned. He felt like slapping her face, like slamming his fist into her jaw. Instead he clenched his fists, terrified at his impulse, and, holding his breath, asked her to choose whatever she wanted, repeating that she was one of their most cherished customers (though "cherished customers" came out as a fierce sneer) and that he would do everything in his power to ensure that she would once again be satisfied shopping at Lindström & Maloney.

The visual artist gave him a distrustful sideways glance. Then he fled to Annie at the register. She stood leaning against the counter, reading. He could see now that she was absorbed in a battered paperback copy of *The Idiot*. She rubbed her right foot against her left shin. They stood there for a moment, him breathing heavily, her glancing at him and returning her foot to the floor.

"So, you're reading Dostoyevsky?"

"Yes?"

"Hmm. I didn't think you were into that kind of thing."

"What do you mean, 'that kind of thing'?"

"I mean *The Idiot*."

"What about it?"

"It's long." Annie stared at him, confused. "And longwinded."

"I don't think so. You've just got to have a little patience. I'm in the middle of the second volume. I've decided to read all the Russian classics. I read *Anna Karenina* in the fall, and after I'm done with this one, I'm going to move on to *The Brothers Karamazov*."

She spoke eagerly now, and rapidly. "I'm trading books with a friend. It's cheaper that way, and then we read the same books so that we can talk about them—I mean discuss them and all that. We meet every Thursday."

"I just can't stand the paper quality in paperbacks. Look at how the pages are fraying along the edge. It hurts my hands to touch them."

"It hurts your hands?"

"Yes, it does. I can't stand them."

"Not everyone can afford to buy first editions."

"Then go to the library."

"But then you don't own the books."

"No."

There was a loud noise somewhere in the back of the store. The visual artist had knocked over a stack of boxes filled with cheap ballpoint pens. She'd wanted something behind the boxes, and they'd all tumbled down. Thomas sighed, composing himself.

"Can I help you with something?"

"I wanted to look at the paper dolls."

"All right," Thomas said, sticking his hand in and pulling out a couple sheets of paper. "Perhaps you need something like this for a collage?"

"Absolutely not!" Then she clapped shut like an oyster. But a few minutes later she left the store with thirty sheets of various paper dolls, rolled together and bound with string.

"What's she going to do with them? That's kind of weird," Annie mumbled, her attention once again fixed on *The Idiot*. Thomas hissed, "Fuck that artist bitch," and restacked the boxes before heading down to the basement. He told Peter that it wasn't very smart putting large sheets of cardboard behind small boxes of ballpoint pens. How are the customers supposed to get to the sheets? Maloney shouted, "Did you get it all out of your system?" And Thomas clenched his fists again. He responded coolly, glancing at the stacks of broken-down cardboard boxes, "I thought you were doing inventory. But apparently not."

Crunching his last chicken wing between his teeth, he imagines the visual artist playing with the paper dolls. Maybe she's not even an artist. Maybe she's insane. His anger only dissipated as he walked around the store, alone, after closing time. At first it transformed into grief, just briefly, and then into silence, or rather, the silence pervaded him. The silence filled me with peace, he thinks, the silence was so calming that my anger became silence. *I shouldn't have acted so immature, but it's too late now.* A fat man and his equally fat daughter climb onto two recently vacated barstools. The girl glances at him, her eyes glinting, her mouth open. Her father tugs on her arm and says something in a harsh tone of voice. The girl stares despondently at her knees. Thomas gives the man a dirty look and slaps his money down beside his empty plates, then hurries out into the bustling May evening. The sky's beginning to darken and several frayed, hazy clouds, blue-black and violet, glide ungodly slow over the city. He checks his cell phone: another unanswered call from Jenny. Since the funeral, he simply hasn't felt like talking to her, though she's tried to call him several times a week. Patricia says that she left a voicemail at the museum, crying and incoherent, and that Patricia then tried unsuccessfully to get a hold of her. Patricia suggested Thomas be the one to call. "It's your sister, after all, not mine." He finds a bench, lights a cigarette, and taps Jenny's number. She picks up at once. She says nothing for a moment, then yells at him.

"After the funeral I had to handle everything myself, and you didn't even text me!"

Thomas asks, "What do you mean, 'everything?'"

"I mean *everything*, of course."

She tells him, more coherently, about Alice's move and the loneliness she now endures, the meaninglessness of daily life, her sleepless nights. "Now I'm all alone in the world, no father, mother, or daughter. Why should I go on living? What reason is there?" she says. "I might as well hang myself."

"Jenny, Alice is alive and well, and I'm here, and Patricia and Kristin and Helena. You do have family, plenty of family, you just need to get used to the fact that she doesn't live at home anymore."

"But no one calls me."

"I'm calling you now."

"Only because I called you. Just admit it. And I don't want to talk about it. Not another word. I can't stand it."

A pause. Jenny sighs. "We're not going anywhere, Thomas. We're always standing still. Always. Always. We're treading water, it's pathetic."

Jenny groans. With his foot Thomas nudges a curled cardboard cup. It rolls beneath the bench. He pushes it out with the toe of his shoe.

"Do you want to come hear Ernesto play tonight?"

"God no."

"I'm going to the show. Alice stopped by today."

Jenny becomes frantic. "How did she look? Is she eating? Has she lost weight?"

"She looked well."

"Did she seem depressed?"

"Nah. She was in a great mood." A pause. Jenny composes herself. "Good," she says. "That she's doing well. Now I just hope she finds a job. *I* can't support her financially on my meager salary."

Thomas tells her he'll say hello to Alice for her, and Jenny grudgingly agrees to let him. She says that Kristin called to invite them up on Friday, they can spend the night in the barn and have a "summer fest," and we need to go. We owe it to them.

"Did you know Dad read poetry?"

"What?"

"Poetry. He read poetry."

"That's nonsense! Who says that? He never owned a book."

"Luc, the one behind the bar at Frank's. Apparently taught Luc how to fish, too."

"Who says that?"

"Alice."

Silence. Jenny breathes. She presses her mouth against the telephone, and hurls her voice hoarsely right into his ear: "I remember how sometimes a boy was with him when I visited. A thin, red-haired boy. But that was many years ago."

"Frank says he was very close to Dad."

"Ha! Dad wasn't close to anyone."

"That doesn't mean Luc wasn't close to him. You were too."

"And so were *you*, Thomas. So *are* you. You can't run away from that. Neither one of us can."

Thomas flicks his cigarette away. "Speak for yourself."

Jenny pretends not to hear him. "Maybe he read in prison. What else would he do? There'd be plenty of time to read quite a lot of poetry during all the years he was locked up, I guess. Imagine him reading poetry in prison. That's a nice thought, Thomas, isn't it? Yes, it is. It's a nice image, I think we should hold onto it." And it's as though he can sense her close her eyes in her kitchen, where she's no doubt sitting in one corner, on one of the tattered, varnished chairs. She's closing her eyes and imagining her father absorbed in a book, every now and then raising his face, a stanza on his lips, as if he just needs to taste it one more time, take it in, understand it, feel the words. Thomas sees it just as clearly, and he pushes the image away in disgust, away from his consciousness, rejects it, because what the hell is that, it's like he's absorbing her made-up image, like she planted that in his head, overtaking an untrue, romantic image like fucking *telepathy*.

"Hmm, yes," Jenny says dreamily, now mild and peaceful, now it's time to say goodbye, and Thomas focuses on the fact that Jenny is ready. As always, they have to go through various phases before Jenny's well enough to say goodbye; she has to feel markedly better than she did before the conversation began. A whole lot of tiny posts need to be in balance so that Jenny can stand suddenly upright, surprisingly strong. Thomas says goodbye and hangs up, then sits there, his mind inert and scattered, looking at small groups of enthusiastic youths going out for a night on the town, dog walkers, and well-dressed men and women returning late, no doubt from the numerous office buildings in the northern part of the city. It smells like spring here. A little garbage, a little wind, a little warmth, something that whirls up, as if from the underground, something invisible, fragrant.

The chestnut trees have long since blossomed and faded, so quickly; he suddenly remembers the sight of their almost vulgar swollen buds when he sat in Kristin's car on the way to Café Rose. Now they're gone. Now there are only dense, rustling treetops, fat green leaves. A rat runs beneath the bench right behind his feet. The cardboard cup skitters. He stands up and decides to walk the rest of the way. Jenny has sucked something out of him, but he doesn't know what. Left a hole in his brain, an empty spot.

The venue is a dark little club with a bar along one wall, a modest stage in the back, some scattered tables, and a dance floor that's already swarming with people, though the band hasn't begun playing yet. Everything's painted black: walls, ceiling, floor. Only the mirrored bar is lit. David Bowie, remixed to hip-hop, thunders from the loudspeakers. Very young men and women wriggle their bodies. Alice sits at the bar gesticulating with her tomato-red drink. Thomas struggles through the crowd to reach her. She smiles and embraces him and says something, he can't hear what, so he only nods and finds the check from his back pocket and pushes it into her hand, which causes her to radiate like a small sun. He sits beside her, and somehow manages to order a beer from the bartender, a young man distinguishable by the impressive Afro protruding thickly and majestically around his handsome face. Two women Alice's age catch sight of her and approach excitedly, greeting her with squeals and hugs, surrounding her from every angle with their long limbs, their chatter and giggling, their cheap jewelry, hair and scarves, and Thomas thinks that maybe he's become hard of hearing, because how can they hear each other when he can't. Hard of hearing and middle-aged. Perspiring, he pulls off his sweater and watches the dancers, who, like one enormous creature, slither in rhythm to the music. The women leave Alice to head in the direction of the bathrooms. One is short-haired and blonde, the other bears a long, dusty Rastafarian mane. Alice shouts into his ear: "THEY'LL BE ON SOON," and he nods again (of course they're on soon, why else would they be sitting here gawking?). All at once he realizes that he is the oldest person in the place. Maybe people think he's Alice's lover, that he's a filthy old pig pathetically reliving his youth. Now she puts her hand on his thigh and leans close to him, shouting: "HAVE YOU EATEN?" He nods twice and barks: "DID YOU GET THE JOB?" She shrugs. "I DON'T KNOW YET, THEY'LL CALL IN THE MORNING." She removes her hand, thank God, and something finally happens on the stage, the music stops, a couple guys are tuning the guitar and the bass, and Ernesto appears in a lumberjack's shirt and shorts, sitting down behind the drums. There are hoots and cheers from people on the dance floor; the stage lights sparkle red and blue. A moment later music bursts into the room and grates at Thomas's eardrum. There's wild applause, the audience hopping manically, the thin little guitarist with bangs puts his mouth to the microphone and begins to sing loudly, crazily, without inhibition. In the middle of this booming, aggressive music Ernesto hammers on the drums, and the crisp roll of the snare follows the kick drum's constant thumps. Ernesto takes every opportunity to bang the hi-hat and drown out the entire band. And then Luc's standing right beside Thomas with his cockeyed grin. It's as if he materialized out of thin air. Alice, who's busy moving her torso, deeply immersed in the music, wraps her arms around his neck, then points at Thomas. And Thomas gives him a measured nod. Luc nods in a friendly way. Then Alice and Luc, or Luke, or whatever his name is, head to the dance floor. The bartender sets another beer in front of Thomas. A man in his mid-thirties takes Alice's spot on the stool, pulling a young girl onto his lap. As they sit swaying, it's clear that they're on something. Heroin, to judge by the contracted pupils. Or powerful painkillers in large doses. Thomas has heard that's common now. They're easy to get a hold of and cheaper than either crack or coke. The girl can't be more than seventeen years old. They lace their fingers together, and he runs one hand up under her peach-colored shirt. The whole time they've got these sheepish grins. Thomas turns his head and watches Luke dance with Alice. He's in complete control of his body, he's elegant and lithe, his hips rocking rhythmically back and forth. There's something snakelike about him, and there's an immense beauty. Alice jumps up and down swinging her arms. And the music gets louder, a guitar solo now, deep notes become shrill become high-pitched, infernal wails; the guitarist treats his instrument as if it were his enemy, then he bends lovingly over it, then he holds it away from his body like a taut coil, his body's a taut coil too, his face cramped up, his bangs flopping with every wild jerk of his head. He growls into the microphone and throws the guitar across the stage floor; people cheer and clap like crazy. He snatches up his guitar and returns to what passes for a melody. The music crescendos, the lights turn green, yellow, violet, Ernesto goes amok on the drums—and the set's over. The band absorbs the audience's cheers and they climb from the stage, sweating. A moment later Thomas is surrounded partly by Alice and Luke, partly by Alice's two girlfriends—who apparently know the wasted girl and her boyfriend—and again he's clumped into a mass of hair and arms and squeals and hugs. They order Cokes, like at a child's birthday party, and when he realizes that Luke's looking at him, he says: "Good to see you," and Luke responds: "Likewise." And then there's really nothing more to say. Luke's eyes glide hungrily around the room, up and down girls' bodies. Alice introduces him to her girlfriends and to the wasted guy, whose name turns out to be Mingo. This Mingo greets Luke and Thomas with a limp, moist handshake and an aloof, half-dead smile. The girl on his lap is Andrea; she went to school with Alice and the girls, and as far as Thomas can tell, she also dropped out. But the other two are still in school. "Come back to us, it's so boring without you two!" says the one with the Rasta hair, and all at once he's terribly concerned for his niece, who's standing there, smiling and radiant, with her slender shoulders, the tattoo crawling up her neck. What will become of her? Is she also doing drugs? And how much more does he *not* know about her? Ernesto arrives, and he's welcomed like a hero. "You guys are amazing, this concert was SO much better than the last one," and so on. Thomas mumbles "Good show," and thinks: *I need to pull myself together,* and orders a beer for Ernesto and whoever wants one. He wants to get away from there right now, he's out of his element. But then this Mingo begins to talk to him in a snuffling, nasal voice. "I grew up right around the corner and you know what? I was really scared of this street when I was a kid. But not anymore." He laughs an odd, soundless laugh. "No. Not anymore. You know what else? It's got something to do with the light. Because it's completely dark in the middle of the street, the buildings are so tall there, y'know. Did you notice that? It's always dark in the middle of the street. That's why I was so afraid, but now I just think it's (he breathes deeply, leans back a little, swaying on the stool) wonderful, like . . . stepping straight into night or death in such a beautiful, beautiful way." Again this silent laughter of his, and his hand resting on Andrea's back. Though her glass is empty, Andrea sucks and sucks on the straw. Mingo shakes his head dreamily, smiling, exhilarated. His eyes are narrow slits. Thomas can't stand it any longer, not for another second, everything in him wants to get away, his heels itch, the muscles in his shins quiver. He pulls Alice aside. "Stay away from Mingo."

She smiles, her head tilted to one side.

"What's with *you*? I've told you not to worry about me. I know how to take care of myself."

"But you should stay away from people like him. Can't you see how he's filled that girl with drugs?"

"I think it's the other way around." Her girlfriends call for her, waving. She glances in their direction, looks impatiently at Thomas. He holds her gaze.

"What do you mean 'the other way around'?"

She smiles. "Exactly what I said. Say hello to Patricia for me, okay? I'll call you when I hear about the job, okay? Thanks for coming." She squeezes his shoulder and hurries back to the group, while Thomas sneaks away without saying goodbye to the others. The air is thick with the smell of body odor and heat; it's like a blessing to step out into the cool evening. His ears are ringing, and in the sky the stars shine like small silver tacks. For a moment he enjoys a cigarette, and then he sees it. Mingo was right. The middle section of the street really is in fact lined with high-rises, and it narrows and curves only to open once more on the other side, where it sort of widens. And in this last stretch it's almost got this small-town feel: smaller, older houses, tiny front yards. But after that, the street runs into a broad, high-traffic boulevard. He ambles through the gorge between the houses (and it really feels like a gorge) and thinks about what Alice said. That it was the other way around. That the girl had filled Mingo with drugs? Does she sell them? And what about Alice? He decides to show up unannounced at her new apartment. Then again, maybe he should just keep away. Should I watch over her now like I've watched over Jenny? But I'm not tired anymore, he thinks, surprised, walking under tall trees, up the boulevard opening wider and wider with its broad green median. I'm not the least bit tired anymore, it's passed. And he who is awake can keep watch. But what good is it to keep watch when it feels like a duty? Does it do any good? At home, Patricia sleeps peacefully under the blanket on the sofa. The TV is on, and the cat meows, lovingly rubbing itself against his leg. Thomas sits in the armchair and closes his eyes. An image pounds through his brain and clutches onto his retina: He sees the fat girl at the restaurant staring at her knees with this strange, hard glare, a look he remembers vividly, physically, in his own eyes: that's exactly how he stared, at his shoes, at the floorboards, at dirty floormats and linoleum, filled with shame, whenever his father yanked on his arm in front of others. And suddenly he smiles to himself, putting his arm around the cat, because he's not the zombie anymore. He's still haunted, as always, but by neither zombies nor his father. This time it's a girl with black eyes and long, shiny hair who's staring at her knees. Now it's himself. And here in the armchair Thomas O'Mally Lindström falls asleep with a sigh, completely at ease, content. A cloud floats across the sky, exposing a sliver of new moon. The cat curls itself, purring, onto his lap.

The following day he rises early. Dressed in a bathrobe and rubber boots, he finds the basement keys in the drawer in the entryway and takes the stairs down. This time it doesn't take him long to find the right unit. He snaps on the light switch to the bulb hanging over the boxes and the microwave, and there he finds the money. Exactly where he put it. Two packets of bills. Even this—entering the basement without fear or anxiety—feels like a fountainhead in his body. It's bubbling in there, running, gushing. There's the money, and here he stands. It's not a nightmare, it's real, and it's just a man and a stack of bills. He closes the microwave and turns off the light, locks the door, and heads back to the apartment. Patricia's still asleep on the sofa, fully clothed, one arm dangling over the side; she's kicked the blanket onto the floor, and her T-shirt has slid up. Each time she takes a breath, her belly moves gently up and down. He brews coffee and feeds the cat, he makes toast and fries an egg and tomatoes in chili and oil. He grinds peppercorns over the food and puts out cheese and jam. He wakes Patricia with a kiss. Still drowsy, surprised at his morning caress, she follows him into the kitchen. The sun's already above the rooftops, and the river flows jade-green through the city.

Patricia takes his hand and smiles, her mouth full of food. "What's got into you?"

"I don't know. But I'm not so sleepy anymore," he says, winking at her. This too is a caress, this wink, which makes her blush. She

Alice says nothing. Then, sadly: "Well. That's all I wanted to say."

She hangs up.

Thomas stands there a moment. Then he turns to Maloney. "Can we give Alice a trial hire for a few weeks?"

"Alice?"

"She's desperate and doesn't have a job."

"We don't have the money for that. You know that."

"Let's go have a beer," Thomas says, collecting their jackets.

Eva and her niece (whom Maloney pines for) have begun removing products off the shelves. It smells of disinfectant and soap. Thomas reminds Eva to set the alarm. The niece pushes her black bangs to the side and looks at them with a pair of sparkling blue eyes.

Thomas hands Maloney a draft beer. "I think we should expand."

Maloney sets his glass down with a thump. "What?!"

"Listen, things have been going pretty well, and I think we should open a branch. A small, exclusive place. I'd like to train Alice, so that one day she can manage the new place."

"'The new place?' Have you lost your mind? We don't even have money for a down payment. What's the matter with you?"

Thomas lowers his voice. "I've got a little savings that I could offer." And now, as he sits there lying, he slugs half of the tall pint down his gullet.

"Savings?!"

"It's always been our dream, right? A chain."

"Yeah, when we were twenty and high on pot! It's ridiculous, Thomas. Even if you have enough to make a down payment, there's still the overhead costs. Not to mention unforeseen costs. And Alice's salary. And . . ."

"I think I can handle all that." Thomas drinks the rest of his beer. Maloney stares at him.

"What the fuck's this all about? You couldn't have put aside that kind of money, I know exactly what you make. There must be something else. What is it?"

Thomas shrugs.

"C'mon, Thomas. Spit it out."

"Can't we just say that it's possible to do this. Let's just leave it at that. I want to give Alice a chance. I'd like to spend my money on it. I want to lead Lindström & Maloney toward the future."

"Toward the future?! Give me a break! Tell me what this is all about. Did you inherit money? Does this have anything to do with your father? Have you lost your marbles?"

But Thomas says nothing more, except that if Maloney won't join him, he'll do it himself. He goes to the bar and orders more beer. They sit for a long time in silence. Maloney stares out the window, as if fixated on the clouds and the rooftops. He sighs. Beer froth forms on his upper lip. Then slowly he shakes his head. "I don't know what's going on with you, but you've been acting strange lately. And now this. I don't get it. Talk to me, man, tell me what's going on. Why has Alice suddenly become so important to you?"

"She's my niece."

Maloney sighs again. "It's impossible to get a straight answer out of you."

After three beers, however, Maloney seems to accept that Thomas really has considered expanding their business. "We'll split fifty-fifty, even if I'm the one fronting the money," Thomas says, clutching Maloney's forearm.

"You *are* crazy," Maloney mumbles, shoving a handful of peanuts into his mouth.

"Come with me to look at some potential locations," Thomas says.

Maloney shakes his head. "Not on these terms. This is your project. If you get it up and running, and if it doesn't cost me anything, I'll gladly go along with it. But not till then. In other words: I want to see it before I'll believe it. And you will *give* me half of the new store." Glancing gloomily at Thomas, a wounded expression on his face, he stands with difficulty and walks out into the twilight. Back in the bar Thomas suddenly grows desperately horny. He wants to fuck someone hard from behind. A tight pussy, a deep and timid asshole. A woman, a man. His cock swells fat and pulsing, a stab of heat spreading to his groin and climbing to his head. He tumbles out onto the street and lights a cigarette. His body astonishes him. It's not even 6:00; he can still pick up Patricia from the museum. Behind the store's tall window panes he sees Eva's niece absentmindedly pushing the floor polisher across the floor. He can just make out a glimpse of her panties underneath her smock.

He barrels through the city with a hard-on. Cherry trees sway over the streets, soft pink and white. They've already begun to shed their petals. Imagining a new store isn't difficult. A simple, modern design, a smiling Alice behind the counter. Thomas pictures the light cascading through an open door, warm and golden. A large glass partition to the street. Alice looks older, poised, her head's no longer shaved. Her shiny hair spills thickly over her shoulders. The image is sharp as a blade to him. Maybe one day Alice can even become a partner. Lindström, Maloney, & Farrokhzad—it doesn't sound that insane. And when he and Maloney no longer have the energy to run the business, she can take over. By that point, maybe, they really will have a chain of stores. He will have to pay in cash. First thing tomorrow he'll start searching for a property. Turning the corner, he sees the museum with its streamlined architecture towering before him. A chalk-white rock in the midst of all the bustle. Two women in summer dresses sweep past him. A couple of mothers with small children sit clustered on a bench, boisterously sharing the contents of a large bag of candy. A man his own age with an apathetic expression on his face pushes an old woman in a wheelchair. A few street vendors shout from their fruit stands. Music streams from a restaurant. Vivid scents: musk, flowers, sun.

Thomas walks into Patricia's office and locks the door behind him. She's on the telephone watching him, surprised. She waves cheerfully. He closes the blinds. She ends her conversation, smiles, and is just about to say something when he grabs her, picks her up, spins her around, and presses her down across her desk. She wants to protest, turning halfway around, but he shushes her, covering her mouth with his hand and lifting her dress up over her back. Patricia kicks at him, she almost seems afraid. Thomas holds the backs of her legs firmly in place with his knees and quickly unzips his fly with his free hand. She gags, biting his thumb. He lets go of her mouth. "Stop it," she says hoarsely. "What the hell are you doing? Stop it. This hurts." She wriggles and flails, shouting, "Let go of me!" He catches a glimpse of her eyes. Again he covers her mouth with his hand, and now she growls, gurgling, and his hand grows wet with her spit. He yanks her stockings and panties down and forces his way into her dry, warm pussy. She fights harder, lashing out with her head, punching her arms backward trying to reach him. But then she grows quiet and passive. He removes his hand from her mouth, she says nothing. She puts her left cheek against her desk. And he fucks her, roughly, yanking her ponytail, he can feel the veins popping out on his forehead. She's limp and heavy as a sack of potatoes, he's thirsty, he pounds his thighs against hers, and it climbs in him, he comes, a white flash, millions of minute stars, heat, he falls across her back. He lets her go, and she begins to cry.

At home later—she'd taken a cab, shocked and raging, while he'd walked through the city, empty, but full of an odd sort of happiness—he steps toward her. They stood looking at each other in the living room, ten feet of space and a cat between them. He steps toward her raising one hand defensively, and says, "Honey. I needed you so badly." Why he says this is a mystery to him. How could he step forward like that, a gesture, after what had happened? Because it's not something you can talk about. It's not something there are words for. When they go to bed after a silent dinner in the kitchen, where she simply sat poking at her chicken filet, she snarls at him suddenly. "You violated me." He doesn't respond. He glides swiftly into a dream. It starts with Alice in a well-lit room, he's bending over her shoulder, showing her something. A finger runs across a sheet of paper, the paper's fibers rising against his skin. Then there's a plateau, desiccated red earth. A boy's naked feet running and whirling up clouds of dust. And the plateau becomes a completely barren lunar landscape under a blue-gray sky. Huge clouds clump together with supernatural speed. "You assaulted me, you bastard," Patricia says angrily, off in the distance. She shoves his shoulder, hard. But he can't wake up.

When he wakes up with a start the next morning, he doesn't know whether this was part of the dream or not. Patricia's making tiny peeping sounds in her sleep each time she exhales. She's slept on the floor at the foot of the bed, her back to him, the duvet wrapped snugly around her. He gathers his clothes and shuts the door behind him. It's quarter past 6:00. He sits on the living room floor and begins to research the commercial properties that are for sale. By 7:30 he's got a good little list. He makes coffee and leans across the kitchen table with his cup. It's drizzling outside. A tugboat lurches slowly up the river, followed by a few kayaks. From below, a flock of sparrows fly up and settle in an orderly row on the rooftop across the street. The rain sheets the glass with a fine film. Thomas puts his cup in the dishwasher and writes "I love you" in capital letters across the front page of the newspaper. He locks the door on his way out.

It's not until he's walking down the stairs toward the train that he understands what he's done. He can feel a hard knot directly under his breastbone, something unyielding that won't go away, and of course the soft sense of shame. Patricia's wide, frightened eyes when she turned to look at him. Her flailing body on the desk. It's so insurmountable, so incomprehensible and unbearable that he grows sluggish, sleepy. Sitting at the window with his cheek resting against the cold glass, he falls asleep. He rides two stops too far. He walks back along the rain-sopped streets. The asphalt is gleaming and dark. He thinks: *The asphalt gleams, dark.* The rain picks up as a thunderclap booms off in the distance. The light from the sky is mottled. Looking up, and through a window in a café, he sees someone he recognizes and he stops in his tracks: It's Jenny, her back to him, talking to Maloney, who raises his mug and blows into it. Thomas lurches to the side, squeezes between the streaked panes of glass. Maloney says something and smiles. He bites into his bun. Jenny turns and regards the rain. Maloney puts his hand on her arm. She's wearing a green shirt, and a scarf around her neck. The furrows around her mouth are clearly visible. Thomas swallows, holds his breath. Then he hurries past the café and sprints the last stretch to the store. The thunder's right above him now, the street suddenly illuminated with a violent crack of white light, followed by another boom, very close, the sound exploding in his ears. He jumps, startled, and paws in his jacket for his keys.

Later, Maloney struts through the back door wearing a yellow rain jacket. He's whistling. By this point Thomas has made several appointments with real estate agents, and before Maloney has hung up his wet jacket, Thomas is out the door carrying Annie's red and white polka-dotted umbrella. "Whoa, this place is CLEAN!" Maloney calls out. "That niece really worked the elbow grease."

Monotonously, the rain persists for the rest of the day, and Thomas tours many dismal properties; it's as though all the life has been sucked from them, or perhaps life has sucked them dry, left them to gather dust. Back rooms yellowed by nicotine. Doors hanging crookedly on loose hinges. Stinking wall-to-wall carpets and small, stuffy bathrooms with rust-caked toilet bowls and leaky tanks. "All it needs is a loving hand," says the young agent, his tie askew. "It's quite a find at this price." Thomas shakes his head and goes outside to smoke. The agent says that he's got a few more places to show him, none of which were in the newspaper. Then suddenly, in one of the streets from his childhood, at 4:00 p.m., as his belly grumbles with hunger, he steps inside a property that calms his breathing—a long-since closed bookstore where he, as a boy, used to buy his notebooks and sharpen his pencils with the big pencil sharpener the bookseller had installed on the counter. It didn't cost anything extra. The bookseller wore a gray smock, and his developmentally challenged son either ran errands or sat on a footstool behind the counter, singing. "What was it you said you wanted to buy a place for?" the agent croaks, "office supplies? I don't want to be a party pooper, but I'm afraid there's not a huge customer base for that kind of thing in this neighborhood." Thomas leans against the wall. "There was a video rental here until recently," the agent says, studying him curiously. "But the owner had a heart attack last summer. The store has been empty for almost a year."

"Who's selling it then?"

"His wife, I believe."

"Can I count on your discretion?"

"Of course," the agent nods.

"To be blunt, I'd like to pay in cash."

"Aha."

"Is that possible?"

"Sure. That shouldn't be a problem. Between you and me, she's ready to give the place away, if you know what I mean." The agent looks at him inquisitively.

"Yeah?"

"Cash settlement. Under the table, in other words."

"Interesting. And what about your share?"

"We haven't announced the sale anywhere, so I don't have any special requirement. Let's say five percent? Cash?"

"And the paperwork?"

"That can be arranged. But that'll be in addition."

"Understood. But I'll get the deed to the place and all that?"

The agent nods. "Yes, we've done this kind of thing before. Or, rather, I have. I run this business by myself."

"Good," Thomas says.

The counter's still there, solid and wide. But the built-in shelves are gone, replaced with a cheap metal variety. A pornographic poster hangs from a single nail and shows an enormous chocolate-brown breast and a pink mouth and tongue. The top of the poster has been torn off, the woman has no eyes. Several posters lie curled up on the floor. Thomas thrusts open the back room door that leads to a large rectangular courtyard with poplar trees and shrubbery. At the far end is a magnolia tree, weighed down by the rain. Here you can see the original floor, uneven planks blackened by too many layers of varnish. "There's good light in here," the agent mumbles, glancing at his watch. "I like it," Thomas says. Except for the counter, there's nothing special about this place. There's a humble quality to the rooms; they're simple, unadorned. Kristin once told him that the reason they purchased the farm was that it had "a good spirit dwelling in it." He feels there's one here, too. Thomas listens closely. Rain drums against the glass. The bookseller's son was named Amando. He used to bite his knuckles whenever he was agitated.

The agent pushes his glasses up. "I've heard there was once a pharmacy here. A long time ago."

"Last time I was here it was a bookstore."

"Well, I guess it hardly matters now," the agent says. "Here's my card. Call me whenever. I'm usually in my car and can come meet you pretty fast."

Patricia has left a message on his telephone. Her voice, stifling a sob, is angry. She asks him to come home immediately, says that she's sick.

Standing in the rain outside the old bookstore, he watches the real estate agent unlock his car. It's Wednesday. The agent gets behind the wheel and starts the engine. It's 5:00 P.M. Thomas lights a cigarette and calls Alice, who answers sleepily. He asks her if she's interested in working at the store. In the beginning it'll be just a few weeks, until they see how it's going. He says that he's planning to open a branch. She says nothing at first.

"What did you say?"

He explains it again, slowly, painstakingly.

She asks about the salary. He says he needs to do some calculations.

"I did get a job."

"What did you say?"

"I have a job. I started yesterday."

"What kind of job?"

"It's just a job." Alice sounds detached now, a little dismissive.

"Were you sleeping?" he asks.

"I was just resting."

"Will I see you at Kristin's Friday?"

"Yes."

"Have you spoken to your mother?"

"She called yesterday. She told me to bring a sleeping bag. Apparently we're all sleeping in the barn."

They discuss whether she has enough money to get by for now, and she believes she does. "If not I'll just borrow some from Luke," she says. "Or his friend."

Another silence. Thomas is about to advise her against that, but decides not to. "Okay, well, I'll see you later," he says.

He can tell she nods when her earring clatters against the telephone. He calls the real estate agent.

"Are you still in the area?"

"Ten minutes," he says.

He arrives a short time later, parking his car and climbing out.

Thomas says he's ready to make an offer. "That didn't take long," the agent smiles. He looks very satisfied. Thomas names a figure considerably lower than the asking price. He believes that he's achieved something important, something meaningful, when the real estate agent, his exhaust pipes spluttering, drives off again.

On the way home he picks up Thai food and white wine. Patricia slumps at the kitchen table in her blue dressing gown. Her greasy hair hangs over her eyes.

"Do you have a fever?"

"No," she says, her voice quivering.

"Then what is it? Are you sick?" He puts a hand on her shoulder. He grasps both of her shoulders and she shakes him off.

"Get the fuck away from me."

"But you said you wanted me to come home? You just called."

She raises her red-rimmed eyes. "That was *hours* ago."

She gets to her feet, points at him, narrows her eyes. "Why did you do it? Why did you put your hand over my mouth? Why would you do something like that?"

He looks out the window.

"It's perverse, Thomas. It's fucking violent!"

"I don't know. I had a sudden urge. I couldn't help myself."

"You couldn't help yourself. You had an *urge*! Don't you hear how fucked-up that is?"

He throws up his hands. "I'm sorry. But can't you please forgive me?"

Patricia takes a threatening step toward him. All at once she seems big and fierce, strong. "You're acting so fucking strange, what the hell's wrong with you? You're acting like a child caught with his hand in the cookie jar." Clenching her jaw, she shakes her head and returns to her chair.

"Of course I'm ashamed. I'm ashamed. I'm sorry. I don't know what came over me. It was overpowering."

"Yeah, let me assure you that it was!" When she lunges to her feet, the chair knocks over backward. "You assaulted me. You're *destroying* us!" She rushes away. Looks at him with disgust. "I'm leaving."

"But I bought food . . ."

"Eat it yourself!" She goes down the hallway and slams the bathroom door. Shortly afterward he can hear the water running. He knocks. "Patricia? Can I come in?" But she doesn't answer, and the door is locked. He goes back to the kitchen. He picks up the chair and sits down. Her cup from yesterday morning is still on the table. Her lipstick has left marks, two red wings on the white porcelain. He watches the sparrows that are once again lined up in a row on the roof across the street. The river: white-green, milky. Some flies buzz around the fruit bowl. He stands up and tosses a half-rotten pear into the trash. A long time passes. Then she's standing in the doorway in a beige jumpsuit. She's applied a thick layer of makeup. Her eye shadow is dramatic, dark, gray-black. Her skin is dulled under a coat of powder. She's wearing her silvery shoes, her party shoes.

"Where are you going?" he asks.

But she only stares at him, sharp and angry, her hands at her sides. "That's none of your business."

She turns on her heels. Then she's gone, the door banging shut. The cat leaps on the kitchen table and sniffs curiously at the box of chicken satay. He calls Patricia several times, but she's turned off her phone. He tries to convince himself that she's just out with a friend, but jealousy and fear gnaw at him, like maggots. Later, he drinks the entire bottle of wine, and even later he stares walleyed at the sales sheet for the old bookstore, and even later than that he reads Celan: "Black milk of daybreak we drink it at sundown / we drink it at noon in the morning we drink it at night / we drink and we drink it / we dig a grave in the breezes there one lies unconfined . . ." He reads Celan, loses himself, images of his father in his cell: his profile, the sharp nose, these words in his mumbling mouth, in his consciousness, his back arched, his face close to the book. He shivers, he stands at the window, he lights a cigarette. He thinks: One could jump. One could fall. As easy as anything, could dig a grave in the breezes. He lurches back, startled. He lies down under the rumpled sheets on the unmade bed; the cat's sprawled at his feet. Water swishes through pipes, the poems jumbled and harrowing his mind. He curls up and sleeps, just as unsettled and troubled, and doesn't awake until there's clattering in the kitchen early the next morning: Patricia has returned.

When they sit across from one another in the kitchen drinking coffee, it's as though they're each hovering in their own worlds. He's held her tight, she's pushed him away. In vain he's tried to get her to say something, anything. She reeks of booze. Maybe she didn't even sleep last night. Her makeup is cracked, her eye shadow smeared. He boiled eggs, she took only one bite. Now she's got egg yolk on her chin. The morning is warm and humid. She hasn't said anything about where she was, he hasn't asked. A ceasefire, Thomas thinks optimistically, letting his eyes wander across the light-blue sky. But what kind of war is this? There are butterflies in the pit of his stomach because he doesn't understand, and he's so desperately trapped in the present that he instantly forgets. He jerks his head. What is this? What do you mean? What does *she* mean? Not a cloud. Blinding sunlight. Rooftops, ships, tiny cars far below, people. An airplane ascending, slowly diminishing in size, carried off by the jet stream. Patricia stirs her teaspoon in her cup.

"You're coming with me to Kristin's tomorrow, right?" he says.

She glowers at him.

"Why are you so mad at me? I said I was sorry. Are you drunk?"

She says nothing.

"I'm getting ready to buy a new store. I want to hire Alice. Show her the ropes."

She looks at him, but her expression is cool and distant.

"Do you have the money for that?"

"Looks that way."

She shrugs. "Well, good luck then."

"Patricia," he says. "Patricia."

The silence is thick and dense, as if it's squeezing them each into their own corner. She stares at the shelf lined with glasses. So he says, "Want to go swimming tonight?"

She doesn't respond.

"Want to come with me?"

"I don't know." She sounds a little hoarse now. She sighs. Her eyes remain fixated on the glasses. He follows her gaze. The cat meows insistently, rubbing itself against her legs. Then it leaps onto her lap.

Leaning forward, Thomas lays a hand on her arm. "Patricia? Don't you want to be with me?" She lifts the cat and drops it, so that it falls to the floor, meowing.

He says, "Let's meet at the little beach at 5:30. Okay?"

She rises slowly and gets ready to go. She brushes her teeth and washes her face at the kitchen sink. Her perfume lingers in the warm, unmoving air: cedar, vanilla. The stench of alcohol. She doesn't say goodbye. She steps into her heels. She slams the front door behind her. As he clears the kitchen, he feels the sobs welling in his throat. He packs two towels in a bag, he feeds the cat and gives it some water. The cat's tail swishes back and forth as it eats, its front legs bent slightly; it stares at him, affronted. He hustles outside and down to the street. His head pounds, his throat's constricted, his vision's blurry. Fucking Christ, he thinks, wanting to slap himself silly. Get your ass together. It feels like walking on sludge, on wet sand, he sinks in, lights a cigarette, leans against a wall, and rubs his head. He can't go any farther, the humidity's extraordinarily high; he clenches his fists. Get yourself together, man. Unlock your bike and get on the fucking seat, unless you've decided to die in the middle of the street. But maybe that's exactly what you've got in mind. A grave in the breezes. You're digging your own fucking grave. Pierced by fear. And he begins to move, the urge to sob subsides, biking through a city shimmery with heat. The peonies are in bloom, the roses, the rhododendrons, the bougainvillea, like glimpses of purple and cyclamen in parks, against the walls of houses, on patios, on balconies. Everything has exploded during the night.

But as soon as he's turned the corner, he sees it. Maloney's standing outside the store talking to a policeman, his face a shiny red hue, his expression gloomy and agitated. A cruiser is parked on the opposite side of the street, and a second officer leans against the vehicle talking on a cell phone; his black shoes gleam in the sunlight, and he taps one foot. The store's front window has been smashed. Glass shards have rained on the sidewalk. A small crowd has gathered: a group of snot-nosed teenagers wearing backpacks, some older women. Annie and Peter are standing together a little ways down the street; they look like two frightened children who're hiding, leaning or tipping toward each other. Annie's practically on her tiptoes.

Maloney strides toward Thomas, who is frozen in place with his bicycle still on the road. Maloney's warm, tangy breath right in his face: "It's all smashed. Everything. I'm telling you . . . even the office computer and our mugs. Our coffee mugs are smashed, the yellow one and the other one." He stops talking and sucks air through his nose. "The one with the little duck. Your *mug*! And the candlesticks—everything." Maloney's lost in thought. Thomas begins to laugh hysterically. "The one with the duck!" But the laughter dies in him as quickly as it'd begun. Maloney's face is lit up with fright. The policeman signals to his colleague standing at the car and heads into the store, glass shards crunching under his feet. A car honks repeatedly. Maloney pulls Thomas onto the sidewalk. The second officer, still on his cell phone, walks past them and positions himself in the doorway.

Thomas asks, "Was anything stolen?"

Maloney looks down, wide-eyed. "I don't know." Then he looks up, angrily. "I just got here, for fuck's sake, how would I know?"

They peer through the doorframe, motionless, quiet, seeing heaps of paper and cardboard. All their goods have been pulled from the shelves. The chandelier dangles crookedly as if someone tried to shoot it down. "A dog walker called the cops." Maloney takes a deep breath. "Early this morning." Thomas nods. Maloney throws up his arms, almost contemptuously. "They were already here when I arrived!" Thomas nods again. "But it's a good thing they're here, Maloney." Maloney gives him a flustered glance, then his eyes dart every which way. The officer sweeps his hand across the countertop. "Palvino?" he says. The second officer reacts. "There's a mark in the countertop," says the officer inside the store. He shouts to Thomas and Maloney: "Do you know anything about this?" Thomas feels dizzy.

"We sure as fuck don't!" Maloney says. "We don't go around carving into our own countertop!" Palvino says, "Watch your language, please." "Sorry," Maloney mutters. The officer turns once again to Palvino: "It looks like a symbol of some kind. Done in a sloppy and clumsy way. Come have a look." Palvino slinks into the semi-darkness. Thomas's heart thumps in his chest. He gulps for air, his dizziness intense. His eyes flicker, and he's forced to lean against the wall for support. Who carved into his countertop? Who? I'm going to faint now. But he doesn't. The register has been broken into, coins are scattered across the floor. The officers talk quietly among themselves. Soon they come outside, and the officer who is not Palvino pulls off his latex gloves. Maloney says, "This is my partner, Thomas Lindström." Thomas extends his hand. The officer's handshake is brief and firm.

"Kagoshima. I've called for assistance." He turns to Palvino: "Go ahead and put the tape up now." To Maloney and Thomas, he says,

"You're not allowed inside until we're finished. I'm sorry, but you'll have to wait to tally up your losses." He gives them a measured, friendly smile.

"Would you like a cup of coffee?" Maloney asks sheepishly, following his reprimand from Palvino.

"Yes, thank you. If you were having one anyway." Palvino opens the door of the cruiser and leans across the backseat. Now it's the pistol in his belt that captures the sunlight.

Maloney totters into the street, calling for Peter and sending him off to fetch coffee. Palvino affixes the police tape. Maloney stares at Thomas, and they shake their heads. Maloney's eyes focus on the floor. Thomas is weirdly lost in thought, watching Annie slowly approaching as if through a kind of filter. With a quivering lower lip and vacant eyes, she whispers, "Was anything stolen?"

"We don't know yet."

A tear falls from her right eye. "Don't cry, Annie," Thomas says, putting his hand on her shoulder. And Peter arrives balancing cups of coffee and a bag of pastries under one arm. The coffee is scalding and bitter. Without a word, Palvino takes two cups and slips under the tape. Maloney's pastry-grinding mouth is suddenly in Thomas's face. His forehead is slick with fine pearls of sweat. "Who the fuck did this shit?" he hisses, and begins restlessly pacing the sidewalk. The sun shines directly on the store now, and the thousands of shards in the display window. Standing in the doorway, Kagoshima asks, "Do you have any idea who might have done this?"

Thomas shakes his head. Kagoshima suppresses a cough. "We'll talk to people in the neighborhood, of course, possible witnesses. There must have been a lot of noise when the window was smashed. But the man who called us heard nothing." The coffee has apparently made Kagoshima cheerful; he's friendlier, gentler. He smiles at Thomas. "Okay then. You might as well go home. Have you vacuumed the store in the past few days?" "Yes, there was a spring cleaning here recently, but that was Tuesday. And no, not in the past few days."

"Then we'll have a look to see how many hairs and fibers we can find. If there are too many, we won't touch it."

"Why not?" Thomas asks. The sun blinds him. Kagoshima is a dark shadow in front of him.

"Too many people go in and out of stores like this. We're not interested in customers' hair. That's too sweeping, and we can't do a full sweep."

"Then what'll you do now?"

Kagoshima sips his coffee. "Our colleagues from Investigations are collecting possible DNA. Shoeprints, fingerprints. Traces of blood, if there is any. I tend to doubt there will be, though. Then we'll run it all through our database and look for a match. It usually takes a day. Getting the paperwork done typically takes at least a week." With the back of his hand he wipes his lips. "I just need to know where you two were last night and this morning."

"At home!" they cry, practically in unison. "We were asleep," Maloney says. Kagoshima nods. "And when were you two last here?"

"Yesterday," Thomas says. "I left early, before lunch. But you . . ." He looks at Maloney.

"I closed at 6:00 p.m. I was the last person to leave."

"And when was it, precisely, that you left?"

"Quarter after. Maybe close to 6:30." Maloney brushes some sugar from his sleeve.

"We'll be finished in about an hour," Kagoshima says and makes as if to go back to the store. But suddenly Peter's standing there. "Has this kind of thing happened elsewhere in this neighborhood recently?" he asks so softly that it's almost a whisper. The others observe him, surprised.

Kagoshima: "And you are?"

"Peter Ohlsson, our apprentice," Thomas replies.

"Aha. No. Not as far as I know. But we'll investigate, of course." Kagoshima nods at length, and the others stare at his round face. Then Maloney straightens himself with a jerk: "But what's this all about? Why did they carve into our countertop?"

"It looks to me like what we call criminal mischief in the first degree. I can't say more than that at this time."

"What does it look like, the thing they carved?" Peter asks.

Kagoshima says, "It looks almost like . . . like a sun with four rays. Four lines radiating from a circle."

"A sun?" Annie mumbles.

"Something like that," Kagoshima says, stepping over the doorframe.

"What if it's a warning?" Peter says, horrified. "The symbol in the countertop?"

"Let's not go there," Annie says softly.

"The symbol in the countertop! It sounds like the title of some ridiculous B-film! Who the hell would warn us, and against what?" Maloney's agitated again. "A sun? That's *ridiculous*! I'm going home now to sleep. I can't deal with this anymore."

"We need to board up the windows when they're done. C'mon. Let's go have a beer." Thomas grabs Maloney's arm. Maloney snarls like a dog and tries to yank his arm free. Thomas gets Peter's attention. He says, "You can go home. You too, Annie. We'll call you later. Annie nods and retrieves her purse from the sidewalk. Peter lifts his hand in a sad farewell. Stooping, walking slowly, they head up the street. "Now let's go get a beer," Thomas repeats. "Once they're done we'll board it up. Okay?"

Maloney doesn't respond. But he goes willingly with Thomas, across the street and into the café, where they sit in their usual corner. Thomas orders two large draft beers. The café's owner wants to know everything about what happened. He gesticulates in disbelief, he shakes his head with regret, he points out the window, he talks up a storm about how unacceptable this is, such a nice-looking store, everything's getting worse and worse, he says, like in the old days, worse and worse, soon you won't even be able to trust your best friend. Still shaking his head, he finally returns to the bar, after having assured Thomas and Maloney more than once that everything's on the house today. Shortly after that they see Palvino calling on the neighboring businesses. And then it appears that the reinforcements arrive: two plain-clothes officers climb out of a green Mazda and shake Kagoshima's hand. Maloney and Thomas say almost nothing, apart from arguing about whether or not they should have a contractor board it up, or whether they should do it themselves and use some of the old boards they have in the back. Maloney absolutely doesn't want them to do it themselves. They agree to do it themselves. The café owner brings them whiskey and more beer. Maloney stares at the store and says, almost grief-stricken: "Now they're searching for blood in there. They're searching for blood in our store, Thomas." But Thomas is distracted and only half-listening. He texts Patricia several times. She doesn't respond. Peter, on the other hand, sends him a text: "I looked up the sun drawing. It's apparently the generic sign for currency, that is, for money." "The what?" Maloney says. "Tell him to knock it off!"

Late in the afternoon, Thomas bikes through the city with two striped towels flapping in a bag on the handlebar. To the west, the sky shines like mother-of-pearl: light-blue with rose-pink and thin bands of yellow. He crosses the bridge with its view of the turbid water far below, rides through the apartment subdivisions on the other side of the river—where the highway cuts through everything like another kind of river, noisy and bright. And after another twenty minutes he arrives at the small beach, six hundred feet of sand and tufted grass. The water is dead calm, and clusters of jellyfish lap helplessly against the shore. The temperature is dropping now. The salty air clings to his nostrils. A flock of black-headed gulls skim the surface of the water with powerful wing strokes. Sitting on the damp sand, Thomas sighs. Then he lies down and closes his eyes. He thinks about the vandalized store. About Maloney angrily hammering boards to the door. About the conversation with the insurance company. He thinks: She's not coming. Patricia's not coming. And all at once he sees a vivid image of his father and himself, naked and entwined, his father old and bony, he a smooth-bodied young man looping around his father's lean figure like a fat, greedy snake. Their genitals hang limply down their thighs: his father's small and curved, his own firm and vigorous. His father slides his hand through Thomas's hair, sniffing at his ear with pleasure, he puts his lips to Thomas's cheek, he presses his mouth to Thomas's skin in one long, parched kiss. They lie paired in the sand. There's sand everywhere. And the sand begins to rise. It rises, and it covers them, buries them, buries this two-headed body and tugs it earthward, the ancient man and the youngling, the sand crashes down upon them like a heavy darkness, and Thomas feels the light disappearing, his father's body growing cold and stiff as he clings to it, melting completely into it, as his mouth fills with crunchy sand that chokes him. He gasps and opens his eyes: There stands Patricia looking at him. She's blocking the sun. She's pulled a green beret down her forehead. Nothing friendly in her expression. They undress and wade, shivering, into the cool water. There's seaweed and the pungent stench of rot, an even layer of stones along the shore, but farther out the bottom grows sandy, the water clear. Patricia is the first to dive under, and she returns to the surface with her dark hair clinging to her back. The subdued underwater sounds do wonders for Thomas. The images of his father vanish, his panic subsides. He skims along the bottom, where shoals of small fish dart past him, and his weightlessness is so invigorating that his cock stiffens. This, a moment's freedom. He collects a large conch and puts it to Patricia's ear. For a few moments, she listens in silence.

Then she takes it from him and throws it as far away as she can. He grips her waist and draws her close. She lets him, but she's limp, her arms slack. He clutches her hips. He feels her belly against his groin. He feels her breathing, feels her breasts squeezed flat against the upper ridge of his belly. Then she squirms free. Scowls at him. She plunges into the water and begins to swim out. He stays rooted in place. Farther up the coast, someone is beaching a rowboat. Orange buoys bob on the water, maybe they're traps. And just like that, in one swift and surprising moment, he's floating above this scene and indifferently observing himself. He's swaying in the air, staring at the crown of his head, registering his receding hairline, watching Patricia slice through the water. Then just as suddenly he's in his body again, and sound returns: the lapping of the water, the squawking seagulls. Patricia's far away now. He thinks about clouds, about fire, about tropical heat, about a swarm of tiny insects crawling in the grass at twilight. Now she turns and swims back to shore. When she redirects to continue along the coast, he swims along. They glide silently beside one another. But Patricia's a much better swimmer than he is, and she shoots through the water with perfect ease, always keeping several lengths ahead. They wrap themselves in their towels and sit for some time, while the sun sinks on the horizon. The sky glows blood-red, the water darkens, a wide, seductive gold road heading straight toward the setting sun. "Look," Thomas says, pointing east, "here comes the moon." He takes her hand. It's wan and wrinkly from the water. The small, pale half-moons of her fingernails stand out clearly. "I love you," he whispers. "Where were you last night?" She pulls her hand away. He wants to say more, but nothing comes to him. A light breeze brushes the grass. Behind them, a few older kids ride by on bicycles, with fishing poles and red plastic pails on their rear racks. The bikes clatter along the uneven path. Their voices are shrill and cheerful. Thomas gets to his feet and begins to dress. He shakes sand out of his socks and hikes his pants over his hips. Patricia buttons her jacket and pulls her beret onto her wet head. She climbs on her bike and rides off without a word.

"I'm as naked as a jellyfish," he mumbles, once he's finally caught up to her and they're riding across the bridge. "I'm a mollusk. It's disgusting." "What?" Patricia barks angrily. The sharp wind soughs around them. "Nothing," Thomas roars. I want to cry, he thinks. I want to sink down in a well of tears, until the well is dry. I am an idiot. I am beautiful. I am nothing. If I aim high enough, I can do anything. I am as empty as a meaningless, automatic sobbing fit.

At home the cat is infuriatingly needy, rubbing nonstop against Patricia's legs. She snaps on the TV and throws herself onto the sofa. He makes sandwiches; she eats hers then slams the empty plate down unnecessarily hard on the glass table. He cleans up. She stands abruptly, goes into the bedroom, and changes her clothes. Then she leaves. When he hears the front door open, he rushes down the hallway, the dishrag in his hand. He catches a glimpse of her silvery shoes and the back of her coat as she disappears on the landing below. He calls after her, "Where are you going? Why are you leaving again? Say something, Patricia!" But she doesn't respond. He falls into the armchair. He can't breathe. He calls her, but she doesn't answer. Then Maloney calls and tells him that the police didn't find a single trace of DNA in the store. Nothing except a whole lot of hair (which they quickly dismissed), and of course Thomas's, Maloney's, Annie's, and Peter's fingerprints. They could tell that someone had sifted through the stacks of paper on the floor, but the perpetrator had worn medical booties or plastic bags on their feet. Thomas goes to the kitchen. Maloney's voice is so familiar that he's almost thankful. He grabs a beer from the fridge. He looks out the window. The city's sea of light radiates in the blue violet evening. "There's nothing left for them to do. There's no trace. The neighbors didn't hear a thing. The windows must have been smashed when everyone was asleep. Why the fuck wasn't anyone awake? There's always some idiot awake."

Maloney continues, "Well, at least we can size up the damage and order new windowpanes. I've called the insurance company. And the glazier. He's coming tomorrow. Fuck," he says, "it was probably just some fucking kids with nothing better to do than smash other people's property."

"You think kids use gloves and wrap their feet in plastic bags when they're seized with a sudden urge to demolish a store?"

"I don't know jack shit about that," Maloney mumbles tiredly. "Shut up and go to bed. I'll see you tomorrow."

On the way back to the living room, as he swills a beer, the phone rings again. It's Jenny. Thomas regrets answering it. She talks non-stop about the coming weekend. What if she can't handle being up at Kristin and Helena's so long; what if there's not enough food—if they've become *vegans*; what if she has an allergic reaction to sleeping in the barn.

"Then just move your mattress inside the house," Thomas says.

"My mattress? How can I sleep on a mattress? With *my back*? I bet they have mice, too."

"Come on, they have cats."

"Maybe they're dead. We haven't been out there for years."

Thomas sighs. "Surely they've got new cats, Jenny."

"And what should I bring them as a hostess gift? Should they each get something, or how does that work?"

Jenny talks and talks, heated, hysterical; she chirrups until, at last, she's calm. She exhales, satisfied, and says good night in a voice practically oozing honey.

Thomas calls Patricia again, but this time it goes directly to voicemail. He sits at the computer and searches for *generic currency sign*. Sure enough, what he finds resembles a sun with four rays. "Popularly called a symbol for money," it reads. "The designator *generic* means, in this case, that it doesn't relate to a specific currency, but rather to money as a phenomenon." For Christ's sake. Despairingly, he stumbles into his cluttered bedroom and curls up under the sheets. A pronounced stench following the day's heat hangs in the air. But he can't bring himself to open the window. One of the blinds dangles crookedly. The cat claws at the door. But he doesn't get up to let it in. In the distance, a church bell tolls 11:00 p.m. He tries to think about Patricia, but doesn't have the energy, he can't deal with it. He dozes off thinking about the vandalized store. He thinks about the symbol carved into the countertop. It's obviously the money they want. His father's money. But who? He imagines a bunch of thugs, hired by Frank and Fatso. But could those two old fools really organize such a thing? He doubts it. He hasn't quite understood it until now, in all its horror, as if he'd hoped it was something else, something that didn't have anything to do with him at all. And maybe it *is* just a coincidence. Maybe there's no connection at all. But he's almost free of the money now. If the sale proceeds as planned. He wants to figure out how it's all connected, but he's too exhausted. His right leg twitches once, then he's asleep.

The next morning the heat's intense again. Thomas can't even eat a piece of toast. Patricia. The symbol, the plastic bags on the perpetrators' feet. He shakes his head. He leans across the kitchen table, opens the window, and lights a cigarette. He calls Patricia, and she answers.

"Where are you?" he asks breathlessly.

"None of your business, really," she says. She sniffles a bit. Is she drunk? There's no background noise. He can't tell where she is.

"Are you okay?"

"Did you just plan on leaving the cat the entire weekend?" she asks, scornfully distant. "You probably did." Her sniffling is gone. She's cold and lucid.

"It's only a couple of days," he says. "I'll make sure there's enough food. Patricia, tell me where you are."

"It'll be lonely."

"It's a cat. We can't take it with us, it'll just run away."

"I'm not sure I'm coming."

"I'll wait for you at the car rental agency at 4:00," he says. "Please come? Darling. I'm so sorry. Truly. What can I do to make things right again?" She doesn't respond. "Say something, Patricia."

"Kiss my ass."

Then she hangs up. He holds the telephone to his ear. The cat stares at him. He wants to lash out at it. But he strokes the bridge of its nose instead. It purrs so hard it trembles. He sits down at the table and glares at the wall. He rises, empties the litter box—which stinks horribly of piss—and dumps in fresh kitty litter. There's discomfort in his legs, and it approaches his stomach. His skin crawls, his guts churn, the back of his head aches dully. He gazes out the window as he calls Maloney. A few streets away, a recently renovated copper roof shines and gleams in the sunlight. Close to the window, a bird flies past.

"What are we going to do?"

"Call Peter and Annie. They might as well stay home today."

"How are we going to get it cleaned up? Where do we begin?"

"Just get your ass down here." Maloney sounds a bit more upbeat than he did the evening before. Thomas opens two cans of cat food and pours water in the creature's bowl. He calls Annie first, then Peter. They're taciturn and nervous, and he can't decide whether they're happy to have an extra day off or not. He shoves some clothes in a duffel bag. Then he finds a shirt in Patricia's drawer, two pairs of panties, a blue dress, tights. He searches for her toothbrush, but it's not there. She must have taken it with her. *She must have taken it with her.* He holds his breath and catches sight of his own face in the mirror above the sink. A pale and rigid mask. He tosses two army-green sleeping bags into a black sack and also takes the trash when he goes downstairs, dumping it into the container before heading toward the station. The heat's always more intense than he imagines it'll be. He can't help but glance around for Patricia. But she must have already left for work. Or is she skipping? Maybe she's even left town? Maybe she's really left him. His pants stick to his balls. In the train he sits across from a girl with coarse hair the color of curry. She's covered with tiny freckles and has a butterfly tattooed on her ankle. When she turns one arm so that it rests on her thigh with her palm facing upward, he sees there's also a tattoo on the inside of her forearm. *The devil likes to play*, it reads. The girl dozes with a fixed smile on her lips; she's got a slight overbite, and Thomas can't take his eyes off her. She seems transparent, as if she were made of glass. One could lift her up and throw her against the doors of the train, and she would splinter into a thousand pieces. Like a casket made of glass, he thinks, like in *Snow White*. She opens her eyes and stares at him. A drowsy, sea-green look. Then her head glides back against the wall, her eyes sailing away. Thomas feels a column of anxiety rising in him. What if Patricia moved out. What if she's *already* moved out. What if she's found someone else.

Maloney's standing outside the store eating fried onion rings from a brown paper cone. The store looks like something found in a war zone, with the rough-hewn boards they'd hammered in place the day before.

"How do we even get in?" Thomas asks, short of breath. He sets his duffel and his sleeping bags down on the sidewalk. Maloney pulls a crowbar from a plastic bag. "With this," he says, handing it to Thomas. "I'll let you play thief." Maloney steps aside with his onion rings.

There's a certain pleasure in yanking off the planks. In that moment right before the nails slip free, the thrust in his biceps and hands feels good. Sweat dribbles down his skin. He licks salt from his upper lip. The planks give one by one, and with a loud crack each falls onto the heap. When he's done they enter the store, crunching on glass shards. "Fuck," Thomas mutters. It's as if they're seeing the mess for the first time. As if they've repressed what happened yesterday. Everything's ripped from the shelves and trampled on. The glass case is open, the keys are missing, each and every one of its twenty-six small windowpanes have been smashed in the same manner. For a moment the two men simply stand, staring. Thomas traces his index finger along the carving on the countertop. Someone had stood here with a knife in his hand. Someone left this message. "Look," Maloney says, pointing at the mountain of silk paper. "And there," Thomas says, nodding in the direction of the expensive gold leaf lumped in a huge ball on the floor, which looks more like a curvy, gilt-metal sculpture cast in the light from the doorway. Maloney chucks his greasy cone onto the floor angrily and walks into the hallway. A terrible wall of heat slams into them when they open the door to the office. The plastic binders with all the balance sheets lie stacked like a colorful mountain. The lamp has been yanked from the wall, the computer screen destroyed. It looks as though someone shattered it with a hammer. Two wounded chairs with broken legs that jut pathetically this way and that. The air is thick, almost sticky, and the dust billows like a swarm of bees as they step inside the office. Thomas falls despondently into the boss's chair. Maloney tries to turn on the fan, but it doesn't work. The cord has been slashed. Instead he opens a window, but the window sticks. Thomas experiences it in slow-motion: Maloney's hand coaxing the hasps and jostling the window until, finally, it slips free with a plop. Maloney sinks onto the edge of the desk and swings his head back and forth, back and forth. "Oh, God," he moans. "What're we going to do?"

"The basement," Thomas mumbles, his voice thick. He's already out in the hallway. But the storage room is intact. No one has been in here. Everything's neatly and tidily stacked on the shelves. The large, rectangular room is cool and comfortable. Maloney sits determinedly on the floor, extends his legs, and rests the back of his head against the smooth wall. "Let's think," he says, his eyes closed.

Thomas lies down on the cold cement floor, and during the next twenty minutes, when they're about to doze off, neither say a word. Thomas doesn't even think of Patricia now, and after this silent, refreshing pause they get to work. Thomas balances two boxes filled with black trash bags up from the basement. They begin in the store. Sweeping everything into enormous piles and shoving it into the sacks. Under some crushed pink pencils with small pony-erasers, on the tips of which have been added lilac-colored manes, Thomas finds the key to the display case. Three hours later they've cleared it all up, and it's evident that nothing has been stolen. Everything has been destroyed. Only a few metal pencil sharpeners and four boxes of ball-point pens are undamaged. As is the display case with the expensive fountain pens. The vandals must not have seen those. They set the trash bags on the street. They sweat and moan. Maloney gets sodas. Thomas fills out the paperwork for the insurance company. They put on music and turn the volume all the way up, and for a moment the atmosphere is almost like when they'd just purchased the store and were fixing it up: bristling with hope for the future—it was energizing and very exhausting. Maloney repairs the ruined lamps and the fan. He fetches the tall ladder in the basement and straightens the chandelier. It really glows when they turn it on. It's as though it brightens the entire situation. The chandelier is their mascot and they love and admire it as though it were a goddess. They consider it a figurehead, like on the prow of a ship, proof of their success with Lindström & Maloney, and have done so since that late evening when they found it heaped on a pile of garbage in front of a mansion in one of the well-to-do neighborhoods in the northwestern part of the city. A weak yellow light shone on the first floor of the otherwise darkened house. They imagined the mansion was occupied by a brittle old widow. They imagined her husband had just passed away. This was soon after they'd concocted the name Maloney. Because Maloney's real name wasn't Maloney. He took the name when they finished their studies. Thomas studied architecture, half-heartedly and restlessly, and dropped out after two years even though he'd gotten a scholarship. Then he began taking classes at the business school and met Maloney. They managed to stay in school for a year and a half, but they quit mid-semester. They had outlandish dreams. A *chain*. A long string of pearls, of beautiful, unforgettable stores like pins on a map stretching across the entire continent, the entire world. A simple concept: Lindström & Maloney. And it would be much *more* than just office supplies, paper—much, much more than that. The name that Maloney's religious parents had given him out there in their oh so pretty white wooden house in the sticks, so many years ago now (Tim Stürtz, nickname Timmy), was too trivial, and they agreed that they needed something more mystical: *a name that was deep as a well.* It was Thomas who came up with it (both the well metaphor and the new name) after they'd been drinking coffee and smoking cigarettes and joints for several hours on the twin bed in his room, scribbling down all the names they could think of in a notepad. Suddenly it came to him: "Maloney!! You're Maloney! Yes, you are! Don't you see it? Lindström & Maloney! It sounds—like a threatening dream, you hear it?! It sounds like something you can't resist. Noir . . ."

"Noir?"

"Yes! Secrets. Rainy weather. Darkness. A well, Maloney, a deep well!" Thomas sucked hard on the last of the joint. At first Maloney looked down at the mattress, then he turned toward the window and stared into the far distance, and at last he leaped to his feet and shouted, "Jesus Christ, you're right! We'll use Maloney. MALONEY!" And it was as if the name was created just for him. Even when Thomas thinks about their friendship before that afternoon—when they sat bent over the notepad, each nibbling on a pencil, on the bed in the dying, weak light of the day, in the messy room, high as kites while the upstairs neighbor argued with his wife and the radiator dripped—he thinks of him as Maloney. He no longer believes the pairing of their names has anything noir about it, but Maloney fits Maloney perfectly.

The office isn't missing anything, either. But all their financial documents were riffled through, and some bank statements from the last two quarters were ripped out and thrown on the floor. Thomas gathers the loose papers, tries to smooth them, return them to the folders. It's clear that someone wanted to check their deposits. He doesn't say anything about it to Maloney. He carries the smashed monitor to the street and sets it down next to the trash bags. The sun's high in the sky, and people hustle past, lightly dressed and full of purpose. The stench of the trash bin on the corner wafts toward him. He lights a cigarette and sits down amid the glass shards on the stoop. He hasn't told Patricia about the break-in. Now he sees it as an opportunity to connect with her. He texts her, and to his surprise she replies at once: "What?? Why didn't you say anything??" "We're cleaning up now, all's well." She doesn't respond. "I love you," he writes, feeling for a moment like a traitor. The feeling passes. Maloney buys shawarmas with pickled chilies and sits beside Thomas. The sunlight blinds them; it flickers through the leaves of the chestnut tree; it sparkles off the shiny hoods of cars and women's hair as they bike past in their colored skirts, their scarves fluttering, shoulders bare. Maloney whistles at a long-legged brunette. She flips him the bird. They laugh. They finish eating. They sit shoulder to shoulder, and Thomas feels the heat from Maloney's big body. We're sitting shoulder to shoulder like brothers, he thinks, and the heat sweeps through him, as if the temperature in his blood has been turned up. Then he stands up and grabs a broom. While he sweeps up the shards, the glazier and his assistant arrive in a dented, yellow van. The glass panels are lashed to the side of the van, in a wooden frame. "And you're certain you don't want thermal windows?"

"Never," Thomas says.

"Burglary-proof panes?"

"No thanks. If sunlight doesn't spill onto the floor, it's pointless."

The glazier smiles. "People usually don't care about things like that. But I'm not gonna complain. It's good business for me." They work quickly and efficiently. They remove old slivers, nails, putty, and wood strips. They clean the rabbet notches, sanding and putty-ing. Carefully, the glazier measures the door pane and cuts the glass on the floor of the van. He arranges the new window in the frame, and the assistant hands him the nails and a small hammer with a square head. Maloney tries to seem interested. "What's that called?" "A glazier's hammer," the glazier mumbles with a couple of nails in his mouth. Suppressing laughter, Maloney looks at Thomas. "Makes sense. A *glazier's hammer* . . ." With a sure hand, the glazier putties a perfect slanting edge around the pane. The assistant keeps an eye on even the tiniest movements, scrutinizing the technique. Then they turn to the store's windows. The assistant's already waiting at the van with suction cups, which they use to carefully transfer the large piece of glass over to the window frame and position it in the rabbet. Then they begin tapping the molding firmly in place along the edge. "There!" The glazier backs onto the street and admires his work. "You can paint the molding right away, but don't go touching the puttied surfaces until they've dried properly. Give it a few weeks. And you said something about a cabinet?" The glazier, a small, stooped man wearing a brown smock, is in the habit of rubbing his chin often, and has a cluster of stiff gray hairs poking from his pointy ears. He shuffles into the store, measures the cabinet panes and, mumbling to himself, jots the numbers into his notebook. The assistant stands off to the side, his hands thrust deep into his pockets. His ratty over-alls are a washed-out blue. They converse about the break-in. Both the glazier and the assistant think it's odd that the perpetrators didn't take anything with them. "It doesn't pay off then, does it? I mean . . . going through all that trouble for nothing," the assistant says, blushing in the same moment the words exit his mouth. He's just a big boy. "Crime never pays, Samir," the glazier says sharply. "No. But it wasn't even theft . . . you know. That's exactly what . . . it *isn't* . . ." The glazier just *looks* at Samir. And Samir lowers his head. The four of them return outside to the sunlight. Maloney says, "It must've taken a helluva a long time to smash everything so consistently. Who would do that, and why?" Thomas feels his stomach squeezing into a hard knot. A sudden, bottomless fear. The glazier and Samir shake their heads, and the glazier fastens his gaze on a point far in the distance. "Meaningless," he mutters. "And that it happened here, in such a nice neighborhood . . ." He falls silent. Samir packs the tools. Soon they drive off in the dented van. Thomas saves the receipt for the insurance company. They admire the new glass partitions and decide that the cleaning job is much too great for Eva to do, even if she brings her attractive niece with her. Thomas calls a company and orders what they call a "post break-in clean up." They can come as early as Monday morning. Which means Annie and Peter can arrive a little later and help put all the products in the storeroom back on the shelves. Maloney surveys the depressingly empty store. "I can't wait to see customers in here," he says. "But I'm not placing any orders now. Not until first thing Monday."

"You want to go over and get a drink?"

"Can't. Have to go somewhere. But Monday. Maybe we should invite Annie and Peter to a company dinner? Call it a kind of perk? Because they're our 'faithful employees'?"

Thomas smiles. "We could do that."

"See you soon," Maloney says, clucking his tongue. He does a few dance steps, laughing, his back to Thomas, before switching over to his standard heavy gait.

Thomas saunters through the city with his duffel slung over his shoulder. He's got plenty of time; the car rental agency is close to the store. He buys an iced coffee and an almond croissant and suddenly feels in really great spirits. She'll definitely come. She answered his text. She responded to me, and that's an opening. The weather is bewitchingly wonderful. The humidity is dropping, there's a light breeze, bright colors everywhere; even the gray stone projects look better today. People have begun putting plants out on balconies. He walks along wondering whether they can swim in the lake up at Kristin and Helena's. If the weather holds, they can. Maybe he should buy something for the twins. He texts Alice; she's on her way there. Maybe they'll have a good time. If Jenny doesn't make any scenes, and if Patricia comes along. If they can make the effort to show that everything's fine with their relationship. *Is* it fine? Fundamentally fine. He has no clue. But the thought of her leaving him makes him so weak, like his entire being is seeping out of him. When he stops to smoke on a bench beneath a tall acacia tree, the real estate agent calls and says "accepted." "Fantastic!" Thomas catches himself shouting. The agent's in his car and can meet him at a nearby square in fifteen minutes. Thomas waits beside a copper statue, coated with verdigris, and white with dove shit, depicting a young man with a raised sword.

Then the agent arrives and Thomas says, "And she knows that I'm paying in cash?"

"Yes. But you'll have to take it as is," the agent says. "She doesn't want any trouble."

"What does she mean by that?"

"Good question. I told her that we'll test for dry-rot and mold. The electrical wires will also need to be examined. She agreed, but very reluctantly. You won't end up with a moldy building or a fire hazard. I know a guy who can look at it over the weekend."

"Thank you. That's very thoughtful. And you're sure that I'll get a valid deed?" The real estate agent nods, tugging at his tie. Thomas thanks him again. They agree to meet the following Wednesday, when the money will change hands. "And the deed will be undersigned," the agent says. The seller will be present. "2:00 P.M. at the location." He shakes Thomas's hand. Thomas sits at the statue's feet and smiles. It's perfect. Right now, just after the business was defiled, Lindström & Maloney gets back on its feet again with a new branch. That'll teach them, the bastards. How's that for rehabilitation. That's how you do it. Thomas trembles inwardly with joy. He can't stop smiling. Alice will have a job and an apprenticeship, a *future*, and it'll also help secure him in his own retirement (he imagines); the money will be removed from the microwave, will be passed on, and his father will be eliminated forever. The old dream of owning a chain (albeit a very small one) will become a reality. All in one fell swoop. And he can get the papers right away, despite the sale being under the table. The seller has, presumably, a few skeletons of her own in a closet. It's perfect.

When he turns the corner of the street where the car rental agency is located, he literally bumps into Frank. Simply smacks his chest into his shoulder. Frank with his slicked-back hair and smarmy smile. The smell of aftershave mixed with cigarette smoke, his sweet, nauseating breath.

Thomas feels a dull thump on his back. "What are you doing in this part of town? We haven't seen much of you lately."

"No." A short pause. And then it just comes barreling out of him. "But maybe you've seen my store?"

Frank looks at him, baffled.

"There was a break-in. I couldn't help but think of you and Fatso. Did you stop by with baseball bats?"

Frank opens his eyes wide, then clucks tolerantly. "Baseball bats?! That's priceless. I've got no idea what you're talking about. Ha! Why would we attack you with baseball bats?! Two old rats like us! If we wanted something from you, don't you think we could easily figure out how to contact you by normal means? *You're Jacques's son.*" Frank looks at Thomas with restrained disgust, his eyes squinting in his angular face. "Though it's hard to believe." He takes a deep breath and lowers his voice to a mild pitch. "I'm really sorry to hear what happened. But listen: We don't want to harm you. I believe I made that clear after the funeral. All we want is to be left alone to mind our own business. We don't want to get mixed up in anything."

For a moment the two men stare at each other like tomcats. Mistrustful, searching. Is there a reason to be watchful?

"Mixed up in what?"

Frank shrugs. Thomas changes his tack:

"How's the bar going? Business good?"

"Sterling." Frank maintains Thomas's gaze.

"And your dry cleaning? Did you find your dry cleaning?"

"I did."

"And what about Luc? Or Luke. He still helping out?"

"Here and there. The boy's got many irons in the fire."

"What does he do anyway?"

Frank pulls his hands from his pockets and straightens up. "Ah, this and that, y'know. He fishes." Frank finally looks away, uninterested.

"Fishes?"

"Yeah. Mostly eel, I think. He's got traps in a couple of places."

"That's not something you can make a living on, though, is it?"

"No, it's mostly just one of his hobbies. That's why he gives us a hand from time to time. Among other things." He glances at his watch. "I gotta get going, I'm meeting someone. Nice to run into you." Frank offers his nicotine-stained hand. Thomas clutches it and holds on tightly. The skin is chapped and cold.

"So you have no idea who could've come by my store? C'mon, Frank."

"Absolutely no idea." Frank turns and strolls calmly—practically leaning backward as though an invisible servant is bearing the weight of his torso—down the street. Thomas watches him go. Sees him stop at a mechanic's and speak to a young man in overalls, who's lugging tires off the sidewalk and into the shop. The two men disappear together into the darkness.

Patricia shows up at 4:15, silent and pale. She climbs into the car without a word. Frank's presence lingers with Thomas as they drive northward out of the city. Patricia says nothing. She can't decide what she wants to listen to on the radio, so she keeps switching channels. At first he tells her everything about the break-in, but she offers no commentary. They eat apples; she remains silent. Around 5:00 they stop at a gas station and get coffee. He puts his hand on her arm and she doesn't remove it. A small opening. He remembers that he wanted to buy something for the twins. He wanders around the store and winds up choosing two large bars of milk chocolate and a video game. He buys enough cigarettes to last the weekend. Patricia has brought a supersized bottle of Rioja. "Good," he says, "there's quite a few of us." She looks away. Standing in a patch of sunlight, she rises onto her tiptoes in her flat, sand-colored sandals.

"I've bought another store," he says. "I get the deed on Wednesday."

She eyes him indifferently.

"Why?"

"Alice is going to be the manager."

"But you haven't even talked to her about it?"

"I did. Sort of. Briefly. And I plan on talking to her about it this weekend."

She smiles derisively. "You've begun smelting before the iron's hot, haven't you?"

"If Alice isn't interested, don't you think someone else will be?" She just glares at him, at such length and with such condescension that it irritates him. "It's a major opportunity for a young person," he says testily.

"Is it now?"

"Yes, you're damn straight it is."

"Relax. Not everyone wants to be a part of the *paper business*."

"Paper business? What's that supposed to mean?"

"Can you try to act normal the next few days? To be honest, it's hard to be around you."

"As far as I can see, you're the one who's making it hard. You're distant."

"And you're not allowed to smoke at a gas station."

He flings his cigarette away huffily.

"Listen," he says. "I've always wanted to have a branch and the opportunity arose. Now we'll have to see about Alice."

She turns away. "I don't understand where the money's coming from."

"Don't worry about it."

"What do you mean by that? That sounds suspicious."

He unlocks the car. "I've been saving up, Patricia. And I bought the new store for a song. It's very simple."

She sits beside him and pulls a nail file from her purse. He starts the engine.

"Where?" she says, her tone still indifferent.

"Really close to where I grew up. In that neighborhood." He turns on the blinker and merges onto the highway.

"Ha! How sentimental of you. You won't have any customers in that area. Who do you think will buy envelopes and fountain pens out there? Frank and his friends?"

He angles the car into the outer lane and accelerates. "There are tons of students."

She shakes her head and continues to do so for what seems like forever.

"Stop being so negative, for fuck's sake!"

He punches a clenched fist against the wheel.

A terrible silence. Then she speaks, her voice low and tense, "You know what. Why don't you just let me out here? I really don't want to be with you. First you practically assault me, then you neglect to tell me something as important as having a break-in at your store, and now this. I've tried to communicate with you for a long time, Thomas. In an ordinary way, the way ordinary people do. But you never even ask how *I'm* doing anymore. We never talk. There's no connection. It seems like you just don't give a shit. And you don't want a baby with me, either." Her voice rises now: "What I'm saying is that you don't want to talk to me, and you don't want to have a kid with me." Then she shouts, "What do you want from me? And slow down for Christ's sake! You're driving like a fucking idiot!"

Thomas grits his teeth and leans forward. He maintains his speed. Patricia emits an angry, animal-like noise and blares the radio as high as it will go. Booming heavy metal from years ago swells the air around them. They zip past green fields and darker wooded areas. Grazing sheep. Beef cattle. Red barns and listless windmills. There's no wind. A murder of crows alight from a treetop and glide across the landscape like black ships in formation. He snaps off the radio. Patricia stares demonstratively out the passenger window, her back to him. Ten minutes later he says, "I'm sorry. I'll get myself together. I promise. We'll have a nice weekend." And when she doesn't respond: "I just can't deal with any more problems, Patricia."

"You're the one creating them," she barks in a deep, intense voice.

"I love you. I fucked up, but I love you. You have to believe me."

The landscape begins to rise. Hills and cliff formations and the mountains' snow-capped peaks farther ahead. "Look," Thomas says. "It's beautiful out here. It's been too long since we've been out of the city. Please forgive me?" She sighs. "Please? Babe?" She looks at him. This is again followed by silence, but slowly that silence grows milder, the atmosphere gradually cooling; he smiles at her, realizes that she's regarding him. She says, "You're a strange man, Thomas." He says, "You think so?" She nods. He says, "I've missed you." She sighs again. He says, "I love you." Some time passes before she says, very quietly, "I know." And like that everything changes. He lays his hand tentatively on her thigh. "I'm actually looking forward to being with all those goofballs," she says in her normal voice. Relieved, he reaches for her hand and puts it on his knee. A few seconds later her hand glides a short distance up his thigh. He braces it between his legs. The hand rests there unmoving, warm and feathery-light. She doesn't remove it. His dick throbs against her palm. *He's* the one who removes her hand, but he does so in order to run his hand up under her dress. He fingers the lace trimmings of her panties. She breathes heavily. "I want you so bad," he whispers. "You're an asshole," she moans, when he slips his hand under the thin fabric. "Not now."

"When?" She's warm and wet. He can almost smell her fragrance notes filling the car.

"Then pull over," she whispers. "I hate you, Thomas."

He goes out of his way to avoid seeming aggressive. But she's aggressive. As she straddles him on the narrow backseat, she slaps him hard in the face with the flat of her hand.

She shakes him and thrusts her groin against his until it almost hurts. She tears at his shirt, and a button pops off. He thinks he smells something strange on her. Maybe she's got another man's sperm in her, maybe another man's touched her skin. This arouses him. "Have you been cheating on me?" he whispers. Afterward the thought is *in no way* arousing. Afterward she pulls her skirt to her knees and smooths it with her hands. She lets him kiss her. He kisses her face, forehead, eyes, mouth, her flushed cheeks. But she's strangely detached now.

They leave the forest road and the half-darkness between the trees. A squirrel scuttles up a tree trunk. The car smells thickly of sex and sweat. He turns on the air conditioning and drapes his arm around her neck. They listen to pop music and chew gum. She fishes perfume from her purse and sprays Thomas with it. "Now you smell like a woman," she smiles. Then she starts to laugh, and she can't stop herself. Leaning forward, she cackles until she begins to tremble. He laughs along, but he doesn't know what's so funny. Yet the bad atmosphere has completely disappeared by the time she, hiccupping, settles into her seat once more and rubs her eyes. "Oh" she says, "Oh, you slut. Everything's so bizarre!" A half-hour later they turn off the road and continue along poorly paved country roads, until they reach Helena and Kristin's driveway. A long, curving gravel track surrounded by pine trees on either side and leading to the farm with the big barn. From up here, you can see the lake on the other side of the grove, which slopes down behind the buildings. And beyond that, marsh and beeches; and farther still, the scattering of fields that stretch as far as the eye can see. A mountain chain in the distance. Smaller mountains closer by. The closest neighbor lives sixteen miles to the east.

While they're removing their luggage from the trunk, Kristin, wearing wooden clogs and an apron, comes outside through the back door. She gives them each a hug and squeezes Thomas's chin. "Let me get a good look at you. How are you doing?"

"Fine. I'm fine. And you?"

"We've been so looking forward to seeing you all." She smiles with an almost quivering tenderness. Her eyes gleam wetly. She swallows. "Jenny's in the kitchen drinking tea with Helena, Alice, and that guy, what's his name again?"

"Ernesto? The musician from the funeral?"

"No," Kristin says. "The other one."

Thomas glances at the house. A soft light emanates from the window in the twilight.

"What other one?"

"You have sheep?" Patricia asks, snatching up the travel bag. Thomas follows her gaze over the field that borders the road. Sheep and lambs graze peacefully. A trace of mist envelops them, dreamlike.

"You better believe we do. Helena makes yarn from the wool, you know. We've got hens, too." She walks ahead of them and calls back, "We'll actually be eating a couple of them for dinner!" Thomas and Patricia glance at each other, slightly apprehensive. "Hens," he whispers, wrinkling his brows. Patricia smiles broadly. Her eyes sparkle with a sudden light. That's exactly how she looked when I met her, he thinks, when I fell in love with her, the freedom she radiated, the confidence. Now it feels as though she's taken a step away from him and lives in a secret world that he doesn't have access to. But she's so *beautiful*. She *sparkles*. Her hips sway from side to side when she walks; he can see her leg muscles straining. He holds his breath. They reach the stairwell, where the twins are standing gawkily behind Kristin's impressive figure. Jenny and Helena emerge from the kitchen, and the hallway's now full of people. They embrace and say hello. Thomas fishes the chocolate bars and the videogame from the plastic bag he got at the gas station, and the twins give him their bashful thanks before vanishing up the stairs with the gifts. Patricia hands Helena the wine bottle. "That'll come in handy," she smiles. And then Thomas catches sight of Luc's face. He's standing behind Alice, a hand on her shoulder. Thomas grows cold, and doesn't hear what Kristin tells him. "Do you?" she asks.

"I'm sorry," he mumbles.

"Do you like especially spicy, dark wine?"

"Not particularly . . ." he says. He hangs his jacket on a hook. The group—still chatting, a large clump of clothed flesh—glides into the kitchen, where a fat-bellied teapot rests amid some sort of arrangement with tea lights in the center of the long, scrubbed, white oak table. There's an aroma of food. A small, plump dog with a dirty pelt wags toward them. It leaps up on one person, then another. "Go lie down, Jupiter!" Kristin shouts. Jupiter waddles sadly over to his basket near the wood stove. An incredibly homely dog. Patricia stands next to Helena in the kitchen and talks to her, one hand resting on her back. From behind, Alice wraps her arms around Thomas. "Uncle Thomas," she says affectionately. "Here we are." She lets go of him, and he turns. Luc offers his hand. He takes it hesitantly. "So you're here too," Thomas says slowly. "Luc."

"Luke!" Alice smiles. "I call him Luke."

"Yeah, it was really nice of Alice to invite me. And when I heard about the lake, I jumped at the chance. I'd like to catch some pike. It's the perfect time for the males."

"But not the females?"

He shakes his head. "They're carrying eggs now. They swim close to shore to spawn when it's a little warmer. So if we hook the ladies, we let them go." He smiles at Alice. She nods and smiles back. A private smile, Thomas thinks with a growing sense of hysterics. He tries to get Patricia's attention, but she's got her back to him, gesticulating eagerly as she talks with Kristin. Thomas turns to Luke again.

"You brought your fishing pole?"

Luke nods. "Sure thing. If we're lucky we'll also get some perch." He looks extremely relaxed in his chocolate-brown sweater that fits perfectly with his eyes and his characteristically thick, unruly hair. Alice gazes at him with admiration.

"So we'll have some fish balls for lunch on Sunday," she says.

"If you catch anything, that is." Thomas says. But now Kristin's tugging at him. "Sit down and have yourself a nice, relaxing cup of tea. You two must be terribly exhausted. I hear that you've had a break-in at the store. That sounds just awful, Thomas."

She leads him to a settle bench, where there's a ceramic mug filled with mint tea and a seat beside Jenny waiting for him. Kristin sits opposite them.

"There you are, you kids. Look at you now."

There are red splotches on Jenny's neck. That doesn't bode well.

"We were just talking about Mom," she says, looking down at the table.

Jenny scrapes at the fingernail polish on her left pinky. There's clattering in the kitchen. Alice and Luke have begun washing lettuce for the salad, while Helena stirs what's in the pans. Patricia's got a dishtowel around her waist. She's skinning almonds.

"Alice really wants to learn more about her grandmother," Jenny says, almost a whisper.

"Well," Kristin says. "I know it's not easy for you, Jenny. But it's understandable, this need of hers. And by now you two must be ready to talk about her. My God, it's been so long." Kristin pushes a bowl of dried fruit across the table toward Thomas, but he has no desire to eat withered apple slices or small, shriveled-up figs.

"And now that Dad's dead . . ." Jenny looks at Thomas, her eyes wet.

"But Jenny. He was gone before he died." Thomas smiles at Kristin.

"I remember how anxious you two always were whenever you visited me in my apartment with the roof terrace. Remember? We used to eat ice cream up there when you came by during the summer. Jenny didn't like strawberry ice cream. Do you remember that, Jenny?"

"But why did we see you if Mom didn't want to see us? Did she even know we were visiting you?" Jenny interrupts fervently, raising her hand to her mouth.

"Of course she knew," Kristin says. "Our father was furious that she wouldn't see you. There was a lot of drama. But he was already an old man by then, you know, and Jacques had custody, so there honestly wasn't much we could do. Like I said before you got here, Thomas, Agnes was at a very low point when she left. And I never saw much of her after that, either. She refused to come back. She believed that distance would make it all go away. Don't you think I tried to convince her to come back? Of course I did, but it didn't help. I was so young. And I only saw her a few times during those years, with the exception of when she was dying. And then it was always me who visited her—"

"Did you bring pictures of us with you?" Jenny cuts in.

"Yes. But to be honest, she didn't want to see them."

Sobbing soundlessly, Jenny lowers her head.

"That's how it was, Jenny. It didn't have anything to do with you two. It was all about Jacques and your mother."

Automatically Thomas reaches for Jenny and pulls her close, as he has so many times before. Her tears don't affect him. What matters is only that he make her stop crying. Alice approaches with a washcloth in her hand and large, worried eyes.

"What's wrong with Mom? Why are you crying?"

"It's just all this about *our* mother," Thomas says. "She'll be okay in a bit. Right, Jenny?"

"Yeah," Jenny sobs, drying her eyes with her sleeve. Thomas makes eye contact with Alice; she nods and heads back to the dishes.

"One time I visited her we did something fun," Kristin says. "God, it was actually really hysterical. Let's have a glass of wine!" She goes off and returns with glasses and a bottle of Bordeaux. She pours. Jenny takes a big swig, tossing her head back. She smiles. The role of victim, Thomas thinks bitterly, it's a rehearsed grimace, a bad habit of hers. Jenny sniffles. Kristin leans back elegantly in her chair, glass in hand: "We'd dressed up in men's clothes and gone to a huge party, the opening of some exhibition. She used to hang out in artist circles, and I'm sure you've already figured out that I was the one who most looked like a man. By the time we arrived we were pretty drunk, and the whole time I had to keep forcing Agnes's hair back up under her bowler." Kristin sniffs her drink.

"You were wearing *hats*?" Jenny says.

"Of course we were wearing hats. Well, but anyway, we were very giddy and pretty self-absorbed. But then there's this very attractive woman who was basically blitzed. She'd probably snorted some coke too—pretty much everyone at that party did—and it seemed like she really believed we were men. She buzzed around us, and then she began hitting on Agnes, in a drunk and sweetish way. We tell her that we're brothers, and I grab champagne for the three of us, and this girl, have I mentioned that she's super hot?" Kristin drinks, laughs. "At some point people begin to dance, and we ask the girl to dance. We have a really great time pretending to dance just like men do, and the girl, she's just crazy about these two gallant brothers she's run into. Then it happens: She wraps her arms around your mother's neck and kisses her."

Jenny: "Kisses her *how*?" And then, shocked: "With her *tongue*?"

Kristin: "Oh, yes. And there's nothing left to do but to continue the joke, so your mother gives me a look of desperation, but she needs to kiss her back. Meanwhile I'm howling with laughter inside. It was just too funny. Your mother's arms are rigid with fear. But what's worse, as the night wears on the girl wants to come home with us. Naturally, I'm really interested in her, so your mother and I squabble in the men's room. She doesn't think it's a good idea at all, but I always won those kinds of arguments, even though I was the youngest. And I won in this situation, too. We managed to get the girl maneuvered to a cab."

Thomas and Jenny hang on Kristin's every word, riveted. From the kitchen Helena calls out, "Are you telling the Chaplin and Chaplin story?"

Smiling, Kristin nods.

"Chaplin and Chaplin?" Thomas says.

"Because of the hats," Kristin says. "Helena thinks we must have looked like two Charlie Chaplins."

"What happened next?" Jenny's mouth is set grimly now.

"Well, we take the girl home. I'll spare you all the intimate details. But after a lot of fuss, I'm the one who tries to seduce her. We're all lying on Agnes's mattress. But in the dark the girl can't tell the difference between us, so she's willing enough at first. By this point, your mother has long since fallen asleep in her fancy suit."

"And she realizes that you're not Mom?" Jenny asks.

"You can bet your bottom dollar on that. But most importantly she realizes I'm not a man! So she shoots out of bed like a rocket and gets dressed."

"Was she ticked off?"

"Oh, yeah. But she was so drunk that it wasn't an especially convincing anger. And even though I was disappointed, it was just so funny that I had to wake your mother. For the rest of the night, we sat there bawling with laughter. Ha! Agnes definitely had a sense of humor when she felt like it. I can still see it clearly. The girl's name was Denise. We were constantly making Denise jokes after that." Kristin shakes her head, laughing, and drains her glass.

Thomas doesn't know what to say. Jenny's folded her arms on the table and dropped her head onto them. She sighs. "Well!" Kristin says, standing. "Is it time to set the table, Helena?" They call the twins downstairs, and they begin to set out the plates and silverware. Luke places a large bowl of salad in the center of the table. "Where can I smoke?" Thomas asks.

"It's okay if you smoke in the sunroom," Helena says.

"Come," Thomas says to Jenny, pulling her along, first through the kitchen then through the enormous living room, with its wood-frame couch and beanbag chairs. Hanging on the wall over the couch is one of Helena's tapestries. Its color scheme is olive-green, yellow, and reddish-brown. Jenny pauses. "Is this a new one? Do you think it's made of wool from the sheep?"

"No doubt," Thomas mumbles, rooting around in his pants pocket for his cigarettes.

"I bet she dyed it herself with plants and bark or something."

Jenny throws open the sunroom doors and sits in a wicker chair. She's surrounded by geraniums. Her salmon-colored dress is stretched tightly across her chest. She crosses her legs and looks at him. "Well?" she says.

Thomas lights a cigarette and sucks the smoke into his lungs. "Why in the world is Luc here?"

She shrugs. "Ask Alice. And his name is Luke."

"He has no business being here, whatever the hell his name is."

"You don't get to decide that. Let me have a drag."

He hands her the cigarette, but she does nothing more than shift the smoke around in her mouth before blowing it out.

"Are they dating?"

"No idea."

"So what then?"

Jenny yawns. "I really don't know, Thomas. Does it even matter?" They can hear the wind in the trees. A breeze. For a moment they both relax and are silent. The weak soughing of the leaves is calming. But then Jenny says, "It's incredibly upsetting for me to hear about Mom. Kristin's so brutally honest. She's totally insensitive."

Thomas ashes his cigarette in a potted plant. "There's no point getting so upset. Can you please stay calm?"

"You be calm!" she says sharply, turning toward the twilight and the towering black pine trees outside. "After all, you're completely paranoid about Alice's random friends. It actually seems like you can't let go of her, Thomas."

She stretches her legs languidly and leans back. "Am I right? You can't let go of her. But you need to." Thomas wants to raise his hand and slap her across the cheek; he clenches his fist in his pocket.

"I think what you're doing now is a massive projection, dear sister."

"A what?"

"As far as I recall, *you* called bawling only a short time ago because she'd moved out. Your life was over, you said. Is your life over?"

"You're so mean, Thomas. So totally mean. You know what? I wish I was an only child."

"I just wish you weren't such a child. You act like one. It's really unbecoming at your age."

She straightens up and stares angrily at him.

"Here you are, you two!" Helena stands smiling in the doorway, dressed in a loose-fitting linen dress. "Time to eat. Come join us."

Jenny gets to her feet. As she passes Thomas she hisses, "Mean selfish bastard." He stubs the ashes from his cigarette in a jar filled with withered chives.

The wonderful aroma of something that has simmered for hours drifts from the kitchen. Herbs, meat, sweet and sour: a thickly condensed scent that instantly relaxes the body, makes it long for food and warmth. And it almost causes Thomas to forget his argument with Jenny; he feels welcomed into the fold, seduced by this fragrance that fills his nose and throat, and he realizes just how hungry he is. When he enters the kitchen, the first thing he sees is Luke and Patricia squatting and talking beside the oven door, which is open. Patricia probes at whatever's inside the oven with her fork. Then he looks right into Helena's alert, gentle eyes. He turns his head and sees the long table, now set. And there, at the table, with a glass of red wine in his hand, is Maloney. Maloney, here, in this kitchen. Thomas halts and simply points at him. Maloney waves. "I told you I'd see you soon!" He stands up and approaches Thomas, grinning from ear to ear. "Gotcha, didn't I?" He taps Thomas on the shoulder. "Jenny invited me. I thought I'd surprise you. We drove up here this afternoon, and I just returned from a quick trip to the neighbor's. Though quick may not be the right word. There's a helluva long way between houses up here. They sent me to borrow some coffee." Jenny leans against Maloney, smiling. "In this house they drink only tea," she says, "and that's not good enough for this gentleman." She beams at him. Now her face seems totally open, and this lazy sensuality seems to pulsate in her supple body. The fabric of her salmon-colored dress shines with the same brightness as her eyes. Maloney wraps his arm around her. "You should've seen the man who opened the door at that farm. Hell, it looked as though he hadn't seen a living person in years. He freaked me out!" Thomas has *nothing* to say; he simply stares at the two, blinking. Has to back away and lean against the kitchen table. "But Thomas," Patricia says, "It's just Maloney." Then she laughs resoundingly. And Kristin says, "A lot of men we've got here now! Usually it's just you, Thomas. And of course the dog." Thomas feels everyone's eyes on him, feels the discomfort, the sweat, his blushing face. A dull rage. Manically he brings bottles, bowls, and baskets of bread to the table. Alice giggles. "He's completely pale," Kristin snorts, "give that poor man a glass of wine!"

They take their seats, and Helena brings the bulky iron pot over from the oven. "*Coq au vin*!" she says, blowing hair off her face. Patricia carries oven-grilled potatoes and parsnips, and there's bread, hummus, baba ghanoush, and olives. Kristin ladles up the food. Thomas glances miserably at Patricia; she tugs him down next to her. Across from them sit Maloney and Jenny, Maloney with one hand firmly planted on Jenny's thigh. Luke sits like a king at the head of the table, as if he had the right. Kristin takes a seat at the other end. The twins pick at their food and are given strict orders to at least try it. Conversation commences. Silverware clinks against the glazed ceramic plates. Luke and Alice have decided to get up early and go fishing on Sunday. But tomorrow they want to go hiking, Alice announces proudly. "You're not usually a nature lover," Jenny says. "Quite the opposite. When she lived at home with me she could lie on the couch for *days*. But apparently that's changed. Now it seems you can't get enough fresh air." Alice pushes her fork through her hummus. "We *are* actually in nature now, Mom, so why not see what it's got to offer?" Jenny gives her daughter an arrogant look. Then she seems to change her mind and nods, smiling kindly. Thomas is amazed they don't begin to argue; everything feels wrong to him. Patricia beams at Luke when he raises his glass and they toast. The *coq au vin* is as tender and delicious as Thomas had hoped. The meat slides easily from the bones, and the sauce is dark and strong. Still, after a few bites he loses his appetite. Maloney tells them about the break-in, and the more wine he drinks, the more colorful are the details. Thomas doesn't say a word. Kristin shouts, "Cheers! Welcome all of you!" She gets to her feet. The twins clink glasses and giggle. Kristin takes a deep breath and looks warmly at each of the guests. "Our family has always been too small. So I'm especially happy to see so many at the table tonight. I hope we'll have a couple of truly wonderful days together. Please make yourselves at home. You *are* home with us." Helena smiles at Kristin, who's clearly moved. "Thank you for the invitation!" Maloney cries out. "My family's extinct, so I'm happy there's room for me." They laugh. Thomas scrutinizes Luke. He eats with careful, regulated movements, scraping the meat from the bones, pushing sauce and meat onto his fork, lifting the fork with a sure hand to his mouth and chewing slowly, mouth closed. His face reveals nothing, no openings. "It's delicious, Helena," Patricia says. "What are we having for dessert?" one of the twins mumbles, biting her frayed sleeve. "Rumor has it that Maloney brought us a frozen custard," Kristin says, smiling at Maloney. "Were you afraid you'd only get carrots and bran crackers up here?"

"A little." Maloney gives a jolly laugh and pours more wine.

"Be happy you're not here during the summer when we only eat vegetables, it's terrible," one of the twins mutters.

"With dirt still on them," the other says.

"From the garden?" Patricia asks.

They nod.

"Your self-sufficiency is impressive."

"There's no one else to provide for us out here in the sticks," Kristin says.

"No, but they also taste better. And it's cheaper. You love our tomatoes, don't you Maya?" Helena wipes her hands with her napkin.

Maya doesn't respond. She gnaws at her sleeve.

"Did you know they raised these cockerels themselves?" Patricia asks.

"Oh my God!" Jenny nearly swallows something down the wrong pipe. "How do you have the heart to do it? Cute little chickens, living and breathing . . ."

"You bet they were living and breathing, hon. Do you think it's any better for hens in cages?" Maloney gulps his wine. "Do you hunt, too?"

"Of course," Kristin says. "I do."

"You actually have a hunting license? And a gun?"

"I sure do. We've got four hares and a deer in the freezer."

"Not to mention a dozen pheasants," Helena adds, nodding proudly at Kristin. "Kristin's famous for hitting the target on every shot."

Alice glances brightly around, from one to the other. "I'm so excited to be here with all of you." Her voice is subdued and delicate.

"Oh, Alice, that's so sweet of you," Helena says, reaching out to stroke her cheek. "We're excited to have you here with us. To Alice!" They toast, then dish more food onto their plates. They pass around the salad. "Great dressing, Luke," and the bread—what an incredible texture. Kristin lights a candle on the windowsill, and Thomas is sent to the utility room to get more wine. He uses the opportunity to go outside and smoke. It's pitch dark. The lamplight is dim, yellow. How dare Maloney show up unannounced. And Luke. What the hell's he to make of Jenny and Maloney *dating?* Are they really dating? He called her *hon.* Thomas feels a faint anger, but only as a sad ripple through his body. Then the grief: No one told him anything. Not his sister, not his best friend. No one wants to confide in him. No one wants to share anything with him. He shivers in the evening cold. I'm lonely, he thinks. I am a lonely fool disconnected from reality. I'm an old, lonely fool who pushes everyone away. I've apparently pushed everyone away. Even Patricia. I'm a complete fuck-up. Here comes the self-pity, and it's ugly. Damn, how it reeks. He grabs two bottles of wine from a shelf in the pantry, where it smells vaguely of onions and earthy potatoes. The kitchen is warm, humming with laughter and conversation. Thomas slides into his chair. Patricia rubs his knee under the table. "Are you okay?" she whispers. He nods, thankful for this little caress, and her smile. He spits an olive pit into the palm of his hand. "Time for coffee!" Maloney rises. "Precious coffee from 'the neighbor.'"

"Let me help you," Jenny chirps, wriggling after him. Alice and the twins collect the dirty plates and set them in the dishwasher. The two girls seem captivated by Alice. They admire her tattoo, and she lets them touch the tiny stud in her nose. They run their fingers over her bracelet. Thomas observes the skinny girls, Alice's young woman's body, their trim waists, their straight backs, Alice's perfectly formed breasts under her T-shirt, the girls' small mounds. They're growing, he thinks, they're transforming. But I'm not.

"Well, Thomas," Kristin says. "Tell me how you've been."

"I'm doing all right."

"You look like a drowned cat, to put it bluntly."

"Thank you."

"Honestly, you look terrible. Have you been working too much?"

"No more than usual."

"Is it the break-in?"

He shakes his head.

"Or did Jacques's death affect you more than you thought it would?"

He shrugs his shoulders, irritated.

"But you've been more down in the dumps than usual," Patricia says.

"What do you mean by that?" Even Thomas can hear how tense he sounds.

"You had to go to the doctor and all that. He had to go to the doctor. He was depressed. I can tell Kristin about that, can't I, Thomas?"

"I'm sorry to hear that, my friend." Kristin sizes him up. "Life isn't for the faint of heart."

"I'm not faint of heart. C'mon. *You* of all people know what it was like for us, what things were like. You know very well I couldn't stand Jacques. I'm not shedding one tear over him, if that's what you think. On the contrary."

"Thomas . . ." Patricia gives him a hard look. Kristin drains her glass and calmly puts it back on the table. "What I mean is that life is *always* full of challenges. Disappointments. Piss and shit. Pardon my language. But what I mean is, you might as well get used to it. No one will throw you a pity party. And especially not at your age. You've just got to get back in the saddle."

"Back in the saddle!" Thomas leans back, shaking his head.

"We've been thinking about having a baby." Patricia sounds suddenly drunk and shrill.

"That sounds really lovely," Kristin says. "I didn't think you even wanted to have children, Thomas."

He mumbles something incomprehensible.

"When Helena said she wanted children, I was up in arms. I was terrified. I didn't want kids. Even though I was a midwife and delivered newborns every day, I didn't *want* any of my own. Now I can't imagine my life without the responsibility. All at once I understood why I must die someday. It's so simple: I'll die so that they can live. And so their children can live. I know that sounds terribly clichéd, but it's the truth."

"It sounds holier-than-thou," Thomas mutters.

Kristin flashes a resigned smile and exchanges a glance with Patricia. She gets up to help out in the kitchen. Patricia's voice is friendly and firm. "You're acting like a grumpy teenager. If you don't get your act together, I'm going home. This is your own family, here, and yet you act like this. Why? I just don't get it. And how can your mood shift so suddenly? We just fucked in the car. This is your last chance, Thomas." She opens her eyes wide: serious, mouth closed. He nods. "Yes," he says. She stands and walks to the kitchen, to the others. He pours more wine, all the way up to the rim of his glass, and drinks the tart, cherry-red liquid in big gulps. "Goddamnit, how can they serve this shit," he grumbles, pushing his chair back. Then he goes out to the barn.

The wind has died down. Apart from the rustling leaves, it's quiet. Standing motionless on the patio outside the sunroom, Thomas listens. Not a cloud in the sky. But he can't see the moon. The darkness seems completely impenetrable. Then he senses something near the house. The cold air is moist and heavy to breathe. From where he stands he can just make out the barn around six hundred feet ahead, a behemoth. He feels uneasy. It's as though something is tugging at his diaphragm, so that he can hardly stand still, as though something manic inside him is rapidly filling with air. Carefully he steps forward. The sheep are gray-white, hazy specks in what must be their pasture. A horse whinnies nearby. He sees the parked cars and some tall trees beside the main house. He tilts his head and glares up at the flicker of distant stars. A cat rubs itself against his leg. He jumps, startled, and stumbles forward until he reaches the decaying wooden barn. He follows its surface with his hands. Here's the sliding barn door, but where's the paddock door? He tries to recall where it is, but nothing comes to mind. The darkness is also in his head, and there's nothing more to do than feel his way forward until he finds it. And so, like a blind man hunched over, his breathing raspy and erratic, Thomas O'Mally Lindström slowly circles the large, enclosed structure. He trips over a branch. His shoes sink into the mud. Splinters jab into his fingers and hands. An owl hoots close by. Something whizzes toward him, then suddenly changes direction. Bats. He bumps into something made of cement. Not until he's halfway around the barn does he finally locate the door. It creaks when he pushes it open. In the middle of the room, there's a large wooden stove with a glass front; a crisp orange fire crackles in it, giving off some light. He feels his way toward the switch and snaps on the fluorescent lights that dangle from the ceiling on thin steel wires. There's the big loom, and the little one. Woven baskets stuffed with thick, soft balls of yarn, along with the various implements that are apparently used to process the raw wool. The straw-colored wooden floors are untidy, and smeared with dirt. A series of rectangular windows run the length of the barn all the way up under the roof beams, forming a kind of band of glass all the way around, except on the far wall where the sliding door is. The light in here must be amazing during the day, Thomas thinks, sitting on Helena's weaving bench. He runs his fingers along the warp's seam. Blue and purple shades, a flowing, expressionistic pattern. The fabric is coarse. This must be one of the large tapestries she's known for. He slumps. The fire crackles comfortingly. Air mattresses lie scattered across the floor, two and two together, with a good distance between each pair; they've already been made, with sheets and pillows and even neatly folded towels on every one. When he was young he slept here quite a bit. He and Jenny. He and Maloney. He and various girlfriends: Danuza, Seline, Beatriz. Back then the old, musty hay was still on the floor and the carcasses of rust-bucket tractors hulked in darkened corners. Thanks to the gaps in the barn's siding, mice and rats were a common sight whenever you woke at night and needed to piss. But the renovated space looks much different now, inviting and clean. They must have insulated the walls before hammering up drywall. Hard to believe they did it themselves. You can do so little for yourself, Thomas thinks, wading across the room to the nearest mattress. He slumps onto it, feeling like little more than a sack of clattering bones. Burying his face in the pillow, he smells the reassuring scent of fresh air and lavender.

He must've dozed off. Because all at once he sits up with a grunt, his heart thumping; someone's in the room. At first he can't see anyone, then he catches sight of Luke beside the wood stove. He's standing motionless, his back to Thomas, staring into the flames and doing something with his hands. But Thomas can't see what. Luke spins toward him suddenly. "Hey, Thomas," he says slowly, as though lingering over the sound of his name. "You already went to bed?" Luke's holding a rifle in his hands. He aims it at Thomas. "Bang!" he says, laughing, low. "I saw a light out here, and I wanted to look at Kristin's guns. They're not exactly new. They're practically antiques. It's a wonder she can hit anything with them." Luke disappears behind the stove and returns empty-handed. "There's dessert. You want to go back in?" Thomas gets to his feet, stuffing his shirt into his pants. Luke steps toward him. Thomas feels weirdly threatened. Exposed. But then Luke hands him a joint. "You got a light?"

They stand in the darkness underneath the awning, beside the pantry. Luke lights the joint and tokes deeply before handing it to Thomas. "Why not?" Thomas mutters, still groggy after his nap. The fat, white smoke smells sweet and good, of herbs and fresh straw. Thomas coughs. It's been a long time since he's smoked pot. "So you and Alice are going for a hike tomorrow?" he asks, puffing on the joint again.

"Do you want to come with us?" Luke says, looking straight at Thomas. These alert hazel eyes, pupils black as coal. For a moment, Luke's face is clearly visible in the light from the pantry. Then he draws back into the shadow again. "We're heading up into the mountains."

Thomas nods without thinking. "What time are you going?"

"Around ten, I think."

"Are you and Alice dating?" Thomas asks, hastily and suddenly.

Luke turns and regards him. Then he chuckles. "Can't say that we are. I think of her more like a cousin."

"A cousin?"

"Yeah, something like that. She's family to me." Thomas can't believe what he's hearing. Alice sure as hell isn't family to Luke. That's an insult.

"What do you actually do? How do you make money?"

"Oh, all sorts of things, Thomas. For me that's the only way to live. It takes many bricks to build a house, so to speak."

Luke takes the joint from Thomas. Their hands touch for a split second. Luke's fingers are long and slender, his skin warm. Thomas pulls his hand away. "And what does 'all sorts of things' mean?"

"It varies. I deal in this and that. I bartend off and on and . . ."

"At Frank and Fatso's?"

"There too. Yeah, why?"

"Just wondering," Thomas says. Luke flicks the butt of the joint into the grass. From down in the grove come the sharp shrieks of birds, the flailing of wings. The sound grows louder. A desperate, hoarse screech, a commotion. "The owl's hunting," Luke smiles, his face once more within the patch of window light, but pale as a moon. Of course it's the owl hunting, Thomas thinks, you don't need to tell me. Fucking know-it-all.

"He hunts them down in the sky, he gives them a grave in the breezes. The sparrows," Luke continues, his voice husky.

"What did you say?" Thomas stares at Luke's half-turned face.

"A grave. For the birds," Luke says, "they don't stand a chance. It snatches them in mid-flight. And then it takes their chicks."

Thomas wants to say something more, something about the poem, something about his father, but he's so edgy and nonplussed that he can't utter a single word. Someone raps on the window from inside. Alice waves for them to come in.

Luke has turned and now looks directly at him. In a clear voice he says, "Did you bring good shoes?"

Thomas scrutinizes him, puzzled.

"Didn't you say you want to go hiking with us?"

Luke waves at Alice and steps toward the door, but Thomas holds him back, gripping his shoulder. "One more thing."

Luke pauses and turns his head.

"Your mother still alive?"

"Why do you ask that?" There's something unpleasant about the way he says it, a kind of snarl.

"Just wondering."

"Why do you want to know?"

"I'm trying to get to know you better, that's all," Thomas says, "now that you think we're family. Now that you quote Celan." Luke smiles as if he's withholding a secret, his mouth closed. He glances at the ground. His lush eyelashes throw shadows on his cheeks. Alice raps again, this time impatiently. Thomas grips Luke's jacket more firmly. "I knew Rose when I was a kid. She was just a young girl then." He feels the pot's effect now and, to his relief, his voice sounds gentle and friendly. Luke relaxes.

"Okay. Yes. She's alive. But I have practically zero contact with her."

"Because you don't want to see her?"

"Maybe," Luke says, grabbing the doorknob.

"Fatso must feel bad about that. He really likes his sister, doesn't he?"

Luke doesn't respond, and Thomas lets go of his shoulder. To Thomas, at the moment the door swings open the inside light appears to wash over them like a wave of ocher-colored desert sand. Alice's smiling face is close to theirs. "We've got frozen custard," she says, holding the door for them. He's high and he's hot. His skin prickles in an especially pleasant way, and he wants to laugh out loud.

He glances down at himself and feels surprisingly happy: His legs move of their own accord, he's gliding forward. He thinks of an old song and recalls every detail of the guitar solo that followed the first refrain—it's as though the band's playing right in his ears. A song from the deepest recesses of his mind, he thinks. Hard to believe it's still in there after all these years.

Maloney dishes out the frozen custard, which Jenny has decorated with canned fruits. Coffee steams in mugs. The twins cling to their mother, but when Alice sits, they flock to her instead. She tugs one onto her lap and wraps her in her arms. It's Nina; the girl blushes, her eyes beaming happily. Maya sits cautiously beside them, and Alice leans over and whispers to her, as if she wants to be democratic, as if she wants to share her caresses equally: It looks as though she's asking her something. Maya nods and glances at the floor. An idiotic smile is now plastered on Luke's face. He greedily shovels dessert into his mouth. His lower lip tugs downward, as if it's trying to locate his chin, making the glistening red flap of skin behind his lip visible. Helena sits next to Jenny. Thomas can't make out what they're saying. What he hears instead is the clack of spoons on the porcelain. After shifting seats, Patricia's now next to Kristin. "Where'd you go?" Maloney asks Thomas, getting his attention. "Were you out looking at the stars? Hey!" He lowers his voice, and leans across the table. "You look like someone *seeing* stars right now. What the hell, were you smoking dope?" And almost as a whisper: "Where did you get it? Is there more?"

"Ask Luke."

Maloney shoots a glance toward Luke, who's ladling more frozen custard onto his plate. He drops a hunk of canned peach onto the floor and leans over to retrieve it, but then gives up and focuses on his new portion instead.

"You could've invited me, O'Mally. What kind of friend are you?"

Thomas smiles goofily and wants to say something. But Maloney stares enviously across the long table and mumbles, "Goddamn, he's sure got the munchies." Luke dries custard from his cheek with his napkin. His red eyes meet Thomas's, and he smiles from ear to ear. Thomas can't help but smile back; it feels unnatural and false not to. The new softness in his face is irresistible.

"It's time for a game!" Kristin calls out, standing. "Come. Shall we repair to the parlor?" There are crimson splotches on her cheeks. She gestures invitingly with her arms. "C'mon! Thomas and Maloney. Let's go! Maya and Nina have prepared questions." And so everyone tumbles more or less tipsy and bubbly into the living room. Alice crawls immediately onto the couch with the twins clutching onto her like a pair of small monkeys. Luke collapses into the big wingback chair before anyone can tell him that's Kristin's seat. Slow on the uptake, Thomas winds up in a beanbag chair that's impossible to get comfortable in; it feels awkward sitting so low to the floor, knees touching his chest. Patricia settles on a footstool, and Maloney brings chairs from the kitchen for himself and Jenny. The low-hanging, rose-pink rice paper lamps cast a reddish sheen over the living room. The dog ambles in and plops down at Maloney's feet. Helena sits, erect and cross-legged, on one of the many lambskin rugs adorning the floor. Kristin stretches out behind her, looping herself around Helena, curling her arm, and resting her head on her palm. "Okay girls," she says, nodding to the twins. "You're up." Maya begins, stuttering, until her sister talks over her. "So, we want to ask you some questions. Or Kristin told us we should ask you about some things (Kristin shakes her head, smiling). First—I mean first question: 'What is your favorite food?'" They respond cheerfully. Maloney shouts, "Anything fatty!" Patricia gives the question serious consideration, thinking for some time before deciding on stewed rhubarb. Closing her eyes, Helena says, "Oysters," to which Kristin makes a surprised face. Luke says, "What? My favorite food? Do I have a favorite?"

"Yes, you do!" Nina screeches eagerly.

"Lasagna. Or turbot. And frozen custard!" Patricia and Helena apparently feel inspired to applaud excitedly. And so it continues. Favorite film. Best friend ("Maloney," Thomas says. "Oh, now I'm not so sure," Maloney responds, causing Jenny to howl with laughter), but when Alice falls silent so too does the entire living room, and then she whispers, "You, Luke" and glances at him, looking lovely. Beneath his giddy pot-mask, Thomas stiffens, his bones stiffen though his muscles are soft, his heart stiffens in its calm rhythm, skips a beat or maybe races ahead too quickly. Something happens that doesn't feel good. "I thought it was Maria," Jenny says, challenging her daughter.

"Not anymore. Now it's Luke," Alice says, lifting her chin. Then comes Maya's next question, and they've reached the end of the game: "Who do you miss the most in your family?"

"My father," Nina whispers. Helena and Kristin look at the girl in dismay. "But you don't *have* a father, we had a sperm donor, you know that, right?" Helena sounds as if she has wool in her mouth.

"That's why I miss him," Nina mumbles, tucking her head under Alice's arm.

"I miss my mother most of all." It's Jenny's turn, and her lips begin to quiver. "I really mean that. I do, Thomas!" She's clearly drunk, her eyes are swimming. "Though I was so little . . . when she *disappeared*. I have . . . a hole inside me where she was. I do!" She lifts her chin, a martyred expression on her face. "Oh." Jenny lowers her head and Maloney hugs her. "You cry so easily, sweetheart."

I'm in a circus, Thomas thinks. An emotional circus. It's a TV show. It's a group therapy roundtable with some sorry psychologist. Then he hears Maya's clear voice calling out his name: "Thomas? Uncle Thomas? Who do you miss the most in your family? They don't have to be dead."

"Nobody," he says. "I don't miss anyone. I'm not sentimental."

"Ha!" Jenny interrupts. "You're a liar. He's unbelievably sentimental. Just like his uncles. He even looks like them. Or he did anyway, back when he was still young and handsome."

"Yes, he does," Kristin says. "I don't know if they were sentimental, but they're the ones I miss the most. My brothers. I miss my brothers."

"That's right," Helena says, reaching back to touch Kristin's knee. "You do."

"Don't you miss Mom?" Jenny asks.

"Of course. You know I do, Jenny."

"Where are your brothers?" Maloney asks, following a silence. You fucking know the answer to that, Thomas thinks. I told you.

"They're dead. Many years ago now. Meningitis. The doctor came too late. We lived way out in the country back then."

"In the big house," Nina says.

"That's right. In the big house. Tom died ten hours after Jon. They were only eighteen. The exact same age as you now, Alice."

Everyone turns toward Alice with her ultra-short hair, sprawled on the couch beneath the wall tapestries. The two skinny girls are twined around her like yarn on a spinning wheel.

"Relax, people," Alice says, grinning. "*I'm* not dead yet."

Kristin and Maloney are the first to laugh. The others follow suit.

"Nope, you're not!"

"Thank God!"

Liberating laughter, Thomas thinks, smiling to himself. His eyes slide shut, his body is so relaxed and heavy that he couldn't possibly budge an inch. And it feels so good, so good. He imagines his two uncles in the big yard, their short blond hair, shiny and glistening in the sunlight, slicked back, their knobby knees poking out of their dark shorts; the twins whom his mother told him about when he was in bed, because he so badly wanted to know about them, because he pestered her; his mother's voice warm and low, maybe she made up all the stories just to make him happy. Tom and Jon, the magical uncles who were now in heaven, the innocent pair who'd played so divinely on the piano in the conservatory, who had such a great future ahead of them. And then: dead, gone, in a single feverish day. The doctor stood there with his bag, unable to bring them back to life. The images flit through Thomas on delicate, flailing wings. "Tell me about the time Tom fell in the lake." "Tell me about Jon! That one about the loose tooth that he swallowed." "Or that time they got a little horse, and you taught them how to ride." "Or when Tom painted a huge tiger on the kitchen wall!" His child-voice is hoarse and extremely close, practically oozing from his adult vocal chords, his throat. He can almost feel his Adam's apple vibrating. He can feel his mother stroking his neck. A mosquito bite itches on his thigh from under the duvet. And there's a wall light with its blue screen, its special evening light. His mother's silhouette on the wallpaper. Later, he's rustled awake by Patricia. She helps him out of the beanbag chair and, with Kristin's assistance, guides him into the cold night, across the yard to the barn, and he struggles to get his long legs into the sleeping bag while Patricia, irritated, sits up, then down, waiting beside him in *her* sleeping bag. All this remains in a foggy haze—until he wakes in the middle of the night to a chorus of breathing, the sleeping flock. He was so incredibly tired, vaguely recalls that Luke resembled a kind of Jesus figure or king sitting in the wingback chair, and that Jenny couldn't stop talking about her uncles, whom she didn't even remember, that Helena missed her grandmother, who'd had a good head on her shoulders, and smelled of oranges (though that could've been something he'd made up), and that he'd thought he was the only normal person in his entire family of bastards and outcasts. Now he believes this was unnecessarily hostile on his part. He's in his sleeping bag, his feet sweaty. Around him it's pitch dark. He's insanely thirsty. He tries to conjure up images of himself as a boy, his mother. But now the images are gone. Something tickles his left ear, he puts his finger in and wiggles it around. When he pulls the finger out, he can hear a zipper slowly unzipping, after which someone stands very quietly, and begins to move searchingly, barefooted, across the floor. He props himself up on his elbows and sees that it's Luke with a flashlight; its bluish cone guides him, a well-lit path leading to the door. Luke gently unbolts the door, then he's outside.

Luke's gone for a long time. Jenny whimpers in her sleep. Someone rolls over, it must be Maloney, judging by the heft of the body. Who knows whether they've screwed here in the barn. An unpleasant thought. Maloney and his sister, bodily fluids, mucus, sperm. At last he falls asleep and wakes to what he believes is a gunshot in the distance, a sudden blast in the night. But now it's silent. Patricia breathes slowly and evenly next to his face. For a long time he lies awake, listening to something rustling near the loom, and now dawn's approaching, trickling through the high windows. He's startled by Maloney suddenly clambering to his feet and stumbling across the floor in his underwear. The door clicks shut behind him. Thomas stands up and follows him; outside the morning's cool and foggy, and he steps barefooted onto the dewy, moist grass. Maloney's pissing spread-legged against a tree. His ass glows white. The sky's ash gray, and the landscape unfolds to every side: there's the lake with the rustling black-brown rushes along the banks, the rickety pier, there the pastures and fields, there a handful of grazing horses with a skinny foal, there the sheep are lying in thick clusters. A wind chime jangles in an acacia tree. Maloney turns, showing his sleepy, sulky face. "Good morning," Thomas says, shivering. Maloney shakes his penis. "Fucking Christ, it's cold," he says, as he makes his way past Thomas, wanting to head back to the barn. But Thomas grabs his arm. "Why didn't you tell me you're seeing Jenny? And that you were coming? I was shocked. That's not good form, Maloney."

Maloney looks straight at him. "You don't need to know everything. Do you? I figured it'd be less of a problem for you to see us together than to hear about it. After all, you've been a little . . . what can I say . . . tense lately. I didn't want to fan the flames."

"Fan the flames? What are you talking about?"

"Thomas, it's 6:00 A.M., and I'm fucking freezing my nuts off. Can't this wait?"

"*Are* you two dating, or what?"

Maloney grins sleepily. "For now, yes. I think so. Yeah, I guess we are. Now get some sleep. You're all discombobulated, man. Sleep's what you need."

Maloney claps him reassuringly on his shoulder and walks, leaning forward, back to the barn. He closes the door carefully behind him. Thomas clenches his teeth and feels his jaw, tense and hard. Except for his socks, he's wearing all of his clothes. Patricia apparently couldn't get them off when she helped him into bed. The back of his skull throbs a little, shooting down into the muscles in his neck, or perhaps it's the opposite way around. He raises his head and gazes across the lake. A gaggle of geese has landed on the bank. They're pecking at the grass. The farmhouse is dark and quiet. The birds aren't chattering. Even the wind chime is silent. The silence is almost terrifying. Thomas strides back to his sleeping bag. Luke's lying on his side, still as a mouse, his back to Alice. His wild red-brown hair is tousled, his shiny, youthful skin gleams with a greenish hue, olive-like. He appears to be in deep sleep. He's got his arms folded across his chest. A tattoo of a heart spiked through with a sword intertwined with green vines adorns his muscular bicep. How pathetic. Does he box? It'd fit the stereotype, Thomas thinks, swallowing a mouthful of air. Someone like him. How clichéd. He stretches out in his sleeping bag. For a brief instant Patricia opens her eyes and looks at him as if from another planet, distant and strange. Then she's asleep again. Soon Thomas himself is asleep, a heavy, dead slumber; he wakes only when Jupiter sniffs at his crotch. At some point he must have kicked his way out of the sleeping bag. He's alone in the barn now. Outside, the sun appears to be shining.

Everyone's gathered in the kitchen when Thomas stumbles inside, the dog nipping at his heels. There're scrambled eggs and bacon and roasted tomatoes. It's 9:30. Helena pulls bread from the oven with potholders. "Who got up early to bake?" Thomas asks. Helena raises her hand. "It doesn't take long," she says. "I've got my good sourdough, and I set it out in the evening." Alice pours apple cider into glasses. Maloney brews coffee. The twins sit at the kitchen table, bent over their bowls of corn flakes. Their long, thin legs dangle and they scowl sleepily. "*I* didn't get up early," Maya says. Jenny enters, dressed in a checkered jacket and skirt. "I don't see how you manage to stay warm up here during the winter. It's brutally cold. And it's May!"

"We have a wood stove. Plus the outdoor wood pellet furnace. We get by." Kristin looks a bit worn-out. Pale and a tad gruff.

"It's super cold up here in the winter," Nina mumbles. "We have to walk around in felt slippers. They're sooo ugly."

"You want to go on a hike?" Thomas asks the girls. They shake their heads and pinch their lips shut. "We hate hiking," Maya says.

"Ah, aren't you two grumpy this morning," Helena says, running her hand over Nina's back. "You need to brush the horses and slice fruit for the dessert." This bit of news doesn't appear to please the two girls.

"Did we stay up late yesterday?" Thomas asks, taking a sip of his hot, strong coffee.

"You didn't," Alice smiles, and everyone laughs as if at a private joke. "You still want to hike with us? We're leaving soon. You can make yourself some lunch."

"Then we'll be rid of all the men," Jenny says, "except you, Maloney." She looks up at him, her eyes gleaming.

"And you," Kristin adds, scratching the dog behind his ear, "Isn't that right, Jupiter?" The dog wags its fat, stumpy tail and waddles under the table.

"No way I'm going for a hike," Maloney says. "Take good care of my friend here. He's not used to fresh air."

Once Thomas has devoured a helping of eggs and tomatoes and finished his coffee, Helena helps him find the cold cuts in the fridge. Everyone's sitting or standing in the spacious kitchen, the windows are pearled with dew, the thin gray-green light is milky and soft. Luke, squatting against a wall, runs his fingers through his hair. "We figure we'll be back around 3:00," he says with his deep, warm, confidence-inspiring voice. "But if we're out later than that, don't worry. I've got a map."

So he's got a map, Thomas thinks. He's prepared. He's dressed like a wanderer in his flannel shirt, shorts, and hiking books. Even goddamn knee-high socks. Probably even has a walking stick. And a canteen. And a fucking compass. It doesn't fit with his tattoo. The boy is many things, he thinks with a shudder, all too many things at once. What's his deal? What kind of creature is he?

"Are you coming, Uncle Thomas?" Alice asks, turning her pretty face toward him. And then they leave. He kisses Patricia and whispers into her hair. "Thank you for putting me to bed."

"Kristin was the one who schlepped you to the barn."

"Thanks anyway." She still has this lone wolf independence about her, and that strangeness he saw when she opened her eyes the night before, and she's put distance between them again. But she accepts another kiss from him, leaning her head against his shoulder for a brief moment.

They drive in Luke's metallic-blue Opel. He eagerly explains that he's spent a lot of time fixing it up. "I got the seats from a friend who works at the incineration plant," he says, shifting gears, "and I traded my way to a new motor. It runs like a dream." Luke stamps on the gas pedal, accelerating. Thomas sits in the backseat. The sun's already higher in the sky, but the light remains murky, as if filtered through a fine-meshed cloth. Luke has chosen a route that's supposed to be well marked. "The inclines aren't too steep," he says. "We can park at thirteen hundred feet above sea level. There's supposed to be an amazing view from the Bearclaw. I thought we could eat lunch up there."

"The Bearclaw?"

"One of the highest points in the area," Luke says. "You can see all the way to the sea."

"You know this area?" Thomas asks.

"A little. But not the Bearclaw. I've only read about that."

They drive for almost an hour, passing small farms and house-clusters with yards like automobile graveyards and free-range chickens pecking at the ground. A gas station, a signpost for some small town. Alice tells them how Kristin has begun working at the hospital, and that she commutes an hour each way. She used to work at the midwife's clinic in one of the villages. She can drive the girls now, so they don't have to ride the school bus. But they have to leave the house by 6:30 every morning. "And they hate getting up early. I think they hate going to school, too. So did I."

Luke stares ahead, his face revealing nothing.

Gradually the thin layer of clouds dissolve and the bright sun beats down on the landscape. New spring buds grow along the shoulder of the road, yellow-green fields extend beyond, and pines speckle the slopes. They turn off the main road and slowly ascend the tortuous mountain pass. With the eggs sloshing around in his stomach, Thomas feels carsick, nauseated. Finally they reach the parking lot and get out. There are no other cars. "It looks like we have everything to ourselves," Luke says, satisfied. Thomas lights a cigarette. It's windy up here, and there's that special mountain silence that's not a silence, but the wind whipping across the earth, through the leaves.

And there's birdsong here, and cicadas, and the buzz of bees and wasps. A thick deposit of moldering pine needles covers the ground. A small swarm of butterflies circle a cluster of purple flowers. The view from here is impressive. A couple of high-altitude lakes, clear green in color due to the calcareous soil below it, and steep black cliffs. But there's vegetation where they stand, and the trail leads into the trees and disappears.

"You guys ready?" Luke asks, shrugging into his backpack. He smiles at Alice and squints for a moment. The bright sunlight makes his eyes appear even more golden. His high cheekbones rise above his smooth cheeks.

"It's so beautiful here," Alice says excitedly, hopping forward. When she moves, her windbreaker swishes. Since her hair is stubbly, her neck seems long. The tattooed snake appears to slither every time she turns her head. "Are you coming, Uncle Thomas?"

Uncle Thomas is coming. Luke takes the lead on the narrow trail, with Alice right behind him and Thomas bringing up the rear. He decides he'll stay in the back. He won't compete with *Mr. Hiker*, won't give Luke the satisfaction. His back aches. He didn't sleep well on the thin air mattress. He runs his hand across his unshaven chin. He didn't even brush his teeth.

Soon he begins to sweat profusely. The trail grows steeper, and now and then they pass between astonishingly precipitous crevasses with views deep into the abyss. Overturned trunks lay scattered across a thick bed of ferns and nettles. The winter storms have clearly ravaged this place and ripped enormous trees up by the roots. The sun's hot and piercing now. Alice sings as she jumps over a babbling brook. Thomas is short of breath. After they've walked for more than an hour, they pause to rest. Thomas doesn't need to lag behind on purpose, it happens automatically. For some time he watches Alice and Luke walking along chatting far ahead of him. What are they discussing? Lactic acid flows into his shins. When he climbs upward, his knees crack, and his lower back aches. By the time he reaches the others, they're seated on the grass drinking water from the bottles in Luke's backpack. Alice bites into a chocolate bar and spreads out her windbreaker so Thomas can sit beside her. They're both sitting cross-legged and it looks as though they could stay that way for hours. But Thomas can't do that, his backache won't allow it. Greedily he guzzles water then plops onto his back, staring into the cloudless, ice-blue sky. He hears a mosquito approaching, and smacks it on his neck.

"Beautiful weather," Luke says, closing his eyes. "Can you feel how thin the air is up here?"

Alice has also brought coffee. They take turns drinking from the thermos cap. Thomas smokes. Luke lies on his stomach and sticks a blade of grass between his lips. As he observes Thomas, he plays with it, pushing it around in his mouth, first the left corner, then the right. "I'm hearing rumors that you're going to expand your store," he says.

"Where did you hear that?"

"From me," Alice says. "I told Luke. That you're offering me an apprenticeship."

"Yeah?"

"But I don't know," she says, putting away the chocolate. "I have no idea what I want to do."

"But you'll only find out what you want to do if you give something a try." With some effort Thomas sits up. "We'll just agree on a trial period. Then you can decide whether it's something for you. You need a job in any case, right? You don't have any money, you said."

She glances down. "Maybe."

"What do you mean by 'maybe'?"

"I'll think about it."

"Don't think too long. I need an answer before Tuesday."

"Before Tuesday?" Luke tilts his head and spits out the grass.

"Yes."

Luke gives him a long, thoughtful nod. "Before Tuesday," he repeats, as if to himself. The way Luke nods, the way he closes his eyes, as if he knows more than he's showing—even though he might not at all—gets on Thomas's nerves. He forces himself not to snap at him. Something tells him that he needs to avoid doing that. Something's at stake between them, Luke's in charge of this hike, he's the one calling the shots. It's best that Thomas know his place, as the tag-along that he is, and it also has to do with his age, and dignity, but Thomas can't quite decipher how it all fits together, what it *is*. It's just this intuition that tells him not to snap. *Do not cause any trouble now.* Luke rolls onto his side and rests his head on his fist for a moment. Then he scrambles to his feet and they all continue up the trail. Though Thomas tries to keep up with the youths, he's quickly soaked in sweat. His feet slide in his shoes. He wipes sweat from his forehead with his arm, then blows at the hair that keeps falling across his forehead. They suddenly encounter a chamois standing on the trail, motionless, perhaps one hundred feet ahead. It's reddish brown, with a darker stripe ridging its spine, and gnarled horns twisting backward. It stares at them, black bulging eyes, nostrils quivering, ears nearly flat against its head. Then it leaps elegantly into the trees and is gone. They've stopped to watch, and Thomas has reached Alice.

"It was a male," Luke says. "They're solitary."

"Solitary?" Alice leans against Thomas. "What do you mean?"

"They're loners. The females live in groups of up to twenty."

"You'd almost think you studied biology," Thomas says breathlessly.

"I just know what I need to know," Luke says, with the precocious air of someone who always thinks he's right. He scratches his arm. "What I need to know. We're almost there. I think we have another half-hour or so, but the path gets so steep soon that we'll have to scale the mountain."

"Scale?" Thomas stops. "What do you mean by 'scale?'"

Luke laughs. "We're ascending a mountain. Pretend you're a chamois. It'll be much easier."

"He looks a little bit like a chamois. A tired little chamois," Alice clucks. "Oh, you look really beat, are you okay?"

Grimly, Thomas asks for a sip of water.

"You can also wait for us here," Luke says. "If you can't go on."

"I can go on."

After they've walked a stretch, the trail curves and abruptly ends. A narrow, grassy clearing followed by sheer cliff walls rises steeply above them. Climbing plants speckle the rock, blueberries or crowberry, maybe club moss. A partridge alights, flapping its wings. There's no trail, but the area is demarcated in red, and you can see worn patches of ground between the markers where others have walked, or rather, crawled. At the summit there appears to be a kind of plateau. The wind cools Thomas's sweaty body. His throat is parched, though he'd just gulped water. He wipes his hands on his pants. Alice and Luke have already begun scaling, and Thomas watches them balance their strong bodies perfectly, their thighs hoisting them steadily and easily upward. They don't falter. They don't need to clutch at the tussocks of grass before they leap like he does. His legs tremble, and he doesn't dare look down. But then he does and it's dizzying. All the way down. All the way down to hell, he thinks. If I slip, I'm a goner. If I make even the slightest misstep. A grave in the breezes. He sniffles, moistens his lips. Toward the west, the mountainside pitches steeply downward, and around two-thirds of the way there he can see a wide, fresh spring flowing into a waterfall. The water rages over the mountain, gushing into the empty space, foamy and roaring, white and angry, but he's so far away that he can't hear it. He realizes that, despite the heat, his teeth are chattering. He heaves himself up, from notch to notch, from one cluster of roots to another. It feels as though his upper arms can't go on, as if he's going to be forced to let go, to fall. Three eagles circle the mountain, riding the wind before swooping into the valley and out of his line of sight. He looks skyward. Forward, he thinks, one small step at a time, no more than that. Up to that rock, that tussock, follow the demarcated area. If he tilts his head almost completely back, he can see Alice's ass. The soles of her shoes are orange. She's cinched her windbreaker around her waist, and she strides confidently; she turns halfway around and looks down at him, smiling. "We're almost there," she calls out. He doesn't have the faintest clue how he manages to scale the rest of the way, his heart pounding, sweat dribbling into his eyes, his breathing raspy. He coughs, and suddenly he's clutching the edge and hauling himself over, and there he sees Luke standing with his arm around Alice. It looks as though he's showing her something, pointing at a spot in the far distance. He's removed his backpack. Thomas gets on all fours and then finally, gasping, he stands up.

"Look," Luke says, "three eagles."

"I saw them," Thomas grumbles.

"Uncle Thomas! You made it!" Alice hops enthusiastically up and down.

"Of course I made it. What do you take me for?"

Alice grins. "Come have a look. You really can see the sea from here. It's awesome, Luke! So awesome. Thank you for bringing us up here." She strokes his arm.

"My pleasure," he smiles.

They stand watching the eagles drift across the sky. But Thomas quickly sits down. Little by little he catches his breath.

"Doesn't your mother live out here somewhere?" he ventures.

Luke nods curtly. Then he unzips his backpack. "I'm hungry," he says.

"Yes, food! And we've got sodas." Alice eagerly begins to unpack. Like a little girl playing at going on a hike, and that's what she is, too,

Thomas thinks. Just a little girl playing grown up. Soon I'll have to convince her to play store.

Luke wolfs his food. He bites into his sandwich. His jaws grind at a measured, rhythmic pace. He doesn't waste a crumb, his fingers don't get greasy. Alice has kicked off her shoes. She's sprawled out placidly, a blissful smile curling at her lips, her arms at her sides. "Ah," she whispers. "Complete freedom." Thomas digs into his sandwich. Rarely has anything tasted so delicious. A ripe tomato virtually explodes in his mouth; its acidic taste, its sweetness, its juice dribbling down his chin and onto his shirt, where it leaves a stain. The ham is salty and dry. The soda fizzes on his tongue. And there's cheese. And a protein bar made with nuts and honey. They share the rest of the lukewarm coffee. It's only at this moment that Thomas begins taking it all in. The plateau's overrun with bristly grass. There are harebells and narrow-leafed thyme and varieties of cranesbill, white, rose-pink, blue. There are low-hanging, richly blooming baby blue eyes and saxifrage plants, with their tiny, yellow, distended inflorescence. There are cacti. Alice finds a small, unassuming white orchid dappled with wine-red dots. He'd had a short-lived passion for botany once, and this passion returns to him now. *Plants in mountainous regions.* Thomas scrabbles to his feet. Feels a tingling sense of joy scanning the countryside; the view is as awesome as Luke promised. You really can see the sea from here. The sandy beaches, a white belt running as far as the eye can see, and the water that almost seems to meld with the sky. He rotates 360 degrees and stares over the green forests, green lakes, green valleys, and green fields. Another mountain chain rising majestically, brown and gray. The snow on its summits. Everything is far away and deep down or high, high up, but also completely, incredibly close. Here, ants as big as fingernails crawl across Alice's naked foot, here reptiles sun themselves on flat stones, here one of the eagles nosedives and comes so close that they can see its enormous wingspan and its sharp, curved beak. Thomas ducks involuntarily. He smiles at Luke, and Luke returns the smile, the smile sliding up his face; there's a gleam in his eyes now, something Thomas has never seen in him: he's exuberant, abandoning himself to the moment. The energy from the food now pumps through Thomas. Here they are at the top of the world, and unexpectedly, like a gift, he feels overcome with joy, which they share in common. Alice giggles excitedly. Luke joins in. An odd solidarity unites them. Because together they've reached the top, because together they are here. It's suddenly very simple and very right. His endorphins rush through him like a cool, refreshing shower, like the first ripple of an orgasm, his fingertips prickle, his feet throb, he breathes deeply and exhales: I am alive, he thinks, I am happy; he laughs out loud and the others laugh, too.

They begin the descent. Now the others can see, if they look up, the soles of Thomas's shoes. He feels his way forward with his feet, sliding only once. It's faster going this way. He stays focused. He doesn't look down. He leaps the last step and lands squarely. The return trip along the spine of the thickly-wooded mountain is far easier than it had been going up, though he can feel his thighs burning, and the ball of his left foot grows especially sore and tired. They walk side by side. Alice puts on her windbreaker again. They chat. The tone between them remains friendly, like up on the plateau. Thomas describes his new store. A little too frenetically, he talks at great length about how he plans to decorate it, how the old countertop will have to be sanded and varnished, how they'll have to dress up one of the walls with a beautiful patterned wallpaper, maybe something with dark-blue and gold? The rest will be painted off-white. And the floor, should he paint it black? Or go with a dark stain? "The back room will be really comfy. You can see huge trees in the courtyard in there. The light's incredible."

Alice seems increasingly interested.

"If you need a hand renovating it, let me know," Luke says.

Thomas scrutinizes him. "You mean that?"

He nods. "Absolutely."

"That's nice of you."

Luke shrugs. Does he seem a little shy now, a little coy? What would she actually do, Alice asks more scrupulously. In her own assessment, she'd be good at helping customers, because she's *service-minded.* She also thinks she could learn how to keep the books. "I'm awful at math, but I can count," she says. Thomas thinks to himself: Now we're playing store. He suggests she come in on Monday, so she can *nose around.* Just five or six hours a day. It'll be a while yet before they open the other store.

"So I can keep my job at the same time," she says, kicking a small, knotted branch.

"You have a job?"

"Yeah, but it's only in the evenings."

"You didn't tell me that. What are you doing?"

"Telephone sales, sort of." She pulls the hood of her windbreaker up.

Thomas eases his pace, so that Luke can pass him. He has a bad feeling about this. He lowers his voice. "What exactly do you do, Alice? What kind of job is it? Please tell me."

She doesn't respond.

"Tell me. You don't need to hide it. Not from me you don't."

"You want me to be totally honest?"

"Yes. Totally."

"It's an escort service. I just answer the phone." When Thomas doesn't respond, she goes on. "That means I'm not an escort, if that's what you're thinking. Not at all."

He stares at her.

"I'm not!"

"Who got you the job?"

"Does it even matter? I've only been there for a few days. I needed the money really bad." She pauses. Then she looks at him from inside the hood. Her face is in shadow. She says, "Mom knows."

"*Jenny* knows?"

She nods. "Yeah. And she doesn't care. I have to make a living somehow, right? It doesn't bother me, it's just a job. It's better than cleaning houses."

They reach Luke, who has stopped to wait for them. Conversation grinds to a halt. They stride down a steep hill, the forest floor dense and dark with lean, lofty spruces, redwood, arborvitae, and evergreens stretching toward the light. They come to a patch of birch forest. Sunlight filters through the leaves, shimmering onto them. Gravel crunches beneath their feet, and from time to time they smell rot, mushrooms, wet ground, and then suddenly the scent shifts to wood sorrel and elderberry. They walk in silence, side by side. Alice pushes back her hood again. Luke tells them about a camping trip he took when he was thirteen, not far from here. At night he and his friend were afraid of bears.

"This was in the fall, right before they hibernate—when they're desperate and hungry. We lay in the tent clutching each other. The next morning we went home. Later I learned they don't even have bears here."

"Did you live up here as a boy?"

"No. We lived in the city until I was nine. Then my mother moved up here with the idiot, so I visited a few times. Mostly I lived with Fatso."

Luke seems more relaxed now, even his body. He's not being sneaky or calculated; his movements are freer, his face softer. Though Thomas's mood briefly darkened at the thought of Alice working for an escort service, he nevertheless believes, at this moment, that things will work out, and even as Luke tells them how he loved visiting Jacques when he was a boy, Thomas can't help but think of the new store, its interior design, its clientele—young people. He can picture it, and the images flit one after the other, coupled with the strong aroma of fresh paint and wood, so he only hears bits and pieces of Luke's story.

"But what did you actually do when you weren't fishing?" Alice asks.

"Oh, just about everything. Often we just sat in the living room watching TV. Sports. Usually. Sometimes he let me drink soda. Or he'd help me with my homework."

Thomas can't believe his own ears. "He did *what*?"

"Mostly history and geography. And he'd tell me about his youth."

Thomas looks at Luke's profile in disbelief. Then he shakes his head.

"What did he say?" Alice squeezes her head between her hands, as if checking that it's still there.

"How he'd carry on at the big dance halls, for one. He never went out without his hat and vest. I remember him saying that. Always his hat and vest. And a newly ironed shirt of Egyptian cotton. Polished, shiny shoes. He showed me a photograph of himself sitting at a long bar with a drink in his hand. Toasting the camera. I still remember his smile in that photo, a big, wide smile. He was very young then, and dark-haired. His hat lay on the bar. It was white. I used to think a lot about that Egyptian cotton, how exotic and strange it was. I'd never heard of Egyptian cotton before. And sometimes . . ."

Luke stares deeply between the trees, as if he's seen something interesting in the forest. "Sometimes there were others too. My uncle and Frank and many I didn't know. I'd sit in the corner listening to the men talk. They'd forget I was there and it wasn't until they were leaving that Jacques would see me and say, You're still here, Kid. Go home, Kid. Then he'd put his big hand on my shoulder."

"So that's why they call you The Kid!" Alice smiles excitedly, as if she's solved one of life's great mysteries. "I didn't understand why. But that's why, isn't it?"

"Yup. Jacques started that. But I was the only child there. Just me and . . ."

"I remember that photograph," Thomas interjects, sounding more curt than he'd intended. "But I've never heard anything about dance halls or Egyptian cotton. He probably just made that stuff up to entertain you. Or to make himself seem better than he was."

"But back then he really *was* like that," Alice says. "That's what Mom told me. That when he met grandma he went to all these really fancy places and that he wouldn't have met her otherwise, because *she* went to those places. Or something like that."

"He met my mother at a costume party thrown by one of her fellow students. She studied art history at that point. Later she dropped out. But when they met each other she was a student. No more than twenty years old. Jacques lived in an apartment near the river, it had a great view, tall ceilings. He had a rich night life, knew everything about it, and she was enthralled by his bohemian lifestyle. They got married. My grandfather was furious."

"What about your grandmother? Was she furious too?" Alice asks.

"She died young. Just like my mother."

"Also breast cancer?"

"Yes."

"What happened then?"

"They had me. Not long after that Jenny came along. He had money then, he worked a bit for his uncle—a goldsmith—but he also dabbled in seedier things. My mother didn't know anything about that. But when Jenny was really little things changed. His uncle fired him after he stole money and gold from him, but he didn't report him to the police—because he was ashamed that his own nephew had swindled him. That's when Jacques began his career in crime.

They moved out of the hip apartment by the river. And he started beating my mother."

"How do you know?" Luke asks. He adjusts his backpack.

"From Kristin. I don't remember it myself, of course. Not really. Just that one time. I must've been four years old."

"But why?" Alice asks. "And why did he hit you? I asked Kristin yesterday, but my mom won't talk about it. She always says that it wasn't so bad. But I can tell she gets really nervous."

Thomas sighs. "Listen, he wasn't very smart. I'm sorry, Luke, I know you have a different image of him, but he just wasn't. He was unscrupulous. Ruthless. My mother was obviously beside herself when she realized where the money was coming from, the money that put food on our table. She was probably hysterical, and so he smacked her. And it just got worse and worse."

Luke and Thomas lock eyes. Once again Luke's words are cool, measured. "Why didn't she just move home to her rich family?"

"I don't think she wanted to go home to her father, they weren't on good terms. But I don't know. There were others, after all. An aunt up north. A cousin. She must have been desperate. She was so young."

"But she just took off?" Luke holds Thomas's gaze.

"Yes. She did. I don't know why. I've stopped wondering."

"Have you really?" Luke asks. He's so close that Thomas can smell his body. His sweat, almost resinous, and even a hint of something like jasmine, something very alluring, that seems to emanate from him.

"Have you really stopped wondering?" he repeats.

"No, you haven't," Alice says. "He hasn't. You can't! Imagine if it were you."

Luke looks at her with an almost startled expression.

"What do you mean?"

"Imagine if it were *your* mother who left you when you were five years old, *your* father who beat you." The look Alice gives him is at once sharp and quizzical.

"But my mother left me too," he says, and now he sounds like a sniffling child.

"Still, you know what I mean. It's not the same thing. You just didn't want to live in the country with your stepfather," Alice says. "My father left as well. That kind of thing happens, it's normal. But seriously, it's not the same as what Thomas and my mother went through. Wouldn't you say?" She looks at Thomas, her eyes wide.

"I don't know, Alice. I don't know what it was like for Luke when he was a kid."

"But where did you actually live when he was in prison? Mom never said anything about that."

"He wasn't in prison when we were little. They never caught him. It wasn't until we'd moved away that he got locked up."

"Why do you think that is?"

Thomas glances up at the trees. "Maybe he just got reckless. Maybe he was just older and had lost his grip. I don't know."

Alice goes quiet, disappearing into her own thoughts. She looks like someone who's been given more information than she can grasp. The path veers, the terrain growing more and more barren; they've reached the tree-line above the parking lot. They walk for a bit in silence.

"In my opinion," Luke mumbles, almost inaudibly, "those who run away are cowards." Thomas wants to say something, something about how Luke himself ran away from his mother, something about how Luke shouldn't say one bad word about *his* mother, but before he does Alice stops abruptly.

"Look! We're already here! How strange, I thought we had a ways to go yet."

There's the parking lot. There's the blue Opel glinting in the sunlight. Alice takes the keys and trots ahead. Thomas and Luke march side by side, unspeaking, and Thomas realizes they're walking in rhythm. He climbs in the back seat. "Thanks for the hike, Luke," he says. "It was a wonderful experience." Luke nods, meeting his eyes in the rearview mirror. He puts the key in the ignition. They drive at a good clip back to the farm. Now and then, to equalize the pressure change, Thomas pinches his nose and blows air. The road declines steeply. And now exhaustion settles in. Alice and Thomas doze on the way home; sleep arrives to the faint accompaniment of rap music on the radio, sluicing into Thomas's mild dreams. In them he's swimming, he's with a woman, he's feeling the sun burning on his back.

As soon as they turn onto the graveled driveway leading to the house, they see commotion on the grounds. Maloney's chopping firewood. His face is flushed, and he's swinging the ax in broad arcs. Helena, Patricia, and Kristin sit drinking tea on the patio. The girls are chasing each other on the lawn with the water hose, and they howl—a shrill, lively, wonderful howl—every time they spray each other, a sound that reaches inside the car. As soon as they've parked, Alice rushes out and joins the twins. She peels off her windbreaker as she runs and tosses it on the grass, and the girls hoot as they spray her, their laughter only increasing. She wrestles the hose from Nina who then, with Maya, runs screeching around the house where Alice can't reach them. She drops the hose and chases them. Thomas saunters over to Maloney, who's standing underneath the lean-to of the woodshed. He cleaves a log with a single blow of the ax, and the split halves fall onto the flagstones, white and dry. He dabs the sweat from his forehead with the sleeve of his shirt. He's soaked through.

"They put you to work?" Thomas lights a cigarette and parks himself on a large rock.

"No kidding. And here I was thinking I'd be lounging in a chair drinking beer all day. Didn't think I'd be doing shit. But I had no choice. And you just took off. How was it out there in nature?"

As Maloney groans and chops firewood, Thomas describes the hike, though he doesn't say a word about how hard it was for him, and he doesn't tell him what they talked about.

"What do you make of Luke?" he asks instead, glancing in Luke's direction. He's removed his T-shirt and is sitting among the women. They're all looking at him as he tells them something. Patricia tilts her head back and laughs.

"I don't really know. He's all right, isn't he?"

"You think there might be something shifty about him?"

"Nah. That wouldn't be my first thought. What do you mean? He gave me a bottle of schnapps as compensation for whipping me at craps that one night. After the funeral. Personally, I think that's good of him." Maloney sets his ax aside and gulps from a water bottle.

"I just can't get a read on him."

"But you don't need to. He's Alice's friend. So what's it matter to you? Jenny seems to like him quite a bit. He got Alice a job."

Thomas stares at Maloney. "He was the one?"

"Yeah. Why?"

"She works for an escort service, Maloney."

Maloney shrugs. "So what? She's not a hooker. I mean, she's got to earn a living somehow. Landing a job's hard enough these days, especially when you don't have any experience."

Thomas sighs, shaking his head. He glances at the flagstones then turns toward the pasture. "I told her she can start working at the store next week."

"What store?"

"Ours, of course. I want her over at the new branch, but we need to train her first. It doesn't cost much to have an apprentice."

"But Thomas," Maloney eyes him. "Hello. We've got Peter. And it's not exactly free, is it? An apprentice *isn't* free." Maloney has made eye contact, and he doesn't look away. "What are you doing anyway? I don't get this *at all.*"

"I hope to increase our profits once we open the new place."

"When *you* open the new place. Besides, what kind of place is it? You haven't told me shit."

So Thomas has to explain to Maloney that he's this close to buying the former porn video rental store. He has big plans with it, he says, and he intends to keep his promise: Maloney won't have to spend a dime, but they'll apportion the surplus revenue equally between them. The place will become part of their company, but he'll be the one buying the property and doing the renovation. Maloney leans tiredly against the chopping block.

"I don't know what to say," he grunts.

"You don't need to say anything. I'll take care of everything. Including Alice."

Maloney glances up at the sky absentmindedly. "It's not exactly the best way to start out as a kind of stepfather, you know, if I'm supposed to boss the girl around every single day."

"You won't have to."

Maloney looks at him sadly. "But Thomas. C'mon, man. We're running this business together. It's not like I can pretend she's nothing more than air, can I? I need to show her the ropes."

"Hey!" Thomas says. "I know what we can do. We'll put Annie in charge of her training. She can do it. She's so organized. It'll be good for her to have that extra responsibility. And if any problems arise, I promise I'll handle with them. How about that? Come on, Maloney. I sure as hell don't want her talking on the phone with horny old bastards every night. We need to give her a chance. What do you say? Especially now that she's your 'stepdaughter'." Thomas chuckles briefly. It rings hollow. His laughter turns into a nasty cough. He tosses his cigarette.

"Laugh all you want," Maloney says darkly. He leans forward and places another log on the block. He raises the ax high over his head with both hands. When it catches the light, the steel of the blade sparkles. Then he lowers the ax until it's hanging suspended between his legs. He says, "I give up. You have to take care of all this shit on your own."

"It's not shit, Maloney. This is a good thing."

Maloney quickly raises the ax again and hacks at the log. "You know how to fucking complicate things, you know that," he mumbles. Thomas strolls away. He grabs a towel in the barn and asks Helena whether or not they still have an outdoor shower. They do. He walks around the barn. From here he can see all the way down to the lake. He undresses. And naked under the tepid jet of water, there in the grass—where he has a view of the shimmering lake and the girls and Alice splashing about in the water near the pier, and the evergreens, and the sheep, who've now moved away from the pasture, closer to the road, grazing on the slope beside the grove, and with fresh, cool air filling his lungs—he thinks with satisfaction: *everything's been resolved.* In the water the three girls are like the Three Graces. Alice's dark skin, the twins' ivory. Alice's ultra-short hair, the girls' long, wet locks. The two nymphets cling to the young woman's body, holding her without letting go, clutching her arms and hands, scrabbling onto her shoulders, piggybacking through the water. Shaking off water like dogs, hopping up and down, doing backflips and disappearing under the pier only to pop up on the other side. No one's allowed to touch those girls, he thinks. *I won't allow any filthy man to touch my girls.* And again he's filled with images: a vision of the new store, his expectations running amok along with a deep, deep sense of peace. The crisis is almost over now. It was a crisis, he thinks in astonishment, watching Alice, who's elegantly swinging herself up onto the pier. A crisis that I've been through. Yes, that's what it was. Just some ridiculous crisis. Maybe he's actually free of it now, totally free, and freer than he's ever been. When the money is spent, he thinks, then he's free. On top of that, I'll have shafted the old man. So that, in the end, he was forced to give something to his family after all, the twisted cheapskate asshole. Now he can pay for his grandchild's education. I've shafted him pretty fucking good. He who laughs last, laughs hardest. Thomas rubs the towel on his bony white body, rubs it hard enough to feel it, and then ties it around his waist. Then he fetches clean clothes in the barn and gets dressed, taking short, rapid breaths. Now I want a goddamn drink, he thinks, heading toward the kitchen where the women, little by little, are beginning to prepare dinner.

An enormous leg of lamb rests on the kitchen table, coated in herbs and drenched in red wine. Just as Thomas walks through the door, Kristin roars with laughter, wraps her arms around Helena, and kisses her neck. "My dove," she says, "That's so *funny*!" But Thomas never figures out what's so funny. Patricia's sitting on a chair in the middle of the room, and Luke's massaging her neck. She cocks her head to one side so that he can reach under her ear. Her eyes are closed, her expression blissful. "Mm, mm, mm," she moans. "Oh, that's so nice." Luke gathers her hair and lifts it off one side of her throat, letting it hang down against her cheek. Thomas tenses up. Outside, Alice and the twins emerge, now dressed. Throwing a red ball. "See," Helena says, pointing through the window at them. "They worship her." The green grass, the red ball, the low sun in the foliage. The girls throw themselves at the ball, running. And inside the house: *Luke is touching Patricia. Someone is touching my girlfriend.* Only now does Kristin see him. He's been standing motionless in the doorway. "Thomas! Why are you standing there like a pillar of salt? Come on in!" Patricia turns and sees him, her gaze veiled and sated. He clears his throat. "I need a drink," he says. "What would you like? A mojito? Helena just got some mint for the peas." Luke maneuvers his hands gently across Patricia's skin. He's squirted a dollop of olive oil on her neck, the bottle's on the floor. "My neck's really sore from sunbathing," she says. "And I've got an awful headache. I couldn't adjust the deck chair."

"That's an old piece of crap. We never use those chairs," Kristin says, squeezing lime juice into a glass. "We don't have time for that out here in the country. Lazing about in the sun doing nothing!"

Luke guides his hands down the nape of Patricia's neck, between her shoulder blades, past her dress. Thomas tries to make eye contact with Patricia, but she only lowers her head, making room for Luke. "I can do that," Thomas says. "I can give you a massage, hon." The words come out edgy, tense. "Thanks, but Luke's much better at it, I think." Then Patricia whispers, "Oh, yeah, right there . . ." Staring watchfully at Luke and Patricia, Thomas crosses the room and leans against the counter. Kristin pours rum and cane sugar in a glass. "Do we have ice, baby?" Helena nods. And Kristin puts the greenish drink in Thomas's hand. He feels a violent urge to tear Luke away from Patricia. He wants to drown him in oil, pour it down his gullet, listen to him gurgle. Jealousy pecks at his chest, and he's close to hyperventilating. "How was the hike?" Kristin asks. "Was it tough? You're no spring chicken any more." She laughs. "Speak for yourself," Helena says. "Thomas will always be a young man to me. *The young man. Our* young man. Luke tells us you got a good glimpse of the coast up on Bearclaw? It's been a long time since we were up there . . ." The two women discuss how they once got lost on that very mountain, because they wanted to veer from the trail; they wanted to venture into the wilderness. "That was back when we insisted on doing everything our own way. We thought everything was so bourgeois, so restrictive—even a forest trail," Kristin says, and Helena chuckles, placing the lamb in the oven. Kristin observes the girls outside playing ball. She says, "The sun's setting now. I think I'll have one of those mint drinks too. Anyone else want one?" Luke and Patricia do. Thomas musters all his strength to bridle his anger. He doesn't know what to do with himself. He can't leave the kitchen. He offers to wash the dishes. "That would be great," Helena says, and begins shelling peas. Beyond the trees the sun burns crimson, and the kitchen is temporarily bathed in a heavy, golden light, it's almost magical—a magical moment—and then the girls come rushing in, their cheeks flushed and sweaty. Alice has promised to braid their hair. "We want *many* tiny braids. With beads!" Maya says eagerly. She's morphed from being a sourpuss teenager to a happy little girl, and she doesn't even realize she's shouting. "C'mon! Let's go upstairs!" The girls thump up the stairwell at Alice's heels, bubbling with excitement.

"Where's Jenny?" Thomas asks Patricia, wanting to connect with her.

"She's probably with Maloney, wouldn't you think?" Helena replies, tucking a lock of hair back behind one ear.

"Isn't he chopping firewood?"

"Not anymore."

"I see them," Patricia says. She stands and gives Luke a thank-you hug. With her head resting on his shoulder, she's looking out the windows above the kitchen table. Thomas scrubs aggressively at a pan. *She's embracing another man, she's smiling happily.* Jenny and Maloney are sitting side by side on the pier.

"What a pair of lovebirds!" Patricia says, letting go of Luke. "Hard to believe they're dating."

"It's so good for Jenny," Kristin says, sipping her drink. "I sense harmony all around this family right now. Isn't that so? Everyone seems to be doing better."

"Better than what?" Thomas slams a breadknife unnecessarily hard into the dish drainer.

"Better than before."

"Better than ever," Patricia smiles, glancing tenderly at Luke. "In any event, my head feels much better now." Luke smiles, and sits reverse in the chair Patricia has vacated. She's staring at the yard.

"Luke sure has many talents," Thomas says bitterly. "You must've really paid attention in school."

"You don't learn how to massage in school, Thomas!" Patricia turns, giggling, and collects her mojito from the table. She's wearing her blue dress, the one he'd packed for her. In it her waist seems narrower than usual, her arms plumper.

"You learn by doing." Luke's voice climbs slowly from the center of his body. "Like most everything."

"I think you have an exceptional talent." Patricia puts her glass down, picks up a dishtowel and lethargically begins drying the dishes. Thomas is ready to explode.

"I like doing things the right way," Luke says, tipping slightly in his chair. "To see things through to the end. One of the many things I learned from Jacques." Thomas tries to catch his breath. He wants to say something, but Helena beats him to it.

"So you're patient? Are you a patient person?" She scrutinizes him.

"I'm not sure about that. I don't know. But when I put my mind to something, I follow through with it. I don't give up."

"Sounds heroic," Kristin says, without even trying to conceal the irony. She reaches across the table and turns on the lamp.

"Or stubborn," Thomas says. "Or simply naïve." Luke tilts his head back and laughs. "Yes! He always said that. *You're a stubborn one, Kid. You'll do all right.* I hope he's right!" His laughter fades. Patricia hands him his drink. He raises the glass to his mouth and slugs it greedily. Thomas shakes his head. "I still don't understand how we can be talking about the same man." But no one seems to hear him. It's getting dark now, fast, first blue, then bluish-black, the trees silhouetted clearly against midnight blue. Thomas puts down the dish brush and takes a deep breath. Going berserk won't do any good now, even if he wants to pummel Luke's face. He lifts his head and looks out the window. He can see the moon now. A curved little hook in the darkened sky. Kristin follows his gaze. "Won't be a cloud in the sky tonight, I think. You'll be able to see what a blanket of stars we have up here."

"They're coming in now," Patricia says, gesturing to the window, behind which Jenny and Maloney are walking hand in hand back to the house. Maloney wedges his face against the glass and grimaces. Jenny yanks at him, smiling and shaking her head. He puts his arms around her, lifts her up, and begins to run, her pale, chunky body squirming in his arms. "He has a lot of energy all of a sudden," Patricia says, quietly, almost forlornly, and Thomas senses envy in her. Does she want to be lifted up wriggling and whining the same way she wants to be massaged by young men and vanish several nights in a row in her shiny shoes? He sips his drink. "Patricia," he says. "Patricia."

"What?"

"Nothing," he says. She smiles and shakes her head.

Patricia retreats from the window, back to the kitchen table. She picks up a stack of napkins and lays one beside every plate that Kristin has set out. "Just have to wait for the lamb now," Helena says, pouring the shelled peas into a pan, where a hunk of butter, a few pearl onions, and heaps of chopped mint are already sizzling. Thomas walks through the living room to the sunroom. He sits on the bench and lights a cigarette. But before he has even taken a drag, Luke plops down beside him in the semi-darkness. And he inches closer. "Can I have a smoke?" he says, drying his hands on his pants. Must be the olive oil, Thomas thinks, handing him his pack. His fucking massage oil. I hope the oil catches fire. When he flicks the lighter, Thomas is surprised by the light in Luke's eyes. As if he's consumed by a huge bonfire raging inside his brain, right behind the frontal bone of his skull. Thomas shrinks back. "I brought you your drink," Luke says. "If you want the rest, anyway." Luke hands him his glass, then takes a long drag of his cigarette and leans comfortably back on the hard wooden bench. Ice clinks in his glass. Thomas fills his mouth with the dregs of his sweet citrus drink, and though the ice cubes are cold on his tongue, the rum feels hot. He turns to see Luke's silhouette. The cigarette dangles from his thick lower lip.

"What do you want?" Thomas asks. "Why did you come out here?"

"Now? I just want to bum a cigarette." In the expanding darkness Luke's eyes glow. "What should I want?" A pause. He blows a spiral of white smoke from his mouth. "Should I want something in particular?"

"No idea. It just looks as though you want something from me."

Luke smiles. He flicks his cigarette away, and it lies smoldering on the flagstones.

"No, Thomas," he says almost solemnly. "You're wrong about that. I'm just happy to be here. I like this family. It seems as though there's room for everyone, and I feel at home."

He looks straight at Thomas. "You want to visit my mother tomorrow?"

"Your mother?!"

"Yeah. You asked about her up on the mountain. So I thought, since we're so close to her house, you know, and since you know her. From way back when. Seems like the right occasion. To go over there. Maybe on the way home?"

"I wouldn't say I *know* her. Besides, I thought you had nothing to do with her anymore."

"I don't. But I've got an urge to visit her all of a sudden. To see her . . . as though from another perspective. With you. And Alice, maybe. Through your eyes or something." Luke leans forward, propping his elbows on his knees. "But I have to warn you: it's a freak show over there. She's stark raving mad."

"So you *do* want something from me after all?"

Thomas has the feeling that Luke shrugs. But he's not sure. There's something suddenly disarming about him. They can barely see each other. The light from the living room, behind them, spills into the sunroom in squares, small squares. Small squares of light falling on the eucalyptus, a few bushes, Helena's lavender and spices, the geraniums. They stare out into darkness. Thomas feels Luke's presence surging around him, a kind of electrical charge.

"You want to come?" Luke asks once more.

Thomas hesitates. "Yeah, sure," he says. And then, "Are you in love with Alice?"

"No!" Luke shakes his head tolerantly. "You *already* asked me that."

"Why *aren't* you in love with her?"

Luke takes a breath and holds it for a few seconds. Then he exhales.

"Because I'm attracted to different kinds of girls."

"And that kind is?"

"Hmm . . . Maybe more hardened. It's hard to explain."

"Try."

"I can't, Thomas."

This electrical charge continues to pulsate from Luke, and it makes Thomas a little dizzy. His scent, too. This odd jasmine-like evanescence, and the bitter undertone of his old sweat: earthy, woodsmoke. What does he mean by hardened? Thomas pictures a few leather-clad bitches, whips in hand, boots crawling up their thighs.

"But *you* are in love with Patricia, aren't you? You seem very happy together."

"We are."

"It seems you've got a good relationship. A good apartment, good jobs. A good life. What everyone wants. She told me she wants a baby. But you're not interested?"

Thomas doesn't reply. But of course he needs to reply. The silence goes on for too long. Luke's breath, light and effortless, and so close. A jab of claustrophobia pings through him. *He's breathing down my neck.* "I can't explain it to you, Luke," he says. "Maybe it's like you and your hardened girls. It's a very private thing."

"A woman like Patricia should have a baby," Luke says emphatically. "Otherwise there's no justice in the world."

"What's having a baby got to do with justice?"

"It has a lot to do with justice."

"In that case, if I were you, I wouldn't try to make myself a judge of that." Thomas stands. "I'm going in to see about the lamb."

Luke trails close behind. When they enter the well-lit living room, they're forced to squint. "I'm starving," Luke says. "I could eat that entire lamb myself. I don't think I've ever had roasted lamb before."

Thomas spins around abruptly, causing Luke to bump against his chest and chin. Luke steps back, a reflex.

"Did Jacques ever take you to Lucianos?"

Luke looks at him, puzzled. "What? Lucianos? No, I don't think so. Who's Luciano?"

"Ah," Thomas says, turning his back on him again. "It's just a restaurant. We ate there sometimes. Jacques, Jenny, and I." He continues into the kitchen. Permeated now by a palpable sense of relief and joy, the kind you feel after taking your revenge on someone; they have Lucianos to themselves. Luke has never been there, and in one way or another it feels as though Thomas is special, and he thinks: It was our place. He didn't take anyone else there. It was only for him and his children, only for us, and Thomas wants to celebrate, then thinks better of it and that feeling of *victory,* of *revenge,* completely overpowers the underlying sense of shame he feels at his petty, childish behavior. But he's suddenly in a much better mood.

Jenny sits at the table waving her beer. She's busy stuffing herself with peanuts and olives. She spits out the stones on a napkin and hands the bowl to Maloney. But he doesn't want olives. Peanuts, on the other hand. He pops a handful into his mouth and swigs the rest of his beer like the experienced drinker he is, one with good technique. Under the table, Jenny's legs slither around his. She's wearing the blue pumps she wore to the funeral, sheer, flesh-colored tights, and the tailored, salmon-colored dress. Patches of sweat stain her armpits. Her hair has a glossy, wheat-like sheen—it's not quite as reddish-blonde as when she was young—and it tumbles down either side of her round face. She's wearing a black pearl necklace. To Thomas, the necklace seems familiar; maybe she's had it for years. Raising his bottle to make a toast, Maloney leans back, scowling. "Maloney's back aches," Jenny says. "But oh, oh, all of you should've gone swimming with us. It was cold, but *lovely.* Maloney jumped off the pier. Didn't you, my love?" He nods. "If I hadn't been so hot after chopping the goddamn firewood, I wouldn't have done that. But swinging that ax was hard work. My arms are completely dead."

"And your back," Jenny adds, trying to blow a lock of hair from her face.

"Thank you, dear Maloney," Kristin smiles. "We'll think about you every time we get a fire going."

"I damn well hope so!" Maloney bellows with laughter. "What about you, Tommy? Did you do anything sensible?"

Thomas sinks into the chair beside him. He's got a view of Jenny's deep cleavage. "I drank a mojito," he says. "I think that's very sensible."

"You could've helped Maloney with the wood," Jenny says, looking coolly at her brother. "He was out there for hours." She wipes her mouth with the crumpled napkin.

"No thanks," Maloney says. "All he would've done is chop my legs off. That man can't handle his tools."

"What can't I do?"

"You'd think you two were brothers," Jenny sighs.

"We are brothers," Maloney says, dropping his arm around Thomas. "So where does that put you, sister Jenny?"

"Maloney!" Kristin gives him a stern look. Then she smiles. "Why *are* you like that? He's always been like that!" She smiles at Luke, who's leaning close to Patricia across the kitchen table. Thomas can't make out what they're discussing.

"Where's Helena?" Jenny asks. Now she looks bored. Her eyes are half-closed, her mouth is open.

"She must've gone to lie down. The lamb exhausted her. It'll be ready in twenty minutes."

"But then it has to sit, too," Maloney says, winking at Kristin. "Right?"

And so on, back and forth. Small talk. Cozy. Rich yellow light, dark steamy windows. The scent of roasted meat wafting from the oven. A dish of orange salad. Laughter now and then. Eye contact with Patricia, and Patricia approaches. He reaches for her, takes hold, pulls her onto his lap. He wraps her soft arms in his. The weight of her body. Luke's all by himself at the kitchen table with his beer, maybe he's feeling a bit dejected, maybe he's on the outside looking in; it's not the worst thing that could happen, Thomas thinks, pleased. He'll learn to leave others' women alone.

The dog bumbles across the room and drops at Jenny's feet. She bends over and pats its back. Maloney stares happily at her heaving bosom. Patricia goes to the bathroom, and Thomas heads to the utility room for a bottle of red wine. By the time he returns, the twins and Alice have come downstairs. The girls proudly model their new 'dos, whipping their hair from side to side, jingling the beads. "You two look like you come from a tribal culture," Maloney says.

"We do," Maya replies, turning. "What do you think this place is?"

"Are we a tribal culture here at the farm?" Kristin wrinkles her brows, stirring the sauce.

"Yes!" Nina cries out. "And you're the chief!"

"Oy," Alice says. She pours herself a glass of water. "That was hard. I've never done so many braids in one day."

"Join the club," Maloney grouses.

"You've been braiding too?!" Alice sips, then sets her glass on the kitchen table. "What have you braided?"

"I don't braid hair out of principle. But I've worked hard. Unlike certain others. So welcome to the hard workers' club. We're a whooped bunch."

"You braid your fingers in mine," Jenny says, yawning.

Alice stands behind her mother. Puts her hand on her shoulder. "You should grow your hair out so you can braid it," Jenny says. "You look like a combat soldier." Alice removes her hand and walks over to Luke.

"No! She looks like a secret agent!" Nina's the one who says this. "Isn't that right?" Nina tugs at Maya, who's still spinning, a dervish, around and around. But now Maya stops: dizzy, wobbly. "No way! She looks totally cool. I want to look like that. When these braids come apart I'm going to cut them off." Then she thumps to the floor and within seconds Jupiter is all over her, licking her face with his long, floppy, pink tongue. Soon, both girls are rolling around the floor with the tail-wagging dog licking them. When the dog begins to hump Nina's thigh, Kristin shouts "Jupiter!" and yanks the dog off. Pointing at the dog, she says, "Shame on you." And it lowers its head. "It's not doing anything," Nina says. "It's just playing." No one says anything. They've all watched with interest. "I don't want it doing that," Kristin says firmly. "It's not appropriate. End of discussion." She pounds the kitchen table with her fist.

"What's going on?" Helena's standing in the doorway in a brown silk shirt, her eyebrows lifted slightly. "Didn't you take the lamb out of the oven?"

And so there's roasted lamb with peas and baked potatoes. The tasty-looking orange salad sprinkled with chopped parsley. Thomas sits between Maloney and Helena, opposite Patricia. Maloney gorges himself. The lamb is tender and seasoned with garlic, the potatoes oozing melted butter. Everyone praises the meal and Helena. "Don't think we eat like this way everyday," Nina says, her mouth stuffed.

"Nah," Maya mumbles. "We almost never eat meat."

"But you've got so many animals in the freezer?" Patricia sits up straight. "Don't you eat them?"

"We do," Kristin says. "But we try to be as vegetarian as possible. As healthy as possible. But it's not true that we never eat meat, Maya."

"Almost never, I said." Maya squashes her potato in the sauce. "That's why we're not growing."

"Maya! Of course you're growing." Helena looks at the girls, both startled and cheerful at once. "You've grown a couple inches this past year alone. What do you mean you're not growing?"

Maya doesn't reply. She lowers her head and shovels mashed potato into her mouth.

"So," Kristin says. "What do you want to do tomorrow? You're staying till the afternoon, right?"

Luke and Alice are going fishing. "I don't have any special plans," Jenny says solemnly. "If the weather holds, maybe I'll lie in the sun and read a magazine."

"Be careful with the deck chairs," Patricia says. "They can be dangerous."

"The weather will be fine," Kristin says, tasting her wine. "But there's supposed to be rain and wind tonight. And thunder."

"That means the electricity will go out just like last time." Maya looks at her mother, defiant. Helena shakes her head. "That's not always the case, dear. Why are you always so negative?"

"That's how kids *are* at that age. Alice was dreadful. Wouldn't you agree, Alice? You were *dreadful*!"

"I wasn't any more dreadful than anyone else. Like you!" Alice points at Jenny and smiles. "We were probably both dreadful."

"Kristin can also be really dreadful," Nina says.

"She can be *dreadfully* dreadful!" Maya snorts sarcastically.

Sitting between Maloney and the gentle Helena, Thomas feels good, he feels comfortable. He scans the faces at the table. There's color in everyone's cheeks thanks to the hot food. Seeing his family makes him happy. He's glad Maloney's part of the family now. Even for Luke he feels a kind of affection. He's just a boy, after all. The light strikes his thick, reddish-brown hair, making it shine like copper. Luke looks attentively at Patricia. She's telling him something, gesticulating gracefully with one hand. It's okay, Thomas thinks. It's okay that they're talking. She sat on my lap a short time ago. She likes it here. And like a swarm of butterflies, or a hot spiral of steam, a wave of tenderness fills Thomas. And so he clinks his glass and gets to his feet. "Dear Kristin and Helena," he begins.

"Us too!" Maya shouts.

"Yes, and you two. Thank you for inviting all of us dreadful people to your house, and for several days at that." Helena laughs. "We're so happy to be here. I was just sitting here thinking that I really do have a family. This makes me very happy. To belong somewhere. I believe we'd all agree that we're very happy to belong here with you." Jenny wipes her eyes and loudly blows her nose. "And though I was a little shocked to see Maloney *here* and together with my sister, well, I couldn't ask for anything better than having my best friend also belong here. So, a toast for Jenny and Maloney!" Everyone raises their glasses, and the girls refuse to sit until they've clinked glasses with everyone. It takes a long time. But finally they're seated again. Maloney calls out: "Thank you for your confidence, father-in-law!" Everyone laughs; tears roll down Jenny's cheeks. With a quivering lower lip she says, "I can't handle all the emotion," and Thomas clears his throat. The wine's suddenly making him feel dizzy. "And Alice: You're our hope for the future. Remember that." He raises his glass to her and winks privately. Nina shouts: "We're also your hope!" "Yes, also you two," Alice says, tugging one of the girl's many braids, "you two are our very greatest hope." "That's right," Thomas says, sitting. Helena refills his glass and whispers, "Thank you, dear Thomas. That was a fine little speech." The conversations continue, cheerful, scattershot; the dirty plates are carried into the kitchen, and Jenny gets more and more tipsy and affectionate, with blotches of red wine forming on her lower lip, blue and dry. From time to time she sniffles, dabbing at her eyes. To the girls' giddy delight, Alice braids Luke's hair. The twins serve the fruit salad that they made themselves. Maloney makes coffee. "The coffee baron strikes again!" Kristin shouts enthusiastically. Jupiter's in his basket, still ashamed. But Helena goes to him, discreetly, and squats down to give him a morsel and a loving pat. This seems to cheer up the old boy considerably.

Everyone's more willing to help clean up tonight. They work at a good clip, and they have fun doing it. The girls chase each other with the dishrags and Jenny regresses to her childhood, kicking off her pumps and chasing Thomas around the kitchen, into the living room, and finally into the sunroom where she smacks him on the back with a towel, so that it stings. "Revenge!" she squeals. "After all these years! You *tormented* me." They have to let the dog out because it doesn't like the commotion. Now it stands outside barking. "If you want to see our stars, then you should do it now," Kristin says, "the weather's going to turn cloudy and windy." Patricia wants to come with Thomas. She's flushed and in high-spirits. "They must've put something in the wine," she says. "I feel like I'm on drugs, like I'm *high*! I'm high." Jupiter leaps on them one at a time, tearing a hole in Patricia's tights. But she doesn't care. She showers the dog with caresses, until it lies down on the flagstones. Thomas lights a cigarette. To adjust their eyes to the darkness, they step away from the house. "It takes ten minutes before our night vision kicks in," Thomas says. "I read that somewhere. Want to go down to the lake?" They step cautiously so they don't trip. After some time they find the path, and at last they can see more than just contours. The lake is shiny, black. The slender moon throws light on the water, but not much. They look into the sky. At the sea of stars. The longer they stare, the more stars they see. "Look," Patricia says. "There are *layers* of stars. A shroud of stars. As if the more you look, the deeper into eternity you see." Eternity makes them dizzy. It's so overwhelming, so frightening, and so magnetically alluring all at once. They have to turn away. Patricia whispers, "We'll die someday, Thomas. That's what you see when you look up there." They walk farther on, along the bank of the lake, where the path isn't a path but trampled-down grass that, every now and then, isn't trampled down. Their legs are wet, the dew has long since settled in. At last they can go no farther, the path is blocked by blackberry and willow scrub. The rushes shiver. They turn around and walk back a ways, then sit on a boulder. Thomas recognizes a few constellations, but not many. Patricia's especially fascinated by Orion's Belt. The three clear, well-lit stars are lined up straight. "You know that some people call them the Three Kings? While others call them the Three Marys? It's a mythical constellation." Thomas didn't know that. But he does remember an episode of *Star Trek*, in which Captain Kirk tells Edith Keeler that a famous poet wants to write a poem with three letters, each of which symbolizes a star in Orion's Belt: "Let/me/help." Or at least that's how he remembers it.

"You watched *Star Trek*?" Patricia asks.

"Everyone who owned a TV watched *Star Trek*. It was on for years."

"Not me. But Orion's Belt is also mentioned in *Blade Runner*. Remember that? How does it go again . . . it's a beautiful passage." He feels her eyes on him. Her face is bathed in darkness. "I've . . . seen things you people wouldn't believe . . ."

". . . attack ships in flames off the shoulder of Orion," Thomas continues, "I watched c-beams glitter in the dark near the Tannhäuser Gate . . ."

". . . All those . . . moments . . . will be lost in time, like tears . . . in . . . rain." Patricia rests her hands on her knees and sighs. "Isn't that gorgeous?"

"You're forgetting 'time to die.' That's what he says at the end."

She stares at the constellation again. "Oh," she says, "Oh."

"Oh what?"

"Oh, everything." She sighs. "I think my buzz is gone. Sucked into outer space." She scratches her leg. "There are mosquitos here. Can we go back?"

Grass crackles beneath their feet. "What do you think about Luke?" Thomas asks.

"He's very sweet. And very young."

"Why did you ask him to massage you?"

She stops to regard him. "You weren't jealous, were you, Thomas? Were you jealous? You *were*. Ha! That's too funny."

"I wasn't jealous. I just thought it was a little strange."

She shrugs. "My neck was sore. And he said he was good at massaging. What's the problem?"

"There's no problem."

They start walking again. "Do you like being here?" Thomas says, taking her hand. "Or are you bored?"

"I'm not bored. I was irritated that you fell asleep during the game yesterday. I was mad at you. But I also didn't care. By this morning my anger was gone. I've really enjoyed being with the ladies." Patricia drops his hand and threads her arm through his. When they approach the house, the dog begins to bark. "Kristin told us a lot of stuff about your mother today."

"What did she say?"

"That she was a wild and decadent person."

"A wild and decadent person. What does she mean by that?"

"I suppose it means she wanted to be free to live life to its fullest. That's how I understood it anyway. She rebelled against her educated, well-heeled family and took off with a charlatan no one liked. She burned all her bridges, Kristin said. So she couldn't come crawling back when she'd had enough of the wild life. She was a proud person. All too proud, Kristin said."

They come to the mudroom and the front door. Patricia squats down to rub Jupiter's back. "That's why she died alone."

"That sounds like a rather theatrical interpretation. Did she tell you about her horoscope too? Or read tarot cards for her?"

"It wasn't meant that way, Thomas."

"What do you mean?"

"I mean she's dead."

"Yeah, she's dead all right. But what does that explain?"

"I don't know. Jenny was happy to hear about her. Even though she cried. There's so much grief buried inside her. Kristin gave her one of your mother's old necklaces. Hard to believe she was only thirty-two when she died . . ." Patricia looks at him. "What is it?"

"Nothing."

"Give it a rest, Thomas. Every little thing pisses you off. Can't you be happy for anyone? Is that what's wrong? Are you miserly?" Patricia straightens up and rests her hands at her side. "Well?" He doesn't respond. Just stands there. "Are you stingy with your feelings? With your family? Do you have a patent on the correct 'interpretation'? Do you see yourself as some kind of police officer for this family? Huh? Is that it?" She looks at him, and he glowers at her, so she shakes her head. "So much for a romantic stroll under the stars. There's very little that's fun with you anymore. Do you know that? There's just bad luck around you these days." She goes inside and slams the door. But she pauses there, her hand resting on the knob. For a moment she doesn't move, as if considering going in or out. Then she returns.

"Thomas," she says. Her voice is different, low and compact.

"Yeah."

"What're we going to do?"

"We can't argue inside, that's for sure." He nods at the brightly-lit windows.

Her arms droop at her sides, all energy drained from her. Under the sharp light of the bare bulb dangling in the mudroom, she looks rumpled, worn out. She gives him a wounded or sad look, he can't tell which. Then she turns and goes back into the house. This time she doesn't return. Thomas sits on the stoop smoking another cigarette. Frogs croak nearby. Midges and moths flit around the bulb above him. His legs are sore following the hike. His butt, too. He doesn't have an answer to Patricia's question. He gazes at the stars one last time, thinking: *That's how it is*, though he doesn't quite know what that means. Doesn't understand it. But that *is* how it is. *I am tamping this half-smoked cigarette out on the flagstones. I am throwing the butt into the grass. I am turning around and lifting first one foot, then the other. I am walking up the stairs, I am putting my hand out, I am touching the doorknob, I am opening the door. The hinges squeal. I am stepping into the entryway. It smells a little sour in here. I am breathing. I am breathing. I am breathing.*

"Was it nice out there?" Kristin comes downstairs just as Thomas closes the door. He nods. "I need to use your bathroom," he says, passing her going up. The walls on the second floor are pitched at an angle, and it's hard for him to stand erect. Up here there's a large bedroom with a king-sized bed, an acid-washed cabinet, dim light thrown from a single wall lamp above the headboard of the bed, and a view of the lake. The twins' dinky rooms, plastered in pink, are teeming with knick knacks, unmade beds, heaps of clothes, schoolbooks, and old toys on the floor. The one is apparently as disorganized as the other. He locates the bathroom at the end of the hall. It's messy in here, too: wet towels on the floor, overturned bottles of shampoo and soap in the shower, a plastic basket filled with rubber ducks and miniature ships—which the twins must have outgrown years ago. He does his business and washes his hands, then looks at himself in the mirror. He looks overheated, sunburned, the whites of his eyes seem yellowed—maybe it's the light. A few tiny nail clippings are stuck to the hand soap. Despite treading carefully, he bangs his head against a ceiling beam on the way down the hall. Pain jabs his skull. The steep stairwell. Someone let the dog back in the house, and it greets him with a wagging tail, then follows at his heels through the kitchen to the living room, where Thomas hears voices and the twang of a guitar. Maya's the one playing it, testing it out haltingly. Then she hands the guitar to Alice and Alice begins plucking chords to an old Bob Dylan tune. Her singing voice is light and pure. Kristin, Helena, and Jenny sing along, and the girls clap in rhythm, and then Patricia starts singing too, and Maloney. His voice forms the humming foundation to Kristin's alto and the others' sopranos. Luke's the only one not singing along. He sits quietly on the edge of the cot watching, uncomfortable and rigid, as though he's embarrassed at the boisterous, unrestrained cheerfulness. Rocking back and forth on her stool, Helena raises her arms above her head, lets them sway to and fro. Thomas settles into a kitchen chair and waves awkwardly to Patricia. She smiles wearily at him. Luke gathers his hands on his knees and leans forward, hiding his eyes beneath his hair. And Jenny says, "Can you believe we still remember every single lyric of those rotten old songs. Thomas used to play guitar too, it sounded horrible. Isn't that right? You couldn't play at all. He's tone deaf."

"But Jenny, as you can tell, has immense and underappreciated musical talents," he says, which makes Alice laugh without restraint.

"I love you all the same, you idiot. You know that," Jenny says. "That's the problem, of course." And she looks as though she's about to cry again, but no tears come.

"So you love him even though he can't play guitar?" Alice teases her mother.

"No. I love him even though sometimes I don't *want* to."

"Hey, thanks. Right back at ya," Thomas says, smiling at his sister. Maloney raises his voice: "I'm going to let you two figure that out together, that's a little too intimate for me." He glances cheerfully at Thomas. Jenny drains her glass.

They sing more songs. The twins do this silly dance, keeling over laughing the entire time. Finally they throw themselves into the beanbag chair. Kristin hammers on the bongo that Helena uses to meditate. Then Maloney and Jenny go to bed. Jenny gives Alice a long goodnight hug, which seems to surprise Alice, who rests her slightly baffled face stiffly against her mother's shoulder, until at last she wraps her arms around Jenny's buxom body and surrenders herself. For a moment she appears blissful. It's 10:30. Maloney bows to the group and keeps close to Jenny as she, stumbling in her high-heels, waves to everyone. Her dress is creased in the back. She's walking *inward*, Thomas thinks, as if she were knock-kneed. They begin kissing even before they're beyond the kitchen door, Maloney practically munching on Jenny's mouth, her hands gliding up under his shirt. Thomas turns away in a kind of stunned disgust. And yet he looks again, but by then they've disappeared from sight, the door slamming shut behind them. "So!" Helena says to the twins, "bedtime." The girls don't want to go to bed, but after some complaining and nagging, they slink away after all. "Goodnight, Uncle Thomas," Nina whispers sleepily.

"Goodnight, Niece Nina. Sweet dreams."

"What do we do now?" Patricia asks, trying to stifle a yawn. "Maybe we should go to bed too?" "Wait," Luke says, standing. Soon he returns with a bottle of tequila. He holds it up to the light so they can see the worm floating in the liquor. "Okay," Kristin says. "I'll get some glasses." They each down a shot. And another. Then Helena decides she doesn't want any more. She laughs and tilts her head back.

"Oh, do you remember that time you had to carry me home, dear? Because *I* remember it! Tequila makes a person so crazy, I went out like a light."

"I carried her on my back. Luckily she was light as a feather," Kristin says tenderly, rubbing Helena's wrist and her imperceptibly pulsing vein. "You still are . . ."

"Listen," Luke says. "Let's recite poetry. You guess the poem and score points for each correct answer."

"Poetry!" Kristin refills her glass, then rolls her eyes. "I don't know any poems by heart."

"Of course you do." Helena arches forward and whispers something in Kristin's ear.

Alice leans back on the couch's pillows. "How many points?"

"Five for the poet's name, five for the title, and five for the name of the collection in which the poem was first published. You get five bonus points if you can name either the year the poem was written, or the publication year of the book the poem first appeared in."

"Huh, that sounds complicated," Kristin sighs.

"What about suites?" Patricia says. "What about literary journals? If it was printed in a magazine before it was published in a book? And if it was *only* published that way?"

"That doesn't count. But you get a bonus for suites. What should we say? Three extra points?"

"Five," Patricia says.

"You must be hoping for a suite, huh?" Alice nudges Patricia teasingly, who's now leaning back with a cushion under her knees. Patricia smiles at her.

"What if you only know the first verse?" Alice asks.

"That's enough. A few lines are enough," Luke replies. He draws columns in his notebook for scoring.

So he carries a notebook in his pocket, Thomas thinks. I wonder what he writes in it? Luke looks at Thomas. "Who wants to go first?"

"We need another drink first," Thomas says. "To kickstart our brain cells."

"Ha!" Kristin slaps her thighs and extends her glass. Though this is her fourth shot, she doesn't seem drunk at all.

They roll a die to determine who will start. Kristin wins.

"Okay," she says. "Pay close attention: *The opals hiding in your lids / as you sleep, as you mysteriously . . . Oh, as you mysteriously . . .*" Kristin hesitates, glancing at the ceiling. "Ride *ponies*! Yes. *Ride ponies, spring to bloom/ like the blue flowers of autumn.*"

Helena blushes a little. The others applaud.

"Wait," Kristin says. "I remember some of the last part too." She squeezes her eyes shut in concentration. "*Only by chance tripping on stairs / do you repeat the dance, and / then, impeccably dressed /*, no, impeccably disguised! *And then / impeccably disguised /* so . . . what is it?"

"*In the perfect variety . . .*" Helena says.

"Oh, yeah!" Kristin snaps her fingers. "*In the perfect variety of / subdued / white black pink blue saffron,*" she pats her cheek after each color, "*And golden ambiance, do we find / the nightly savage, in a trance!*"

"Wow!" Alice blurts out, "That's awesome. Who wrote it?"

"Yes, who is it?" Kristin's eyes gleam.

"You remembered it," Helena whispers, squeezing Kristin's knee.

"The nightly savage, in a trance," Luke mumbles. "I pass. I don't know it."

"Come on! Thomas?"

Thomas shakes his head. They are silent. They glance curiously at each other. A new suspense, tension in the room.

"O'Hara," Patricia says. "I don't know where it was published the first time. But I'm guessing it was in the collection *Meditations in an Emergency.* Wasn't it published in 1957? I can't remember that at all. But in any case, it was in *The Collected Poems*, published after his death."

"That's right. It was in *Meditations in an Emergency*," Kristin says. "1957 is also correct. Well done!"

"What's the title of the poem?" Luke has his pen ready.

Patricia shakes her head. "No—I can't remember that."

"Yes, you can, c'mon, babe." Thomas is beginning to enjoy this game.

"May I help?" Kristin asks.

"No. You're not allowed." Luke is stony. He spins his pen around in his fingers.

"Well, I'm going to anyway. It was written to a female friend of his. She was in your line of business, Patricia. Sort of. He wrote more poems to her over the years."

"Including a sonnet," Helena adds.

Patricia considers. "Oh . . ." she says. "Oh! It's right on the tip of my tongue, I have it . . . Is it . . . hmm . . . is it . . . it's Freilicher. Jane Freilicher. Isn't it? The painter?"

Kristin nods. Alice and Thomas clap.

"But what's the name of the poem?"

Patricia doesn't know. "Something with Jane," she suggests.

"Yes, but *what*?"

"To Jane?"

Kristin shakes her head. Luke regards Patricia. "You give up?" She nods.

"*Jane Awake*," Kristin says. "Doesn't she get a point for getting half the title right?"

But Luke says no. Fifteen points for Patricia. You've got to follow the rules. A short discussion ensues about the fairness or unfairness of the rules, then they continue playing. Helena goes on and on about how important this O'Hara poem was for her and Kristin when they met, but no one's really listening. Kristin needs to choose the next player. She points at Alice.

"Me?"

"Yes, you!"

"I don't know any poems."

"Of course you do. I guarantee you memorized some lines in school."

Alice bites her lip. "Any kind of poem?"

"Yes," Luke says. "Any kind."

How goddamn poetic of him, Thomas thinks. The schoolmaster of poetry. A schoolmaster in *every form of poetry.* He feels laughter bubbling in his throat, rising, but he restrains himself, because now all goes quiet. Alice begins earnestly and stutteringly to recite: "Humpty Dumpty sat on a wall / Humpty Dumpty had a great fall / all the king's horses and all the king's men / couldn't put Humpty Dumpty together again."

"Oh!" Helena says excitedly. "No! I've completely forgotten what that is."

"Well, it's not really a poem," Alice says shyly.

"It's a rhyme," Luke says. "Is it the same guy who wrote *Alice in Wonderland*?"

"Lewis Carroll? No," Kristin says.

"I don't know who wrote it. I just remember it from when I was little."

"Then you don't get any points," Luke says.

"Yes, she does!" Kristin shouts, "Nobody's guessed the writer yet."

"That's because it's an age-old nursery rhyme," Thomas says, "and nobody knows who wrote it. It's probably been passed down via the oral tradition."

"It was in one of my books when I was a kid," Patricia says. "I can still remember the illustration of the egg-shaped creature in the tree. It wore suspenders and had a strange hat."

"It's called 'Humpty Dumpty,'" Alice says softly.

"Five points to Alice!" Kristin's animated now. "Otherwise I'll veto."

"You can't do that," Luke says sternly.

"Call it a draw, at least. C'mon Luke," Alice chides. "I don't want minus points."

"Can you get *minus points*?" Kristin is genuinely perturbed.

"No," says Luke. "You can't get minus points."

"Come on then, Luke. Give her a point. This is only a parlor game," Thomas says. "And she *knew* the title. You're cheating!"

Luke regards him, irritated. "Of course the player should know the title of the poem she's reciting."

"I don't entirely understand why you have to," Kristin says. Luke makes a decision then, it's clear, and he does an about-face like some other Humpty Dumpty. He smiles. "Fair enough. Five points to Alice."

Alice cheers. They pour more tequila. Helena goes off to the kitchen for olives and salted almonds. "But who *is* Humpty Dumpty?" Alice says, gulping her drink. She spreads out on her stomach, exposing a strip of skin between her T-shirt and jeans. "Who the *hell* is Humpty Dumpty? How bizarre!" She laughs so hard she begins to cry, her shoulders heaving. "A dumb little egghead."

"It's Maloney!" Thomas shouts, suddenly very drunk on tequila. "It's Maloney sitting in a tree waiting for someone to rescue him."

"And his savior's *Jenny*!" Patricia practically howls, kicking off her sandals so she can tuck her legs beneath her on the couch.

"Jesus Christ, now I can taste that fucking worm!" Thomas jiggles the bottle and breaks into laughter, and thinks of that *Blade Runner* quote about memories that will disappear like tears in the rain, and that's not at all funny, it's a deep, deep well, and under the well: darkness, death, but if he stays out of the well, it's fun. There's Maloney as Humpty Dumpty, there's Luke—and for crying out loud, his real name is *Luc*, he recalls, *Luc* and not in any way Luke, it's a goddamn pantomime to call him Luke just because fucking Jacques did—*he*, Luc, is the *Schoolmaster of Poetry*, and everything's funny: a glance at Kristin, the laughter rolling off their lips, Alice shaking and drooling as she lies there on her stomach. "What's going on?" she gasps. She finally gets up on all fours, turns, red-faced, her eyes glazed. Luke pinches his lips impatiently before raising his voice, "Are we going to keep playing? Alice, who do you pick?"

"Ah! Why am I so drunk all of a sudden?" Kristin looks as though she's fallen off the moon. They laugh at that too.

"Who do you pick, Alice?" Luke asks again, annoyed.

"I pick Helena," Alice nearly whines. And Helena can't help but smile; it takes a long time before they settle down.

"Okay," Helena says. After drinking water from her green glass, she takes a deep breath.

"Sorry, but I need to light a cigarette," Thomas says.

But *Thomas*! You can't do that." Helena looks shocked.

"Sure he can," Kristin says. "What are we, Calvinists?! Give me a drag."

And so it continues. They pass the cigarette around, and then it's Helena's turn to recite. "This genre means a lot to me. It's part of my meditation. It's connected to my work at the loom. To the images. To harmony and disharmony." She glances at the others through the semi-darkness, meeting their eyes, while her own smolder and glow.

Her beauty is a rare flower, Thomas thinks, a passion flower, gone quickly, until it blooms again, a new flower, ephemeral and unforgettable. Now I'm thinking these thoughts, he thinks, surprised. What kinds of thoughts are they, *passion flowers, rare beauty*—from *Humpty Dumpty* to *unforgettable*. Meanwhile Helena goes on: "I don't know if you understand what I'm saying, but the tapestries represent, for me, the expression of a lifelong act, a slow and rather humble act, but one that's totally spontaneous and unforeseen, deeply expressionistic, the byproduct of a single unruly movement or thought." Helena stares at a point above their heads, her face inscrutable. "It's probably the closest I'll ever come to eternity," she says, her eyes darting to Alice and rousing her. Alice and Patricia seemed to have zoned out during her long monologue. Patricia's lying with one arm over her eyes.

"But what poem are you going to recite?" Alice asks sleepily, staggering to the coffee table and scooping up a handful of almonds. She pops them into her mouth.

"Right. Okay. Listen . . ."

"Haiku," Luke interrupts tensely, leaning forward in his seat. "You're talking about haiku."

"You're a very bright young man," Helena says following a brief pause. She smiles warmly at him. "But do you also know the poet and the publication year? That's the question, after all, as I understand it."

"You don't get any points for guessing the genre," Patricia says, shifting her arms from her face to the crown of her head. "You didn't say anything about that anyway."

"No, I know" Luke says defensively, "I just knew it was haiku."

"Luke's so smart he doesn't need his head," Alice giggles.

"Listen to Helena!" Kristin can't help but shout.

And Helena recites her poem: "*Midfield, / attached to nothing, / the skylark is singing.*"

"That was short," Alice says, lifting her eyebrows.

"It was beautiful. Beautiful!" Kristin, still boisterous, pats Helena's thigh.

"Learning that kind of poem by heart would be easy, I think," Alice says, rubbing her head.

"It's Basho," Luke says. "1644-1694."

"What do you mean by that?" Thomas stares at Luke's pale, rapt face.

"That's correct." Helena smiles at Luke. "It's the year of his birth and his death. He died in 1694. Basho's probably Japan's most important haiku poet. You could say that he invented the form."

"What kind of bullshit is that?" Alice mumbles.

"What you recited reminds me of Buson's most famous poem. The one with the temple bell." Luke leans back in his chair. "Do you know it?"

"Of course I do! Everyone does!"

"Not me," Alice says.

"Me neither," Thomas says, fishing a black olive out of the ceramic bowl.

"Well, it goes like this: '*Butterfly / sleeping / on the temple bell.*'"

Helena ecstatically twirls a lock of hair around her index finger.

"Because there are winged creatures in each poem? Is that why you think they're similar? I don't get it." Alice sits cross-legged, hands around her feet. "But I think I could definitely write those kinds of poems. It wouldn't take longer than a few minutes to write those, tops. Hey, maybe I can be a poet!"

"Basho said that haiku is what happens at this place at this moment," Luke says, and Helena nods, understanding. "That's exactly right," she says, her index finger twirling faster and faster around her lock of hair.

"What's happening right now is that we're piss-drunk in this house!" Alice says, throwing herself back onto the couch. Thomas stifles a laugh. She's right. But Helena continues enthusiastically:

"That's what it's like working at the loom. Basho had this theory about the clash of the eternal with the transient. He said that each element should be present in every single poem . . ."

"Okay, that's enough." Alice covers her ears. "No more haiku for me."

"Especially no more haiku theory," adds Thomas. Helena laughs, winking at Luke. "Okay. We can talk about it tomorrow then."

Kristin raises her voice: "And the winner is Luke! But he didn't say the name of the poem. So he won't get any points for that."

"We need special rules for haiku. They don't have titles and it's hard to know precisely when they were written, or where they were published."

"Luke's absolutely right," Helena says.

"Of course you can," Patricia suggests, "if you're an expert."

"But Helena and Luke apparently aren't," Thomas blurts triumphantly. They all laugh, and Helena shakes her head, smiling at the boisterous, ignorant lot. Thomas stands, roaring: "I HATE HAIKU!" Which causes Alice to get to her feet and hop up and down on the couch, so that the pillows slide to the floor as she howls: "Hi-ya! Haiku-Helena!"

"That's enough!" Kristin cries. "STOP!!"

Helena decides Luke should get ten points for knowing the poet's name, birth year, and death year—though everyone else protests vociferously. Helena also suggests that he should get a special bonus for his "surprising knowledge of haiku," but that's shot down immediately, with boos and foot-stomping. Kristin's about to leave the room, scowling at Helena. "It's undemocratic," she hisses, standing with her arms at her sides. "You can't just introduce an absolute monarchy!" Helena pulls her down beside her, then plants a kiss on her cheek. "The children are here, you can't just leave." Luke preens at hearing Helena's praise. He stretches his arms toward the ceiling and cracks his knuckles, and for one moment that's the only sound they hear. Then the wind whooshes outside. Like a storm. The wind blows and whistles and drives a branch against the roof, clawing it. Helena walks to the window. "Some weather . . ." "Who are you going to pick, Helena?" Luke asks. Kristin, no longer agitated, fills everyone's glass. They toast. The heat in the living room is intense; it feels as if it's coming from inside themselves. Though he's a little dizzy, Thomas's mood improves; he lights another cigarette and exhales long, blue spirals, *columns of smoke*, he thinks woozily, *a fucking skylark pips*, and then he's overcome with such a forceful laughter that he swallows his own spit down the wrong pipe. With her flat, strong hand Kristin repeatedly claps the coughing, half-choked man on his back. "What was so funny?" Alice giggles when he's finally more or less himself again. She takes the cigarette from him and pulls at it until the cherry glows red. But before he can answer, Luke repeats in a firm voice: "Who do you pick, Helena?"

Helena points at Patricia, and Patricia sits bolt upright in her chair. Her hair is untidy, tousled, and she's a little unsteady. While lying on the couch her dress has slid up her legs, and now she tugs it down, so that it lies smoothly over her hips and thighs. She's fetched a book from the shelf. Holding her hands over the title and the author's name, she says, "Ladies and gentlemen! Listen to this music!" She giggles, doubling over. She rolls her eyes. Then she reads aloud, hesitantly, clearing her throat from time to time; the tequila sings all over her Ss. "*Saxifrage, the great horned owl, milk, / irrefutable as lightning, the rock, / thick with doves, the southerly wind, / yolk, bromine, why not, / and as far as I'm concerned, lightning, yes, / whale and lightning, they stand firm, / let us build upon them, / they are worthy of an ode.*" Patricia inhales and holds her breath, then she smiles and curtsies, but as she leans forward her chair tips and she screams in fright, flapping her arms, and Thomas barely manages to grab her before she falls. The book thumps to the floor.

"Enzensberger," Luke says mechanically. "'Ode to Celery.' First published in *The Local Language*, 1960."

"You've got to be kidding me," Patricia says, impressed. She sits down. "You're not a newbie at this, are you?"

"Are you hurt?" Helena asks worriedly. Patricia shakes her head.

"It's totally cheating to read from a book. Anyone can do that!" Alice is upset.

"Normal people can't remember every possible poem by heart, can they?" Kristin says. "We'll just have to bend the rules."

"I didn't know you read poetry, babe?" Thomas says, his voice still rusty following his coughing fit.

"I don't. But I did once. You know that. I was very into Enzensberger at one point. For a long time." Patricia stares dreamily at the night-darkened window, which mirrors her image like a veiled angel or a ghost.

"Sounded a little like haiku to me," Alice sniffles.

"But it isn't, my dear," Helena says with a sigh. She stretches her legs.

"You're all so smart and well read. All these old poems . . . Why isn't anyone reciting *new* poems? Some recent poems? It's sad." Alice groans. Then she yawns, so that everyone can see her reddened uvula. "Oh, how sad . . ." She crumples into a fetal position and watches the group, her eyes half-closed. From time to time they glide shut.

"You're the one who should know new poems, Alice. You're young. You should teach them to us," Helena says gently, touching Alice's ankle.

"What I like about the poem," Patricia interrupts, straightening abruptly, "is . . . the *celebration* of life, you know? The earthly life with egg yolks and southerly wind and owls and celery. You know what I mean?" There are red blotches on her cheeks now. She crosses her legs.

"That's how the other poems were too," Alice mumbles. "Southerly winds and midfields and soft-boiled eggs . . ."

"Twenty points for Luke. You're in the lead." Kristin picks up her nearly-empty glass.

"He's led the entire time," Helena smiles.

"Do we have any candy?" Alice asks sleepily.

"We're here now, aren't we?" Patricia looks at Thomas, narrowing her eyes. "You and me."

"That's right," he says. "You and me. We're here right now." And then he adds, "No matter what. Right?" He holds her gaze, wanting her to give him a sign. But she lifts her head, tilting it all the way back, a mysterious smile etched onto her lips. Then she stands and wobbles out of the room.

"The big question tonight," Helena says, "must be how in the world Luke knows so much about poetry. You should study literature, man!"

"It's Jacques," Thomas says. "It's all because of Jacques."

Helena shakes her head. "Unbelievable . . ."

"Thomas is right," Luke smiles, moving onto the couch beside Alice. "It's all Jacques's fault."

"It's my turn now." Kristin sets her glass down with a thud.

"But you've *had* a turn, Kristin!" Alice peers from behind the pillows, wagging her finger—*no, no, no*—clucking her tongue, glowing, smiling, laughing.

"Yes! But now it's my turn again! Listen up. *This* is how you capture life. This one is . . . like the waves on the ocean. I hope I don't stumble over this. I only recall a small chunk of it by heart. It's difficult stuff, this . . . No, I'm getting the book." And before Luke or anyone else can protest, Kristin has begun reciting. She has removed her scarf and wrapped the book in it, so they can't see the title. She's on her feet. Standing in all her grandeur in the middle of the room. The tall, straight body, the sinewy arms. The effortless elegance she carries around like something she was born with. She recites loudly and lucidly, bobbing her head rhythmically and systematically, which, considering her growing inebriation on tequila, defies all reason. Her hair, thick and gray, swishes from side to side. "*Even the children remember that as a year in the slums, threatened with change, where the speakers in the vans invited theft. Sticky finger licking chicken. Clichés and lamentation. We were floating the logic in a rushing medium. I want to be free of you, in order to do things, things of importance which will impress you, attract you, so that you can be mine and I can be yours, forever.*" Kristin rolls through the text. My mother could have been here, Thomas thinks, right here, beside her sister. She could have resembled her. She could have enjoyed Kristin's ferocity and enthusiasm. She could have loved it or recognized it. Or she could have been irritated. But then he thinks about what Patricia said about his mother, that she was wild and decadent; that's not how he remembers her. How does he remember her? Was she distant? Was she loving? Was she gentle and motherly or high, drunk, strange, unreliable? Was she irascible? Did she play with him for hours? Did they build things with blocks? Did she teach him how to draw a house? Did she leave him to fend for himself? He doesn't remember. He remembers only these tiny glimpses that have always haunted him: the feel of her raw tweed dress when he sat on her lap, the smooth nylon stockings, her rounded knees, the distracted way she ran her hand through his hair. But what *was* her hand like? He can see her standing in the little kitchen, her back to him. Now she turns her clear blue eyes to him. She hands him a plate of sliced apple. He closes his eyes. The stories about her brothers, her soft voice. He would often reach out his hand and touch her earlobe, rubbing it between his index finger and thumb; sometimes she let him do this, sometimes she didn't. And her laughter, which seemed to come from somewhere else, another room, maybe the living room. Her laughter, and her light, easy footsteps across the wooden floor. He hears Kristin: "*A child is a real person, very lively. They are like plump birds along the shore, standing, watching the local flags snap. It is the sea salt in our blood. A mere drop in the cup. A mirror makes it turn over.*" He's riding in a bus with his mother. She's wearing a light-blue jacket. The baby is Jenny, and the baby's drooling. He hears clearly the chugging of the bus's motor, the swoop of the door opening and closing, every time the bus stops. Can hear someone talking in the seat behind them. He feels lonely or insecure and clutches his mother's jacket. She stares out the window. She's wearing sunglasses. But it's raining outside, the water's sliding down the glass. And it's dark. Where are they going? And *is* this really a memory? Can it be considered a true memory? No. He shakes his head and empties the bottle into his glass. She's nothing but a jacket and stockings and a plate of apple slices that are already turning brown. He cannot grasp her presence. It doesn't work. "*It seemed that we had hardly begun and we were already there, watching people for an instant framed in windows, never finding out what happens to them, or what they mean.*" Kristin beams. Alice is asleep on the couch. And Luke, deep in concentration, sits on the edge of his flimsy chair. Patricia has returned now, and she leans against the doorframe. She looks spent. "*The air we breathe: the air we breathe ranging in size contains flakes of sound, dark, silence, and light.*" Kristin claps the book shut and glances around the room victoriously. Helena begins to gather glasses and bowls, which she places on a black lacquered tray. No one says a word. "None of you know that poem?" Kristin asks, shocked. "C'mon! That can't be. Patricia?"

She shakes her head.

"Luke?"

"Never heard it before."

"Ignoramuses!" Kristin plops into the beanbag chair, sighing. She squeezes the shrouded book against her chest.

"I'm going to bed now," Patricia says, exhausted, "It's 1:30 in the morning. Are you coming, Thomas?"

"No," Luke says firmly, unexpectedly. "He's staying. We're not quite finished with the game."

Thomas looks at Luke, and Luke stares insistently at him, insistent and challenging. "Luke's right," Thomas says. "But I'll be there soon." He wants to stand up and take Patricia's hand, he wants to apologize, to do something, kiss her, but she's already gone. Luke covers Alice with a blanket. Helena helps Kristin out of the beanbag chair and hands her the empty bottle of tequila. After they've said goodnight and are on their way out of the room, Kristin turns abruptly in the doorway, yelling: "It was LYN HEJINIAN, YOU MEATHEADS! From *My Life*! A masterpiece! First published in 1987. Three hundred thousand points for me. You don't know shit about poetry!" Her eyes glow. She gestures threateningly with the empty bottle, so that the dead, alcohol-soaked worm bounces up and down, smacking against the glass. She shakes her head resignedly. From the kitchen Helena calls for her, friendly but firm, and Kristin curses under her breath, tromping off in her soft moccasins.

Thomas and Luke go outside to piss. Standing side by side in the wet, cool night air, they splash their urine against something that, in the dark, resembles a bank of earth or an anthill. Wind cuts through the treetops. They stand close to one another. They're quiet. Thomas's mouth is dry. Wind whips through his hair and his shirt, which fills with air and lifts from his back like a sail. He shivers. The sky seems pale with light. Huge cloud masses scuttle swiftly toward the northeast. Luke zips up his fly. They walk single file back to the house. They get beers in the utility room. "Let's go to the sunroom so we don't wake up Alice," Luke suggests. The bench is hard and the sunroom cold, but Luke pulls pillows and wool blankets from the couch in the living room. Thomas lights the candles resting in some small, amateurish ceramic candleholders, which the twins must have made when they were in kindergarten. A gust of air wends its way through the glass partitions, causing the flames to shoot up until again they shrink, flickering weakly. The wind howls outside, shivering in the trees. Luke uncaps the beers with his lighter, and they light cigarettes. Thomas lays a quilt across his legs, and Luke drapes a blanket around his shoulders, now like an Indian chief. Although Thomas feels less drunk, a headache already thumps behind his left eye. An awl in his head. He stares at the plants in the room, standing in pots, their branches and leaves outstretched. It smells strangely of geraniums, smoke, and candlewax. Luke turns abruptly toward him. With a soft, low voice, he says, his words threading the air between them: "*What did I / do? / Seminated the night, as though / there could be others, more nocturnal than / this one . . .*"

"Celan," Thomas says, interrupting him. "But I don't know the name of the poem, or what year it's from. I just recognize the tone."

"'All Souls.' From *Language Mesh*, 1959," Luke says before Thomas has completed his thought. "Your turn."

Luke's eyes radiate heat. Thomas can smell his breath. Once again there's this jasmine-like fragrance in it, almost like a sweet tea in the midst of something fusty and sharp. Thomas can't remember a single strophe of anything at all. The only thing he knows is Celan's "Death Fugue," and that's too easy. Luke would guess it at once. Shakespeare, he thinks. Come on, remember some lines of a sonnet. Or Dickinson. Dickinson or Rilke. Lorca. Luke waits patiently. He drinks his beer and ashes his cigarette. He leans back on the bench and turns to face the storm, the night. But Thomas doesn't know Emily Dickinson, Lorca, or Rilke by heart. And why would he? He's read very little poetry, and then mostly because the small volumes are often beautiful, and published on first-rate paper. He's caressed the books more than he's read them. The font type, the margins, the paper's weight, the cover design—this is what he looks at. There's nothing left for him to do but give up and utter a few lines of "Death Fugue." But not the first lines. There's a microscopic chance that Luke won't remember the entire poem. He clears his throat. Luke gives him an encouraging look, then smiles. A small, kind smile. And

Thomas focuses on the sight of the poem, the way he sees it on his shelf at home. Imagining it, he scans the page in his mind. Then he says: "*He calls out jab deeper into the earth you lot you others sing now and play / he grabs at the iron in his belt he waves it his eyes are blue / jab deeper you lot with your spades . . .*" Thomas can't remember any more. "*Jab deeper you lot with your spades . . .*" Thomas sputters to a halt. A smile spreads across Luke's face, exposing his teeth. "*You others play on for the dance*," Luke continues, nodding; he's enjoying this very much, apparently. "That was easy," he says. "Paul Celan's 'Death Fugue.' *Poppy and Memory, 1952*."

And on and on it goes, Thomas gives up, Luke recites indefatigably. Once in a while Thomas guesses correctly, but most of the time he's wrong. And usually it's the poets' surnames he gets right, not the titles, not the given names, not the publication dates. Luke seems to expand on the bench, filling more and more, he seems kinder, more animated. Meanwhile, Thomas's headache gets worse.

"Do you even understand the meanings of the poems that you know by heart?" Thomas asks at one point. Luke shrugs and pops open another beer. "That's not important. What's important is knowing them. Almost like counting sheep when you can't sleep."

"What do you mean by that?"

"I don't really know. I've just learned them. Jacques made me practice when we were fishing. It was a kind of sport to him. Sometimes he would tell me that his head swarmed with poems, as if they plagued him. Other times they made him . . ." Luke sighs, wrapping the blanket tighter around him.

"What? In good spirits? Happy?"

"I don't know." Luke stares straight ahead. "But I think so. In prison he always crammed poetry. When I visited him, the first thing he'd asked was whether I'd learned this or that suite, and whether I'd brought this or that book for him. We had a kind of . . . fellowship with the poems." Luke breathes slowly, in and out, from deep within his belly. "It was something we shared—even when he was in prison and we couldn't fish or anything."

"Strange," says Thomas. "Fucking strange." He shakes his head and swigs the last of his lukewarm beer.

"Are you tired?" All at once Luke sounds gentle and jittery. But he doesn't look nervous. Only happy. Big and happy and gracious.

"We can do a few more," Thomas says. He doesn't want to disappoint him. Luke gathers himself and closes his eyes. For a moment, he seems like a sprinter waiting for the official to fire the starter's gun. Extremely present and alert, but at the same time mentally withdrawn, into his body. "*Why, if this interval of being can be spent serenely / in the form of a laurel, slightly darker than all / other green, with tiny waves on the edges / of every leaf (like the smile of a breeze)—: why then / have to be human—and, escaping from fate, / keep longing from fate? . . . / oh not because happiness exists, / that too-hasty profit snatched from approaching / loss.*"

Since Thomas doesn't stop him, he keeps going. Thrusting the words, rhythmic and strong. Rocking back and forth. Lifting his head and lowering it. Thomas gets goose bumps and feels a sudden tenderness for the young man beside him, so vulnerable suddenly, or so it seems, but maybe he's wrong. *"Look, I am living. On what? Neither childhood nor future grows any smaller . . . superabundant being / wells up in my heart."*

They fall silent. Listening to the wind. A lucid thought pierces Thomas: *Is he my brother?* The notion startles him. Is Luke my brother? Is that it? Luke—exhausted, quizzical, but also proud—looks at Thomas.

"Applause," Thomas says, carefully touching Luke's shoulder. "Not too many can do what you do. Rilke. It must be one of the elegies, but which one? I haven't a clue."

"The ninth."

They smoke another cigarette. Luke tucks his legs underneath him and hugs his knees. The cigarette glows and the lights flicker. Thomas regards Luke. They don't at all look alike. Except in height. *What if he's my brother*? Warm and cold, his lungs floating behind his ribs, as if there was suddenly all too-much air in them. "Rilke," Thomas says. "They say you'll need to spend your entire life studying his work if you really want to understand him." Luke doesn't comment on that. He's oddly distant now. Outside it sounds as though the wind has transformed into one large, greedy mouth.

"Well," Thomas says, "It's almost bedtime for me. Aren't you getting up early to fish? Or have you changed your mind?"

Luke will go fishing. Thomas stands. But it's as if Luke's consciousness returns to the situation and the sunroom. With renewed energy, he insists on reciting yet another poem. The goodnight poem, he calls it. Against his better judgment, Thomas returns to the bench, swaddling himself in the blanket. He's had enough poetry. And this new, nagging idea—that Luke could be Jacques's son—careens in him like confusing, off-key notes. Luke's different now, freer, and it's obvious that he knows this poem from beginning to end, and could probably recite it in his sleep.

"*We two, how long we were fool'd / Now transmuted, we swiftly escape as Nature escapes, / We are Nature, long have we been absent, but now we return, / We become plants, trunks, foliage, roots, bark . . .*" And a little further along in the text: "*We are two fishes swimming in the sea together / We are what locust blossoms are, we drop scent around lanes / mornings and evenings . . .*" Thomas eyes Luke. Luke's face opens, his jaw slackens, his eyes looking calmly ahead, his left hand keeping rhythm, tranquilly tapping the arm of the bench. Thomas allows him to repeat the entire poem. At last Luke turns to him, and his voice is deep and hot in Thomas's ear. It feels as though Luke's eyes are boring right into his brain, but there's also a question behind them, a kind of prayer, almost: "*We are snow, rain, cold, darkness, we are each product and / influence of the globe, / We have circled and circled till we have arrived home again, we two, / We have voided all but freedom and all but our own joy.*" When Luke is finished, it's quiet. But he continues to stare. Thomas hears Luke's breathing, even imagines he hears his heart beating. Suddenly it's all too much. Too intimate. Too constricting, as if both the poem and Luke's gaze were an invitation written in invisible ink; is that what he's saying? Thomas thinks, shifting in his seat. Is he telling me we're brothers with that poem? It's unreal and strangely obvious at the same time. "Very nice," he says. "Who is it?" Finally Luke draws his face back.

"Whitman. Walt Whitman. You don't know it?"

Thomas shakes his head.

"It's one of my favorite poems," Luke says softly. "If I can put it that way. I recited it to myself at Jacques's funeral. It played on a continuous loop in my head. It's calming, I think, or something like that."

So he does have a favorite poem, Thomas thinks. Then he considers the poem's meaning. He inches away, and Luke sets his feet on the cement floor again, then leans forward and braces his hands against the edge of the bench.

"Maybe he thought about it too," Thomas says tentatively. "Jacques, I mean. When he realized he was dying."

Luke shrugs. "I don't think so. He just died. Collapsed." Then, with more urgency, he leans backward and slides his arms along the bench, one of which settles right behind Thomas's neck. He says: "You know that prison guard at the funeral was the one who kindled Jacques's interest in poetry? He loaned him a book. Many years ago. Later he helped him order books from the library." He looks at Thomas. Half his face is in shadow, the rest glows in the flickering orange-yellow light of a candle. The other candle has gone out.

"So a convict and a guard were both held in the vast, life-enriching clutches of poetry?" Thomas says. He can't help but laugh, briefly and hoarsely. "That's too funny!" But Luke doesn't think it's so funny. He presses his lips together, tilts his head back, and gathers up his hair.

"Well, there's no doubt who the winner of this round is," Thomas says, conciliatory. "Not to mention the first. You're really good, I'll give you that. I'm happy that Jacques gave these poems to you—that he gave anything to you at all." Thomas regards Luke, searching for some sign in his face, in his eyes, something to reveal who he is, and who his father is. But there's nothing to see. Thomas gets to his feet. "Are you coming?"

Luke shakes his head. "I'm going to sit here a while," he says quietly. "If I can have another of your cigarettes?"

"Just don't burn the house down," Thomas smiles. "Goodnight, Luc. Good to spar with you." Luke flinches at the sound of his real name, but he doesn't respond. "I didn't offend you, did I? What I said about the clutches of poetry?" With small gestures, Luke indicates that Thomas didn't offend him. Then he smiles tiredly, lowering his chin. And as Thomas begins to go, his headache throbs with merciless precision. He's not drunk anymore, but apparently he's already got a hangover. It must be 3:00 in the morning. He ambles through the house, then cautiously outside, into the wind. This time he finds the barn door without any difficulty. Shortly afterward, he's lying on the saggy air mattress beside Patricia, listening to the peaceful sounds of bodies sleeping near him. The sleeping bag warms up quickly. Patricia grinds her teeth. No way he's my brother, he thinks, and now it seems insane that he'd convinced himself of the opposite only a moment before. He can feel in his bones that he has no genetic connection whatsoever to Luke. No kinship. Not even a sliver of a doubt. Calm now, he rolls onto his side. Takes a deep breath. I've dived into a sea of bobbing people, he thinks sleepily. I'm bobbing in a sea of people. Right before he falls asleep, he's suddenly gripped by panic. What if Luke really burns the house down? But of course he won't. And the wind whistles and howls.

By the next morning the wind has died down, and the sun's shining through an almost cloudless sky. Thomas wakes to the sound of bleating sheep. He looks at the clock—9:00 A.M. Though he tries to fall asleep again, he can't. He's nauseated and his mouth is pasty: a dry taste of dog food and vomit. But he didn't vomit. And luckily his headache is now more of a dull throb than actual pain. Patricia's getting dressed. Pulling her blouse over her head, buttoning her skirt in the back. Thomas sits up. The others have left their bedrolls. Jenny and Maloney have carefully folded their blankets and towels. "Morning," Patricia says. "You look like an old man."

"I feel like an old man," Thomas mutters, turning his face away. She walks off. He gets to his feet. His clothes reek of smoke. When he goes out to the yard, the light's very bright. He squints at the sun and stands there a moment; everything seems bleary, flickering. Finally he regains focus. The sheep stare at him. They're gathered in a large, bleating mass on the other side of the fence. On the patio, Kristin sits dressed in a bathrobe and sunglasses, drinking coffee with Jenny, Maloney, and Helena. And now Patricia steps out of the sunroom, a mug in her hand. Thomas O'Mally Lindström cuts across the lawn, planting his big feet step by step in the wet, dewy grass, his arms swinging listlessly at his side, thinking about the poem Luke read last, the so-called "goodnight poem." He wonders about it. He thinks about French fries smothered in thick mayonnaise, about burgers with enormous pickles. He notices the rowan trees' feather-like leaves, a blackbird landing on a gnarled apple tree, Patricia sitting down and saying something to Kristin. Can feel the heartburn just under his ribs. The light like confetti when he slips under a shedding lilac. Finally he reaches the patio, and finds a seat beside Helena.

"Oh," he groans. "I feel a little dizzy today."

They discuss the good weather, the arrival of summer after an unrecognizable spring, last night's competition, the long drive home. They laugh wearily at one of Maloney's jokes, which falls flat, then they simultaneously zone out. Thomas gets coffee and buns smeared in butter. Maloney concentrates on spooning a bowl of yogurt heaped with a generous portion of sugar into his mouth. "Where are the girls?" Patricia asks.

"They're still asleep," Helena says. "Anyone want aspirin?" She looks at Kristin, grinning. Kristin grunts something unintelligible.

"Awr," Jenny says, stretching. "That air mattress thoroughly beat me . . . I've slept terribly . . ."

Alice and Luke have gone fishing. Helena heard them rummaging around in the kitchen shortly after sunrise. They stand. Carry their mugs in. And the morning passes packing cars and cleaning the house. Sleepily, the twins descend the stairs at 11:00 A.M. and are promptly sent out to feed the chickens. Thomas walks down to the lake, but Alice and Luke aren't anywhere to be seen. He shuffles back. The others are seated on the patio again. Patricia gets a sunburn rather quickly. She wiggles her toes with her legs up on a chair. Thomas lays a hand on her warm, naked shin. He can't find his cigarettes. He discusses hiring Alice with Maloney once more. Maloney's pretty much resigned to it. Jenny gets involved, she's distrustful, but thinks that overall it's a good idea. "If it has to be this way," she sighs, "then I suppose this is as good as anything else." Kristin opines that Alice ought to go back to school. Helena says, "Leave the girl alone now. She's only eighteen."

"Exactly," Kristin snaps, her hangover clearly making her testy. "She should get an education, for God's sake. Like everyone else!"

"Everyone else . . ." Jenny says pointedly. "I don't have any education."

"Sure you do! You studied nursing!" Kristin sounds very irritated now.

"For one semester only. But I never finished. Nobody encouraged me to continue."

"We did too," Thomas says. "Don't start that again."

Appalled, Jenny stares at him with round, martyr eyes.

"But Jenny," Helena soothes, "you've done all right, though. You've always had work."

"But not as a nurse! Anyway, that's not the point. Can't you let Alice figure things out for *herself*? Why do you need to get so involved?" Jenny's on the edge of becoming hysterical.

"I'm going down to stack some wood," Maloney declares, removing his T-shirt so that everyone can see his big white belly. Helena's aghast at the sight. His gut apparently stops all conversation. They gaze at Maloney in silence, watching him trundle toward the wood pile. Then they discuss the vandalism at the store, and Thomas realizes that he's hardly thought about it since they left the city. Kristin speaks up and loudly tells them about a breech birth that went horribly wrong. She doesn't spare any of the gruesome details. Most children are born at home up here, she explains, and it's not always possible to reach the hospital if there's an emergency, because the distances are too great. She'd called for a helicopter, but it was too late. Patricia shudders. "Usually everything goes as it should," Helena smiles. "Now don't be scaring Patricia. Kristin says that you two are thinking about having a baby? It's lovely. I miss having little ones in my life. Perhaps we could become grandmothers of some kind?" Helena glances happily at Kristin, and Kristin gives her an exasperated, unfriendly glare.

"I can't imagine Thomas as a father . . ." Jenny says.

"Here they come!" Patricia interrupts, pointing down toward the lake. Rising to her feet, she shields her eyes from the sun with her hand. Alice and Luke appear. She: easy-going and slender with her ultra-short hair. He: calm, and as though conjoined with the earth, wearing shorts and rubber boots. Their fishing poles rest on their shoulders, and Luke's carrying a bucket that seems heavy. Maya and Nina run toward them, Jupiter barking at their heels. "I think they caught something!" Patricia says cheerfully. "So we can have minced fish-balls for lunch."

Yes, they can. Luke has caught a medium-sized pike and four small perch. He seems rather pleased. The women shout excitedly, all except for Kristin, who sneaks away. Luke and Alice sit on the stoop and clean the fish. Luke teaches Alice just how to avoid cutting herself on the sharp spikes the perch have on their gills and dorsal fin. He uses the knife skillfully. Tosses the fish heads to the two wild cats who, drawn by the smell, have approached. Luke explains how he had to fight the pike. The perch, too. "When they have a good bite on the hook, they can really put up a struggle," he says, wiping blood from his hands with a paper towel. "But that just makes it more fun." According to Alice, Luke is the most amazing and talented and professional fisherman there is. "What did you do, then?" Nina asks Alice.

"I watched Luke and kept him company. But unfortunately I didn't catch any fish myself."

"Yes, you did," Luke says.

"Okay, but you had to take over the line for me." She looks at the twins. "I couldn't hold it! It was the pike. It got away the first time, but Luke hooked it again."

"You can't possibly know it was the same pike," says Nina.

"Of course you can," Luke says. "And do you know how we know? It told us its name."

"What was its name then?" Maya widens her eyes in anticipation.

"Samuel the Fat Pike was its name." With sunlight glinting in his eyes, Luke looks at the girls, who can't hide their pleasure at this moment.

Luke and Alice carry the fish to the utility room, where they are filleted. Luke tells them that pike can be difficult to strip entirely free of bones, if you don't know the technique. But he knows how, of course. What makes deboning difficult, he explains, has something to do with what's called the Y-bones, because they're curved. Then he begins to explain at length. Thomas can't concentrate anymore. The little troop has followed them out, and now stands appreciatively observing Luke and his knife. "I think we should fry the whole perch," he says. But Samuel the Fat Pike will be minced. Patricia churns it through the mincer then dresses it with flour, dill, and lemon zest. Soon the aroma of fried fish spreads through the house. Helena prepares a remoulade sauce, and the girls slice lemons into wedges. Maloney's called in to fry the perch. While trying to flip one in the air, it lands, to the girls' immense pleasure, on the floor. Maloney throws it right back in the pan again—making the girls even more giddy. Jenny sits in a chair doing nothing. She looks exhausted, and yet not. Her arms are pink from the sun. Now she picks up the newspaper and browses it absentmindedly. The way she does, stooped, as if the world didn't interest her in the slightest. And maybe it doesn't, Thomas thinks. He's recruited to whip up a salad of carrots, cabbage, and chopped hazelnuts, and he wants to force Jenny to help him, but decides against it because it seems too childish. "How about we eat outside?" Helena suggests. "We'd just need to move the table out of the sunroom." Luke will do that. Helena sends Nina upstairs to get Kristin, who returns soon after with pillow marks on her right cheek and a tired, worn-out expression on her face. The minced fish balls seem to raise her spirits. In short order they're seated on the patio together, a faded parasol over their heads. The bread is passed around. The butter is fresh and yellow. And the fish couldn't be any tastier. They divide the four perches. Their skin is crunchy and the meat firm. The fish balls are light brown and juicy. You can taste the flavor from the lemon zest. There's no end to the superlatives thrown Luke's way; he beams at the boundless admiration and praise. At last Maloney takes it upon himself to interject some crude observations to draw attention away from the young man at the end of the table, who has each of the women in the palm of his hand. Thomas glances at his friend, relieved. Blinking, Maloney asks about Kristin's hunting license. "Let's talk about killing animals," he says, "not little fish, but large mammals with horns and visible genitalia!" Thomas can't help but notice Luke shrink a bit. "I also want to learn how to fish," Maya whispers, leaning against Luke. "Next time," Luke says, standing abruptly. He saunters into the shade and lights a cigarette. He seems hunted now, restless, his eyes darting uneasily across the meadows and fields, as if he's suddenly thought of something very unpleasant. It's Thomas's cigarette pack he's fingering. Though he was only offered a single smoke last night, he must have taken the entire pack.

The twins cry when they say goodbye to Alice. "Nothing ever happens here, and *now you're leaving*!" Nina whimpers. She has to wrap them each in a bear hug and give them some of her bracelets before they calm down. She rides with Jenny and Maloney. She has to work in a few hours. And Thomas remembers what she does, the job she performs. He doesn't like the thought of it. He quickly arranges to meet with her at the store Monday morning. "Remember to call Annie and Peter!" Maloney calls, popping his ruddy head out the window. "Company happy hour tomorrow!" Jenny waves her scarf, which, like a salmon-colored wimple, is thrown hither and thither by the wind as Maloney's red Toyota finally putters up the driveway. Then Luke says, "You want me to drive first to show you the way?"

"Way? Way to what?"

"To my mother's. Did you forget?"

Luke glowers at Thomas reproachfully. Patricia doesn't understand. But there's nothing to do: Thomas promised to go with Luke.

Patricia didn't, and she quickly says that she needs to go home to the cat, which has been alone all weekend. Suddenly and swiftly Patricia presses her lips to Luke's mouth, after which she disappears into Kristin's embrace. Thomas tries to suppress his gasp. For a long moment Patricia holds Helena's hands in hers. He strives to get Patricia's attention; she doesn't look at him. She smiles to the girls, though. What *is* it? Is she flirting? Trying to provoke him? Or just showing Thomas how completely indifferent she is to him? She gets into the rental car. Thomas blocks the sun with his hand and once again attempts to make eye contact with her, without succeeding. Patricia's already driving away, and Helena puts her arms around Thomas and whispers, "She's an exceptional girl, take good care of her." Thomas is going to ride with Luke. He doesn't really want to, especially now, but everything's happening so fast. Kristin says, "Goodbye, little Thomas. Don't do anything your aunt wouldn't do." And then there's nothing left to do but climb into the seat beside Luke; he's already put the key in the ignition and revved the engine. The wheels stir up clouds of dust, and Kristin and Helena and the twins take an instinctive step backward. Luke accelerates, making the bumps on the gravel road feel extra hard; Thomas's head is slung back when he turns to wave at the women and the gangly girls, who with their small, slender braids look even more gangly and perplexed than before.

Luke drives fast. He doesn't say a word. Sunlight sweeps over the landscape with inexpressible beauty. At first Thomas wants to say something, compel Luke to tell him about Patricia's intentions. But he changes his mind; it would be the dumbest thing to talk to Luke about that. It'd be best to seem unaffected, as though nothing were amiss. Because something tells him that Patricia's the problem, not Luke. So Thomas watches the scattered green fields and gradually feels his body relaxing. He's tired after the long night, the many poems, the tequila. He closes his eyes, dozes with his chin resting on his chest. When Luke stops the car on the side of the road, he jerks awake.

"What's going on?"

"Nothing," Luke says dismissively. He sits with his hands on the wheel and stares ahead. Soon he starts the car again and steers onto the road.

"Don't you know where you're going?"

"Yes."

Thomas observes Luke out of the corner of his eye. The small freckles in his face are light-brown, finely drawn against his olive skin. The lush eyelashes, the delicate marzipan-like curve of his ears. There's a little dust in his hair, along with some flakes of dried leaves.

"Did you call your mom and tell her we were coming?"

Luke shakes his head. He seems determined. And there's nothing more to say. They drive for half an hour in silence. On either side of the car are vast fields, pastures with swampy areas, the forested mountainsides far in the distance. They pass a small gas station, a few large farms, some low houses made of wood. It really is a thinly populated region. Thomas forces thoughts of Patricia out of his mind. Then Luke exits the main roadway and drives along a complicated network of side roads, until he suddenly slows, then finally turns down a long, winding driveway. A house comes into view, or rather, a shack. In several places a window has been smashed, replaced with cardboard instead of glass. The roof looks dangerously warped. It's a wooden house painted red, but the paint's chipped and the foundation is covered in green lichen. At one end of the house, a loose board juts out, revealing the rotting core. An old moped lies flipped on its side on the lawn, along with a wheel-less wheelbarrow and something that resembles a stack of rusted iron, which turns out to be some bedframes and various broken farm implements. Luke parks the car. But he doesn't get out. He lets out a deep sigh.

"You think anyone's home?" Thomas asks cautiously. Luke shrugs. "Come," he says, opening the car door. "Maybe she's inside." Standing in front of the house is a simple wooden table, a bench, and a ramshackle garden chair with cushions made of a pale-yellow material, which at one time had been patterned with something like orange tulips. Beer bottles are scattered around the yard. A bucket with rainwater and cigarette butts. A broom, a shovel, a ruined fruit-picker leaning up against the doorframe. Luke leaves the car door open, strides through the tall grass, and grabs the doorknob. It's locked. Thomas walks up beside him. They peer through the windows. The kitchen's a dreadful mess. With the outdated electric stove and a big dirty pot on the kitchen table, it looks awfully sad in there: dirty dishes; a loaf of sliced white-bread, the bag opened; a package of margarine—also opened; a hunk of half-buttered bread; and a large knife beside it smeared with margarine. As if someone was interrupted while preparing breakfast. Old newspapers litter the floor. They walk around the outside of the house. Blankets are heaped on the unmade bed in the bedroom, the living room is dominated by a large TV and a battered couch—on which a pair of curled up cats are sleeping comfortably together. Another room apparently serves as a kind of storage space. Here, various pieces of furniture are piled one atop the other, along with cardboard boxes and plastic bags scattered pell-mell, spider webs, junk upon junk. Topping the stack is a child's broken highchair. "Why would they have a highchair?" Thomas asks. "Do you have younger siblings? Or is your mother a grandmother?"

"It's mine," Luke says, pulling himself away from the window, into the sunlight. "From when I was small. I don't know why she brought it up here."

They sit on a bench smoking cigarettes. Thomas doesn't dare say anything about the place; he's not sure how Luke will respond if he says anything negative. And it's hard to formulate anything positive. He feels bad for the kid; did he really grow up in such a dump? Or were things better when Rose still lived in the city? He can't bring himself to ask. Luke closes his eyes and takes a deep drag on his cigarette.

"Does your mother live alone here?" Thomas asks. "No idea," Luke says. "I haven't seen her for a long time. Let's go." He stands and begins strolling slowly, as though despondent, sluggish, toward the car. Thomas flicks his cigarette butt into a bucket and follows him. Just as they click on their seatbelts, a small van comes into view on the winding gravel drive. Luke's hands grip the wheel. His knuckles are white. The van approaches, jouncing and spitting exhaust fumes. Now they can see two people in the front seat. One must be Rose, but even when the van passes right next to them, Thomas can't recognize her at all. Luke doesn't move a muscle. The van comes to a halt, and a man climbs out with difficulty. He's compact and heavy and wearing a thick, quilted vest over a brown sweater, though the temperature is well above 70 degrees. Clipped to his belt is a large ring of keys. His shoes are tattered, his face puffy. He wanders slowly around the van and opens the door for Rose. A pair of long, thin legs poke from the car now. And then the rest of Rose appears. She's a tall woman, just as Thomas remembers her, but now she's emaciated and frail. She's wearing leggings and an oversized, floppy shirt that's a nondescript bluish-green. At the center of her shirt is the washed-out print of a pink apple. Her hair, once shiny and reddish-orange, now tumbles around her face like a pallid nimbus, discolored and dry. For a moment she stands silently, as if finding her balance. Then she turns toward Luke's car, still wearing her sunglasses. "Honey," she says in a strangely slurred voice, "is that you?" Finally a kind of life stirs in Luke. He glances quickly and expressionlessly at Thomas, then climbs out of the car. Thomas frees himself from his seatbelt and follows him. They stand under the baking sun, and Luke shoves his hands into his pockets. The man says, "So you're Luc." And Luke's mother comes clattering—that's how it seems—clattering on her long, delicate bones, the flesh still somehow clinging to them, clattering into a clumsy embrace of her son, who looks as though he doesn't know what to do with himself. "My child," she mumbles.

"My boy." Then she lets go of him. "Why don't you ever visit your mother?" The man, meanwhile, begins carrying plastic bags into the house. They must have gone grocery shopping. Rose removes her sunglasses, revealing her face. It's easy to see the similarity between her and Luke: the caramel-colored eyes, the freckles. But her mouth is narrow and pinched sourly, trembling now. Behind it a row of small, yellowed teeth. She finds her cigarettes and a lighter. She coughs, spits in the grass, then slowly lifts a cigarette to her lips. Her upper body sways a little. Either she's drunk or on something. Pills, maybe, something deadening. Every now and then her eyes glide shut, and she tips so far backward that it seems she'll fall over. But each time she manages to right herself at the last instant.

"Mom," Luke says. "Mom. Why are you high already? This early in the afternoon for God's sake. Who's giving you the pills?"

"Stop talking nonsense," Rose says. "I'm doing fine." Her head pitches slightly. "Mind your own business." She looks at Luke. She narrows her eyes the same way he does. A cold and accusatory glance.

"We're leaving. Come on, Thomas." Luke hurries to the car. But halfway there he stops and spins angrily toward his mother. "I want to punch you, but I'll do you the huge favor of leaving you alone. Fuck you," he shouts, threatening her. "Fuck you, bitch!" And for one moment Thomas is afraid that he'll actually attack her. His rage makes him ugly. His face is flushed red, his body tense as a bow. He's frightening to look at. Luke yanks on the door handle, gets in, guns the engine, and begins to back out of the driveway at high speed. Thomas runs after the car and leaps in. Rose, hunched over, angles toward the house. The man comes outside carrying a case of beer: A man with a heavy case of beer in his hands, a sheepish expression on his face, the brilliant light above the warped roof of the house, and Rose, plopping down on the bench now, her back to them. Turned in his seat at a 90-degree angle, Luke keeps an eye on the road behind them. Cussing and swearing. They crest a small hill and barrel down the other side; the house is out of sight. Thomas is relieved to have escaped that place. As he studied Rose's vacant eyes, his headache had returned with renewed vigor. The entire situation so horribly painful. So hopeless. He rolls down the window. Fresh air rushes in and mixes with their own odors. They reverse all the way to the road. Luke doesn't say a word. He seems more embittered than angry now. After a while the atmosphere in the car becomes almost unbearable. Thomas tries to think of something to say, but it feels as though nothing can cleanse the air, so sullied as it is by Luke's bad mood. And Thomas himself is shaken over seeing Rose in that state. Gone is the sixteen-year old, long-legged girl with baby fat. Fatso's fun little sister, the nanny, who played crazy games with him while Jenny took her mid-day naps, who tickled him until he cried with laughter, who took them down to the street where she hung out with her friends, while Thomas sat on the stoop watching the older girls pass Jenny between them tying small bows into her hair. And later, during pre-pubescence: Rose, a radiant young woman the stuff of wet dreams. There was something different about her, something vibrant that no one else could offer, not anyone he knew anyway. But Rose is no more. Rose is a wreck. Life stinks, Thomas thinks, leaning back dejectedly in his seat. They're back on the road again. Soon he sinks into a torpor-like state of sleep, headache, and old hangover. He dreams disconnectedly, of something that happens inside a spacious fancy apartment, a party it seems. Mashed up against the wall of a narrow corridor of raucous, boisterous people, struggling for breath, skin glistening with sweat. A strong whiff of secretions emanating from human bodies. Sizzling pork fat on a cast-iron pan. A hunk of meat splatting in the center of the pan. A fantastic aroma wafting from it. He arches forward, over the stove. Someone slaps him on the back. Snoring loudly, he wakes himself up. Three quarters of an hour have passed. Luke snaps on his turn signal and enters the highway. He's driving too fast. He's leaning over the wheel. "Fuck," he says.

And not a word more until they reach the city. But then it's as if he relaxes. Loosens his shoulders and his jaw. Moistens his lips with his tongue. Breathes calmly through his nose. The tension inside the car slowly dissipates. Luke turns the radio on. And Thomas thinks almost happily: He's back. They listen absentmindedly to a program about the prenatal care of penguin parents. Soon Luke glances at him, giving him a sad little smile. *I am filled with love,* Thomas thinks, shocked, as a geyser of heat rises in him. Thomas is overcome, hot as flames now—as if he's been cleansed from the inside by an all-consuming fire—with a powerful and uncontrollable urge to find his way into Luke's body: a finger between his thick lips, a finger in his ear. To push inside him from behind. To taste Luke, everything that can't be seen with the naked eye. To seek a way into the parts of him that keep him alive. The same parts that help him taste, chew, swallow, digest, listen, smell, breathe, expel waste. It lasts only half a minute. Luke looks at him worriedly. "Are you okay?" he asks. "Should we stop somewhere and get some water? Your face is all flushed." Blood roars in Thomas's ears. He shakes his head. "No, it's just the heat. It'll pass soon." But the heat from the shame that follows doesn't pass right away. He imagines Patricia sprawled across her office desk, sees himself grunting behind her, then her tears. What is it? Is it violence? Is it him? Distractedly he stares at the suburbs as they race past: apartment complexes, football fields. Shame courses through him, and it's not until Luke finally becomes talkative that it goes away.

"Maybe now you get why I can't stand looking at my mom," Luke says, and Thomas nods. He understands. "What kinds of drugs is she on?" "No clue," Luke replies, "pills, no doubt. And lots of alcohol. She'll die in her own shit."

"Were you hoping she'd be better?"

"I don't know." Luke stares at the road. "No."

"Was that how she was when you lived with her?" Thomas asks carefully.

"I don't know. No, not quite that bad. But she'd often lie in bed for days on end. I was too young to comprehend what was wrong with her, I was just used to it. It started before we moved to the country, but it wasn't this bad." Luke speaks fast, frenzied. "I mean, she was drunk a lot and there were hangers-on at our house smoking bongs during the day, but she was young, and she was employed now and then. She managed."

"But you moved in with Fatso when you ran away from home?"

"Yeah."

"How old were you?" Thomas tries to piece Luke's story together, but it seems to him there are holes in it.

"Twelve."

"What you told us when we were on the mountain—all that about you and your friend getting lost—was that before or after?"

"After. Sometimes I went up there to visit her when I lived with my uncle. I still had a few friends there from when I was in school."

"Did you miss her?"

"I guess so. But she lived with a psychopath. So things didn't go so well. One time I kicked him in the head, and he had to be taken to the emergency room. After that I stayed away. Luckily he punched his ticket last year."

Thomas looks out the front window. The sky is brightening into a soft yellow; it's already late in the afternoon. "She was so full of life when I knew her. But that was a long time ago."

"People change," Luke says brusquely, scratching his arm. "Just like you say Jacques did."

"Did *I* say that he changed? No, you're the one who says that."

"He changed for the better, apparently. That's not the case with my mom." Luke stares dejectedly ahead. Then he sighs. He pulls his sleeve down over the white, swollen mosquito bite on his arm. He shifts in his seat. "Fuck it," he says, turning up the volume on the radio, which is playing reggae music.

"Are you really interested in helping remodel the new store?" Thomas asks following a short pause.

"Of course."

"I'll pay you."

"You don't need to do that."

"Of course you should be paid." For some time there's silence. The city begins to emerge: multiple interchanges and ramps leading traffic in different directions on several levels. One moment they're above the city, seeing the river and downtown, the next they're under it, on the same level as the poor devils who live right next to the highway. Gradually they merge into the chaos of streets, alleyways, and expansive boulevards. Though it's Sunday, there's a great deal of activity here compared to where they're coming from. It's overwhelming. And liberating. Thomas shudders. Why did Rose's boyfriend, or whatever he was, have all those keys on his belt? What did he need them for? Maybe they're keys to all the places he's ever lived in his life. He didn't exactly look like someone who had a job that required such a huge keychain. Strange. Keys to hell, Thomas thinks, smiling to himself. To the many chambers of hell. When they stop at a red light, he stares at a construction zone. A massive crane stands unmoving, its bucket floating high above the streets, swaying slightly in the gentle breeze. Some guard dogs are running around, barking. They pass the cemetery where Jacques is interned, in an urn somewhere. "Where do you live?" Luke asks. Thomas gives him directions. "You live in *that* part of the city?" There's awe in Luke's voice. They discuss the store. They exchange phone numbers, so Thomas can contact Luke if he needs to. A text from Alice beeps into Thomas's cell: "See you tomorrow morning." This perks him up. He remembers that he'd promised to call Annie and Peter about the so-called company dinner; he'll text them instead.

Luke turns down Thomas's street. "The good life," he says. "Can't be cheap living here." He can't hide his envy. Luke glances curiously up at the buildings, ducking his head to see better. He parks in front of Thomas's building. "Number 76?"

"Yeah," Thomas says. "This is the place. Want to come in?"

"No thanks." Luke straightens up. "I need to get going."

Thomas turns to Luke. "Thanks for the ride." It's an awkward moment. *Should I hug him?* Instead he claps him on the shoulder. It feels wrong. "No problem," Luke says, giving him a passing smile. It's not until Thomas has already stuck his left leg out on the street and planted his foot on the ground that Luke suddenly says, "Maybe he just didn't understand you." Stopped in mid-stride, Thomas turns back. "What do you mean?"

"Maybe Jacques just didn't understand you." Luke narrows his eyes just like Rose had a few hours earlier. Cold, rejecting. Thomas gulps for breath. "Maybe you got on his nerves."

"I really don't think it's that simple," Thomas says with as much composure as he can muster. He climbs out. Before he can even shut the door, Luke pulls it closed from inside. "See you later!" he shouts. He's one big, pleased smile. He guns the engine and speeds off down the street. Let him imagine he's special, Thomas thinks. But *why*? Why did he say that? He didn't need to. No, it's not even worth thinking about. Still, it takes him some time before the sense of betrayal leaves him. Also the feeling that there is something fundamentally wrong with him. An age-old feeling and a recurring theme in his life so revolting that he could vomit. A little shit like Luke. Now it's not only inconceivable that he'd wanted to penetrate him, that he'd ever felt that way, the heat flushing through him—it's disgusting and terribly embarrassing. Thinking of it nauseates him, overwhelms him with self-loathing. Standing on the street, Thomas can't find the energy to set his body in motion. He lifts his arm and studies it as if it belongs to someone else. Two women regard him curiously when they walk past. He observes his arm. He lowers his arm. Twilight closes in on him, growing denser, fluffy, green. But there's still daylight. A heavenly light: the sky is yellowish, violet, soft. *It's summer,* Thomas thinks. And all at once tears fall from his eyes. It's so pathetic. Even in the midst of his crying fit he's aware of how pathetic he is and how endlessly sad and true everything feels. His entire face dissolves, his mouth and eyes twitch. Here come the tears, and they're huge. They wash over him, a cascade of liquid salt and animalistic noises. He can't control himself; here he is, firmly glued to the same flagstone on the sidewalk, snot barreling down his chin, the tears sounding foreign and loathsome and much too old, the tears are an old man, something beautiful and shiny breaking apart before growing ugly and shapeless, an old man no one wants to look at, for God's sake, unarticulated, raw grunts climb up from the depths inside him, and now he wants to scream, his scream will put an end to his shame, *but there's no end to shame*, he thinks, and he's losing it, it's wrong, all wrong, but then, in a split second, he recognizes self-pity as something that packages up his crying, puts an end to his tears, hides the pain, *encapsulates the pain*, and *then* he gets a hold of himself. He has nothing but contempt for self-pity, that much he knows, even now. Hell, he thinks, I'm no better than Jenny. A neighbor strolls down the street, a newspaper tucked under his arm. He greets Thomas warmly and Thomas returns the greeting, his face turned. With the sleeve of his shirt he mops his wet cheeks. Finally he pulls the key from his pants pocket and lets himself in. The apartment smells dusty and stuffy. It's baking hot. The hallway light is on. There's the bag they brought this weekend, and there are her shoes. But she's not home. Only the cat, which meows neurotically, rubbing hard against him. Thomas brings back his right leg and kicks it, and it slides across the slippery parquet floor. It smashes against the wall, yowling, and falls over. It looks confused. Then, with difficulty, it gets to its feet and slumps away. Thomas notices, almost gleefully, that it's limping a little on its right back leg.

By Monday morning his mood hasn't improved much. When he awakes, Patricia's fast asleep at his side; stripes of sunshine slip through the cracks in the blinds, partly lighting up her face and the white bed sheets. Her eyelids quiver as if she's in the middle of a dream. Tentatively he puts his hand on her belly, but she rolls onto her side with a sigh and goes on sleeping. The cat's still hobbling. Thomas doesn't stick around long. He rides his bicycle. It looks as though it'll be a very hot day; the air is humid: thick, clammy heat. Where does Patricia go at night? The question opens a chasm in him: He pictures her in the arms of other men, at a dance club and dizzy with alcohol; he sees her naked in some dark bedroom, alone on a dark street, drunk and exhausted and hailing a taxi as she stumbles along on high heels. The tip of her tongue. Shiny, parted lips. Her face in subdued light. Her lustful gaze. He imagines her enjoying another man's cock. He's out of breath, and not because he's zipping along on his bike but because his desperation encloses him in a tiny room, restricts all movement, and he feels something squeezing against him on every side, compressing his body into a tapering shape he can't escape. But as he enters the store, he sees Alice and she gives him a big smile. That helps. Everywhere he looks the store is dazzlingly clean and spotless, and the shelves are already being stocked. Peter and Maloney came to work early, and now they're practically emptying the stockroom in the basement, hauling box after box of product upstairs. Alice is helping Annie by putting everything into place. She embraces Thomas. Annie says, "It won't take long when there's two of us." And it *does* go fast. They're finished before lunch. There are empty spaces on a few of the shelves, but they've got to order more product. They do that while eating their lunch in the office. Annie and Alice chat up a storm and really seem to like each other. They've taken their sandwiches outside, in the sunlight. Customers ask about the break-in, there's lots of talk, and the atmosphere is pleasant all day: connections, warmth, Thomas feels better and better. "Thanks for the wonderful weekend," Maloney says, throwing some crumpled-up envelopes into the paper basket, "they're great people, your aunts. I'm still wiped out after chopping all that goddamn firewood, but it was a pleasure being up there. It's good to breathe some fresh air, for once."

"Maloney," Thomas says. "Maloney?"

Maloney looks up. A pause, a glance. "What?" he asks, low. His smile vanishes abruptly, like someone fearing bad news.

"I think Patricia's seeing someone else."

"Oh, Christ," Maloney blurts, relieved. "I thought it was something serious. That you were sick or something. You look like an undertaker. There's no way she's seeing someone else. As affectionate as she is to you? What are you thinking?"

"Is she affectionate?"

"Yes! Don't you have eyes in your head?"

"She goes off at night. She's gone every evening."

"Have you asked her where she goes?"

"She won't tell me. She doesn't respond."

"Oh. Well," Maloney says, "I don't think you should take it so seriously. Maybe she just needs to go out and get blitzed. Would that be so strange? You've been a rather heavy burden on everyone these past few months. She probably just wants to have some fun."

"I think it's more serious than that," Thomas says, staring at the floor. Maloney shrugs. "What do I know," he says, rubbing an eye. "You need to talk with her." Thomas nods weakly.

"Stop pouting like a little boy who needs consolation, okay? If you have issues to work through, see a shrink or something. Did you reserve a table at the restaurant?"

Thomas nods again. "Yes," he says. "Yeah, you're right." He collects himself, straightens up, walks out of the office, and guides Alice on a proper tour of the store. He shows her how to work the register, where to find the bags, how to do various procedures. At a quarter past 6:00 they close shop. All five of them stroll to the restaurant, a twenty minute walk. It's a beautiful night and mild, the temperature almost like that of skin—like being in a soft and compliant world, the body merging with it; there's no limit, the light is speckled green, soft, odors hang unmoving in the air: trash, car fumes, the acrid stench of fast food deep-fryers and, every now and then, rose bush, honeysuckle. People sit on their stoops enjoying the first really warm summer evening; the city's alive, teeming with life. Alice's legs in a pair of cut-off jeans are bare, she's walking beside Peter and talking with him, she seems so natural and comfortable, energized. And Thomas is seized with pride. Then he thinks of Patricia again. She hasn't called him all day. His fears return. But just as they've sat in the soft restaurant chairs, she texts him: "Still at work. Going home in a few hours." What a relief. They order cocktails and appetizers. Peter's gray eyes gleam once he's drained his first gin and tonic. Alice describes the poetry reciting competition at Kristin and Helena's. Annie has never heard of anything that strange. "What poems did you read?" she asks. Alice can't remember, but then she recalls Haiku-Helena and begins to laugh, so Thomas explains it to Annie and now she laughs, too. "I've never cared much for haiku," she says. "But have you read Bella Akhmadúlina?"

"Bella Akh . . . ?"

"Akhmadúlina. A poet. She's wonderful."

"Annie's in a Russian phase," Thomas explains, passing the tuna tartare around the table.

"If you want, you can borrow one of her books from me."

Alice nods, surprised. She would like that very much. "Peter's also part of my reading group now," Annie says. "Isn't that right, Peter?"

"Yup," Peter says, carefully setting his knife and fork down.

"Jesus," Maloney says, shoveling grilled squid onto his plate. "Since when have all our employees become so literary?"

"I think we've always been literary," Peter says quietly.

The main courses arrive. Maloney's ordered a steak with Béarnaise sauce to accompany "the good red wine," as he calls it. Annie's ordered lobster and Alice tries a bite; she's never had lobster before, and she likes it. She dives into her breaded chicken breast. They quickly work through several bottles of wine. Peter becomes chattier and chattier. He gesticulates with his hands as he describes how horrible he was at ballgames in school. "But I really got into gymnastics," he says, "and I'm still very good at it."

"Gymnastics!" Maloney shouts. "You do gymnastics? I can't fucking picture you doing that."

But Peter has won several semi-professional competitions during the past few years. Alice thinks being that good at something is totally cool, and wishes she was. And Thomas thinks it couldn't get any better than this. Here she sits eating lobster and drinking white wine, getting offers to read poetry, maybe even the chance to attend a gymnastics meet or a book club discussion. She's clearly enjoying herself. She'll say yes to working for us, he thinks, maybe they could even let Annie run the new store; surely they can manage the original store with just Peter. That's not a bad idea. It could be *the women's store*, and he can shuttle back and forth between the two. Once again he's jolted by a sense of pride and elation. They're all a little buzzed and chirpy. It's almost 9:30 P.M. Annie, Peter, and Alice talk about wild animals. A few years ago Peter saw a white tiger in a zoo. "Are they albinos?" Annie wants to know. Peter explains how they're recessive mutants of the Bengal tiger—which is to say, a subspecies. "Do you have a girlfriend, Peter?" Maloney asks out of nowhere. Peter blushes. "That's Peter's own business," Thomas says. But Maloney keeps at it. "What about you, Annie? You have a boyfriend?"

"Yes," she says in a clear voice. "I do. I just moved in with him."

"Congratulations," Maloney says.

"Maloney's dating my mom. Isn't that crazy?" Alice returns her napkin to her lap as the dessert is brought in. "So he's, like, your stepfather?" Peter interjects, confused. "I'm over eighteen. I don't need a father anymore," Alice says. When she puts a spoonful of moist, coal-black chocolate cake into her mouth, she closes her eyes in rapt pleasure. Thomas tells them all about the new store. Annie seems very interested. She asks a bunch of questions: When will it open? Where is it located? Will it carry the same products? Thomas offers to take them all on a tour once the sale is final. Maloney says nothing. He stares absently at Thomas. "Have you actually considered moving in with my mother?" Alice asks him. "What?" Maloney says. "I don't really know. Maybe. At some point." "You've always lived alone. Would you be able to stand it?" Thomas says. With his spoon, he pokes at his crème brûlée. "Would you be able to stand living with Jenny?" Maloney smiles sheepishly. He's in love, Thomas thinks, he's really in love with her. Thomas's cell phone rings at that moment. At first he can't hear anyone on the line. Then he hears strange noises. A clattering or struggle. Is that the sound of clothing? Or did someone butt dial me? And now, a kind of whimpering—or is someone singing or mumbling in the background? The sounds in the restaurant are so loud that he can't really separate them from what he hears on his cell. He steps onto the street. "Hello?" he says. "Hello? Who is it?" No one answers. But now it sounds as though the telephone on the other end slams against something hard. The call is dropped. He stares at his cell. When he sees Patricia's number on the little screen, he grows cold with fear.

He calls her several times but doesn't get through. He stumbles into the restaurant and pulls Maloney into the coatroom. "What's wrong?" Maloney breathes, glowering at Thomas, irritated. "Say something, man!"

"She called. There were only noises."

"Who?"

"Patricia. Only noises . . ."

"What kind of noises?"

"It sounded as if her cell phone was thrown, I can't get ahold of her." Thomas clutches Maloney's shirt with both of his hands.

"What are you trying to tell me, Thomas? What kind of noises? Did it sound like she was with someone?"

"What do you mean?"

"A man. Was she with another man?"

Thomas hadn't even thought of that. He stares at Maloney, his eyes wide. "Yes," he says, "maybe. But . . . Oh, no. What should I do? I thought . . ."

"What did you think?"

"I don't know. That she was in danger."

With his head cocked to one side Maloney smiles. He drops his hand onto Thomas's shoulder.

"Go home. Then she'll have to explain. That's all there is to it." He squeezes Thomas's shoulder. A kind of rough caress. "This kind of thing happens even in the best of families." He follows Thomas out to the street. "Take a cab," he says, "leave your bike here." Thomas continues fumbling with his bike keys. "Leave the bike here!" Maloney raises his voice. Thomas turns and looks at him in despair. "Get out of here," Maloney says sharply. "I'll think of something to tell the others."

Maloney trudges back into the restaurant. Thomas stands helplessly staring at the traffic. Shortly afterward an empty taxi approaches, and soon he's on his own street. She's been with another man, he thinks, full of heavy, almost stunned grief; she has another man, I was right, I knew it, and now I've heard it. I've heard her having sex with another man. I'm not angry. I ought to be raging with jealousy, ready to pound her and her lover. He's slack and amazed. There's nothing between himself and the world, the temperature's the same, everything's merging. For the third time the driver asks Thomas to pay up. He's impatient. Thomas hands him the money and climbs out of the cab. He fishes his keys from his pocket. He unlocks the door. He punches the elevator button, can't deal with the stairs. He waits. The elevator—with its familiar whirr and clatter—rattles down the shaft. But there's another noise now. Behind him. Whimpering, breathing. He turns, stares down the stairwell to the basement, where it's pitch dark. Makes out some kind of bundle in the depths. The basement door is ajar. "Help me," a voice whispers, very weakly. "Help." It's Patricia's voice. The elevator comes to a halt with its little *ding*.

He guides her toward the light. She's naked below the waist. Her eyes see past him, an empty gaze, zombielike. He gathers her clothes and ushers her into the elevator. She's pale as a corpse. When they reach the apartment, she goes directly to the bathroom and turns on the shower. "Who took your clothes off?" Thomas asks, grabbing hold of her. "You can't take a shower, Patricia. You need to be examined." She wriggles free of him and returns to the shower. He tugs her back and embraces her. She cries soundlessly. "I'm calling the police," he says. He doesn't know how to console her; he searches for the right words, but doesn't find them—there are no words he can trust. Her entire body trembles, ice cold, in shock. Still this vacant stare. Abruptly she dashes to the sink and throws up. Afterward he gives her a bathrobe and holds her again. He asks, "Should I call the police, or do you want to wait?" She doesn't want to wait. She washes her face in cold water and brushes her teeth. Scrubs her teeth for a long time. She plops down at the little table in the kitchen. He makes her a cup of tea and asks if she's eaten. She hasn't, but she doesn't want anything. He regrets asking the question. "Did you know him?" he says carefully. She shakes her head. Shrugs her shoulders. "I don't know. No. I don't think so." She looks at him. "I can't be in my own body," she says. "I want to shower." She seems more calm and composed now. Two officers arrive thirty minutes later. Thomas has wrapped Patricia in a blanket and positioned her on the couch. He's sent from the room while the officers talk to her. He jams his ear against the door and hears snatches of her incoherent account. She came home from work and was attacked from behind opening the door from the street. Everything happened so fast. A man shoved a towel in her mouth and hauled her into the basement. That's where he raped her, on the concrete floor. She screamed, but no one came. She managed to call Thomas. But the man grabbed the cell phone from her hand and flung it. "He yanked at my hair. It hurt. Everything hurt. I screamed, but no one came, no one came. He . . ."

"Yes," one of the officers says.

But Patricia says nothing more. A few minutes pass. Despite the heat, Thomas is freezing. His heart gallops like a wild horse behind his ribcage. Someone entered his girlfriend's body. Was close to her, forced her. Someone sullied her, besmirched her, caused her pain. She's been *violated*. It's completely unreal. He squeezes his eyes shut. Now he hears Patricia speaking again. They ask her if she saw the perpetrator's face. No, he was wearing some sort of black hood. She couldn't see his face. "And he had gloves on, I could feel them."

"How old do you think he was? Could you tell?"

"He wasn't very old. He was . . . it was . . ."

"Yes."

Thomas hears her crying again.

"I don't know!" she sobs peevishly. "I really don't know! I couldn't see his face!"

Her tears subside.

Long silence.

"Did he threaten you?" one of the men asks.

"Did he say anything. Did you hear his voice?"

And a short time later: "He said absolutely nothing to you?"

She's probably shaking her head in response to these questions. Their voices are so low that Thomas can't catch what's being said. The two men exit the living room and tell him that he should drive her to the hospital. She needs to be examined for traces of DNA. In the meantime, they'd like to see where the rape occurred. They'd also like to take Patricia's pants, panties, and shoes with them. "Do you have a car?" one of the officers asks. Thomas shakes his head.

"Then we'll call an ambulance."

She says very little during the short drive to the hospital. She stares out the window at the darkness. Once in a while her lip quivers. He holds her hand and doesn't know what else to do. He wants to embrace her, to lie on top of her, to protect her, to warm her, but he's afraid she'll feel trapped, that she won't be able to stand the physical proximity. The medics seem so solid, everything they do seems right, they make Patricia smile faintly, they inspire in her a sense of security. They don't turn on their flashing lights, they drive slowly and calmly through the city, chatting reassuringly. Patricia doesn't want to leave the ambulance. But the man who'd sat beside them persuades her, and he explains to Thomas where they need to go. They wait in a long, green hallway, the fluorescent bulbs on the ceiling juddering as if an entire colony of cockroaches has taken up residence inside them. Finally her name is called. It's a female doctor who'll examine her, thank God. She guides Patricia gently through a door. Thomas texts Maloney: "she was raped." He writes the word *raped*, and it cuffs him upside the head like a baseball bat, and he gasps, as if only now does he understand what has happened. He pictures this masked monster pulling his girlfriend into the basement and having his way with her, he pictures his gloved hands holding her wrists, clutching her throat. What if he had killed her? He could have killed her. Maloney calls him up, shocked, quietly frightened, ashamed that he'd led Thomas to believe she'd voluntarily been with another man. "I'm so sorry, Thomas," he practically whispers, "tell me if there's anything I can do for you two." Thomas requests that he look after Alice in the store, since he doesn't figure he'll be at work tomorrow. "I'll call Jenny," Maloney says.

"No, don't tell anyone. I don't know if Patricia wants anyone to know."

And then he sits and waits. Time seems to stretch endlessly. But according to the clock on the wall, only twenty minutes have passed. Soon Patricia returns. She says nothing about the examination. She says nothing at all, and he doesn't dare ask. At home she takes a long shower before they go to bed. Afterward her skin is red from the hot water; it looks as though she scrubbed herself with the nail brush. She doesn't have many injuries, just a few scrapes and some bruising on her buttocks and the backs of her thighs, which she must have gotten when she was thrown down on the concrete floor. Before she crawls into bed, she pulls on stockings and a long-sleeved woolen jersey. She pops the sleeping pill the doctor gave her. She breathes rapidly, inhaling quick bursts of air. Then she falls asleep. Thomas, on the other hand, lies awake half the night, because he realizes in an instant—an instant that gashes time, burns itself into time like hell's roaring flames—that the break-in at the store and the rape might be connected. The apple core in his father's apartment, the slit armchair. All of it might have something to do with him, and the money in the microwave. Rigid with guilt and fear he lies breathless beside the sleeping Patricia. And he took what he wanted from her roughly at the museum, against her will. He held his hand over her mouth, forced himself into her. As if he were giving her a foretaste of what would happen to her tonight. As if he himself had incited violence against her body. As if the violence surrounds them now—he brought it into their lives. The ransacked store. The symbol on the countertop. Patricia's beautiful face, stiff and empty. Her freezing cold body, exposed from the waist down. Someone had waited for her. Someone had planned it. Why else would you cover your head? Why else would you wear gloves? Or was it just a coincidence? Why didn't he ask the police if a serial rapist was terrorizing the city? I hope there is, he thinks desperately, I hope it doesn't have anything to do with me. He imagines the two assaults against Patricia, one of which he was responsible for. Here she's sprawled across her desk on her stomach, trying to turn, biting his hand, and here she's lying on the basement floor, on her back, a figure leaning over her, blocking her face from view. Holding Patricia's wrists in an iron grip. The images are soundless and repetitive, an endless stream of images, two situations, time looping from one to the other: Patricia deprived of the opportunity to decide for herself. Deprived of the opportunity to say no. It's unbearable. Thomas gets out of bed and wanders the apartment, restless and unhappy. The cat follows him with its eyes from its seat on the couch. Not until it's almost morning does Thomas glide into a short, uneasy slumber, but Patricia wakes him at 6:00 A.M. The sleeping pill has worn off. She's drenched in sweat. It's at least eighty degrees in the bedroom; the sun is up.

There's something strange between them now—mornings in the little kitchen, evenings when they make dinner, on the couch watching TV, or lying in bed in the stuffy, sweltering bedroom where their clothes are more often heaped on the floor instead of in the laundry basket. Thomas feels it but he doesn't quite understand it. Now, seven weeks after the rape, Patricia seems calm—serene even. Her sessions with the psychologist are over, the immediate shock having been worked through; she's eating and sleeping again, she's gone back to work, she's *functioning*. But she's distant, and this distance seems to intensify with each passing day—something dreamy, silent, foreign. And despite his more or less good intentions, Thomas can't get through to her, can't make contact. June turns to July, and July is hot as a sauna. During the day it's humid, scorching, the air as motionless as a cloud of hummingbirds on tiny fluttering wings. Heat shimmers, melting the asphalt, making people dizzy and hallucinatory. The city reeks. It's been eighteen years since the temperature has been measured this hot. And now it's Wednesday evening, and once again they're standing beside the oven preparing a simple dinner in silence. Patricia rinses lettuce, Thomas stirs tomato sauce. They boil water for the pasta. The sun's setting, but its absence doesn't make much of a difference; nights are thick and heavy, sleep restless and horrible, and here, enshrouded in steam from the boiling water, and the gas burners, sweat pours from their bodies. Patricia's hair is wet, her naked shoulders gleaming. Thomas glances at her. He longs for her presence, her caress, her concern. Patricia slices a cucumber. He dries his hands on a dishtowel, and he's unable to resist the urge to wrap his arms around her. But the embrace is clumsy, and Patricia stiffens at his touch, like so often. Once again he's afraid to get too physically close, to overstep her boundaries, after what happened. He lets go and settles on putting his hand cautiously on her arm.

"How do you feel today, hon?"

"Fine." The paring knife whacks the cutting board in quick, hard strokes.

He removes his hand and tries to make eye contact, but she's focused on preparing the salad. "I wondered if you could help me order the flowers for the grand opening?" he says. A short pause. She dumps the lettuce and cucumbers into a white bowl and pours olive oil into another. "But I guess you'll need to see the room first, and the colors. You still haven't seen it yet. We could ride over after dinner? Would you like that?"

"I'm too tired," she says, squeezing lemon juice into the oil.

"Is it the heat?"

She shrugs and whips the dressing together. The timer goes off. He strains the pasta and mixes the tomato sauce with the spaghetti.

They sit on opposite sides of the table. She ladles a huge portion of food onto her plate and gobbles it hurriedly, greedily.

"Patricia," he says. "Will you tell me how you really feel?"

"What do you mean *how I really feel*? I just told you I was fine."

"You seem a little sad, I think."

"Sad? I'm not sad."

"You sure?"

"Of course I'm sure, otherwise I wouldn't say it. I'm just tired."

She shovels spaghetti into her mouth. Tomato sauce squirts, leaving a red stain on her white tank top. Thomas pushes a few soppy leaves of lettuce around his plate. He's not hungry.

"I know I've been gone a lot recently. It's been stressful getting everything sorted out at work, you know. The new store's opening on Tuesday, and the floors aren't even finished yet. I'm sorry."

"You don't need to be."

"But I am."

She shrugs, ladling another portion of spaghetti onto her plate. He watches her. She's deeply suntanned. Fine, miniscule lines surround her eyes and mouth. Since the rape, there's been something rigid about her. As if her expression is unchanged. She moves her mouth only when she speaks or chews. She glowers at him. "What? Why are you looking at me like that?"

"I'm just looking at you, hon."

"Can you stop asking me how I'm feeling all the time? To be honest, it's a little irritating. How are *you* feeling?"

"Sorry."

"Every time you ask it's as if you want to remind me to feel bad. But I don't feel bad any more." She spears a chunk of cucumber with her fork. "I'm past that. It's over."

"But," he says. "But . . . can you really get over it this fast? It hasn't even been two months. Don't you think that you . . . that you're just repressing it?"

She gives him a tolerant smile. "For God's sake, Thomas! Don't you think I know best how I'm doing? I'm not repressing anything, honest."

Later he washes the dishes. She turns on the TV and throws herself on the couch with the cat. It sprawls across her belly, its paws resting along her breasts and hips. It's purring. The woman and the animal are completely relaxed. But when Thomas enters the living room, she gets to her feet. "I'm going to bed."

"But it's only nine 9:00!"

"I'm dead tired."

She gives him a hasty peck on the cheek. A short time later he hears her brushing her teeth. Then she closes the bedroom door. He pours himself a tall glass of whiskey and stares out the window. Again he has this constricting sense that the vibes in the room are all wrong. As if everything is unsaid, held back: an ominous silence. He feels rejected. He goes down to the street to smoke. The evening's humid, the air stagnant. He feels powerless. A flock of rambunctious teenagers scoot past, ignoring him; they're completely absorbed in themselves, hopping and bopping along without a care in the world, laughing, pushing, shouting. He gives them a wistful, envious glance. *If only they knew what awaits them.* But you shouldn't think like that, it's vile, he thinks, *the store*, think about the store instead, the cool, freshly painted walls, the smell of varnish. He closes his eyes and slips into a moment of bliss: cigarette smoke encircles his head in the still, moist air, and he imagines himself standing behind the counter welcoming new customers, showing them around, punching the first sale into the register. And Alice is smiling, rolling the handmade paper into brown tissue, securing a red and white-striped string around the package with a practiced hand and handing it to the customer. He opens his eyes. He flicks his cigarette butt away, and when a little later he peeks into the bedroom, Patricia's fast asleep, her hair on her face. The hallway light illuminates her head and upper body. Every time she breathes, fine strands of hair shift slightly. Her breasts seem larger. Then she rolls on her side with a grunt.

The next morning Thomas hears Patricia leaving the apartment at 7:30. The heat gives him a headache. Even now, this early in the day, the heat is intense, enervating. When he walks into the kitchen, he sees that she's forgotten her cell phone. There's a bowl filled with dried oatmeal on the small table. She no longer drinks coffee in the morning, but she left the package of mint tea open, and steam billows from the kettle. He picks up her cell and palms it. He's *already* glanced through her call list. One day when she was especially distant, he even dialed some of the numbers. Mostly women answered, girlfriends, though once he got the voicemail of a man he didn't know. Luke's number is there too. It doesn't appear that she's ever called it. But why would she have Luke's number? He puts the cell down, makes a pot of coffee, and then takes a shower. Soon there won't be any clean clothes left, either in the dresser or the closet. He doesn't know why, but they've pretty much stopped doing laundry—neither bothering to do it. Irritated now, he gathers his clothes off the floor and stuffs them into the washing machine in the bathroom. How hard can it be? She doesn't clean anymore, either. The living room floor is dusty, littered with cat hair. He sighs. Still half-naked, he grabs his shaving kit. Just as he's about to rinse the shaving cream off his face, his eye falls randomly on her toiletry bag. Tubes of lipsticks and eye shadow, a large powder brush. He spots the little silver perfume flacon that he gave her on their one-year anniversary. A sentimental moment: *we were happy back then*. He sighs again then dries his hands. He fishes up the flacon, but drops it and it falls back into the toiletry bag, and he has to set the bag in the sink to root around between the tiny cases and pencils and tubes, and just as he finds the silver flacon, he notices a piece of flat white plastic that doesn't look like anything else in the bag. He lifts it out. It looks familiar, but what is it? He rolls it between his fingers. And then, all at once, to his horror, he understands what he's holding. A pregnancy test. Two small pink lines side by side indicate that the test is positive. There's no doubt about it. Positive. He shakes it. Stares numbly at it. Then he drops it as if it were poisonous.

Thomas chain smokes in the kitchen, still undressed, clammy and shaky, cold-sweating in the brutal heat. First the shock and then *it can't be true.* Out to look at the test again. Back to the kitchen. Later comes an overwhelming fear, but most of all this: Patricia never said a word. She must've known for some time. But she hasn't felt the need or the duty to involve him in such a big and dramatic event. Something so *significant.* Something so frightening. But then the thought comes to him like a revelation: Of course she'll have an abortion. Immediately he feels calmer. Of course she will. There's not a woman in the world who'd run the risk of having a kid possibly conceived during a vile, violent assault. He sits down. And remains seated for some time. And yet another encouraging thought strikes him: Of course that's why she hadn't said anything, she'd decided to have an abortion without anyone finding out. She'd wanted to *protect* him, and as he considers this, he feels a strong sense of tenderness and relief. Poor Patricia. He slurps his cold coffee. He gets dressed. Poor, poor Patricia. "You poor thing," he mumbles. "That's why you're so quiet and tired." *Now I understand everything.* The tension between them, her insatiable appetite, and chubby cheeks—he'd wondered about that—this gradual *roundedness*, her swollen breasts. She's just pregnant, she must be feeling awful. Almost invigorated, he devours a banana and crackers with ham before gathering his things. A text message dings on Patricia's cell phone, and he can't help but read it. It's a reminder for a gynecologist's appointment at the hospital today at 4:30. His heart thumps. She's having an abortion today. That must be the explanation. Tenderness swells in him again. Christ, he thinks, I'm going out there to hold her hand. I won't let her lie there all alone with her shame. Her terrible, painful shame. Under no circumstances. He imagines her loneliness: Patricia alone and pale in a hospital bed, suppressing tears. The more he imagines how awful her loneliness must be, the more his shrinks. He notes the name of the doctor and the department, then puts the dirty dishes in the machine. He feels a sudden urge to scrub the entire house, clean the windows, arrange bouquets of aromatic flowers in every room. And he'll do laundry this weekend. He'll empty the fridge and clean it. We'll start afresh, he thinks, it seems so easy and obvious. This is an opportunity, a real chance to show how much he cares for her; she needs him now, and he will dote on her, tend to her needs, take care of her. His fear and his anger are gone. As he dries every surface of the kitchen with a cloth, as he strips the old bedclothes, he feels strong and purposeful. He takes out the foul-smelling trash when he finally leaves the apartment. It's 9:15, and the sun's already brutal and intense.

Thomas crosses the city on his bicycle. Traffic is sluggish and irritable. Cars are snarled up, and honk at each other without restraint. Rush hour is draining in such weather. His pants cling to his thighs, his swollen feet—slick with perspiration—slide in his shoes, and his eyelashes grow wet as sweat trickles continuously from his hair and forehead. Though he keeps wiping away the sweat, his hands are damp, too, and it doesn't help much. When he turns down the street where the new store is located, he sees Alice and Luke sitting on the stoop drinking Cokes. They're both wearing shorts and faded, paint-splattered T-shirts. The roar of the growling floor polisher slips through the open door. While the floors are being polished, Alice and Luke have been painting the façade, the two window partitions, and the entrance. Tomorrow the floor will be stained and varnished. He climbs off his bike and leans against the wall, breathing heavily. The new awnings provide some shade, but zero protection from the heat. "How's it going?" He almost has to shout above the noise. "You've got a lot done already!"

"It'll just need one more coat once the paint's dry," Luke says, looking up at the masonry. "We'll be finished tomorrow." They polished and puttied nicely before they began painting. When the floors are done, only minor details will remain. The cabinetmaker figures he'll be able to install the shelves and cabinets by the end of the week. The first shipment of products will be delivered on Monday morning. "It'll look awesome," Alice says, setting her drink down. "That light-green color over there, it's practically transparent, like water in a pool or something. It's a good thing you chose that instead of the creamy one. That would have been asinine."

"It's a whitewash. That's why it's almost transparent." Thomas sits beside her and takes a pull of her Coke. "Jesus Christ—it's hot," he groans. But Alice and Luke don't seem to be bothered by the heat or the humidity. A thin film of perspiration beads their faces, and they have that special kind of paleness that comes from being in this kind of heat, and it only makes them more attractive, as if they too were painted with whitewash. But their eyes are bright and lively, and they seem energized. They crawl up on the ladders again and continue working. Thomas goes inside to talk with the craftsmen. Particles of fine, yellow sawdust from the floorboards cling to the panels and the baseboard. Inside it smells of fresh paint and new wood. He thinks of Patricia, how he'll squeeze her hand, stroke her hair. He takes a deep breath, filling his nostrils with the aroma he's longed to smell: *The new store.* Just as he'd imagined it. With his eyes closed, he runs his hand over the countertop. It's smooth and a little oily from the last treatment. The register's in place. He bought it for almost nothing at an auction; it's from the 1920s and pretty as all hell. He scans the bright room, absorbs it all, before walking into the back room, where the men are in the process of polishing the floor. They shut off the machine when they see him.

"A package came for you a few hours ago," one of them says, a young man with sideburns.

"Will you be done polishing today?"

The young man nods, the older man scratches his head.

"We'll tally up the totals the day after tomorrow, once you've stained and varnished," Thomas says. "I'll pay cash. The cabinet-maker's coming Saturday morning. I expect the varnish to be dry by then. Remember to give it five coats, as we agreed. I can tell the difference between four and five coats, just so you know." The young man gives him a crooked smile. "We'll stain soon," he says. The older man snaps on the machine again.

The package contains a ceiling lamp with an enormous, rounded screen of plastic enveloped in linen. It looks like a globe, overcast with clouds made of slender threads or fibers. When there's a bulb in it, he thinks, maybe it'll look like a huge belly with a fetus inside, the skin stretched taut over a small light. Thomas shudders at the thought and goes back to Luke and Alice. "Have fun. Call me when you're done for the day."

"How's Patricia doing?" Alice asks.

"Good."

Luke sweeps his broad brush back and forth across the wall. "Tell her we said hello," he says, smiling.

"Lock up when you're done!" Thomas shouts as he traipses down the street. Alice waves.

Maloney's apparently talking to Jenny, a private and tender conversation consisting mostly of sounds and sighs, but also "I love you" and "I can't wait." When Thomas clears his throat, Maloney ends the call, looking rather foolish with his idiotic grin. They start the day's tasks. Over the course of the summer, Peter set up the store's website. He seems very glad to be entrusted with the responsibility of webmaster. Thomas designed the site himself, and now he asks Peter to post the announcement of the new store. During the summer there are fewer customers. They drink coffee on the stairs after lunch. Annie and Peter chat about their literature group, Maloney texts with someone—no doubt Jenny. Thomas wonders whether he should take flowers with him, for Patricia. Maybe it's inappropriate. But he wants to make sure there are fresh roses for her when they get home. She loves white roses. He sighs in relief. He thinks: *The nightmare will be over soon.* It'll be like old times with him and Patricia. Everything's behind them now: his father, the money, the break-in, the rape. All that shit, over. When Alice and Annie are comfortable running the new place, he'll invite Patricia on a trip. He'll propose to her. Maybe they can even have a baby. And he'll suggest that they move, so she won't have to be confronted every single day by the place where she was assaulted. Because of course she shouldn't have to. First thing tonight he'll begin looking for another apartment. Thomas stretches his legs, buzzing with anticipation at this new life, which seems so light, and he thinks about how everything that he wished for at the beginning of the year has slowly become reality: a new store, Alice as part of the new store, Jenny less bothersome and lonely—now that she has Maloney—and his revenge on his father complete. After all, he's the one who paid for it all, in cash, with crisp new bills, and Thomas hopes Jacques turns in his grave every time Thomas spends some of the money. A new apartment, maybe with a balcony, maybe larger than the one they're in now, which should be put up for sale as soon as possible.

Late in the afternoon he rides his bicycle to the hospital. The sunlight is thick and golden, and as sticky as melted butter, as dripping honey. Thomas pumps the pedals hard, already out of breath. The air's so heavy that it almost hurts to breathe. The cabinetmaker has agreed to work the entire weekend; the shelves and cabinet doors were stained at the factory—they just need to be installed—and he'll suggest to Maloney that they remain closed on Monday so everyone can help tie up loose ends and stock shelves. It'll be a joint effort. Enthusiastically he thinks about how important it is to strive for a flatter, more elastic company structure, so everyone can shift easily between stores. He'll talk to Maloney about that, though he's still keeping his distance and considers the branch Thomas's project. But won't that change when he finally sees how successful the new store will be? Thomas is certain that they'll markedly increase their revenue. He veers from the road and bikes up the hospital's wide driveway, pebbles leaping into the wheels. His bike skids on the gravel. The lawn is yellow, baked-dry. The sun is harsh. He's thirsty. His tongue clings to his teeth and the roof of his mouth. He locks his bike to a light pole and pushes through the revolving doors. He finds the slip of paper with the information he needs and asks for the gynecologist's office. He takes the elevator up to the fourteenth floor and walks down a long hallway, passes through a set of glass doors, and strides from department to department, listening to the faint rumble of the air conditioning. It's pleasantly cool in here, a waiting room with a small group of people clustered over a newborn baby, visiting hours, apparently, a woman in the last stage of her pregnancy dressed in a bathrobe and supporting herself against the wall as she inches forward in small strides, another set of glass doors, and at last he arrives. The doctor's office door is open. He's sitting behind his desk. Patricia's back is to Thomas. The doctor looks up, sees Thomas. "Yes?" he inquires. And Patricia turns. Startled, she stares at Thomas. Thunderstruck, disbelieving, her eyes wide. "Can I help you?" the doctor asks kindly.

"What are you doing here?" Patricia's voice is harsh, almost a hiss.

"Do you two know each other?" the doctor asks, surprised.

"Yes," Thomas says, entering. "I'm her boyfriend." And to Patricia: "You forgot your cell phone, hon, I couldn't help but notice the message from the hospital." He puts his hand on her shoulder. "And I don't think you should be alone with this."

Patricia glowers at him, her mouth agape. She shakes her head. "I know what's going on," Thomas continues, gently. "I found the pregnancy test this morning." He sits in the seat next to Patricia.

"That sounds a bit dramatic," the doctor says, chuckling as if it were funny. "But I'm glad you're here. We've been discussing the advantages of having an abortion in Patricia's situation."

The older, dark-skinned man has kind brown eyes. Patricia looks down, slumps in her chair. The doctor says, "I can only repeat what I said last time, Patricia. You need to consider this thoroughly. Consider the consequences of a pregnancy possibly stemming from a rape. You may think this way now, but later you might have serious issues to contend with. Also for your child. Even if you weren't impregnated during the assault, perhaps your child will always remind you of it."

Thomas doesn't understand. He glances searchingly at Patricia, but she looks away.

"What?" he says. "I don't quite follow."

"Patricia hasn't decided whether she wants to have an abortion or not," the doctor responds, eyeing Patricia earnestly. "But I *strongly* recommend it."

She lifts her head and says to the doctor, "No."

A short silence. "What?" Thomas says. "No to what?" Thomas turns wildly from Patricia to the doctor—who tilts his head almost in apology before cocking it to the side—then back to Patricia. "Are you saying . . . that you want to go through with the pregnancy?" He feels sucker-punched, and it practically knocks the wind out of him, because now it occurs to him that he might soon be a father. Head spinning, he clutches the armrest. No one answers him. "But can't we can take a test to find out if I'm the father? That's possible, right?"

The doctor leans back in his chair.

Patricia shakes her head.

"You want to keep it?" Thomas's voice is shrill and thin. "Why haven't you told me? Patricia! You *need* to have an abortion."

She shakes her head again. "No," she repeats in a firm voice.

"But it is possible, right," Thomas glances urgently at the doctor, "to take a paternity test and find out who the father is?"

"We'd need to do a amniocentesis," the doctor says. "And Patricia doesn't want to do that."

"What?" Thomas says, taken aback, turning to Patricia again.

The doctor continues: "We couldn't even do the test until the fifteenth week, and then it'll take another two or three weeks before we have an answer. By that point in a pregnancy, abortion can be very traumatic, especially if one is already a little vulnerable." He gives Patricia a friendly glance, then folds his hands in his lap. "Patricia has known about her pregnancy for some time, and during that time she has chosen not to do an amniocentesis. But the problem of course," he emphasizes, "is that once the baby is here, well, it's here. Regardless who the father is." Patricia shifts uncomfortably in her seat. Thomas stares darkly at the floor, blood swishing through his ears, thinking he's going to faint. "In other words," the doctor goes on, "the problem, right now, is that you need to make a decision based on this uncertainty."

"I don't consider that a problem," she says. "I don't consider it an uncertainty. It's not important to me who the father is. I never saw his face. I have no idea who he is. But this is *my* baby." She puts her hand on her belly. "And I want to keep it."

Thomas can't believe his own ears. He tries to get her attention, but she stares stiffly out the window.

"I know you think it's an advantage that you never saw the rapist's face, and of course I understand what you mean," the doctor says calmly. "You won't necessarily be able to recognize him in your child's features. But I still think that it's very troublesome. And you," he nods in Thomas's direction, "how do you feel about Patricia's decision?"

"Me?" Thomas looks unhappily at the doctor. "I'm extremely shocked! Patricia," he says. "This is insane! You're not at all yourself yet."

"I'm absolutely myself," she answers coolly. Thomas's head aches and there's a corrosive, icy chill running up his spine. He implores the doctor as if the doctor could help: "But this is absurd! I can't . . . we haven't even discussed this! I didn't even know that you were pregnant! She never said a word! Why didn't you *say* anything? For God's sake!" Thomas shouts. Patricia ignores him. The doctor clears his throat, visibly uncomfortable. To Patricia he says, firmly, "You've gone through counseling, right?"

She nods.

"Did you discuss the pregnancy with your therapist?"

She nods again. "Of course I did." Then she says nothing more. The silence hangs heavy in the anonymous office. Thomas wants to say a whole lot more, but he can't. He feels his blood pounding in the large vein on his forehead, like light, fast clouts with a hammer, his headache intensifies, he glances about desperately and sees a stuffed owl standing on a cabinet beside the door, near the ceiling. The glossy black eyes stare across the room, at once sharp and dead. "Well," the doctor says. "If you've made your decision, then you've made your decision. But you can still call me if you change your mind. We have some time yet." He slides his business card across his desk. "Call my cell phone if I'm not here."

Patricia starts to get to her feet. "I just hope you come to a consensus on the best way forward," the doctor says. "I understand you two have wanted a baby for some time." He looks at Thomas and smiles, but his eyes are not smiling. "Good luck." And Thomas wants to scream that he never wanted a baby at all—and certainly not one some monster of a man may be the father of, a kid conceived during a violent assault against the woman he lives with, a kid who carries that violence inside even before it's born. But he doesn't say anything, he just nods at the doctor and follows Patricia out. She's already on her way down the hallway. "I hate hospitals," she mumbles when he reaches her. "It smells like illness and death here." And still he can't talk. Everything's spinning around in his head, the rape, the pink and goopy little creature that'll be pulled out of Patricia, and all of it happened behind his back, and why? She walks faster every time he catches up with her, and that provokes him. "Stop," he snarls, grabbing her arm. "Look at me!" But she pulls free and continues without looking at him. He marches in front of her and forces her to stop. "Could you fucking look at me? What's going on?" A nurse in white clogs passes them, a stack of folders in her arms. She frowns disapprovingly at Thomas. "Why won't you look at me? It's one thing that you didn't tell me you were pregnant, but another thing entirely that you just sit there and . . . and . . . and say out of the blue that you don't care who the father is! That you *don't care*. What do you mean by that? You say it means nothing to you! So you don't care about me? Do you not care about me?!" That last part he nearly screams. "Stop shouting," she says measuredly, shoving him aside. She keeps walking hastily forward. The elevator is filled with people. Going down, the butterflies in his belly nauseate him, and for a moment he almost throws up. He stumbles after Patricia through the foyer, and when they exit the hospital, it's as if they slam into a wall of unbearable heat. Thomas gulps for breath. "You need to talk to me," he says, almost tearfully. He grabs her hand. "We need to talk." He guides her to a bench, she sighs wearily. Reluctantly she sits at the far end. She raises her eyebrows a little. "What do you want?" she asks, indifferent.

"What I want? After all this? Don't you think we have a whole lot to discuss? For one thing, I'd like an explanation." She smiles contemptuously. Just one moment in the sun and he feels so hot it's as though his blood is boiling; his headache's splitting his skull in two, as if his cranium has become too small, as if the tissue in his head is pressing on the helmet of his skull. Patricia shoots him a cold glance.

"You'd almost think you hate me," he says. "Do you hate me?" No answer. "Why do you hate me all of a sudden? Haven't I helped you and supported you as best I could?"

"Just stop it." She looks up and regards a ginkgo tree's columnar shape. "What do I want?" she says, calmly. "Why do you keep asking me that? You just heard what I want."

"But this has got to be a joint decision! For God's sake, we live together! I love you!"

"Oh, do you now?" she says, still without looking at him.

"Maybe we can have a baby together, one we know is ours. Later. That's mine. Okay? Why are you so stubborn? Please look at me, Patricia?" Her eyes linger briefly on his, then she turns back to the gingko tree.

"It's very simple," she says. "I want a baby. I've wanted a baby for a long time—unlike you. Now I'm pregnant, and obviously I don't want to have an abortion. Is that so strange?"

He stares at her profile. Her beautiful, aquiline nose and her fine little ears, from which a single white pearl dangles in a slender filament of gold. He loves her ears.

"Yes," he says. "I think it's very strange. There's a strong possibility that you got pregnant that night. *No* normal person would run the risk. I just *can't* understand how you can even *consider* having the baby, especially when you can take a test and actually find out if he was the one who got you pregnant."

She turns her head and looks him straight in the eyes. "What would I do with that knowledge? I'd still have to give birth, either way. To a dead child, mind you."

A pause. Once again he feels a surge of powerless rage, a hatred of this fucking fetus that's sloshing around in Patricia's body, that has possessed her, that has fucking possessed her, he thinks, sweat rolling off him. He says, "Then you've got to put it up for adoption. If you're going to be so fucking obstinate."

For an instant her eyes spark to life. There's a brief flash of terror, which is followed again by a cool, stiff expression. "I hope you don't really mean that." He shrugs irritably. "What else?" "You know what?" she says, slowly raising her right hand while turning toward him. She points at him. "You listen closely." Her voice is low and savage. "I know better than anyone how to live with what happened to me. Don't you lecture me. Don't you make demands. Don't you ask me to *put anything up for adoption*. I want to have a normal life again. And I will. A life more normal and joyful than my last few months with you." She lowers her finger, but continues to stare at him. "I have my reasons for not involving you in this, Thomas." She studies his face. His nose, mouth, chin. It feels very uncomfortable. As if she's gauging him. As if he were a stranger. Then she looks into his eyes.

"I've rented an apartment near the river," she says. "I'm moving out. I'm moving, Thomas. I'm leaving you, and that's how it is." He opens his mouth to talk, but nothing comes out. "That's how it is," she repeats. She stands, clutches her green suede bag, and hurries across the scorched lawn. He remains seated on the bench, in the sunlight, unable to move. "Patricia!" he shouts after a moment. He gets clumsily to his feet. "Patricia!" With all the strength he can muster in his lungs, he roars her name across the hospital campus. But she doesn't turn around.

When she's out of sight, he slumps onto the bench. Everything's unreal, blurry. He buries his head between his knees. A normal and joyful life, she said. The opposite of a life with him. In the morning, when she goes to work, before he's gotten up, the little click of the lock when the door closes. *Not a word of goodbye*, he thinks, furious. He has difficulty catching his breath. And yet he lights a cigarette, the nicotine clawing at his throat. Thoughts and images swirl around in his brain, his headache growing more and more intense: Patricia, naked in the shower, smiling as he hands her a towel; Patricia sitting opposite him in the kitchen one winter evening, a glass of wine in her hand; private conversations they've shared while lying in bed in the dark of night; the sensation of gliding into her; the wet softness of her mouth; her hand on his back. Is he the one who impregnated her, in the car on the way to Kristin's, maybe, or on her desk in her office? Or is it the lover he suspected her of being with all those nights in May when she didn't come home? And: *Why does she have Luke's number?* Now he pictures Luke's oil-squirted hands sliding across Patricia's skin, there in Kristin's kitchen. Did she have an affair with Luke? The rapist left his sperm in Patricia, but the police couldn't find a match in their database. They have nothing at all, no traces, no description. Thomas shakes his head slightly. Patricia's voice early one morning: "I think of it as a bad dream. I won't let him mean anything. Not one *thing*." Thomas flings his cigarette and arches forward, resting his head in his hands. The sun is burning his back and the nape of his neck. And Jesus, this past Monday when he came home from work, she was sitting on the basement stairwell just like he's sitting now, her head in her hands, silent as a stone pillar. It startled him, he hadn't seen her until after he'd been waiting at the elevator for at least two minutes. She hadn't made a peep. "What are you *doing*, Patricia?"

"I wanted to see the place where it happened." She turned her head slowly to look at him. And then she'd shown him exactly where it happened. Around thirty feet down the hallway that runs between the storage units. Not far from the microwave and the money. She'd lain down on her back. "I lay like this," she said, her voice lucid, "right here. I don't think it took very long, but it felt like . . . like an eternity." She lay there, unmoving, her eyes closed and breathing heavily. Didn't even flinch. It had made him terribly nauseated. When they were back in the apartment, he threw up in the kitchen sink as she chugged orange juice directly from the carton. "You're so thin-skinned," she said. And shortly afterward, as she wiped her mouth on her sleeve, "I've signed up for karate. You should too. It strengthens the spirit."

"The spirit? What do you mean by that?"

"Karate helps you focus and it empowers you. It's not just self-defense. It's a lifestyle."

"I'm not interested in changing my lifestyle," he replied.

"No," she said. "If only."

And now, here on this bench where he sits hyperventilating, crouched over, boiling hot, dripping with sweat, writhing, his headache pounding intensely, he thinks that by then she'd already made up her mind. Of course she had. All that stuff about the spirit and karate was a critique of him, which he hadn't understood at the time. *She was ridiculing me.* Rage bubbles inside him again. But a moment later he's sobbing hoarsely. *She's leaving me.* She *has* left me. A chasm. A black hole to disappear into. *My life is vanishing.* A hand settles on his shoulder, startling him. A muscular porter in uniform looks at him worriedly.

"You shouldn't sit in the sun. It's too hot. Get under the shade, so it won't make you sick."

"I *am* sick!" Thomas shouts, sobbing. He leaps to his feet and seizes his bicycle, then flees from the hospital as fast as he can. His eyes flicker, his vision wobbly, blinding white spots, sensory overload, he pounds the pedals as if the devil were on his heels, his headache feeling like a tight-fitting cap outfitted with razor blades. He races through a large intersection, and the sun thrusts its unbearable light right in his face, an eighteen-wheeler drives straight at him, an eighteen-wheeler is about to run him over, it nearly catches his back wheel, the bike rack, but he dodges it, he dodges it at the last possible moment, the cars are everywhere now, and he's propelling forward like a rocket, disregarding the red light, he's shouting and screaming at the truck driver, at all the others, giving them all every dirty hand gesture he knows, outstretched arm, middle finger, and: *cuckold, Christ,* "Fuck you," he screams. "Fuck you all!" But after another fifteen-hundred feet he's about to keel over, he doesn't have any more strength, and suddenly he's dizzy. His entire body weak, he careens down a side street, his breathing raspy and dry; it feels as though his eyes are being squeezed out of their sockets, the tremendous pressure from within, from the brain, his bicycle tips over, he crawls across the dirty flagstones of the sidewalk, props himself against the base of an apartment building. Sitting with his back against the wall, right beside the building entrance, and now he really feels nauseated. Dreadfully nauseated. His gut fizzles and bubbles. He spits up a small quantity of greenish bile. He can barely see anything now, everything's a gray-white mass. He feels the wall against the back of his head. He's freezing in his sweat-soaked shirt. His teeth chatter. His cell phone rings in his pocket. And then he passes out.

"Hello," a man's voice says from far away, and he can feel soft pats against his cheek. "Hello? Wake up. Can you hear me? I think he just fainted." Slowly the voice reaches Thomas in his pitch-black depths. "But is there a pulse?" says another, softer voice. And then: "Oh, good." Thomas forces his eyes open, the sunlight is bright. He stares right into a mouth filled with perfect white teeth, and the mouth speaks again: "I think he's waking up. Hi! Welcome back. You fainted. We've called an ambulance." And the other voice: "Did you hit your head?"

It takes a little while for him to understand what's being said, but when he does, he runs his hand over his scalp—no, no pains. He shakes his head. A man in his early thirties stands over him. Behind him is a woman, a stroller, a large white dog. The man and woman are both smiling at him. "Glad you're all right," the man says, helping him to his feet.

In the ambulance they take his temperature and pinch his skin. "Red and dry," one medic says privately to the other. "Not much fever, badly dehydrated, low blood pressure." He's wheeled into the emergency room and put in a bed with green linen, shielded from the other side of the room by a curtain the same color as the sheets. He's given an IV, and the solution drips slowly into Thomas's parched body. The nurse smiles and assures him that he'll feel better soon. He tells Thomas that a doctor will stop by shortly to check on him. Until then he should rest. And he does. He dozes immediately, and dreamlike sequences mix with the sounds around him: low voices, people walking past, a suppressed sob, trolleys clattering with instruments, and the periodic screeching of a baby. He feels his body sinking into the mattress. Senses his breathing growing even. He has only *one* thought: I want to lie like this forever. Nothing can disturb me here. Send me back to the darkness, to peace. But the doctor disturbs him not long after. There's nothing wrong with him—apart from lack of fluids and heat exhaustion. The doctor examines the bump on his head and doesn't believe it's anything to worry about. "Do you have a headache? Dizziness?" No, not anymore. They're both gone. "We'll keep you here for a few hours. When you're sufficiently hydrated, you can go home. And remember to drink plenty of fluids in the future. Eat some salt, eat something sweet. It is *summer*," he says, a trifle irritated. "One of the hottest in many years." Thomas nods. "Eighteen years," he says softly. The doctor exits the room, pulling the green curtain closed and leaving Thomas alone in his little green shelter. He closes his eyes and thinks: Don't sleep, don't sleep. What if I have a concussion after all, he thinks.

Then he falls asleep.

It's almost 9:00 p.m. when Thomas leaves the hospital, walking right past the bench where Patricia left him. Stooped, he trudges across the desiccated grounds, and the heat is nearly as intense as it was during the afternoon. He doesn't have any interest in going home, but he has even less interest in doing anything else. He can't stomach the thought of staying at Maloney's or Jenny's. He doesn't want to explain, doesn't want to drag anyone into the chaos his life has become in the course of a few hours. Alice has called and left a message. They'll finish painting in the morning. Only four days remain until the store opens. Thomas progresses slowly through the streets. The fresh fluids in his body have done him wonders. Maybe Patricia's at home in the apartment, and they can discuss this properly. On the train home he decides he'll be calm. Not get bent out of shape. The new store is the most important thing now; he's got to remember that, he can't have a meltdown. He considers his condition for a moment, but it's as if the heat exhaustion and the hysteria have completely drained him of emotion, his unease is gone. But he's hungry. He stops at the tapas restaurant and eats standing at the bar. He stuffs himself with chorizo, shrimp, and aioli; he asks for ham dressed in garlic and parsley, for fried calamari, stuffed chili peppers, and roasted potatoes in tomato sauce. When he comes home, Patricia's not there. The living room's crammed with moving boxes. Thomas takes a cold shower, smokes a cigarette, and thinks about how, in the future, he'll be able to smoke wherever he feels like it. He can fucking smoke in bed, if he wants. He stares hatefully at the cat, who stares back. "What?" he says. "What do you want?" It must understand that Thomas doesn't want its company. With its tail raised, it walks out of the living room, and soon he hears it scratching in its litter box in the bathroom. Exhausted, Thomas lies down on the clean sheets. She can kiss my ass, he thinks. She can sail away on her own fucking sea. The fucking bitch. But then he's close to whimpering again. He rolls onto his side, pulls himself together, and glides again into a hybrid state: Now he's awake. Now he's asleep. One moment he's dreaming that he's walking with Maloney through a kind of tunnel or tube. But it's also like being under the sea. And he hears the faint whoosh of cars on the street. Maloney laughs. The next moment he opens his eyes and gazes out the window. The blinds aren't closed, and he sees the illuminated windows in the building across the street. It'll be hot when the sun comes up, but he can't bring himself to get out of bed to close the blinds. Then he finds himself in some sort of music competition, a TV show. He's standing on stage. He's playing the saxophone. He's showered with applause. A woman with a pageboy haircut thrusts her glistening red lips toward him. Is that a feather boa tickling his chest? When he wakes, the cat is curled across his belly. In disgust he shoves it over on Patricia's side of the bed and gets up to take a leak.

Already at 7:00 A.M., he hears her shoving moving boxes around. Groggy with sleep, he has almost forgotten what happened, but then it returns, a storm raging through his body; his stomach clenches, his throat constricts. The bedroom is dark, he can't remember closing the blinds. Maybe she did it. Maybe she was in here while he slept. He sits up in bed. The bed is moist with sweat. He stands in the living room doorway, buck naked. Patricia glances up at him, then continues stuffing books in a box.

"Don't take my books," he says.

"Of course I'm not taking your books."

"Why are you doing this to me?"

"I'll be picking up the rest of my stuff on Saturday, once I get the keys to my apartment. Luke promised to help me move."

"Luke?"

She looks at him. "Yes, Luke. And one of my colleagues."

"Whose name is?"

"Whose name is Kamal." Briefly she scrutinizes his nakedness. "Aren't you going to get dressed?"

"No."

"Oookay." She grabs another stack of books off the shelf.

"So that's just it?" he asks. "Is that all you have to say to me?"

"What should I say, Thomas?"

He turns and goes to the kitchen. He starts the coffee, drinks a glass of pineapple juice. He lights a cigarette. Smoking, naked, he returns to the living room and stands right in front of her. "For one thing you could tell me if this is only about the pregnancy, or whether you stopped loving me a long time ago. And you could tell me whether you're seeing someone else. Is there someone else? Where were you all those nights?"

She sighs, then sits on the edge of the sofa. "It's very simple," she says, surprisingly mild. "It's been hard for a long time, and when you assaulted me at the office, that was the last straw. I couldn't forgive you, however much I tried, because it was violent, Thomas—no matter how you look at it. That became totally clear to me after I was raped. What you did to me was an assault. And no, I'm not seeing anyone else. I've been out having fun, I've met different men, but I'm not seeing anyone. And I'm not interested in having a relationship with anyone. I want to be alone. I have this great need to be alone right now." She leans back and drapes her arms across the spine of the sofa. "I'm not actually mad at you. I was yesterday because it was a stressful situation."

"So what is it?"

"I said it was simple. I want to have this baby, and you don't. So we can't live together. And besides," she looks up at him, "I've also realized that we're two very different people. You were raised in an entirely different environment, and, to be totally honest, I think there's some kind of cultural divide between us."

"A *cultural divide*? What the hell are you talking about? It's low of you to bring my childhood into this. That's really punching below the belt, Patricia."

"Call it whatever you want then." She props her legs up on the sofa and wraps her hands around her knees. "That we've 'grown apart.' Or that you have something inside you that . . . that I can't deal with."

"That you can't *deal with*?"

"Bottom line is, I'm moving out, and I'm going to have a baby, and you aren't."

"And what if it's *mine*? If I'm the father?" He hears his voice, hoarse and all-too shrill. Aggressively, he ashes his cigarette on the floor. "What then? Huh, Patricia? What will you do then?"

She stands, and continues packing. "I'm taking the sofa," she says. "You can have the dining table and the chairs."

He snorts and walks out of the living room. Irritably puts on his clothes. The espresso machine sizzles and bubbles on the stove; he pours a cup and drains the coffee in one mouthful, though it burns his throat. He has no appetite anyway, only anger. But then he remembers what he'd decided last night, *to relax*; he stares at the river, *focuses*. He thinks about the store, *the store, the grand opening, Alice*, and soon he feels better. He calms down. He doesn't *want* anything to do with that baby she's carrying. That's how he's got to think of it, as an *impossibility*, it's impossible for them to be together, and it's *her* decision, that's the reason, he's got to hold on tight to that. He brushes his teeth. He returns to the living room and says, "Don't take all the towels. And I want the bed." She nods. They glance at each other. A brief second of something that reaches all the way down inside them, a togetherness, but also distance, as though they're standing on opposite shores of a lake, recognizing with sorrow that they cannot cross it, no matter how much they might want to. "Where are you staying now?" he says tiredly.

"With Jules and Tina."

She bends down and closes the box. He says, "Take the cat with you. I'll put it down if you don't." She sighs and yanks tape across the box flaps. "I really will."

It's not until he's down on the street with his keys in his hand that he realizes his bicycle is still wherever he left it yesterday. He can't even remember the name of the street.

Although he tries to resist, the thoughts still slip through when he plucks a package of letter paper from the basement a little past lunchtime. Did Patricia call Luke because she wanted him to help her move? Or is there another reason? And what does "I've met different men" mean? What the hell does it mean? How many men has she met? And did this begin a while ago? Has she been unfaithful to him before? He's never heard anything about this Kamal. What the hell, why would she end their relationship just because he made one mistake, forcing himself on her that day? Didn't he have a right to? Weren't they living together? Fucking stuck-up bitch, pampered whore, she didn't have what it takes. He's about to boil over with a black slush of hatred and jealousy. But also: Hey! We've been together for five years. Isn't that worth something? He swells with indignation. He wants to deck her. To punch her in the belly, smash that fucking demon that's growing inside her, a parasite in her flesh. Slap the shit out of her, put her in her place. His nostrils quiver, his breathing constricts. He tries pushing the thoughts away, the same way he pushes boxes from one place to another. Back to the actual: that he's *blameless*. But the baby. The cause of their break-up. A small, stubborn blob of mucus in Patricia's uterus that is stealing her from him. He stands silent, completely drained, empty. Ashamed of his violent fantasies. And yet a moment later, with all his might, he wallops an empty box with his clenched fist. His hand pierces the cardboard, leaving a hole. He kicks the box. Then Maloney sticks his head through the hatch and asks if he's hungry. Annie's going to bring sushi on her way back from The Other, which is what they're calling the new store. "The food'll be here in twenty minutes." Once the boxes are organized, Thomas crawls up the steep stairwell and plops into the boss's chair in the office. Maloney's on the phone with a salesman. When he ends the call, Thomas says:

"Patricia's gone. And pregnant. She wants to keep the baby. And I was at the emergency room yesterday. With heat exhaustion. I can't remember where I left my motherfucking bike."

Maloney looks at him without comprehension. "What are you *saying*?"

"Patricia's moving out."

"But *why*?" He sits on the rickety chair opposite Thomas. "What happened?"

Thomas shrugs. "I suppose it's because she wants to keep the baby, whether the dirty fucking rapist is the father or not. She's packing her things. She's rented an apartment."

"When did you find all this out?"

"Yesterday. Before I went to the emergency room."

"Thomas," Maloney says. His face looks as though it's going to fall apart, concern and sadness consuming him. "I don't even know what to say. Are you all right? I mean, was it serious? Since you went to the hospital?"

Thomas shakes his head. "I just fainted. I forgot to drink water. Listen, I don't want to make a big show out of all this with Patricia. Don't want everyone knowing about it right now. By and large, there's not fuck-all to say about it." He studies his hands. "Maybe it's a good thing."

"What's a good thing?"

"That she's moving out."

A short silence. Maloney regards Thomas, and Thomas considers his own large, knuckly hands, which resemble his father's to a tee. He looks up again. "What's most important is making sure The Other is off to a good start. Which reminds me—I need to order wine . . ." He reaches across the table for the telephone, but Maloney puts a hand on his. "I've already done that," he says. "I spoke to the cabinetmaker too. I've decided to get involved in all this. Jenny convinced me. You can't do it all by yourself, especially now, when . . . fuck, I'm really sorry, Tommy."

"What did you order? Sancerre?"

"Ten bottles. He said it tasted like grass and vanilla. Sounds pretty damn good, eh?" Thomas gives him a mistrustful glance. "What did you say about your bike?" Maloney asks. "You don't think she'll come back?"

Flushed and out of breath, Annie comes through the door wearing a yellow summer dress and carrying two large paper bags. "Sushi!" she says, setting the bags down. "It's looking really nice over there, now that the floors have been stained." She smiles at each of them. "Peter!" she shouts. "Food!" It's as if The Other has put everyone in a good mood, as if the place makes everyone expansive and happy. He's never heard Annie shout so enthusiastically. I want to be happy and buzzing with joy too, Thomas thinks, lifting a maki roll with his chopsticks. He glances at everyone. They're absorbed in their sushi, Peter desperately trying and failing to snare something with his chopsticks. Maloney uses his fingers, Annie carefully dips a piece of salmon in soy sauce. Sitting in the midst of a community, Thomas feels a little better than when he stood in the basement fifteen minutes ago. And the new store tugs at him. He feels a powerful urge to see the freshly stained floor. He decides to stop by on the way home. *On the way home.* It feels as though he doesn't have a home at all anymore.

The floors are shiny as a mirror, and dark—just as they should be. Luke and Alice are putting away the painting supplies: the façade is done, it's white with a faint trace of green, which, to his enormous satisfaction, really creates a connection to the color of the walls inside the store, as he'd hoped and believed it would. Standing in the doorway, Thomas regards his new place, so clean and humble, as though it's waiting to be moved into, like a bridal chamber, or a bride on fresh, clean sheets the very first night of her marriage; he imagines shelves and cabinets and the products that will soon neatly fill them, all the life that will be here. Alice puts a hand on his shoulder. She's standing behind him, and seeing what he's seeing. She's been such a quick learner since she started; it's easy for her, the customers like her. She understands the business intuitively, but she also has a strong aesthetic sense, which he imagines she inherited from him. She's grown with the tasks, and he's already convinced her to quit working for the escort service now that she's got a real salary. She's also begun to write poetry. She's thinking about signing up for an evening writing class. Thomas looks at her. "It'll be great," she says. Her hair has grown out, it's standing straight up, black and thick. The little stud in her nose reflects the sunlight. Everything happens so fast at that age. Thomas remembers himself as a young man going through a melancholic, apathetic, insecure, aimless phase that became, in a very short time (after he met Maloney), energized: a feeling of freedom and independence, *to have a goal.* Alice has a goal now. She'll stand behind the counter in this store, and some day maybe she'll take it over. He hasn't told her that, but it's the plan. Lindström, Maloney, & Farrokhzad. To be eighteen years old and shake the past off you with a carefree shrug. That's how it felt. And that's how Alice looks now, as if she's shaken off her mother, her father, and her entire childhood in one simple motion: cleansed and free. "Thomas," she says, "How's Patricia? Is she back to work?"

"Yes. And she's well." He almost says more, but stops short. Alice eyes him expectantly. "She's doing really great, in fact," he says.

"I don't understand how anyone could get over something like that. It's amazing."

"Yeah. But she's strong. You two wanna grab a bite?"

Thomas locks the door, and they find a tiny joint nearby that serves small dishes and salads. There are only four tables; they sit next to the window. The heat's so intense that none of them are especially hungry. It's almost 7:00 p.m. Thomas orders cold beers all around. Luke and Alice chat, and suddenly, watching Luke, who's partly turned toward Alice, seeing his back in the threadbare white T-shirt—the smooth skin of his upper arms, the tattoo of the heart pierced by a sword, his moist, sweaty hair that's nearly the same color as tiger pelt, his sonorous voice, and his big hand now lying heavily on the table—it swells in Thomas again: this mad desire, prickling and stabbing and dizzying, but only for an instant, like lightning or a shooting star, a powerful flash. Then it's gone. Thomas clears his throat. "I want to pay you two for your work," he says. "How many hours did it take?"

Luke shakes his head and pops a wedge of lime into his beer bottle with his thumb. "I don't want anything. I told you this was a favor."

"C'mon, Luke, I'm sure you can use a little extra cash?" But Luke shakes his head stubbornly.

"Besides, it's only small change," Luke says, sipping his beer.

"What do you mean?"

"I mean . . ." Luke cocks his head and looks at Thomas. "I mean that the hourly wage for an under-the-table painting job is pretty low." He breaks into a big smile. "Wouldn't you agree?"

"Yes," Thomas says, confused. "I guess so."

"If I'm going to make money," Luke goes on, leaning back in his chair, "then I want to make big money."

"And how will you make *big money*?" Alice asks sarcastically, rubbing her eye. Her hand is speckled with white paint.

"I have a few ideas."

Alice: "If a person wanted to earn a lot of money, that person must start small, then save in order to loan more and . . . invest. Am I right?" The expression she gives Thomas is one of earnestness.

He nods. "Yes. The rich are rich because they are stingy enough to save. And save more. And take advantage of the system."

"Exactly," Alice says. She challenges Luke with a stare.

Their food arrives. Grilled chicken for Thomas, hamburgers for the others. Alice holds her burger with both hands, takes an enormous bite, and asks: "What do you plan to do then, Luke? Tell us."

"Wait and see," Luke says, shoving a French fry smothered in ketchup into his handsome mouth. Thomas looks at Luke, and Luke meets his eyes before narrowing his own. "Are you looking forward to the opening?"

Thomas nods.

"Does it have anything to do with fishing?" Alice tries, biting into a pickle.

"Ha!" Luke laughs with food in his mouth. "I don't think you can get rich doing the kind of fishing I do. Besides,"—and now his grin is gone—"I've actually been saving money. Just not enough."

"Enough for what?" Alice asks.

"Impressive," Thomas says, chewing a piece of tough chicken that activates his gag reflex. He holds it in his mouth a moment before he finishes chewing it and swallows.

"Come on, Luke," Alice nudges him, "what is it?"

There he sits in the evening light, suntanned, with all his freckles and his amber-brown eyes. His curly, disheveled hair—now long and paler from the sun—falls over his eyes. His scent reaches Thomas's nostrils, this mysterious aroma of flowers blended with many other smells: sweat, dirt, sourness, something almost bitter. Once again he feels this knot of desire.

"But . . ." Alice scrutinizes Luke.

"You might as well let it go," Luke says.

"You're so weird," Alice says, swishing beer around in her mouth. Luke rocks back in his chair, a self-confident expression etched onto his face. "Well," Thomas says, "then I would like to say something." He simply can't keep his mouth shut. "I might as well say it now. You'll learn sooner or later anyway. Patricia and I have split up. She won't be coming on Tuesday. I just wanted you to know."

They stare at Thomas, dumbfounded, but there seems to be something cheerful in Luke's eyes too, a flash, and then it's gone. And maybe that's something Thomas imagines because he's so attracted to him. Because yet again he's unbelievably attracted to him, and it feels like that time in the car, after they'd visited Luke's mother, a powerful urge to force himself into his body, behind what's visible, wanting to be consumed by him; Luke exudes and discharges steam, that's how it feels. He drops all four legs of his chair back on the floor now, precise and elegant; he looks so damn appealing, and there's this unpredictability about him—which almost scares Thomas. "There's nothing particularly spectacular about it," Thomas says. "We've agreed that it's the right thing to do. It's a mutual decision. I guess you could say we've grown apart." He knows how stupid this cliché sounds, this pathetic lie. "That's the way it goes. And she's also pregnant."

Alice sets her fork down, gasping. "*What* did you say?"

"She won't get an abortion. We don't know who the father is. In any case I don't." Alice continues to stare at him, her eyes wide, and she is silent, almost contrite. Then she looks down at her hands and scratches at the paint. A short silence. Luke watches Thomas light a cigarette. He's barely touched his salad.

"Does it make any difference?" Luke says slowly. He dries his hands meticulously with his napkin. "I mean, a baby's a baby, right?"

"Luke!" Alice pushes her half-eaten burger away. "You can't say that! Jesus! Put yourself in Thomas's shoes!"

Luke smiles. "I'm sorry, Thomas. I didn't mean it like that." Yes, you did, Thomas thinks. That's exactly what you meant, and why did you say it?

"I was just being funny." Luke grins.

"But it's *not* funny!" Alice shouts, gesticulating wildly.

"But hey," Thomas says. His eyelids narrow to slits, and deliberately he takes his time before adding, "Patricia mentioned you've promised to help her move?" Luke glances at him quickly, and Thomas continues, "That must mean you already knew we split up. She must have told you? Why didn't you say anything?" The silence isn't awkward, but hard and intense. Thomas pins Luke with his eyes without blinking.

"What?" Alice looks at Luke. And then at Thomas. "What *is* this?"

"No," Luke says at last. "I didn't know anything. She just asked me if I would help with some boxes. I thought she meant the museum or something. You know, old catalogues and whatnot." Thomas keeps his eyes drilled on Luke. "It sounds strange," he says. And Luke can't look at Thomas anymore. He turns away. "I just wanted to help."

"It doesn't really matter to me," Thomas says. "You should help her move."

"I just wanted to help her. Like I'm helping you paint." Luke looks at Thomas, now with a child's open, innocent face. And then abruptly he needs to leave. "Thanks for dinner," he says, and offers his hand formally to Thomas. Does he feel a tiny bit of shame now? Discomfort? Did Thomas catch him red-handed? In any case Luke hustles away, without a glance back, even when Alice thumps on the window with her knuckle as he walks past. "Do you think he was lying?" she asks.

"I don't know."

"Bizarre." She stretches the "a" in the word and her eyes widen. "But that wouldn't be like him. He's never lied to me. He's all about honesty."

"You two still aren't dating?"

"No!" Alice smiles warmly. "And we won't, either. I haven't even kissed him or anything. I'm seeing someone named Eli now."

"Eli? What happened to Ernesto?"

"That's over. A long time ago. Eli also writes, like me."

Thomas regards his niece, pretty and straight-backed and covered in paint.

"Imagine that, Alice—you writing poetry."

Then Alice wants to go home, too. She's tired. She still lives with Luke's friend, but he's never there, she says, so it works out nicely. She wants to find her own place, now that she actually has a regular paycheck. Thomas counts his money and pays her generously for painting. "Buy a dress so you'll have something new to wear at the opening. It brings luck."

"Who says that?"

"I do."

Smiling, she shakes her head. "There's no way I'm going to be squeezed into some dress, I'll have you know."

"Don't say anything to your mom about Patricia and me, okay? I want to tell her myself."

"Of course." She leaves. It looks like a thunderstorm is on its way. The air is oppressive and dense. Thomas drinks his third beer. He's the only customer in the restaurant, and the waitress is cleaning up. Though it's still pretty early, he needs to go home soon; if not he'll end up sloshed, and that's no good. He's still a little under the weather following his bout with heat exhaustion. And Luke lied, Thomas is sure of it. Something's going on, he just can't tell what. But he simply can't envision Patricia dating him. And what about all that money he was talking about? Or the savings he's got, the plan? If Luke has been with Patricia, he'll kill him. Thomas examines his hands. Luke, bent over Patricia. His pink tongue slithering into her mouth. He clenches his fists. *I'll kill him.* Still, Luke's presence clings to him like a yearning he doesn't understand. He feels his cock rising insistently against the crotch of his pants. He pays the bill and leaves.

The cat hisses at him when he returns home. It's standing at the far end of the hallway staring at him with its yellow eyes, its back arched, its tail stiff and bushy. "Hey! Chill the fuck out," Thomas says. Patricia apparently fed it, but it hasn't touched the food. The litter box has also been changed. She damn well better take that fucking cat, he can't stand the sight of it. Now it's sitting in the windowsill watching the sky. The apartment is quiet in a way Thomas doesn't like. Unlived-in. He's alone here. He'll be alone from now on. When he gets home at night, everything will be as he left it in the morning. There will be no more surprises. There will only be what I do or don't do, he thinks miserably. Only my own fucking mood. In the living room the boxes are sealed, stacked, and shoved against the wall near the hall. He peers in the bedroom closets. She's taken all her clothes. Her creams and makeup are also gone. And many of the pots, pans, and kitchen utensils. She must have been pretty efficient. Maybe she had help. Not Luke, because he was painting all day, Thomas thinks, almost relieved. He sees how she tried to disassemble the sofa, the open tool box is on the floor beside it, but evidently she couldn't figure out how to do it. If the store resembled an empty room calmly awaiting, then the apartment is the exact opposite: Something that's been ripped up, consumed, something sad, drained of life. Standing in the center of it all, he doesn't know what to do with himself. Then Jenny calls.

"I got a strange letter in the mail today," she says.

"What do you mean?"

"There's no sender, and the letter has only five words."

Thomas's heart pounds, and he slumps onto the coffee table. "What does it say?"

"It says: 'Say hello to your brother.'"

"*Say hello to your brother*?" he whispers. "Nothing else? Is it handwritten?"

"No. It looks like a print-out or a copy. According to the postal stamp it was sent from somewhere here in the city. Isn't that odd?"

Thomas says nothing.

"Are you there, Thomas?"

"Maybe it's from Frank and those guys."

"Frank?" snorts Jenny. "Why would *he* send a letter like this? To *me*? He can just write directly to you, if he wants anything from you. And why would he? What does this mean? *Say hello to your brother.* It doesn't make any sense. Does it? Well anyway, I'll give it to Maloney tomorrow, so you can see it."

A pause. Their breaths on each end of the telephone.

"How's it going otherwise?" Thomas asks in a small voice.

"Great! Did I tell you that we're moving in together? We've toured a row house in the district behind the cemetery. There's even a backyard. With an old pear tree."

"Congratulations." Thomas swallows.

"How are you two doing? Is Patricia feeling better?"

"Yes."

"It's so awful, Thomas. I can't even imagine it. Tell her I said hello. We could all go out some night, if she wants. Tell her. We could go to Luciano's."

Jenny's voice is light and mild; she says goodbye and prepares to hang up. "See you on Tuesday," she says, no trace of instability of any kind, and he hears someone snap on the television in the background, must be Maloney. Thomas is rigid with fear. He sags on the coffee table, unable to move. It's clear to him that the break-in, the rape, and now the letter to Jenny are somehow connected. It's got something to do with the money, with *him*. Someone's warning him. Him, Thomas, and no one else. Someone knows I've got the money. He listens to his own rapid intake of breath pumping like a little locomotive run amok, barreling down the tracks without a conductor. Will they ambush him, kill him? And who the hell is it? Once again he recalls Frank jabbering about his dry cleaning, which he claimed he'd left at his father's apartment. As if he'd ever dry-cleaned anything in his life, the way he dresses: wrinkled shirts, faded jackets. There's still a lot of money left in the microwave. He has to get rid of it. But no. It won't make any difference. Feeling completely powerless, he gets to his feet, stumbles into the bedroom, and throws himself on the bed. It smells nasty and stuffy. He tosses and turns. *But they can easily bust the lock.* He gets up and latches the security chain on the door. He nearly trips over the cat on his way back to bed—it's lying across the doorway in the darkness—and it hisses loudly when he whacks it with his foot.

Back in bed and now it's pouring outside, rain lashing against the window panes. He can't stay still, everything's spinning in circles. Thunder rumbles, a lightning bolt flashes and lights up the room, and soon a powerful boom jerks him upright in bed, startled. He sneaks around the apartment, turning on lights, smoking, drinking whiskey, listening to the rain, keeping an eye on the door, staring out the windows, trying to watch TV, then back out to check on the door again. And gradually the stormy weather passes, following another short, powerful burst, and then the night falls silent. Close to 3:00 A.M. he finally falls into a light and dreamless sleep, which lasts until quarter past 6:00. He thinks something wakes him. A noise. He lies completely still in bed, listening. But there's nothing. Unease fills him. He practically leaps out of bed and, once again, walks around the apartment, but there's no one. He takes a shower, paranoid that someone will force his way in, like in a film, a shower curtain smeared red with blood, a singing, unsuspecting person enjoying a shower, and then: dead and maimed. He listens carefully, shuts off the water, listens again, turns on the water, hurries to rinse shampoo from his hair, stands silently on the tiled floor, cautiously opens the door. Walks into the living room, the kitchen. But it's only him and the cat. Outside the sky is gray. The rooftops are dark after the night's rain.

At 7:00 A.M. Patricia pushes her key in the lock. The chain's still attached. She eyes him through the slit in the door.

"Thomas? Let me in."

She stands in the doorway. Her hair is pinned up, and beneath her thin blouse her breasts are hefty, enormous. He feels an urge to embrace her, to hold her close to him, to whisper in her hair. But then he sees the tightness in her face, the rejecting, irritated eyes.

"Why did you have the chain on?"

"Why are you here so early? Can't you show a little consideration?"

"I want to do something before I go to work." She gestures with her arm. "What's that thing on the door?"

"What are you talking about?"

"This thing. You can't see it from there."

He walks out onto the landing. She pushes the door halfway in. There's a mark carved into the wood right above the knob. The exact same one that's on the countertop at the store. The currency symbol. Four lines radiating from a circle. Blood rushes to his head, makes him dizzy.

"What is it?" Patricia asks.

"No clue," he says.

She enters the apartment. He stares at the symbol. His pulse thumps in his ears. It happened last night. Someone was here last night. Or this morning. Maybe whoever did it's on the floor above right now. Thomas darts upstairs. There's no one. Nor is anyone one flight below. He hurries back, closes the door, and methodically locks it. Stands listening. Not a sound. He heads to the kitchen, to Patricia. "I can't have that cat anymore, it's driving me crazy," he says breathlessly.

She scoops up the animal and caresses it. Speaks to it in a low voice, lovingly. "Little kitty. Didn't you eat your food?" And to Thomas: "I can't take it to Tina and Jules's. It's too much."

"Too much! It's goddamn too much for *me*, all this. Then you'll have to move to a hotel or home to your mother."

"My mother's in a nursing home four hundred miles away, in case you've forgotten."

"I'm kicking it out! I'll dump it on the street if you don't take it with you. I mean it, Patricia."

She steadies her gaze on him. "You've become such an unlikeable person, Thomas." Then she puts the cat back on the floor and begins removing pots from the cabinet. She turns on the radio and blasts the volume. He puts on his shoes and leaves. He stops to scowl at the symbol carved into the dark wood. Someone has been here, someone stood right here and scratched into his door, while he was on the other side, so close. His fingertips tingle and prickle. He stumbles down the stairs. Sobs uncontrollably for a moment, filled with grief, anger, confusion. And then this powerful fear above all else. He's afraid of what's coming for him. He's certain now: Someone's trailing him closely. The gutter is rimmed with rainwater; it's a little cooler than in previous days, but the humidity's still extremely high. Feverishly he paws around in his pockets. His cigarette pack is empty. He buys a croissant, but doesn't eat much of it. There are few people on the street this morning, and it's quiet and gray. Only a little past 7:30. He can't shake the feeling that someone's watching him. But all he hears are his own steps. Unlike on the street, the train teems with people. He squeezes into the hot, swarming mass formed by the cluster of bodies, and he imagines someone stabbing him with a knife as he stands here. It would be so easy, so soundless; the perpetrator could hop off at the next station unnoticed, and disappear. He can easily imagine the young man with the stubbled face doing it, the way he leans against Thomas with all his weight each time the train rounds a curve. Or the older man over there, with his pigtail and buggy eyes, who every now and then glances at Thomas. It could be a woman, could be the girl dressed all in black with the baseball cap. He's practically waiting to be assassinated. His saliva has apparently dried up; he swallows and swallows, but it doesn't help. Four stations before his actual stop he squeezes onto the platform, right before the door closes. He dashes up the stairwell. Almost in surprise, he realizes that no one's following him. He trots the rest of the way and locks himself in the store. He tries to do his usual morning routines, his hands trembling. He sits down in the office, it's a quarter past 8:00. At last Maloney arrives, and drops the letter on the desk. It's a printout. *Say hello to your brother.* Even the text on the envelope is printed. It's an average, cheap envelope, standard size. Copy paper. Thomas holds the letter up to the light. Just as his sister had said, it was sent from here in the city, from the central post office. "Can't you take it to the police? Talk with that guy, what was his name again? The one who came here when we had the break-in? What if this has something to do with that? You never know."

"Kagoshima."

"Yeah, him. Go over to the station, Thomas. They need to see this, it's too damn weird." Thomas doesn't respond. "If you don't, I will," Maloney adds.

"I'll go over there in a bit."

"You want coffee?"

Soon the new coffee automat's making slurping, clicking sounds, and Maloney returns with two paper cups. He sits down. "Looks like you didn't sleep a wink all night."

"I haven't."

Maloney gives him a worried look. "You've certainly got a lot to contend with right now. Have you talked to Patricia?"

"Nope. Why should I?"

"Break-in, rape, break up, what the hell's going on?" Maloney shakes his head regretfully. Thomas regards him. There's something buoyant and fresh about Maloney despite his girth; he's clean-shaven, wearing a spotless, light-blue shirt. Which even seems to be ironed. "And now this letter. What's going on?" Thomas picks up the letter and leaves the store. The police station isn't far away. But of course he goes in the opposite direction. He took a whole lot of money that should've gone to someone else. He can't tell Kagoshima that, for

Christ's sake. He's backed himself into a corner. It tears at his flesh, an urge to flee, a stab in his chest. He walks around the block and sits on a bench, but he can't stay still; he stands, has to smoke, he trudges down to the water—which looks so ungodly disheartening today, cloudy and motionless, hardly a ripple on the surface. He returns to Maloney. "They're looking into it," he lies, "but from what they can see there are no fingerprints." The floor guy calls, wants to settle the bill. The day passes, and mostly Thomas mopes, cursing himself, thinking angrily and vulnerably about Patricia, and then again: *But the whole thing's my fault*, the rape, his fault, and it's too late now, he can't get her back, he can't get rid of the money, and it's so obvious that he'll soon get a visit that won't exactly be a social call, and what can they do now other than punish him brutally? All he wants is to go back to the hospital and lie there, in that green hollow, safe and sound, gliding in and out of sleep like a newborn, someone looking in on him, fluffing his pillows, adjusting his blanket, taking care of him; the nights will be long and peaceful, no one will look for him there, no one will find him, he'll be among strangers, he'll be a stranger himself—that's the only relief he can imagine. "Maybe you should go on a trip," Maloney says as they're closing up. "Maybe as early as next week, after we've opened The Other. Go to the casino or something. Get your energy back. You look like a ghost."

"That's exactly what I am," Thomas mumbles, turning off the chandelier. "Hey," Maloney says. "The casino is the *perfect* solution! There's alcohol, hot babes. You'll forget all your troubles at the gaming tables. Unless of course you lose everything, but fucking hell, it's fun. Do it, man!"

"Jenny tells me you're moving in together?"

"Yeah," Maloney smiles. "She fell in love with this place with a pear tree. Did she tell you that?"

Thomas wants to tell him that he's happy for them, that it's courageous of Maloney to finally move in with a woman, that it's fantastic, but he can't muster the energy. He's already on his way down the street when Maloney finishes locking the door. "Where are you going?" Maloney calls out. "Don't you want to get a beer?" "I gotta run," Thomas calls back, but his shout is nothing more than a peculiar whistling, and when Thomas turns the corner he begins to sprint. He runs, faster and faster, he sprints through the city, sweaty, out of breath, red-faced, he runs as if fleeing from a huge beast that could rake its massive claws through him at any time and flay him open, slicing straight through the vulnerable flesh, tossing him around as if he were a child's forgotten toy, trampling him into the dust, splitting him apart, until he's utterly shapeless, nothing more than a bloody pulp, a black mush shorn from skeleton, and the skeleton is easily yanked apart, crushed, destroyed.

Thomas goes to a bar. He orders vodka. He sways on his feet, and every time he sips he thinks of Celan's death fugue: "*Black milk of daybreak we drink it at sundown / we drink it at noon in the morning we drink it at night / we drink it and we drink it / we dig a grave in the breezes there one lies unconfined . . .*" And he keeps drinking. He considers war and persecution and extermination: to be forced to dig your own grave. The Holocaust, mass-extinction, the black brands of history. He thinks of how everyone bears this brand. With frightening clarity he sees that it's not just the exterminated who bear it, but the exterminator as well. Always. He shivers, trembling. To carry it with you. And the dead, who are gone, who haunt the living. Dead father, dead mother. He thinks of his own life, a suddenly splintered life, and he can't determine when it began to splinter and change shape, to lose its substance and direction. He thinks of his own life as a war, he thinks of his unknown persecutors. But after the fourth glass the alcohol gives him a merciful gift, swaddles him in a robe of unfeeling, he's pain-free now, he pinches himself on the arm, not even that hurts, he sighs loudly, relieved, drains his glass and looks around the bar, and there, in a dark corner, he thinks he recognizes a familiar face, lit in the glow of a nicotine-yellow basket lamp. Very slowly the person raises a cigarette to his mouth, and then he lifts his face. His eyes are glazed. He's on more than alcohol. Looks straight through Thomas with his wasted heroin stare. And now it occurs to Thomas who this person is, it's Mingo, the man at Ernesto's concert who was tripping on acid, the man with the street like a gorge, the one with the girl sitting on his lap. Now he remembers what Alice told him: that it was the "exact opposite," apparently the *girl* is selling drugs, not Mingo. He's sitting by himself, drinking a cola. Slumping on the bench with the lit cigarette dangling between his fingers. He seems to have forgotten it. With his hair plastered on his head, he looks far more wretched and skinny than the last time Thomas saw him. And there's the girl exiting the bathroom. What was her name? Anna? No. Andrea. She says something to Mingo, slides onto the bench beside him, nudges him to get his attention, nudges him again, hard, an elbow to his side, and then, very slowly, he fishes something or other from his pants packet and gives it to her. She drops it into her bag, gets up, and leaves without a word. But Thomas can see her standing on the sidewalk. She seems to be texting someone. On his bench, Mingo appears stoned, his head dipping against his chest. He drops his cigarette on the floor. A couple seated at a neighboring table turn to him, irritated, and the man extends his leg and stamps out the cigarette with his foot. Thomas orders another vodka. Andrea's talking on her cellphone now, pacing back and forth. And when Mingo soon threatens to slide all the way down—he's sagging at an odd angle between the bench and the floor, twisted around with one arm sticking straight up—the bartender kicks him out. Mingo tumbles onto the sidewalk. Andrea steps around him. And Thomas can't see anymore. Maybe Mingo's sitting down, or maybe he's fallen. Thomas turns his back to the street. The bartender returns, shaking his head in consternation. "Fucking junkies," he says. "I'm sick and tired of them."

His father would get tanked at this bar whenever he had money in his pocket. It looks the same. Just as smoky, dark, and filthy. He and Jenny would sometimes get a cola whenever they marched up here and waited for their old man to be coaxed into going home. They always sat beside the door. The bartender's name was Vladimir. He was a gentle man, who asked them about school and told them stories about his childhood near the sea. His father had been a fisherman. He would raise his eyebrows and laugh, so that you could see the black spaces between his missing teeth; the stench from his mouth was overwhelming, rotten, disgusting, like shit. He told them, "Mind your schooling, no matter what. Education is gold." Sometimes he gave them crackers and salted almonds from the drawer under the counter. Fatso used to help them drag their father home. Their old man was silent and withdrawn whenever he got piss drunk, his legs would fail him, and his breathing sounded like a bellows, but he wouldn't say a word. You weren't supposed to get in his way, don't say anything, don't be a pain. "Be invisible," Thomas whispered to Jenny, and so Jenny learned to be invisible too. In the mirror on the wall behind the bar he can still see Andrea pacing back and forth. *Invisible as a ghost. Like stars in daylight.* Andrea pacing back and forth, back and forth. The bartender turns up the volume on the music. Thomas is sloshed. He watches the young blonde girl in the mirror, eyes transfixed. A man comes up beside her. Thomas wheels around. Through the tall window he sees the two figures clearly. At first he doesn't believe his own eyes, but there's no doubt: It's Luke. Luke runs his hand through his thick mane of hair, Luke kisses Andrea on the cheek, Luke pushes the glass door open with his back and steps into the bar, followed by Andrea in her white, loose-fitting clothes, her purse slung over her shoulder. Thomas quickly turns his back to them. They sit next to the door, near where he and Jenny usually sat. He observes them in the mirror. They're leaning across the table, talking, and so close that their foreheads nearly touch. Then Andrea fishes something from her purse and discretely hands it to Luke, after which he stands and leaves. The whole transaction takes, at most, two minutes. Andrea lights a cigarette, leans back in her chair, stretches her legs, kicks off her sandals. For Thomas there's no doubt: that was either money or drugs that just passed between them. He drains his glass. So that means Luke is involved in drug trafficking. And now, when he thinks about it, tries to think, despite his inebriation, it becomes clear to him that Mingo must've paid Andrea for drugs—he'd clearly scored a fix—and that she probably then called Luke, who came to claim his share of the money. His thoughts whirl swiftly now. Because that means Luke's a criminal. And his father's last job, or whatever the hell it was, might've been drug-related. Maybe Jacques began pushing illegal narcotics in his old age, maybe that's why he got nailed for such a long sentence. Thomas sits numbly on the narrow barstool. Or was it actually *Luke's* job? Maybe his father was just playing along? Did he take the fall for Luke? Or did Luke threaten him to silence? Did Luke betray him? Does this mean Luke was the one—and here Thomas almost forgets to breathe—that Luke was the one responsible for Jacques's death? *He killed my father.* His thoughts race dramatically, he sucks hard on his cigarette. Vodka pumps through his bloodstream, anesthetizing him. But his brain leaps in every direction at once. He sees his bloodshot eyes in the mirror. Looks at his cracked lips, and the huge sweat stains under his armpits. Luke, during their hike, telling them about Jacques's shirts of Egyptian cotton. Jacques and Luke reciting poetry to each other while keeping an eye on their fishing lines, their blanks, their reels, the sea gray and calm. The old man knocking someone down, lifting a blunt object above another's head as Luke flees. A backyard, a stairwell, a long room. Luke aiming a pistol at someone. His father in handcuffs. Thomas is immersed in his images: Luke with his caramel-colored eyes, Luke with his heart tattoo, his sword, his brawny biceps, his flexing muscles, handing a joint to Thomas as an owl hoots. Here he's on the ladder painting the façade, here he's ransacking the store with uncontrollable rage, here he's carving that fucking currency sign into the door of Thomas's apartment. Luke, Luc, The Kid. Thomas gulps two bottles of sparkling water in rapid succession and gorges on a handful of chips. Then he pays. Andrea's gone. It's hot outside. He can smell himself, rancid sweat, old smoke. Silence above the drunken noise from the bar. He thinks he sees Luke turning down a side street, and races after him. And when he reaches the corner: another glimpse of Luke, turning down another side street. But when Thomas gets to that spot, he doesn't see him anywhere. For a moment he doesn't know what to do. Maybe he's hallucinating. He turns around. Wanders aimlessly through his old neighborhood, and his thoughts pound maniacally in his head: If Luke knows about the money and thinks it belongs to him, then *Luke's* the one who wants it, there can be no doubt; *he's* the one responsible for the break-in, the letter, the rape. Thomas stops, gasping. If Luke raped Patricia. If he . . . wearing a mask, gloves. Patricia on the cold floor. Gloves that he also used during the break-in at the store, so meticulously planned and calculated. He understands everything now. Luke didn't want money for helping to fix up the store, it wasn't enough money for him; he has *other plans.* His secretiveness. The dangerously unpredictable, the wolf-smile, but also: smiling, handsome Luke surrounded by all the women on Kristin's and Helena's patio. The scent of jasmine drifting over the fusty, bitter earth. And his own desire for that scent and Luke's smooth, strong body. Hatred churns in Thomas like a tornado. *He deliberately seduced me*, he thinks, and he seduced Patricia too. She's got his number, she kissed him on the mouth when they said goodbye that Sunday out in the country, he's helping her move.

He raped her. His hatred is so intense that Thomas almost can't contain it. Sweating profusely, he tramps through the streets with his long, furious strides. It's 10:00 p.m., Friday night. He's still so drunk that he's not afraid. He passes his old school and stares into its dark courtyard; the enormous linden tree is still there, the benches along the wall. He walks past his father's apartment building and studies the darkened windows; there's a light on in Mrs. Krantz's place. A squirrel scoots across the street. He thinks: I've seen through him. He feels something resembling joy. He pushes on. He knows he's half-crazy. An odd, pure feeling of seeing everything from a *new* perspective. He's floating above the world. He looks down at it, his eyes clear and sharp. And then a faint but niggling sensation that he's out of sync with everything. But now, again: *I'm holding the long end of the fucking stick.* At last he finds himself standing before the new store. He sits on the stoop. He checks his cell phone. Jules left a message: "Hope you're okay, buddy, give me a call." Patricia writes: "The cat's at Kamal's." He roots around in his pockets for his key, then unlocks the door, trips over the doorstep, and tumbles over the big cardboard box with the lamp inside. There he lies moaning on the newly varnished floor. He's hurt his knee.

Thomas texts Patricia: "Was Luke the one who raped you?" Patricia responds: "What are you talking about?? Are you drunk?!" He doesn't reply. He sits on a stepladder, his head in his hands. He chugs water from the bathroom tap. In the back room he glances out at the courtyard. A silver willow glows ghostly white next to the clotheslines. The pleasure he'd felt at figuring everything out slowly leaks from him. What remains is a cold loneliness. He can't tell anyone about this. Here he sits in his newly occupied property, which he has haggled, stolen for himself, purchased under-the-table, and if he confronts Luke himself? Thomas closes his eyes. The silence is dense, quivering. If he confronts Luke himself? He can't handle the thought. He touches his sore knee, rubs it through the fabric of his pants. A cold, cold loneliness. Cold as death. "*He sets his pack on us he grants us a grave in the air.*" Luke set his pack on us, played his sick game. Set his pack on the entire family. But especially Thomas. He yanked him around the menagerie, made a mockery of him, probably amusing himself, observed Thomas at a distance and amused himself. Thomas glides down the wall into a seated position, and leans his head against the window. He thinks: *Maybe I can beat him to it.* His telephone rings.

"Sorry I'm calling so late," Luke says with his deep, calm voice. "But there's something I want to talk to you about. Can we meet?" Pause. "Are you there, Thomas?"

"Yes."

"Are you at home?"

Thomas doesn't respond.

"You're at the store, right?"

"How do you know that?"

"I walked past a little while ago and saw the lights. I'll be right over. Two minutes."

Thomas can't move. Two minutes. He can't even run away. Terrible panic. *He's going to kill me.* Not until Luke's fumbling at the door does he clamber to his feet. For a moment he considers ignoring him, but then he'd just smash the door down, just as he smashed the door during the break-in; there's no way around it, and in the middle of his tense fright, the flicker of hatred, there's also a sense of relief—a kind of release, for now *everything* will come to a head: not just his relationship to Patricia, but also the uncertainty, the fear, and the relentless guilt. Maybe he will cease to exist, and even that seems like a welcome freedom. But a moment later the thought's replaced with a very real dread of death. Luke raps on the door again. Thomas reluctantly lets him in. Luke shakes his bangs from his eyes. "Hi," he says. "I brought a six pack." He edges past Thomas and stops in the center of the store. "These floors have really turned out great. How many coats did you say it was?"

"Five." Thomas stands behind him, ready to defend himself if Luke should turn and charge him. Luke's fast as a snake. But Luke doesn't turn, he continues into the back room. "Isn't there a chair in here? Bring the stepladder with you. I'll sit on that." Thomas arranges the stepladder on the floor beside the window and drops into the chair. Luke removes two beers from a bag and pops the caps with his lighter. "Want a smoke?" he asks. They sit with their beers and their cigarettes. A short silence. Thomas's heart thumps so hard in his chest that he's certain Luke can see it. The painter's lamp floods the room with bright white light. They regard each other. Hard shadows slant across Luke's face. "I have something I want to tell you," Luke says. "I've actually wanted to tell you this for a long time, since right after Jacques's was buried, but of course I didn't know you back then . . ."

"Before you say shit about anything, there's something we need to discuss," Thomas says, his voice low. It's as if there's no oxygen in him. He inhales sharply through his nose.

"I think it's best that I start."

"I don't think so."

"It's serious."

"Not as serious as this."

"I'm not sure about that." Luke sips his beer. "Let's settle it then. Rock, paper, scissors?" He extends his hand.

"What are we playing for?"

"Who gets to talk first, of course!" Luke smiles. "Two out of three?" Thomas looks directly at Luke, who appears to be calm still, but also nervous. His eyes wander. Thomas raises his hand, and the tips of Luke's fingers briefly graze his. They play. Luke wins the first round with scissors. Thomas wins the second with rock. And in the third and decisive round, Luke wins again, covering Thomas's stone with his paper, grasping it and squeezing and chuckling. "You're too drunk! Winning is impossible when you're drunk."

"I'm not drunk." Thomas pulls his hand back.

Luke's laughter subsides. Again the intense, pulsing silence. Thomas recalls the sensation he felt when the enormous body seized him in the basement the night Jules and Tina visited. A huge zombie body, and it feels as though he can hear its heavy breathing nearby, ready to snatch him and crush him in its embrace. He can almost hear the resounding voice shouting at him: *Who's there?* "Well," Luke says. "This is a little hard for me to say. But . . ."

Here it comes, Thomas thinks. He's going to confess, and then he's going to jump me. He crouches forward, ready to defend himself.

Luke glances at the floor. "I figured you wouldn't believe me if I just told you. So I've brought some . . . hmm . . . some evidence with me." He pulls a crumpled-up slip of paper from the breast pocket of his short-sleeved shirt.

"*Evidence*?" Thomas doesn't understand. "What?"

"Just look at it," Luke says softly, thrusting the document at him. He cocks his head. Thomas is handed a sheet of thick, yellowed paper. He unfolds it. It's obvious what it is: a birth certificate. Issued almost twenty-three years earlier. *Luc Dupont.* Born the eighth of November. Mother: *Rose Dupont.* Father: *Jacques O'Mally.* Thomas rereads the last part. Rereads it again. Father: *Jacques O'Mally.* So he was right after all when he thought Luke was his brother. He looks at him, indifferent. "What am I supposed to make of this?"

"That. That . . . because," Luke says, eyeing Thomas. As though sucking him in with his velvety-smooth eyes, his face both disarmed and vulnerable. "Because Jacques is my father. We're brothers, Thomas." A shy little smile spreads across his face. "I'm your brother."

Thomas stares at him. "So what?"

"And Jenny's my sister. It's been so hard for me to say this and . . ."

Thomas glowers at Luke. Luke nods. "I couldn't say it. But tonight . . ." Thomas thinks: Yet another way to manipulate me. Yet another sick maneuver in his game. Thomas stands abruptly, filled with a sudden, mad rage. "Stop!" he roars, startling Luke. "STOP FEEDING ME ALL YOUR BULLSHIT!" Quick as lightning, he grabs Luke and yanks him up, pulling him close. "Haven't you done enough already? Huh? Who do you think you are? Haven't you done enough?" He gives him a jerk. "So you want a little brotherly love to prance around with? Do you think I'm stupid, Luke?" Luke stares at him, frightened. "I saw you tonight with that little pusher-chick," Thomas snarls. "I saw her handing you money, you miserable shit. I'm very aware of what you've got going on." He shakes Luke hard, then shoves him away. Luke stumbles backward. "So that's how you earn your 'big money,' huh? I *knew* there was something wrong with you. You're nothing but a dumb fucking loser, just like your mother. And your 'father.' Ha!" Again he shoves Luke, forcing him back.

"You don't understand," Luke whispers.

"I sure as fuck understand!" Thomas hisses. "Stay away from my family, you psychopath!"

"But Thomas," Luke gives him a confused look. "All I wanted was to tell you we have the same father. Is that so bad? I haven't asked you for anything. When he died, when they told me he'd died, I asked that you and Jenny not know anything about me. I wanted to tell you myself."

"And you suddenly wanted to communicate something, huh? Normally you like to tell me things in quite another way." Thomas raises his arm threateningly. "*Quite* another way . . ."

"But," Luke takes a step closer, "it's not my fault that Jacques got my mother pregnant. It was random. It was . . . fate. I didn't know until I was twelve." Another step closer: "But he took care of me. He helped me . . ."

"Shut the fuck up!"

"But he did."

"I don't give a shit!" Thomas roars. "And the two of us," he points at Luke with a trembling finger, "we're *not* brothers. You got that? You'll get nothing from me, nothing!"

"But I'm not asking you for anything." Luke seems to be on the verge of tears now. He walks dejectedly over to his birth certificate and scoops it off the floor, puts it in his pocket, and sits down on the stepladder. "Why are you so mad at me? It's not my fault. There's no reason for you to hate me."

Thomas is suddenly at a loss for words. He parks himself in the chair opposite Luke. "No reason for me to hate you?" he says, low, almost inaudibly. "I can fucking assure you that I have a reason."

Luke looks at him, bewildered, then fingers a cigarette from his pack. "But why?" He lights the cigarette with the blue lighter, his hands trembling. "What have I done to you?" Thomas drains his beer. He regards the young man who's calling himself his brother. He feels sick. He recalls that constricting feeling he had when the two of them sat on the bench in Kristin and Helena's sunroom. "*We have circled and circled till we have arrived home again, we / two, / We have voided all but freedom and all but our own joy.*" How pathetic. He was trying to give him a sign, to explain how they belonged together, to seal their brotherhood—the day before he raped Patricia! And what he said when they returned to the city, about his father not understanding him, that Thomas got on his nerves, and Thomas cried afterward, his shame and despair. It's *sick*. Luke has been a monstrous bastard the entire time, and as his brother it's even more vile and disgusting. Contempt swells and swells in Thomas. Luke says: "I was always by myself when I was a kid. I dreamed of you a lot, of you and Jenny. I used to imagine what you were like." Thomas is close to retching. "Did you really see me with Andrea tonight?" Luke glances at him, a sad look in his eyes. "I'm really sorry about that." At *that* Thomas leaps to his feet, shouting and screaming: "*Now* you admit it, huh? You fucking rapist!" Luke regards him, puzzled, but now there's also something uneasy in his eyes; he wants to say something. But Thomas gets right in his face, screaming. "Was it hot raping my girlfriend? Huh? Did you enjoy it? Did you feel big and powerful? Was it fun sending that letter to my sister, or ransacking my store? What is it that you think you deserve, Luke? Tell me. But when it comes right down to it, maybe you don't have the balls. Maybe you don't know how to do anything else but stand there fencing with your fishing pole and reciting stupid poems? Is that all you learned from your beloved father? That's great, Luke, great! Catch a little fish and stammer a little poem. Fucking recite fucking haiku, and then go out and fucking destroy my life!" Thomas approaches Luke, and Luke gets to his feet, lurching backward a step. Thomas towers over him, feeling immensely powerful; he moves closer, so close to Luke's face that he notices his almost vaporous heat, the scent of his skin. "But apparently you've also learned how to rape," he hisses. "You're much worse than Jacques. All that money you'd like to get your hands on—he hid it well. And it doesn't seem like he hid it for *you* to find, because if that were the case, he would've told you where the money was, don't you think?" His voice grows louder and louder. "But maybe you thought you could just pick up your prize later? Was that what you thought? That's what you thought, right, Luke? That's how you treat your 'father' and 'brother.' Fuck you!" Luke's face is dark and emotionless now. He squints in that way of his, his eyes glistening and repulsive. Thomas looks at him, at the body he's desired and dreamed of. It's just flesh now, malevolent flesh, his disgust is total. Thomas advances and wraps his hand around the back of Luke's neck, pulling his head close: "But there was just that one little problem—that I beat you to it. I beat you to it, Luke. Too bad. You'll get nothing. I'm not sharing with you. I'd never dream of it." Thomas breathes rapidly. He's hot, his muscles tense. Luke's face is so close that it blurs into a pale oval, his irises dark stains against white. With a swift motion Thomas lifts his right arm, draws it back, and punches his clenched fist with all his might against Luke's jaw. Luke tumbles backward. "Get out! And don't show your face around here again!" Thomas kicks at him and manages to land a blow to his thigh; he kicks again, but this time Luke gets out of the way. Before Thomas knows it, Luke has him pinned to the floor, and is sitting on top of him with his hands clasped around his throat. He's young, and so strong that Thomas doesn't stand a chance. He restrains Thomas's arms with his knees, pressing them against the sides of his body. Thomas tries to get a foothold on the floor, but his leather soles slide on the smooth, newly varnished wood, and no matter how much he struggles to free himself, Luke doesn't budge. He snarls at Thomas, spitting words between his teeth, his jaw already beginning to swell, red and shiny: "So you're accusing me of screwing your girlfriend? You mean like this?" Luke makes sexual gestures, driving his groin against Thomas's. "You think it was like this?" He drives again, and Thomas manages to slip one arm loose. He goes for Luke's eyes, but Luke jerks his head back. Thomas squeezes his fingers into Luke's chin. Luke releases Thomas's throat with one hand and again braces Thomas's arm under his knee. At the same time, he presses Thomas's head against the floor with the other, holding his sweaty hand over his mouth and nose. And then once again he's clutching Thomas's throat. "So I fucked her and got her pregnant? If that's what you think, then that means she's going to have my kid, Thomas. Have you considered that?" Thomas gasps for air. His feet skate helplessly on the shiny floor. Luke stares at Thomas with pure hatred: "You know what I see when I look at you now? I see a real shit. You think I want a shit for a brother?" He jerks his head. "Ha! No! My mistake! Who the hell would want you for a brother?" Luke bares his teeth, then laughs brusquely and hysterically. "Nobody! Nobody wants you!" He laughs hysterically again, then tightens his grip on Thomas. Thomas's chest heaves and heaves. Luke stops laughing. Thomas clutches his own thigh, pushing off, using all the strength he can muster to shove Luke's knee away with his elbow, and actually manages to free his arm, and now the other arm. He tears at Luke's arms and hands to get them away from his throat. And when he finally succeeds, he goes after Luke's face and eyes again. But Luke leans over Thomas and pushes his cheek into his. His voice is unbearably close: "Because you have no honor, Thomas. You don't even know how to take care of your girlfriend." Thomas hammers on Luke's back, punches his ribs with his fists, grips a handful of his hair, thrashes about under him, but Luke won't be moved. Instead he presses his cheek deeper into Thomas's. The sharp cheekbone, the swollen jaw. "It's no wonder Patricia left you. You're not a real man, Thomas. And you know what?" He lifts his head and gives Thomas an ice-cold stare. Thomas feels weak, his skin prickly, and his head's light as a balloon. Still he tries to shove Luke off him with his free hand, but he doesn't have the strength. "I hate your perfect shitty life and your tiny ridiculous stores. Who the fuck cares whether a wall is painted white or gray? You can take it all and shove it right up your sorry ass." He squeezes Thomas. It feels as though his eyes are going to pop out of his face, as if they're pinned on stalks. Thomas's throat gurgles. "You don't give a shit about your own family," Luke hisses, "and now that I think of it, I almost think I hate you." He nods, smiling grimly. "I do, Thomas. I do *hate* you!" Thomas can barely breathe now. He lashes desperately with his head, rips and punches Luke's arms, but he can't wrest himself free. "I fucking hate you." Luke hocks a wad of phlegm onto Thomas's face. At first it's warm and soft, but it quickly turns wet and cold. Thomas wriggles in Luke's grasp, his arms pawing for the floor, and one of his hands miraculously finds the ladder, and it falls on the two men. When the ladder connects with Luke's back, he briefly loosens his grip on Thomas's throat, and Thomas uses the opportunity to rip Luke's hands away. Gasping for air, he throws Luke off. He tries to get up, and whirls onto his side, but Luke grabs him again; they roll around on the floor: Luke knees Thomas in the groin, and Thomas twists Luke's arm over his back, Luke bites Thomas's right ear, and Thomas screams in pain. Then Luke's sitting on top of Thomas again, his hands around his throat, but this time Thomas's hands are under Luke's; he tries to pry them off as best he can, and Luke isn't able to tighten his grip as much as before. He can't quite stop Thomas from breathing. They're close to the wall now. Thomas's head bonks into some empty cans of varnish, which the workers left behind. They skitter around noisily between them. "Was it you?" Thomas's voice is hoarse and thin. "Say it," he croaks. "Was it you? Did you do it?" Luke laughs. Opens his mouth and smirks. His battered jaw looks grotesque in the bright light, bluish-red, abnormal. "Was it *me*?!" He drops his head back, grinning. He glares at Thomas with a demented expression on his face, an evil clown, madness in his wide eyes: "Rock, paper, scissors, Thomas! I win! Give up. It's too easy beating an old fuck-up like you." Thomas's anger grows again now, and maybe that's why he's so inattentive for one moment, a short, short moment that allows Luke to get a better grip. And now Luke's able to squeeze his hands tighter around Thomas's throat. Thomas gurgles, the pressure behind his eyes is unbearable. He kicks his legs and thumps Luke's chest, claws at Luke's face, is almost lucky enough to jab a finger into Luke's eye, but Luke's fast and moves out of the way. Desperately Thomas tries to find something to strike him with. His hand smacks against a can of varnish, it's empty, and then another can, also empty, and now he hears something rattling around, in this one here, a screwdriver. He snatches it up. Luke says, "How was that again? You didn't want to be like Jacques, right? Now look at yourself." He sneers. "And now you feel bad for yourself. Oh, how *awful* for poor little Thomas." Thomas holds the screwdriver in his hand, out of sight, beside Luke's hip. He's making raspy, squeaking sounds. Luke's voice becomes distant and indistinct. Thomas's vision is going black. And with his last remaining strength, Thomas makes one single, sudden movement, swiftly raising the screwdriver and sinking it into Luke's throat. It penetrates his skin surprisingly easily and disappears into his flesh. Luke lets go of Thomas, and clutches his throat. For a moment, his eyes are shocked and lucid, and then comes the fear of death. Horrible rasping and clucking sounds escape him. Thin jets of blood pump from him and splash across Thomas's face and torso with each beat of his heart. Warm blood drips into Thomas's mouth and he pushes Luke off, then with some difficulty he scrambles to all fours. He coughs and coughs, deep sounds rising from the barrel of his throat; he gasps and spits, his throat is dry and raw as sandpaper. Another coughing fit and he's about to throw-up, hoarsely gulping for air. He clambers to his feet, wobbly. Luke's lying lifeless on the floor of the well-lit room. Blood has stopped gushing from him, but it's pooling around his body now, a large red flower. The dark, polished floor, the red flower. The bright light on Luke's face. The bruised jaw. His wide open, dead eyes. Thomas is terribly dizzy. He struggles to breathe. In and out. In and out. Come on. In and out. His heart thumps. Oxygen fills his lungs. He slumps over the figure on the floor. He hugs Luke close: his blood smells metallic, fresh. Thomas buries his face in Luke's greasy hair. He can feel his own hot breath.

He is alive.

Author's Acknowledgements

Thank you to the Danish Arts Foundation and the Danish Arts Council for their support as I was writing this book. To Leif Aidt, Søren Harbo, Naja Genet May, Line Miller, Finn E. Nielsen, and Simon Schwaner for their research assistance. To Pejk Malinovski and René Jean Jensen for their new Danish translations of Paul Celan and Walt Whitman. To K. E. Semmel for his hard work translating this book into English. To Katrine Øgaard Jensen and *Asympote* for publishing a portion of this book. To everyone who read and provided feedback along the way. To Kim Lykke, Mette Moestrup, Eigil Bryld, and a very special thank you to Simon Pasternak, my Danish editor, for his invaluable guidance and mental first aid.

Naja Marie Aidt was born in Greenland and raised in Copenhagen. She is the author of ten collections of poetry and three short story collections, including *Baboon* (Two Lines Press), which received the Nordic Council's Literature Prize and the Danish Critics Prize for Literature. Her books have been translated into nine languages. *Rock, Paper, Scissors* is her first novel.

K. E. Semmel is a writer and translator whose work has appeared in the *Ontario Review, Washington Post, World Literature Today, Writer's Chronicle, Southern Review,* and elsewhere. His translations include books by Karin Fossum, Erik Valeur, and Simon Fruelund.

Open Letter—the University of Rochester's nonprofit, literary translation press—is one of only a handful of publishing houses dedicated to increasing access to world literature for English readers. Publishing ten titles in translation each year, Open Letter searches for works that are extraordinary and influential, works that we hope will become the classics of tomorrow.

Making world literature available in English is crucial to opening our cultural borders, and its availability plays a vital role in maintaining a healthy and vibrant book culture. Open Letter strives to cultivate an audience for these works by helping readers discover imaginative, stunning works of fiction and poetry, and by creating a constellation of international writing that is engaging, stimulating, and enduring.

Current and forthcoming titles from Open Letter include works from Argentina, Bulgaria, Catalonia, China, France, Israel, Latvia, Poland, South Africa, and many other countries.

www.openletterbooks.org